FATED TO FLAME

S. A. GLADDEN

RUNNING
Wild
PRESS

CONTENTS

Fated to Flame text copyright © Reserved by S. A. Gladden
Edited by Rebecca Dimyan

All rights reserved.
Published in North America, Australia, and Europe by RIZE. Visit Running
Wild Press at www.runningwildpress.com/rize Educators, librarians, book clubs
(as well as the eternally curious), go to www.runningwildpress.com/rize.
ISBN (pbk) 978-1-955062-53-4
ISBN (ebook) 978-1-955062-54-1

CHAPTER ONE

HELLENIA

The crackling of fire was the primary sound in the sacred chamber, putting Leon Exousia's mind at ease. He kept to himself naturally, but it had become more of an occurrence for him to find himself seated on a cushion, staring at the bluish-white hue of the magical flame in front of him. The priestesses that regularly tended to the altar had departed not too long ago, leaving the lingering scents of myrrh and sandalwood burning in the small urns nearby. The gentle curls of the incense smoke created a myriad of patterns in the flickering light, catching his eyes as his mind drifted a million miles away.

His thoughts touched briefly on his father, as they were wont to do whenever he turned introspective. High Lord Vretiel Exousia's death had come much too sudden; Hellenians had exceptionally long lifespans, and while he knew his father had been approaching the tail end of his, the sickness that eventually claimed him left the realm in a state of shock and ripe with gossip. While Leon had been prepared for much of his life to succeed his father, it didn't mean that he felt ready to do it now.

It also did not help that there was a more pressing concern on his hands, one that weighed on him heavier than his newly assumed position as High Lord.

The Flame was dying.

"I knew I'd find you here, moping." A playful voice echoed through the room, accompanied by approaching footsteps. They stopped just behind Leon's kneeling figure. "It's lower than it was even yesterday."

"I know." Gold eyes reflected the dull spark of the magical flames on the dais in front of him, while his lips turned downwards in a frown. Turning his head slightly to the sound of the newcomer, Leon raised a dark eyebrow. "Have you come to lecture me, Elliot?"

"Me? No..." Elliot drawled with his usual smirk splayed upon his full lips. Spiky, ice-blonde hair was his bread and butter, contrasting starkly with his deep skin tone and blood red eyes. He was unusual for a Hellenian, tending to lean heavily towards human trends in fashion and mannerisms while preferring to wander amongst mortals than he did his own kind. Yet, he weathered any gossip and odd looks with the charm of a demon who knew exactly where he stood, and that was thankfully by the late High Lord's son as he had since they were little. "You know I don't lecture. I'm just telling you to get off your ass before the Draconians beat you to it."

"Not like they could if they wanted to; we hold the Spark, after all." Leon rose from the cushion, stretching his long legs and giving his wings a quick flutter before returning them to the usual folded position against his back. It was a sign of disquiet that he hated displaying, being a demon that preferred to keep his emotions close to his chest. But hailing from the royal line meant that his wings were his crown, noticeable to all in shape and style as signal to his importance to his people. "You've come to tell me what I already know, I see."

Elliot unearthed his hands from his pockets and gave a good-natured shrug. "Someone has to say it. And even though I know that it's not obvious to most, I know you're feeling Lady Selene's death pretty hard, too. She wasn't just another Prime to your father... it was real, what they had." His voice dropped a bit of its usual lilt. "That shit almost never happens."

Errant fizzles and popping noises from the faltering Flame filled the silence that stretched between the two friends, each lost in his own sphere of thoughts for a moment. Elliot was correct in his assessment, and it made the resulting tragedy that much worse. Leon had seen the change in his father from the first time he had encountered Selene; he had become softer, smiled often, and liked to visit the human realm for more than just duty. Selene had given him a reason to learn the world she grew up in and explore life beyond the gothic hills of Hellenia.

And now, they were both gone. Her heart had been broken with the loss of her love, and even though Leon did his best to tend to the widowed Queen, nothing could replace what had been taken from her. It had almost been a relief to see her pass into the ether to join Vretiel, because at least then she was free from mourning.

Unfortunately, it also meant the premature fading of the Flame. Ideally, they would have had at least another century of passage between the realms granted, but the Flame died with the Prime, starting the cycle anew. Leon just thought that he would have more time to prepare for the sacred quest. *The absent Gods have other plans, evidently.*

"Listen. I don't know why you're even hesitating. Any other demon would be jumping at the chance to seduce the next Prime. What's wrong with you?"

The new High Lord gave a sigh and shook his head a bit. "I've never done this before. It feels... odd."

"So? Humans are *easy*. Just throw a bit of charm in there,

smile just right, and they follow like puppies," Elliot described, his black nails glinting in the ambient light as he mimicked an animal dutifully trotting behind its owner.

Cutting him a sharp glare, Leon made a tut of disapproval. "I'm not like you. I don't go out snagging a new woman every night for fun."

"... well, *that's* rude. You say that as if I'm a common whore. Which wouldn't *technically* be wrong, but still..."

"Oh, save it. You aren't helping."

Elliot let his expression finally settle into something less playful and more subdued, peering at Leon with a surprisingly perceptive gaze. "I'm worried. Not for Hellenians, because we're resourceful. But I *am* worried for *you*. You're fresh into this High Lord business, and while I *know* you know what to do, it's different when everyone's looking at you. You gotta be strong for a whole race of people, now. The time they've given you to grieve has a limit, and that wick is burning fast. No pun intended," he finished, gesturing ahead to the wilting Flame.

A muscle in his jaw twitched almost imperceptibly as Leon's golden gaze shifted from his best friend to the ground. "You're right."

"I know I'm right. Just making sure you don't lose sight of yourself."

Sucking in a breath, Leon turned back to the Flame and reached out to it with one hand, his long black fingernails curling into a simple motion as he concentrated a bit of magic into his actions. In turn, the light flickered dangerously low, almost going out and plunging the room into darkness before climbing back up to its previously held level. What emerged was a solidified, glowing teardrop, pulsing slightly from within before dimming to a dull hue. It settled in Leon's palm, warm and smooth like freshly blown glass as he studied it pensively, knowing what had to be done next.

"Would you mind accompanying me to the Dreamweaver's coven? They should be able to assist in narrowing down the general location of the next Prime."

Elliot grinned boyishly, his lapse into a serious demeanor already brushed away. "Oh, you *know* you don't have to ask me to go see a bunch of women. You just lead the way." He turned on his heel and followed Leon out of the chamber, reaching out to clasp a reassuring palm on his shoulder as they walked out into the courtyard.

The light that never seemed to progress past sunset cast comfortable hues of orange tinged with purple on their bodies as they moved, the cobblestone path leading them on their way. Elliot glanced over at his friend, light glinting off of the curved horns on his head as he did so. "Are you nervous about all this because of Rina? I mean, now you're gonna have to get up close and personal with the new Prime pretty soon, and I know what she did to you probably doesn't make it easy."

Leon blinked at the mention of his ex's name. *Years have gone by, and yet at the mere mention of her, my body tenses as if thrown into ice cold waters.* "I'm simply overly aware that it will be difficult adjusting to the human realm."

"Uh huh. You know, if you had come with me every time I went to the human realm, maybe you wouldn't feel this way. I could've taken you to a whole *bunch* of places to loosen you up. Some of these places would even give Sustina a run for her money with how many luscious women-"

"Not interested," Leon cut him off with an exasperated sigh. They reached his carriage, and he nodded to the driver as he opened the door to step inside. "You've always found a better home with the humans than you have with your own."

"Well, you can't blame me, all things considered," Elliot said with a wry smile as he settled in next to him. "My father didn't exactly make me feel welcome, so I looked elsewhere.

You could say I have a personal investment in keeping this Flame lit for Hellenia, even if you don't."

"I understand." Leon's mind drifted back in clouded depths as the carriage rolled along to its destination. His fingers fidgeted every so often until he settled for clasping them in his lap as he trained his gold eyes out of the window, looking at the familiarity of the land that they moved along. He wished he felt more secure in his upcoming task, but it didn't even seem real to him, yet. He lost track of how much time had passed since they got in the carriage, and it seemed that it was but an instant that it was pulling up to the building with a distinctively curved roof.

Both of the men disembarked and walked up the few steps to the wooden door, where Leon lifted his hand to knock. Right before his knuckles made contact with the hard surface, it swung open, revealing a dark-skinned statuesque woman with piercing violet eyes and sheer black robes.

"High Lord. I was expecting you."

"And not me?" Elliot interjected, putting his face in an impressive pout.

"Lady Viviane," Leon bowed politely, then unearthed the teardrop jewel from his pocket. "I require your assistance in finding the area in which the next Prime is located. I plan to start my search for them as soon as possible."

Viviane gave a single nod and turned, leading the two men down the dim hallway within.

"She never acknowledges me," the blond-haired man lamented, sighing wistfully.

"That is a lie; she does, sometimes. She just neglects to give you the response that you crave," Leon glanced over to him and gave him a slight smile before focusing back on the task at hand.

The next room Viviane led them to was awash with natural light offered from a ceiling latticed with trusses as if the design

6

was purposefully unfinished. Strings of crystals hung from them, glittering and sending small pinpricks of light along the stone walls. The priestess's long braids swayed against her back as she took her seat in front of a wooden table laden with different artefacts important to her craft, and her slender fingers reached out to hover over a small loom laced with haphazard glittering strings.

"The Draconians have already sensed the waning of the Flame. I expect for them to make preparations soon." She looked over her shoulder at Leon. "You've tarried nearly too long."

Before Leon could say anything in rebuttal, she turned and grabbed a small but sharp ceremonial knife that was laying on the table beside her. With a modest flourish, she pressed the tip of it into the pad of her right pointer finger, where a drop of blood welled in its wake. Viviane then pressed her digit to the string, the red liquid trailing down to land on a knot that filtered to another. As a seemingly random pattern formed in the midst of the trail left, the priestess's eyes were slightly unfocused, fixed on the far wall, seeing beyond what was physically there. As the light fractured from the crystals flitted over her skin, both Leon and Elliot were frozen in their places watching Viviane, eagerly awaiting her answer.

"I have the Prime's location." Her slender hands fell gracefully to her lap, and she blinked multiple times before turning to look at Leon. "In a day's time, I should be able to pull the correct combination of runes to place you within the general area. As the gods would have it, it seems to be in an area your father once frequented."

Elliot looked over to Leon. "That makes it a bit easier. If Vretiel was there, then he probably had a safehouse nearby. We don't have to waste further time getting set up."

The High Lord nodded, his skin feeling cool with building

anxiety over how quickly things were progressing. "Indeed. Is that all, Lady Viviane?"

She looked up at him with her piercing gaze then, holding it for a moment too long before replying.

"For now, High Lord."

"What about for me?" Elliot interjected, batting his eyelashes coquettishly at Viviane.

"...Leave."

Leon held back a small snort at Elliot's expense, watching his best friend's face fall almost comically. "Thank you. I will be back at the manor, awaiting your guidance on the portal runes."

He couldn't shake the feeling that there was a lot that Viviane wasn't telling him. But to be fair, that wouldn't be unusual; she often saw beyond the veil of what was to what could be and discerned appropriately what to say to others. Leon just couldn't help but want to know what awaited him once he crossed over to the human realm.

"You worry too much, you know," Elliot said as they exited the Dreamweaver's enclave. "You'll *love* the chase, trust me. You'll do just fine."

"... I hope you're correct on that, dear friend."

CHAPTER TWO

HUMAN REALM

"What you up to?"

"Gonna head out to the library for a little bit. There's some more research I wanted to do on a corset pattern..."

"Ugh, girl, why don't you come over and we'll pop open some of this cheap ass wine I got and watch a movie or two? You know, what normal people do on their days off."

Jasmine Walters sighed as she put her cell on speaker in order to walk over to her closet and grab something that wasn't pajamas. "I thought you already knew I wasn't 'normal', Kim."

"Yeah, but a bitch is tryin' to help you! Going from musty books to a pile of fabric all the time *can't* be good for your health."

"Maybe so... but I'm not gonna change, boo. It's what I like to do." She thumbed her way through a variety of clothes before settling on her favorite hoodie and pulling it out. "But I'll tell you what... if I successfully make this corset that I want, then I'll celebrate by coming over and doing the girls night thing, how about that?"

"I'ma hold you to that, then. See you at work in a couple of days?"

"Bet."

Jasmine laid out a comfortable pair of jeans on the bed along with the hoodie she unearthed, then made her way to the bathroom while maneuvering around the scraps of fabric and other tools that constantly littered her living space. After brushing her teeth and washing up a bit, she looked at her reflection and was sorely unimpressed with the state of her wild hair.

Every time I don't feel like dealing with this, I regret not looking into lace fronts. She sighed while grabbing her paddle brush and some coconut oil spray to wrangle her coils into something manageable, lamenting her lapse into laziness that caused her to neglect putting on her silk bonnet the night before. Jasmine called it a day after changing out her paddle brush for a softer one, smoothing her edges down before pulling the bulk of her hair into a bun.

Less than fifteen minutes later she was dressed, had locked up her apartment and headed out into the public, the fresh air biting slightly with the promise of frosty winter that was right around the corner. Debating on whether or not she wanted to be lazy and call a rideshare or take the bus, she finally settled on the latter as there was no rush. Her wireless earbuds were charged, her favorite playlist was bumping, and it wasn't long at all before the bus dropped her off only a few short blocks from the main library in the heart of downtown.

Stepping into the old halls of the renovated building never ceased to be calming for her; it was one of the few places where Jasmine could just tune out the cacophony of the world in favor of what lay within the pages of any book she could get her hands on. Her mission for the day revolved around researching how best to mimic the style of an 1840's corset she had in mind for an outfit that she was sure she would never have the opportunity to wear anywhere but her own living room. She made a beeline for the stacks, passing by rows of books with well-loved spines that made the area smell like woody incense. *I kind of wish Kim would give me more credit; I could easily be a complete homebody and look all of this up online from my laptop at home, but I choose to get out the house.*

She gave a kind nod and a smile to the librarian that knew her by sight as she breezed by, squinting at the spines of historical fashion books before pulling out a few to peruse. An empty table near a window was where she settled down to scour the pages, making notes as she read. Time traveled rather quickly when she was so immersed in her work, only getting up to gather more materials to spread out around her as her brain moved into overtime. Eventually, the grumbling of her stomach was what disturbed her quest for more information, and she sighed as she leaned back in the wooden chair and stretched back until she felt a few discs in her spine realign after being hunched over for so long.

"Alright... well. Food, and then back at it." She carefully piled the books she gathered and walked them over to the librarian, who promised to hold them for her while she ventured out for sustenance. The transition from indoor fluorescent light to bright sunlight was a bit jarring, and she blinked a bit before taking out her cell and thumbing in a quick search for a good bite to eat. *Oh, that café I always told myself I would try is open for lunch... today is as good of a day as any.*

At least, that was what she thought until she arrived and saw the amount of people milling about, realizing too late the folly of choosing such a popular place to eat lunch. It was crowded, loud and terribly busy; all of the things that reminded her of the job that was waiting for her after the weekend was over. Unwilling to leave and find another place that maybe didn't have as good of a menu, Jasmine stuck it out long enough to order a sandwich to go and was quick to snatch up the plastic bag and slip away as soon as it was ready. The introvert in her relaxed the moment she left such a busy environment, and she found herself in a nearby park to sit on a bench near a large tree to devour her lunch undisturbed.

The weather was just on the cool side, rustling the leaves above her, but it was just right for her tastes. What *wasn't* to her tastes was the copious amounts of avocado that had been heaped on her turkey club, and she winced at her prior haste in just picking something to eat instead of actually reading what the ingredients were.

"Why do people eat these damn things," Jasmine muttered to herself, peeling the insanely popular fruit off of the bread with the tips of her fingers. "Greasy, wet compressed grass lump ass avocados. Biggest con of the century was getting folks to think that this shit ever tasted good..."

"I don't care for them, either."

Jasmine froze at the introduction of a voice that wasn't her own. *The fuck? There was literally no one around when I sat here.* With her fingers still pinching a slice of avocado, she slowly shifted her gaze to see just who it was that rudely butted into the conversation she was having with herself.

CHAPTER THREE

"Apologies. I didn't mean to interrupt your lunch. But... I'm new in the area, and I'm wondering if I could join you for a moment?"

Jasmine simply stared up at him with a perturbed look on her face, blinking multiple times at the stranger in front of her. No one ever approached her unless it was to ask for yet another discount on already discounted goods at the major retailer she worked at, let alone someone so dastardly attractive. Her brown eyes traveled along the impeccably fitted dark blue, nearly black suit that covered his body, accented both by the red dress shirt he wore underneath it and the silver brooch attached to one lapel of the jacket, a chain connecting to the other side. To top it off, his skin was as smooth as the photoshopped models she flipped past in fashion magazines, the dangly silver earring made her think of some pop star, and his sense of style was making her feel like she really should have at least chosen a hoodie that didn't have a frayed hem.

"Uh," she cleared her throat. "Naw, I'm good. I mean... yes, I'm fine. I mean..." Things were going downhill faster than a mudslide in California. "I don't exactly know what I can do for you."

The gentleman blinked, his head tilting slightly in confusion while causing the sunlight to pick up on the hints of auburn in his otherwise dark locks.

In the very awkward silence that followed, Jasmine had already made up her mind to start packing up her belongings. She wasn't done with her lunch, but that didn't matter. Everything about the encounter felt odd to her, and after the initial shock of being approached had passed, her street smarts were kicking in and telling her to vacate as soon as possible. He didn't look dangerous, but that didn't mean anything. Her instincts didn't let her buy the lost tourist act he was putting on, either. "Never mind. Listen, the weather is chilly, but this bench is nice. I warmed up the seat for you, even. So why don't you just pop a squat, appreciate the day, and I'll be on my way."

She fumbled for a little while with her things, patting herself down as she walked away from the area with her heart hammering in her chest. A small part of her felt bad for being so quick with her exit, but he caught her off guard and was way too well-dressed to be anything but odd. *Who in this day and age just walks up on people like that in the city? Ain't he afraid he's gonna get shot?* Adjusting the strap of her bag on her shoulder, she chanced a peek over her shoulder...

... and saw that he was following her.

Oh, shit. Jasmine slightly quickened her pace. Her mind was reeling with worst case scenarios about crazy men and the women they ended up murdering or luring off into some kind of sex trafficking scheme, and she wasn't looking to become a statistic. She didn't carry mace with her, and while she regretted not being better prepared, she did take a look around her and realize that she was less secluded and in plain view of the foot traffic nearby. Not knowing what else to do, Jasmine steadied her frayed nerves and stopped, turning to face the man in preparation to confront him. "Look, what do you-"

"I'm sorry. I didn't mean to scare you at all. After all of the time you spent picking the avocados off of this, perhaps it would be a waste to leave it for wild animals to scavenge."

Feeling her cheeks tingle in embarrassment, she tentatively reached out to take her forgotten Styrofoam container. With a wary glance up at him, she was once again blown away by how immaculate he was, as well as the genuine look of apology in his chestnut-colored eyes. Jasmine was still wary, but at least she felt a healthy amount of shame in how she acted earlier.

"Thanks. I guess it's my turn to apologize to you for darting. I don't know if you realize this, but it's not a good idea to just walk up on people you don't know like that."

"Ah." He appeared to think on it. "What would have been the correct way of approaching you?"

Jasmine pursed her lips slightly, unsure of how to really answer that without coming off even ruder than usual. She couldn't get over the almost childlike innocence in how he asked anything of her, and while she still had suspicions that it was all a ruse, she relaxed enough to remember the manners that got her through the strenuous life as a customer service representative at a retail store.

"We can, um, start over, I guess." She paused, and then extended her hand. "I'm Jasmine. And you?"

The way his face brightened with a radiant smile of relief was almost criminal to her as he accepted her hand. "Leon. It's a pleasure to be properly acquainted, Jasmine."

As soft and warm as his hand was in her own, she worried that her constantly clammy skin would be off-putting to him, taking her hand back as soon as she could without appearing hasty. "Are you sure about that? I *did* dash on you a second ago."

"I am. Your initial response was understandable, in hindsight. Being in a city this large is slightly overwhelming to me." Leon took a moment to look around, his awkwardness giving leverage to his story. "It's caused me to approach a complete stranger and risk her throwing unwanted avocados at me."

At that, Jasmine actually let out a laugh. His mannerisms were odd, his speech patterns kind of old-timey, but that little zing of humor actually served to let down her guard a little bit more. "I'm gonna consider avocado slices as viable weapons in the future now, thanks to that. So, um... did you have anything to eat, yet?" Her eyes picked up the details in his suit now that he was closer. There wasn't one stitch out of place, one bit of fabric that seemed to be any kind of polyester blend. *He didn't get this getup from any old department store; that's a wonderfully crafted pick stitch I see on his suit.*

"Ah, no... I hadn't thought about food until you mentioned it." He looked apologetically down at the boxed sandwich he had scared her into leaving. "Although I wouldn't want to trouble you with a meal. I'm sure you can make do with what you've already gotten..."

"It's alright. You said you're new around here, so why don't I take you to where I got this thing and you can see if it's anything you're interested in." Jasmine turned on her heel, not wanting to stare at him any longer than she already had. Unlike when she went there alone, she counted on the café being full enough to make her feel safe leading a complete stranger to lunch. "So, uh... let's go, then."

She paused to point out random buildings and landmarks, watching him nod thoughtfully as they went, and carefully gauged his reactions for anything out of the ordinary. However, the more they went along, the more she realized that he truly seemed as new to things as he claimed. His eyes took in the surroundings with a guarded sort of awe, and it made Jasmine wonder just where he came from.

"Here we are, Lumi's Cafe. Four and a half star rating on Yelp... as you can tell by how full the place is right now," she gestured through the window at the people seated within.

As they stepped into the establishment, Jasmine immediately noted how a lot of the patrons stared a bit too long at her companion before reluctantly going back to their food or conversations. It made her a bit on edge, since she wasn't the type to attract attention to herself in that manner. She waved to a host to seat them, hoping that her nervousness would wane eventually. *We really must seem like such an odd match.* She caught sight of their reflection as they passed by a decorative mirrored section of the wall, managing to stop herself from shaking her head slightly at how unexpected her afternoon became.

"I... may have overdone it a little without realizing," Leon said as he slid into the bench. "I often end up wearing what I like, without a thought of how it'll look to others. I'm sorry at any unnecessary attention I draw to us."

Jasmine couldn't help but lift an eyebrow at that. *Really, he didn't think of this before he left the house? He must come from a rich family or something that keeps him in upper-class circles.* "It's alright. I'll just consider it practice in ignoring what other people think, because I'm sure I could use it." She couldn't help but feel bad for him. His apparent level of obliviousness was strangely endearing, and it helped take a few notches off of her natural suspicion as a result. She picked up one of the laminated menus and slid it in front of him, pointing out a sandwich she hoped he would like. "This one doesn't have avocados. It's likely what I should have ordered the first time I stepped in here, but I wasn't thinking. Or, if you like sweets, they have a decadent dessert section here, all house-made." Jasmine turned the menu over and tapped her finger on the corresponding section before smirking. "But I don't think anything here is as fancy as you are, though."

"It doesn't have to be fancy," Leon reassured, hiding a bit behind the menu as he lifted it to better assess what the restaurant had to offer. After a moment of silence, he looked over the top of it at Jasmine with a sheepish smile. "But it may be better if I go with your recommendations, as I don't think I'll be able to make a choice within this century."

With a shrug, Jasmine settled on a flat bread sandwich and a wrap for the two of them to share. The waitress came around, giving her an odd look since it hadn't been too long ago that she had walked in for a take-out order. But as soon as she noticed Jasmine's terribly handsome companion, her criticism faded into obvious interest that made Jasmine feel preemptively exasperated. She eyeballed her nametag, wishing "Whitney" would just take their order and put it in without trying overly hard to sell them on extra things. She didn't relax until Whitney sashayed away.

"Man. Homegirl was *working* it. I'm pretty sure she wanted to leave you her number at least three times during what should have been a simple order."

"She wanted to what?" Leon blinked in surprise, and then to Jasmine's dismay, immediately turned to look to where the waitress walked off to. It didn't take long for him to make eye contact with her, poised by the cash register and looking like she was supposed to be putting their order in but was caught in a daze. As soon as Whitney realized that she was found out, she dropped her pen, then dropped the notepad she used to write their order down on, gathered them both up, and scurried back to the kitchen to finally complete what she was getting paid to do.

"... I see."

Do you, though? Jasmine shook her head, turning her attention back to the menus and stacking them neatly before putting them off to the side. "Well, um, after this I gotta head back to the library before it closes and pick up some books I set aside."

"What are you reading now, out of curiosity?"

"Um, it's not a novel or anything. It's historical fashion. I like old stuff. Gothic era was dope. Victorian as well. Edwardian also wasn't too shabby. Basically, anything that would be a pain in the ass to make today, I'm into."

"Oh, *those* kinds of clothes?" His eyes lit up earnestly at her answer. "You could say I have a similar niche with that sort as well. Have you fashioned your own?"

Jasmine was never gladder for her deep skin tone, as it was hiding what would have been the brightest blush ever. He didn't know how personal he was getting with his questions; her interest in fashion was hidden from most of the people in her life, since what most people considered fashion was way more modern than what she liked. "Sort of? It takes a lot of time, especially when you have to work a hard job just to earn the coin to be able to afford even the smallest accents. I'm a bit of a perfectionist too, so it's a slow process."

She felt oddly embarrassed just speaking about it in front of him. Leon being interested in the same things as she was should have been more exciting to discover, but she was far too aware of the social distance that existed between them. His attire told Jasmine his aesthetic and that he definitely had the money to support it. Meanwhile, there were days that a McDonald's meal could hurt her pocketbook if she spent too much on a yard of good fabric. Fiddling with her fingers, she gave a little self-depreciating sigh. "But it's alright. One day, I'll have the closet of my dreams. Today just won't be that day."

Leon gazed at her thoughtfully, and Jasmine felt oddly scrutinized under his intense gaze. Right around the time when she would have awkwardly begun tapping her fingers nervously on the surface of the table, he spoke again. "I know you'll achieve that, some day. I'd be interested to see what you've done thus far... if you're comfortable."

Why is he talking like we're going to meet again? She just blinked at him for a moment, then decided to change the subject before thinking too much on his offer. "Maybe. Anyway, what brings you out to mingle with the peasants?" Jasmine teased, feeling out the attractive stranger in front of her. "Looking to find ways to better adapt to the poor man's dress?"

His eyes crinkled into a bit of a laugh at her question before he looked off to the side. "It likely wouldn't kill me to get out more, that's for certain. You could say that I've lived a... sheltered life. I suppose I am rather embarrassed about it." He turned his head to look back at Jasmine with a sheepish expression. "Thank you for taking pity on a man completely out of his element."

Before she could come up with a reply to that, their food arrived, and by the looks of Leon's shocked expression, he was not expecting the sheer quantity of it. And to be fair, neither was Jasmine. She was sure that she didn't order that much, and she wasted little time giving Whitney a knowing side eye as she laid out everything with scarce an inch to spare. Leon, for what it was worth, simply was enthralled by what was in front of him.

"Oh... goodness."

"Yeah," Jasmine muttered as Whitney sashayed away after slipping a piece of paper under the plate closest to her unlikely companion before walking off. "Thanks to your admirer, it seems like we got a lot more stuff on the house. I hope you enjoy."

She pulled her soda closer to her and sipped idly as she

tried not to stare too hard at Leon switching his gaze from plate to plate as if he had never seen slightly upscaled café food before. He placed his napkin in his lap in a practiced manner, then picked up the fork and moved it to the plate of French fries. Then, as if he had an epiphany, he set the utensil down and tentatively picked up one of the fries with his fingers before placing it in his mouth.

"Gotta love starches, right?" Jasmine chimed in, reaching for one herself.

"Ah. Yes," he agreed, nodding to himself before continuing to eat them. He might have seemed somewhat hesitant in the beginning, but after chewing for a bit, he reached for another. Then another one. He wasn't uncouth in that he shoveled tons of food into his maw, but he methodically cleared the plate of all of the fries until he reached over and discovered that there were no more.

"I... well. Those were amazing," Leon said, flushing a bit at how fast he ate them. "I'm sorry, I should have offered you more."

"It's alright. It's not like we're suffering for food, here. Not having fries won't end me." Jasmine didn't know how Leon did it, but he managed to scarf down an entire plate of fries while looking cute and wearing the most fashionable suit she had seen in years. The longer she spent around him, the odder it seemed that someone so effortlessly beautiful was even entertaining her. *I'm missing something, here. I know it.* "Although if you want to get a refill, I'm sure we can call your new *friend* over to see if she can get you more."

Leon flashed an expression that was more like a pained wince than a smile at the mention of the waitress. He looked down and picked up the tiny piece of paper that had been shoved underneath one of the plates in front of him. "What is this?"

"Oh, let me see," Jasmine reached out and took it from him, her eyes scanning the girly handwritten numbers complete with hearts in place of dashes. "This would be our server's personal phone number. I knew she was gunning hard for you."

"...ah," Leon said before lapsing into awkward silence. Jasmine tilted her head slightly and furrowed her brow as she looked at him. *Did he really not know what this was? Seriously, how big is the rock he was living under?*

"Forgive the abrupt change in subject, but something just occurred to me. I had family that frequented this city in the past, and they spoke highly of a shop that offers quality fabrics. Would you like to go there with me? With your hobbies, I am sure a woman like you would appreciate it. It wouldn't be today, of course... but later, perhaps? Just to look?"

Jasmine nearly forgot her general wariness when he mentioned going to a fabric shop. "Don't tell me it's Brodeur's." Leon's surprised blink and slow smile in response was all she needed to know, and she let out a little shriek before catching herself with hands clamped over her mouth. It was all she could do to not get up that very moment and forget about all the plans she had for the rest of the day in favor of checking it out. "That's really nice of you," she said carefully after getting herself together. "Only if you're free, though." *One whole 80-hour paycheck could afford a yard of silk at Brodeur's.*

"Of course. Otherwise, I wouldn't have offered," He smiled charmingly, and Jasmine wished he would stop turning her heart into a frantic marching band whenever he did that. "But first, we should get going. I'm unaware of what time the library closes, but I know I've taken up enough of your time today as it is." Leon picked up the tiny clipboard with the bill taped to it before Jasmine could protest, sliding gracefully out of the booth and over to the register where the waitress almost dropped everything in the vicinity scrambling to meet him there. Jasmine propped her elbow up on the edge of the table and watched everything happen with great interest.

"The meal was lovely. Thank you," Leon began politely, sliding her the clipboard with money nicely lined up with the edges of the check itself. Her eyes nearly bulged out of her skull when she saw that he had casually paid with a crisp $100 bill, which was way over what the meal itself cost. Whitney rushed through all of the proper protocol to check the bill for authenticity, placed it underneath the main drawer with all the other large bills, and had counted out the brunt of the change to give to him.

Then the waitress nearly jumped out of her skin when his hand closed upon her own instead of simply taking the money.

"You're a beautiful woman, Whitney. You deserve the love and attention of a man who can give you everything that he is. Take my advice to heart... even if that man can never be me." Leon spoke to her gently but clearly, finishing with a kind smile and calmly removed his hand from hers, leaving the folded paper she had left for him on top of the money. "Everything you hold is yours. Please take care."

He turned on his heel and make his way back to the table where Jasmine was waiting for him, seemingly oblivious to the amount of eyes that were on him as he did so. His gaze was fixated on the exit as he extended a balletic hand to her expectantly. "Shall we?"

Jasmine felt as though she was in some sort of twilight zone. The cafe that was usually bustling with commotion now felt too quiet as they stared at the figure Leon cut as he patiently waited for her response. *I can't believe he swerved her and then expects me to just take his hand. Way to put me on front street, sir.* She still couldn't completely comprehend what happened; she was fully expecting him to be the kind of rich boy who would take anything that was offered to him, including multiple admirers.

But now, she was stuck with a room full of awkward stares and silence, so she hurriedly grabbed her things, scooted out of the booth, and grabbed Leon's outstretched hand just to nearly drag him out of the cafe, her entire face feeling like it was on fire from embarrassment.

"Does the library close soon? Is this the reason for the rush?" Leon asked, adjusting his pace easily to match Jasmine's.

"No, it doesn't. I just..." she slowed down, dropping his hand and heaving a sigh of exasperation. "Why did you do that?"

He blinked. "Do what? Pay for the meal? I believed it was customary, as you have taken the time out to assist me. Should I have not?"

Jasmine wanted to pull out her hair. "No, not *that*. The thing with the waitress. You put us both on blast, Leon."

His expression only deepened into further confusion. "On... blast?"

"Yeah. You brought lots of attention to Whitney and me doing what you did. I don't know if the poor girl is gonna emotionally recover from that rejection, and I'm not sure if I can ever step foot in that place again."

At that point, Leon was looking so deeply apologetic that Jasmine immediately felt bad for even saying anything at all. As a woman, if she was in his shoes then things would have been dealt with quite differently, and she supposed if he really wasn't interested in pursuing things with Whitney then there was very little that could have been done to make it *not* awkward. *Still though... that was the most dramatic way to ever let someone down.*

"Look, don't worry about it. I'm not stressing anymore. These things happen sometimes, and to be honest I don't think

I would have gone back there anyway. The food was good and all, but nothing I can't get elsewhere."

Leon gave a nod, his shoulders visibly relaxing. "Well... the French fries were exceptional."

Jasmine couldn't help it; she started giggling. He was so earnest in his statement, like he didn't know that literally any other place in town could serve him similar. *Well, shit... maybe he doesn't. He's so oblivious.* "Yes, they were. But I can show you better."

His eyes lit up. "Really? Is that something we could plan for after Brodeur's?"

"...sure. I'm free tomorrow. Did you want to meet here, on the steps?" Jasmine gestured towards the library that had just come into view.

"That would be acceptable."

"Alright then. Just give me your number, and I'll text you when I'm ready." She reached into her pocket to pull out her phone, and then gave Leon a sidelong glance. "And, um... not to knock your amazing sense of style here, but you can be more casual. You'll attract less attention that way."

At that, Leon gave a small chuckle. "I will definitely see what I can do."

CHAPTER FOUR

Making sure she left a nice tip for the driver from the app, Jasmine scooted out of the back seat of the car and made her way to the library steps to wait for Leon. A part of her couldn't believe that she was actually agreeing to meet with him again, since she still wasn't sure what to make of him outside of the fact that he was strangely endearing in his awkwardness and too damn attractive for his own good. But the promise of going to the best fabric shop the city had to offer was too good of an opportunity to pass up for a budding seamstress such as herself. *Yeah... this is definitely how I get kidnapped.* She chalked it up to the fact that she wasn't close with anyone who shared her hobby and was too skittish to visit the shop on her own, knowing how upscale the fabrics were. But going in with Leon was a good shield; he exuded enough high-class energy that she could hide behind that while she browsed, if nothing else.

Leaning against one of the railings on the steps, she shot off a quick text to Leon to let him know she arrived, and then slipped the device in her pocket and looked up to the clear blue sky as a cold breeze ruffled her freshly pressed hair. Jasmine had decided that if she was going to go anywhere with someone as sharp as Leon, it would be best for her to put a little bit of effort in her appearance. Instead of a hoodie, she settled on wearing a tan leather jacket with a plain black shirt underneath, with fitted jeans instead of leggings. She had a few "nice" things in her wardrobe that rarely ever saw the light of day, considering her life was mostly staying home if she wasn't in a uniform for work.

Speaking of work... Kim is going to eat all of this up when I tell her about it later. She couldn't help but smile to herself when she thought about what her friend's reaction would be, then got pulled right out of that thought by the vibration of her phone going off. *I know that's Leon. He must be close.* She stood up straight and started scanning the people walking by on the sidewalk, hoping to notice his tall, distinctive figure as he approached.

It wasn't difficult to spot him.

Despite not wearing another type of immaculately tailored suit, Leon's version of dressing down still made him look like he had walked off of the cover of a magazine. The hoodie he wore was quite fashionable, made of dark grey fleece that fitted his upper body snugly, with the sides along his ribs lined with eyelets that were laced with a knit cord that added to the look. It zipped to the left side rather than directly down the middle, which gave it a neater appearance. One hand was in the pocket of his dark colored jeans, while the other held his cell phone. Squinting a little, Jasmine noticed that Leon was one of the few men that actually had a hanging charm from the device, and it seemed to glow of its own accord. In an effort to not spend too much time gawking at how effortlessly handsome he looked, even while being "dressed down", she smiled and waved as he approached.

"You look nice," Jasmine gestured to his outfit. "And the cell phone charm is a nice touch."

Leon tilted his head in confusion before looking down at what was in his hand. "Ah. Yes." He placed the phone in his pocket. "You look beautiful, as well." Without missing a beat, he reached out for her hand and lifted it to his mouth, brushing his lips across her knuckles gently. "Your hair is different, today."

"Yeah, I cleaned up a little," Jasmine laughed, trying to distract herself from the tingles his kiss left on her hand. She didn't know anyone else who did something like that non-ironically, and who wouldn't look like a superfluous fool while doing so. "I couldn't be out here embarrassing you looking raggedy like I was the other day, especially since we're going to Brodeur's."

Leon furrowed his brows. "But you looked beautiful yesterday, as well. Your hair being curly or straight does not change that."

"... oh, well..." Not only was she being complimented by a handsome man, it was genuine, and that threw her for a loop. "Thank you. I know the store isn't too far from here, but did you want to call a ride or do you mind walking?"

"Walking doesn't bother me. It also helps me orient myself to the city better, and I would do well with the familiarity."

As they made their way down the sidewalk away from the library, Jasmine kept sneaking glances at him out of the corner of her eye. A part of her wished that she was as unscrupulous as her friend Kim, who certainly would have taken a picture of him to thoroughly examine and gossip loudly about within select company. But instead, she settled for admiring his high cheekbones and heavy jaw line set within his lightly burnished skin tone until she figured that it would probably be prudent to use the time it took to get to the store to ask him about himself.

"Where are you originally from?"

Leon merely blinked, but Jasmine could tell that he tensed up a bit. "Ah. You could say that I am from someplace rather far from here."

"Really? Like... you talking about another state or another country?"

"... yes."

Jasmine squinted at him, pausing in her inquiries only to make room for other pedestrians coming the other way before continuing to press him. "So, what do you do for a living? What brought you into the city? What are your parents like? I hope you know that I'm gonna keep pressing you, so you can keep being vague if you wanna."

Leon slowed to a stop and turned to her then, reaching out to take her hand in his. "Jasmine... I understand your curiosity. I believe if I were in your shoes, I too would be immensely curious and fairly wary. It is much to ask, but I must beg for your patience with me in the interim."

She looked down at their joined hands, then back up at him with a guarded expression on her face. Jasmine didn't like being in the dark, especially when it came to strangers popping up into her life. While she no longer thought that sex trafficking was in her future if she continued hanging out with Leon, it didn't mean that she was happy with how avoidant he was about himself. "Alright, then. You got a week."

"Pardon?"

"You heard me. My patience only lasts a week, and then I'm playing hardball." She patted the back of his hand before retrieving her own. "Those are my terms, take it or leave it."

Leon's expression turned distant for a moment before he finally cracked a smile. "Agreeable."

"Oh, that was easy. I thought you'd fight me harder."

He shook his head before walking again. "On the contrary, I know a good bargain when it's offered. At the very least, it means that we will be seeing each other again within that week's time. I see no loss in that."

Jasmine barked out a laugh in disbelief. *There must be something wrong with this guy, finding it happy to spend time with someone like me.* "It's settled, then. In the meantime, you at least have to deal with me drooling over fabrics in Brodeur's."

Eventually, they did arrive, and the small bell above the door dinged loudly as Leon pushed the door open for Jasmine to go first. For once, she didn't find herself distracted by his flowery shows of chivalry, since the moment she stepped foot into Brodeur's itself, all of the fabrics and trinkets within took precedent.

"Welcome," a voice called from the small counter near the front of the store, belonging to an older man with hair gone almost completely grey. He adjusted his gold-rimmed glasses and smiled at the two of them as they approached. "Is there anything I can help you find today?"

"Just browsing..." Jasmine said, her voice light and airy as she took in the decadence of the supply the store had. She previously only had the guts to look into the window and fantasize about having the type of money it took to outfit her resources before swiftly moving along the moment she thought someone would have seen her from inside. But now that she was in... she could do hardly anything but stare at the floor to ceiling bolts of fabric organized by not only color but make, matched by the exorbitant trims and ribbons that complimented each swathe of textiles. From the outside, the storefront looked rather unassuming, but the inside of the establishment opened up into an impressive expanse framed by artfully stained wood and lined with globe lights to give the shop a warm glow. Besides the full selection on display, Jasmine adored how Brodeur's made her feel as if she were walking through a vintage parlor in Paris.

She lingered over the clearance racks first, fingering a silk chiffon swatch that drifted across her skin like butter. It was an accident that the tag ended up in her palm in the process, and it was definitely unintentional that her eyes skimmed over the price per yard as well. But it wasn't a mistake in how she winced and gently put it back in its place, knowing that how much she wanted of it would have likely cost her a whole month's rent. *Designed by Jakob Schlaepfer it may be, but I ain't dropping over a thousand dollars on this.*

Leon moved to Jasmine's side after nodding at the shop owner, pointing out the chiffon that she kept fondling. "What would you make out of this, out of curiosity?"

"Maybe a blouse, even though making eyelets for buttons are a pain," she replied easily, her mind and eyes still enthralled by the treasure trove that was in front of her. "But this is just too gorgeous. See?" Jasmine rolled out a length of the silk chiffon she had been not-so-secretly coveting. "It drapes well, and it's light enough to layer if needed. But this *color*... it suits you, I think." The deep blue fabric shimmered in the light as she held it up to him as if fitting him for an outfit.

Leon looked down at the swathe of chiffon that was being plastered to him, smiling warmly. "It is definitely my color," he agreed, watching her barely hide a sigh before rolling it up and placing it carefully back on the rack. "Jasmine, I know you've come here to dream. And while Mr. Brodeur's clearance items are also of top quality, as thanks for introducing me to the wonder of French fries, please don't worry yourself about the price of things you may want. I'd prefer you have what you need to create as many masterpieces as you'd like."

Jasmine's brain took a moment to catch up to what he was implying, and when it did, she stared at him with her brown eyes wide and in shock that he would offer to do such a thing, let alone putting into perspective that he had *that* kind of disposable income to purchase anything in the store as it was. "What? Oh... no. Nope. You lured me here just to look, remember? Nothing more." Her fingers trailed along a scrap of fabric she had recently put back on the pile to which it belonged. "I really am okay with just browsing. I don't have the time I want to make anything soon enough, and it would be unfair to start hoarding pretty things just because they exist."

She was doing a hell of a job trying to convince herself of all of her words. Her entire being called out to the loads of materials that the shop had to offer, and she forced herself to settle on just three small things that she knew she could afford. Turning around with them in her hands, she raised an eyebrow at Leon and gave him a look before he could get any ideas. "I've budgeted for this, at least. You're not allowed to touch it."

His hands lifted in surrender. "I concede. However, I do recommend taking part in the loyalty program." He reached over her and slid an information card in her direction, with a pen to follow. "There will always be more sales, and once you reach a certain amount of purchases, you'll be able to put points towards any fabric you like for free. I don't believe you can turn *that* down."

Jasmine really couldn't argue with him at that, and it was simple enough to fill out while the owner rang up her purchases. She still felt fairly self-conscious being in such a nice shop, but she couldn't deny that it was worth it. Glancing up after sliding the completed form back to the old man at the cashier, she noticed Leon studying her thoughtfully and fought to not feel flustered. His gaze was one that was naturally intense, and she wasn't sure if she would ever get used to his attention on her.

Once the purchases were properly bagged, both of them waved and said pleasantries to the owner before turning for the door, with Leon trailing not too far behind her with the palm of his hand hovering just at the small of her back. Once they were outside, Leon paused.

"One moment, I forgot that I had something of my own I wanted to inquire about. I will return shortly."

As Jasmine watched him go back into the store, she got a random idea and flicked through her phone contacts until she came across Kim's number.

"What's up, you coming over?" Kim said without preamble when she picked up.

"Unfortunately, not today. I'm out with this guy, and-"

"Hold up... you *what*? You out with a whole *man* and ain't said nothing until just *now*? Girl, I should beat your ass for-"

"You can do that later, I just wanted to ask you if you wanted to go to the Ren Faire with me next week."

Kim snorted. "Please, you know I'm not about that life. What the hell I'm gonna do walking around with all them white folks dressed up in old clothes doing weird shit?"

Jasmine glanced quickly back into Brodeur's to make sure that Leon was still occupied with the owner. "What if I told you that you could meet the guy I'm out with right now, if you went?"

"Oh, word? Do he got a hot friend, too?"

Jasmine paused, and then heard the bell ding behind her. Covering the mouthpiece for a moment, she turned to Leon just as he was coming to stand next to her. "Hey, do you have friends? Okay, specifically... a friend?"

Leon looked surprised by the random inquiry, but

answered her nonetheless. "I do. He frequents this... ah, area much more than I. Why do you ask?"

Nodding, Jasmine turned away from him and uncovered her phone. "Yeah, he's got a friend. So are you down?"

"Say less. Just lemme know what weekend or whatever it's on, so I can decide whether or not to call out sick or actually put in a PTO request. Depends on who my supervisor is that day, you know."

"You a mess, girl, but I love you for it. I'll hit you back later." Jasmine ended the call and put her attention back on the perplexed Leon. "Sorry about that. So, uh... I was wondering if you wanted to go to a Renaissance Faire with me. We have them seasonally in the area, and before you mentioned being interested in seeing the kind of stuff I make. It's the best opportunity for me to show you that hobby of mine."

His brown eyes lit up. "Really? I would be honored."

"Cool. Oh... I was asking about a friend because I just asked my girl if she wanted to go, too. She said she'd only come if you had a cute friend."

"Ah, I see. Elliot should meet those requirements easily. He does tend to be a bit much, however. I wouldn't want to leave a poor impression on your companion."

Jasmine snorted. "Oh, don't you worry about that. Kim knows how to roll with the punches. For right now, let's get going." She held up the bag she got from Brodeur's. "I'm excited to possibly find things to add to my garb for the upcoming event."

"Garb?"

"Oh, you don't know nothing about that, huh? Well... let me prep you a little bit while we walk on over to this shopping area I know that's nearby. I'll show you the difference between the stuff that's in Brodeur's and what most people consider fashion. You uh, might not really like what you see, fair warning." Without thinking about it, she looped her arm through his as she directed him towards the mall.

"Is it that atrocious?" Leon asked, and the look of concern on his face caused Jasmine to giggle.

"Just uh... promise me you won't act out too bad at the sight of polyester, okay?"

CHAPTER FIVE

"He *what?*"

"*Yes*, girl. I have literally never seen a man so damn offended over a piece of clothing in my life," Jasmine told Kim emphatically, leaning against a nearby tree trunk. "It became kind of like a game where I started pulling out different cheap, ugly shirts and shit, pretending that I was interested in them before he eventually had enough and literally dragged me out of the store. I thought I was gonna piss myself laughing at him."

Kim shook her head, sending a fluttering cascade of braids over her shoulders as she did so. "He really hates fast fashion, huh? So, from what I'm getting is that this dude is probably rich, right?"

"Yeah, but... I dunno, girl. He's nice, but he's a little weird."

"Weirder than you in this get up?"

Jasmine snorted and smoothed down the black lace that overlaid the soft sateen underlayer of her skirt, watching the hem of it brush against the lace up leather boots she only wore when she had an excuse to dress up in garb. "Yeah, only he's a lot better looking than me. You'll see."

Kim had opted for regular modern clothes, consisting of a long-sleeved shirt and jeans, which did look odd next to Jasmine and her well fitted corset and skirt. It was to be expected, and Jasmine also didn't make it known that Leon and his friend had to dress up either. Not only did she not want that kind of pressure on the two of them to just take in the experience, she was also afraid that Leon would go even more overboard and show up in something largely overdone and overpriced compared to all of the regular people who made their own costumes during the span of months or years.

"I hope his friend cute and rich, too. A bitch needs to pay off these student loans, ya heard?"

Shaking her head, Jasmine pushed herself off of the tree trunk and squinted through the people milling around, lining up to get into the venue. She was just about to get her phone out of her satchel to double check to make sure that they didn't get lost on the way to the fairgrounds, when she saw Leon's distinctive figure parting through the groups of people. It helped that he was tall, and it also accentuated how differently he moved when Jasmine could observe him amongst others. She didn't know how else to describe it other than strangely regal; he moved with purpose, and those that were in front of him seemed to instinctively move out of his way.

She was so enthralled with watching him approach that she was startled by Kim reaching out and grabbing onto her arm hard enough for pins and needles to start up in the tips of her fingers.

"Girl... who... who is *that*??"

"Leon and... his friend, I'm assuming," Jasmine replied, her mouth feeling like she just swallowed a handful of cotton balls. Evidently, Leon must only associate with similarly extremely attractive people; she looked on at his companion, dressed more casually than Leon in a T-shirt and jeans, yet still making it look as though he was on a catwalk. It was easy to see even from the small distance that the two were complete opposites of each other.

"Leon is the taller one, I'm guessing from what little you told me. But *bitch*, where he find a fine ass brotha like *that*? And is Leon Native? He look Native-"

"Girl, I dunno, and hush," Jasmine swatted Kim's death grip off of her arm and used it to wave at the men approaching. "You made it!"

"Indeed. It was easy enough to see where to go with the crowds coming this way," Leon stopped a few paces in front of Jasmine and looked over her outfit. She fought back the urge to immediately assume a self-conscious stance, the fear of her handiwork not being up to Leon's previously discovered picky tastes in the forefront of her mind. It was only when he smiled sweetly, taking her hand in his and kissed her knuckles that she relaxed. "You look beautiful, Jasmine. You made this, yes?"

"Sure did," she said as she did a small twirl, showing off the embroidered vintage leaves on the front of her brown bustier, accented by swiveled bronze clasps that served no functional purpose but to add to the aesthetic. She didn't prefer for her arms to be completely exposed, so she fashioned a small bolero to put on over it all. Jasmine's hair was swept up into two high buns, edges properly slicked down for once in her life, and accented by a tiny fascinator on a headband for ease of wear. The thought of makeup was something she balked at when she considered that she would be walking around a humid park full of people, but she capitulated with a light lip gloss and mascara.

Of course, nothing that she could do to clean up nice could ever compare to how Leon looked on any day, it seemed. Yet, his approval meant more to her than she would admit. Jasmine forgot that there were other people there for a moment until Kim loudly cleared her throat, and she blinked. "Oh, um... this is my friend Kim. We work at the same shitty department store together, and she definitely makes the work day go a lot smoother for me."

"Nice to see the man who captured my girl's heart over a weekend," Kim said boldly, causing Jasmine to stare at her incredulously. "Do you know how hard it is to get this chick to leave her damn apartment? I been trying for years. I'm actually kinda jealous."

Leon chuckled and reached out for Kim's hand as well, which she gave with an amused look on her face while she watched him kiss her knuckles, as well. "My apologies. I understand that she is often preoccupied with her craft, which is why she prefers to keep to herself. Looking at what Jasmine has crafted with my own eyes, I can only be supportive in this and repentant that she's taken time away from what she loves to show me around this city." He turned towards his companion. "Let me introduce my friend, Elliot."

Jasmine looked over and met the honey-colored eyes of the newcomer, watching him scan her from head to toe in a way that she would have rebuked had it come from any other man. When he approached her and took her hand, it was more casual and seductive than anything Leon had done. His thumb made absentminded circles on the back of her hand as he smiled charmingly at her, and the only thing Jasmine could do was stare at him.

"Glad I finally get the pleasure of meeting someone else who can tolerate Leon for long periods of time," Elliot said, his voice confidently smooth with a rolling undertone of chocolate and allure. "Jasmine, right? You're *cute*. No wonder Leon waxes poetic about you."

"...w-what?" she stuttered, glancing over at Leon. The other man cleared his throat and looked slightly embarrassed, and that just made Jasmine even more bewildered. *I didn't even do nothing but give this man French fries and show him bad, modern fashion.*

"Please forgive him. I mentioned before that he can be a bit much." Leon shot Elliot an exasperated look. To that, his friend shrugged nonchalantly and released Jasmine's hand, still grinning.

"I see my reputation precedes me. Must mean I'm doing something right." The blond turned towards Kim then, and his eyes slowly raked over her figure. Jasmine glanced at her friend then, watching as she predictably preened under the lecherous scrutiny by flipping her hair braids over her shoulder. "What's your name, baby?"

"Kim. Make sure to memorize it, 'cause I don't want no other bitch's name coming out your mouth when I take you home tonight."

It took all of Jasmine's self-control not to let out a loud bark of a laugh, not only at how forward she knew her friend could be, but also at the look of absolute shock on Leon's face when she said it. Elliot simply lifted his eyebrow in amusement, obviously thrilled to be in the presence of a woman who seemed to be on the same vibe he constantly was.

"Now that everyone's acquainted, I suppose we can go in," Jasmine said, fishing in her satchel for the passes she got for everyone. Stepping up to the entrance, she smiled at the person working the gate and handed them over, collecting the stubs and waltzing into an area transformed to another time.

It had taken Jasmine awhile to feel comfortable going to Renaissance fairs, despite the fact that her interest in sewing period-style clothing fit right in with what was flaunted at events like that. A combination of never really having a set group to go with, as well as being one of the few non-white participants that frequented the fair were major reasons for her hesitance, but eventually she just made herself go, anyway. There was something about the smell of roasted turkey legs, the sound of jousting, and the plethora of overpriced merchandise at vendors that kept drawing her in, on top of scouring the patterns that the costumers wore for anything she could fit into any of her existing projects. The area in which the fair was held had been entirely transformed with permanent structures, refaced with old-timey décor and surrounded by personnel that stayed in character as they passed by.

"So, umm... the reason I thought you'd find this interesting is because you can really see medieval and Victorian fashion on display somewhere outside of the internet or old books," Jasmine explained, gesturing to a pair of regents walking by in bustled skirts and high-updos. "There's also a lot of different shows going on, like singing or juggling, and then in the center of the park there's jousting."

"I see," Leon said, his eyes combing over everything. "And this event is held once a year?"

"Yeah, as long as there's no natural disaster or lack of funding. Lots of people look forward to taking a break from modern society and stepping back into a different time. There's a freedom in just being someone else for a few days, and even for those that just visit, it's nice for them to see how they think people in old England lived."

"... did old England have *that*, though?" Kim said, gesturing to an impressive suit of armor worn by someone passing by. The details were immaculate, but it was very easy to see that everything from the helmet down to the red lightsaber they held was meant to portray the iconic Darth Vader.

"Uh... well, no. But, I guess the faire has just become a hot spot for anyone who likes to be someone they're not. There's even Vikings and pirates around, so things aren't exactly authentic." Jasmine shrugged, then saw a booth with gowns and other accessories that she started meandering over to. "I just thought that you'd enjoy seeing something like this."

Elliot winked at her then. "You already know him so well."

I wish I did. I don't know shit about this man. Jasmine busied herself in one of the racks, perusing the stitching and patterns on a few robes, but found herself sneaking looks over at Leon to try and read him. She could tell that he was interested, and thankfully wasn't looking over anything with the thinly veiled disapproval that she had seen when she had dared take him into a mall. But every now and then, when particularly elaborate costumers waltzed by, a slight smile appeared on his face that made her feel like he appreciated being there.

Moving through the festival, Jasmine was sure that she paid more attention to how Leon reacted to things than the actual event. It felt sneaky, but since Leon was so close lipped about anything regarding himself, it caused her to resort to trying to read his mannerisms to get a better idea. But no matter how hard she tried to discreetly source out anything to latch onto, she wasn't coming up with the answers she sought. Where did he come from? What was his deal? And why was he so willing to do these things with her? As they meandered over to grab some food, Jasmine watched Kim and Elliot hit it off and joke about the things that they saw, and it made her wonder if she was really just that much of a hermit that it made her automatically assume regular methods of human interaction were odd.

It was difficult for Jasmine to make friends due to her reclusive hobbies and general disinterest in being terribly social. If she and Kim hadn't been in work orientation together, then it was highly possible that they never would have been friends. Taking that into consideration, Jasmine focused on just enjoying being out with the company she had. She led them to a small mead tasting in the corner of the park, asking Leon which flavors or brands he liked best while Elliot decided to buy whatever bottles he thought looked nice. They were able to catch a jousting match on the way back from that, joining in on the cheers from the audience whenever someone was unseated. Leon was attentive and polite, asking a few questions and deferring to her knowledge on what the significance of certain attractions happened to be, and it was nice to be able to talk with someone in the flesh that was honestly interested in a hobby of hers.

"I think that's about all the highlights of the faire. There's some more stuff that we could check out, but I think it would be more of the same." Jasmine adjusted her bolero. "If you guys want to head out now, that's fine with me. Would probably be a good idea anyway to avoid the rush when the park closes."

Leon nodded and opened his mouth to reply, getting interrupted by Elliot. "Whoa, look at these!" He slid his arm from its place around Kim's waist to walk over to a shop showcasing handmade weaponry. The vendor smiled as they approached, letting him walk right up to a western one-handed sword hanging on a far wall that was beautifully crafted with distinctive molding on the handle.

"Is it okay if I touch it?"

The vendor nodded. "Of course! All of the ones that I wouldn't want the public handling are behind the counter. This one I made several years ago, when I was testing out different forging techniques. I've since done better, but I keep it as a reminder of how far I've come."

Elliot carefully lifted it from its perch, palming it to examine it closer before turning to Leon. "Brings back memories, doesn't it?"

Jasmine raised an eyebrow and looked over to Leon, who was carefully guarded with his expression as usual. "I suppose it does."

"Say what now?" Kim asked, stepping over to her friend. "Y'all used to make stuff like this, or what?"

"More like practiced with them. This looks a lot like the sword he used when he was younger." Elliot grinned while holding it up to the natural light. "Amazing that I'd find something so nostalgic in a place like this."

Jasmine traded a look with Kim before glancing at Leon once more. "When were you gonna tell me you did swordplay?"

"I... it is only a... hobby of mine," Leon said awkwardly, giving off the same uncomfortable air as when Jasmine had drilled him about his life on the way to Brodeur's.

Before Jasmine could press him, a flash of light caught her eye and she turned just in time to see Elliot actually toss the weapon at Leon. His reflexes were fast, and he easily caught the sword by the handle before it seemed like he realized what he was doing.

"How about we give the ladies a little show?" Elliot grinned, reaching for and retrieving a basic rapier from a stand.

"Oh... oh, *no*, y'all... we don't... you can't, uh..." Jasmine stammered, horrified at just the astonished look the poor vendor had on their face at the audacity the outgoing man had to even suggest such a thing with their wares.

"Elliot." Leon's voice was stern, an implied weight to just that word that made Jasmine shut up and instinctively take a couple of steps back. Kim shifted the bag of mead that she was holding to her other arm and pulled her even more out of the way, watching the blond approach with the same devil-may-care attitude he seemed to naturally exude.

"C'mon... this is your time to shine. For old time's sake."

Leon didn't make a move to engage, but neither did he seek to release the sword he had from his fingers. Elliot took that as his cue to lunge at his longtime friend, and as a reflex, the composed man parried with just a precise lift of his arm.

Jasmine couldn't believe what was playing out in front of her eyes. While it became instantly obvious that neither of the men were slouches in the sparring department, she couldn't help but be more focused on how Leon countered and moved. The same fluidity that she had glimpsed whenever he did something as normal as walking transferred easily to his sword work, keeping his posture straight and strikes controlled in a way that belied the kind of skill she only previously saw in people who dedicated a significant amount of their life in honing. Elliot remained mostly on the offensive, continuing to press Leon from as many angles as possible, not seeming to mind that every attempt seemed telegraphed on his part.

"Bitch... there's a crowd forming," Kim hissed into Jasmine's ear, and a quick glance to the side of her confirmed that people passing by had stopped what they were doing to look at what was happening.

Meanwhile, Leon took a step to the right to avoid another jab. "Stop."

"Oh, you know there's only one way for you to get me to do that," Elliot's tongue traced his lips, excitement evident in his eyes. "Stop being so damn reserved and come at me like I know you can."

From there, the roles reversed in their dance. Leon switched from guarding and parrying to striking, and the clanging of their weapons rung out through the area. More people had gathered in the interim to watch the impromptu swordfight between two visitors that rivaled the ones professional performers put on at the fair. Elliot held his ground, but it was evident that he was under pressure trying to find room to counter in Leon's onslaught. Eventually, he saw a window of opportunity, feinting to the left before slashing across through the space between them, causing Leon to bend backwards at the waist to avoid it at the last second. But in return, Leon turned that moment into his coup de grace, taking advantage of Elliot's overextended position to catch the handle of the rapier on his blade in an upwards strike. A gasp went through the crowd as the thinner sword launched into the air and spun, just for Leon to hook it on the way down with the tip of his own angled perfectly through the hilt.

Jasmine didn't realize she was holding her breath until the crowd surrounding them burst into excited applause, and she released the tension she had in her lungs in a sigh that nearly deflated her. Kim moved from her side to go to Elliot, while Leon walked back into the open-air shop and laid both swords on the counter in front of the shell-shocked vendor.

"Please accept my deepest apologies for the scene we have caused," Leon began, but was stopped by the shop owner waving a hand impatiently.

"Are you kidding? Not only was that the most action any of my weapons have seen, that was incredible. Are you a part of the swordsman's guild in the area? Or out of town?"

Jasmine watched intently as Leon gave vague answers, hoping to catch a tidbit or two, but there was nothing more to be gained. When he turned around to come back, she could tell that Leon was *pissed* that he had been goaded into such a display.

On one hand, Jasmine didn't blame him. She would be mortified at attracting so much attention to herself like that. On the other, she was overcome with the reignited need to know more about Leon and his secretive background. As he approached with a stormy look, her eyes instinctively avoided meeting his gaze and instead traveled down to his blouse.

"... oh, shit. Your shirt," Jasmine pointed out, and he stopped walking to follow her gaze to the blouse he had on that was missing a button. Evidently, one of Elliot's strikes rung true enough to completely cut the threads that once held it there, creating a conspicuous gap.

"Marvelous," Leon replied sardonically. The glare he shot Elliot made Jasmine twitchy on his behalf, even though the blond didn't seem too concerned about it.

"Uh... don't worry, it's a quick fix. I got stuff back at my place that can take care of it."

Jasmine didn't bother looking over at Kim; she could feel the way her friend was staring at her and she absolutely knew that she would be requiring a call about everything later. Instead, she remained focused on Leon, not knowing if she dreaded a rejection or an acceptance more.

She got her answer after a few more moments of tense silence.

CHAPTER SIX

I t wasn't until Jasmine was putting the key into the lock on her apartment door that she really let herself realize what she was doing.

She invited a near stranger over to her place without a second thought. And he accepted.

"Excuse the mess," she said as she stepped inside, inwardly hoping that she didn't leave anything too embarrassing out in the open. "I don't have company over like, at all, so I always keep unfinished projects laying around."

"It's quite alright. You are doing me a favor, after all," Leon said as he closed the door behind him. He bent down and unlaced his shoes, placing them next to Jasmine's boots before entering the main area. She watched him out of the corner of her eye as she slipped out of her bolero, placing it on the back of the couch as he took in her quaint space.

"It's no biggie. As I said, this is what I do for fun, so it's good to be able to put it to practical use. Did you want anything to drink? I have water, juice, and a bit of soda."

"Water would be preferred, thank you." He took a seat on

the couch, and let his eyes settled on a picture frame on the end table next to it. "Are these your parents?"

Jasmine walked back into the living room with a glass of cold water. "Yeah. That was when I graduated from college. Thought I was gonna stay close by, and then after a few months of me just twiddling my thumbs not knowing what I was going to do with myself, I packed up and moved all the way across the country to try my hand at this adult thing." She laughed. "Can't say that I thought I'd end up where I am now, but I'm not mad at it. I call back home when I can to touch base."

Leon studied the picture for a moment longer, and the smiled softly. "That is good that you keep in touch. My father and I weren't terribly close, but I felt his passing heavy on me nonetheless."

"Damn. Sorry for your loss. What about your mom?"

"Ah... unfortunately, I've never met her. There is a high possibility she is still alive today, but we would be nothing but strangers to each other."

Well, at least he's being somewhat less close-lipped about his life. Shame it seems to be so damn tragic. "Do you miss having a mother figure in your life?"

A bit of silence stretched until he responded. "I don't know if I can miss what I never had, in that sense. This isn't to say that I was completely devoid of feminine presence; in my formative years, a family friend by the name of Sustina gave me what would be the closest to a motherly influence."

Nodding, Jasmine processed what he told her and then gestured for him to stand. "Don't mind me standing in for your mom in helping to mend your clothes after you've gone out and rough housed with your friend. Hand over the shirt, sir."

Leon made a sound of assent, and diligently unbuttoned his blouse with the efficiency of someone who was accustomed to disrobing in front of others. As for Jasmine, she inwardly wished that she had the same amount of decorum as he managed to have, but she could feel her eyes widening the more skin was revealed. By the time that he had the garment off and was handing it to her, it took her a moment to reach out and take it from his fingertips.

"... thanks," she said while turning away from his half naked figure to scurry to her nearby work desk. Although he wasn't extremely cut, Leon was still the most fit person she had ever had the pleasure to know, let alone to be shirtless in her own living room. Forcibly shoving the image of his chest out of her mind, she grabbed a repurposed jewelry box full of needles and other sewing supplies out and rustled through it. "So, what else can you tell me about your home life? Or should I wait until the one week trial period is officially up to drill you on this?"

She heard him chuckle, followed by the soft sound of him sitting back down on the couch. "My home life was nothing orthodox, as you've probably guessed. My upbringing lays many responsibilities on my shoulders, and it is a wonderful breath of fresh air to experience simply *existing* for once. I have you to thank for much of that. Your presence is calming."

Jasmine paused in the middle of picking out a needle, her eyebrows furrowed a little as she parsed what he said. Leon was nothing but an enigma to her, and although she supposed that he was sharing bits of information about himself, it only served to leave her with more questions that she was dying to ask, but knew she still had to tread lightly in order for him to talk at all.

"I'm calming? Man, tell that to the general public when I'm at work while they're yelling at me about using a coupon that expired three years ago. They would *not* agree with you."

"They haven't gotten the chance to know you. The right people can change even the stoniest of hearts, if given the opportunity. For example, in my late father's final years, I watched him turn into a person I never thought he would be."

"Really, now?" Jasmine held up different spools of thread to the fabric of the shirt, seeing what would match the best.

"His marriage was arranged; structured for convenience and nothing more. My father tended to be terse, strict, and difficult to emote. He loved me to the best of his capabilities, but I cannot say it was always warm." He paused. "But Selene made me realize that perhaps it only takes the right person to change the most unmovable man."

"She definitely sounds like his soulmate. Do you two still talk?"

"Unfortunately, she passed not long after my father. A broken heart can lead to death as surely as any illness."

Jasmine threaded the needle, glancing over at Leon in intervals. His gaze had become distant and blankly focused at the dark television screen on the opposite wall. There were a few emotions she could read in his face, the foremost one being wistful. She never thought about it, but Jasmine realized that she took her parents for granted. Just the thought of losing them one day was something she refused to consider, and Leon had weathered so much in what she assumed to be a relatively young life.

She left him to his thoughts, not knowing what to say as she put the brunt of her focus on attaching a button. The plastic of the one she had definitely did not hold up to the quality of the others that seemed to be made out of something like stained ivory, but the shape was uniform enough to blend in at a glance. *God, with how offended he was to see polyester, I hope he won't flip out over this button.*

She wasn't sure how long it was until she was carefully snipping the excess thread from her handiwork, but she pushed her chair back from her bench and stood holding the garment out at arm's length, squinting at the lay of it. "Okay, let's see how this works."

Leon got up and stood in the center of the room, taking the offered shirt to slip on his shoulders. As Jasmine's fingers went to work straightening his collar and pulling down the hem, she chuckled to herself.

"You've done this before, haven't you?"

"Pardon?"

"Having someone dress you is normal. You have your own tailor, don't you?"

Leon cleared his throat. "Yes. I do."

Bougie ass. I called it. Keeping up her inner banter as well as talking with him helped her not focus on his abs as she buttoned him up. "So, I've got 'allergic to synthetic fabrics', 'has a personal tailor', and 'swordfighter' on my mysterious Leon Bingo sheet. Anything else I'm missing?"

"I'm a passable dancer."

"Oh, you can twerk?"

"... I don't follow."

Jasmine snorted, knowing that joking with him on some things would go right over his head. "Never mind. I'm assuming formal?"

"Yes. It was part of my upbringing."

"Oh, cool. I've never tried, and that's probably for the best. I wouldn't want to literally step on somebody's toes."

Leon gently clasped his hands over hers as she was moving towards the top two buttons on the shirt. "It's quite simple. All you need is a good lead. Let me demonstrate."

"O-oh, but-"Jasmine stuttered, unable to stop him from repositioning one of her hands on his shoulder while taking the other in his own.

"You've done me this favor, so let me return it." Leon's other arm drifted to her waist. "We'll go slowly, so you get used to my cadence."

I guess this is just what we doing, now. Jasmine stood stiff as a board, overly conscious of his hands on her the entire time. He took a measured step back, and she stressed too hard over which foot to place forward before overreaching and nearly slamming into his chest. Leon moved again, as fluid as always, and she tried not being so clunky with her movements by comparison.

"Leon, I don't think I'm cut out for this."

"Nonsense. *Feel* what we're doing instead of thinking about it. The energy is there, you just have to follow it."

While she inwardly grumbled about it being easier said than done, she applied his advice to the best of her ability. Eventually, she was able to move without much hesitation, and once she could somewhat anticipate Leon's movements, she could relax a bit. Dancing without music was odd, but the rhythm he set held her attention as they moved around a small section of her living room.

"In my experience, all formal dances start from this base. If you have a satisfactory partner, you'll find yourself passable at most of them in a short time."

"I see. I'm glad you're my partner in this, then."

Leon chuckled, angling her into a turn. "As am I."

Jasmine wasn't sure when they had stopped moving, but suddenly she was looking up at his face and was shell-shocked by what she saw in his expression.

Leon had always been someone with a striking gaze. Perhaps it had something to do with the fact that he was unearthly alluring and it had taken Jasmine enough time as it was to look at him directly without feeling odd about it. But with their recent outings, she had grown used to the various expressions that animated his face. His kindness and childlike curiosity of the world around him was always in the forefront.

So, she definitely was not prepared at all to meet eyes with a man who was now looking at her like he himself just realized that he had the capacity for desire. His lips were slightly parted, eyelids narrowed only a smidgen, but enough to give his brown eyes a lidded appearance as he met her gaze without blinking. The casual mood that permeated the room had shifted into something heavier, making Jasmine's heart beat faster and mouth drier.

"I..." Jasmine licked her lips, which caused Leon's gaze to flicker down towards her mouth for a moment. She was in full deer-caught-in-headlights mode, stuck between her sensibilities and the fact that she was still a woman who couldn't help but be attracted to such a fine specimen. Her brain didn't help by supplying the image of his bare upper body again, either. *Should I...?*

A sudden loud buzzing jerked both of them out of the odd spell they were under, and she blearily looked over to her cell phone jostling itself along the surface of her worktable where she left it. Leaving Leon's embrace had her feeling empty without his warmth, but her heart only started getting back to a normal pace once she was out of his personal bubble. Jasmine checked the screen, seeing that it was from the main office of her apartment complex.

"Hello?"

"Hi, is this Ms. Walters? You've got a package here for pickup. We plan to close up the mail room soon, so we're giving you this courtesy call."

"Oh, really?" Jasmine didn't recall ordering anything offline, but the least she could do is see if it was a mistake. "Okay, give me a few minutes, I'll be right down."

As she placed her phone back down on the table, she saw Leon straightening his cuffs out after buttoning the last of his shirt. He looked up at her and smiled in his usual kind way, the energy of the previous moment dissipated. "Thank you again, Jasmine, for your assistance. The fix is flawless."

"I'm glad. Sorry the button is plastic, though; I don't have *that* kind of fancy stuff laying around here. But when you get back to your tailor, just have them replace it properly."

Leon chuckled. "No... I think I'll keep it as is. A good memory for a pleasant day."

Jasmine didn't let it show how much that touched her, knowing how finicky he was. She grabbed her keys and led the way out of her apartment, walking with Leon to the front of the complex where she would have to split off to go to the office.

"So, um... I'll... catch you later, then?"

"I would hope so. Thank you once again for the excursion." Leon took her hand in his and kissed her knuckles, and Jasmine kept thinking about what it would have been like to feel those lips on hers. "Please take care."

"Ah, you too!" She called after him, watching his lithe figure round the corner and out of sight, heading towards the main road. Then, she remembered that she was on a time crunch to pick up her mysterious package and hustled inside the main office.

She was half expecting it to be a mistake until the attendant came back with a large box for her. Balancing it in her arms was a bit cumbersome, but it wasn't too heavy as she fit the key into her apartment door and swung it open, letting it close behind her before plopping down on the couch to examine the package.

After a moment's hesitation, she unwrapped the brown paper around the box and stared blankly at the ribbon embroidered with the shop name that held it together. Jasmine pinched the edge of the strand and tugged, letting the ribbon fall slack and allowing her access to its contents. She finally made herself blink dry, surprised at the neatly folded swathes of fabric that laid within: the coveted chiffon made by Schlaepfer being the first things she saw. The note that was left was a simple copy of Brodeur's return policy, or rather stern lack of one.

"...that motherfucker did NOT."

Jasmine wasn't one for gifts. It made her feel guilty in a strange way that she never really considered. Perhaps it was because she liked to work hard for everything that she had, even if it wasn't much. And as she sat in a decent apartment surrounded by the things she loved and collected on her own, the box in her lap was making her feel a complicated mix of emotions.

Shifting it to the cushion beside her, Jasmine reached for her cell, scrolling to Leon's contact and preparing to type out some blistering admonishment for him doing exactly what she didn't want him to do. She was one sentence in before she thought better of it and deleted the message. Jasmine went to Kim's number next, wanting to tell her about it, but then paused before sending it as well. *She'll probably just tell me there isn't anything wrong with a man wanting to spoil me.*

Jasmine massaged her temples slowly before getting up and walking over to her fridge. There was a bottle of wine within that she made sure to ration not only for her liver's sake, but also for frugality. Grabbing a coffee mug from the cabinet, she uncorked the container and let the red liquid unceremoniously plop in.

As she sipped her wine and let the warm haze of the first touches of alcohol cloud her system enough to relax her muscles, she walked over to where her work schedule was pinned to the wall and pinpointed the next day she had to do some sleuthing.

There is something I'm missing, and I know it. Fuck his secrecy, I'm gonna find out what I can.

CHAPTER SEVEN

The weather was growing cooler as the season progressed, which made Jasmine pull her thicker jacket around her body as she walked down the street. Once she reached her destination, she pushed open the door, causing the sound of the bell to ding into the depths of the shop. Taking a quick look around, she was relieved to see that she was the only one in. The owner of Brodeur's looked over the rim of his glasses at her as she tentatively approached the counter, putting down his steaming cup of coffee to smile warmly at her.

"Good to see you again, young lady. Is there anything I can help you with today?"

Jasmine pushed her cold hands into her pockets, worrying her lower lip with her teeth. The butterflies in her stomach fluttered now that she was truly faced with what she came to do, and she swallowed before replying. "Maybe."

"Maybe?"

"I'm actually not coming to ask about fabrics or anything. But I *am* wondering if you know anything about the guy I came here with last time. Leon?"

"Not much, I'm afraid. I didn't even know his name before you mentioned it." He blinked once, and the smile he wore toned down a notch. "It isn't every day that someone comes into my store inquiring about a person they seemed to be quite familiar with."

"Yeah, and it isn't every day that people drop thousands of dollars of fabric at my door from your shop, either." Her brown eyes cut towards the owner suspiciously. "He didn't know where I lived until after I got the package, and you're the only one I gave my address to. You really out here giving personal information to people you don't know?"

The shop owner couldn't hide the repentant flinch at her shrewd tone and piercing gaze. "It's complicated."

"It's about to get more complicated for you if I don't understand what's going on, Mr. Brodeur."

Sighing, he straightened up in his seat and appeared to contemplate his next words. "Are you out of contact with Leon?"

"No. But with as much as he *doesn't* tell me about himself, I might as well be left on read." Jasmine leaned on the counter, looking a bit tired. "Listen. Leon's real nice, but I just met this dude. He's buying me things like he's after something. I don't know what he does for a living... and I guess I'm just looking for reassurance that I'm not going to end up on the next episode of Unsolved Mysteries messing around with him. Your textiles are amazing, Mr. Brodeur, but they aren't worth me becoming a statistic."

Nodding slowly, he picked up his coffee cup and sipped on the warm contents for a moment before replying. "That is completely understandable. I can tell you that the unsolved mystery here would never be you, if that helps."

"I... guess? But how do you know?"

Mr. Brodeur paused while his eyes went past her, gauging

at the foot traffic outside of his shop. "While I might not have known him personally, I know well enough to recognize his family name. They have done business with my family for generations."

I knew this dude was loaded. Inherited wealth makes sense. "Is he famous?"

"No. He just comes from a very old and seclusive family. If you were to look them up, I doubt that you would find anything. Believe me, I've tried."

"So what you're really saying is that if I *were* to be kidnapped, I'd just disappear and no one would ever find me anyway... but I'd be rich?"

He actually burst out laughing at that, the lines around his eyes crinkling. "If you'd like to take the pessimistic route, I suppose. But with as honorable as I know my family to be, I doubt that they would find themselves catering to anyone unscrupulous."

"I see," Jasmine nodded. It wasn't a lot of information, but just being able to talk to someone else about the mysterious person that appeared in her life made her feel a little better about everything. "Thank you, Mr. Brodeur. Sorry for coming in on a hundred, but it's been weighing on me for a while. He doesn't seem to know much about this city, but he knew your shop, so I came here to... well, get some answers."

"It's understandable."

"I was nice to him for a spell and now he's just in my life like he intends to be a staple in it, somehow. Leon just... skirts anything about his life to me, but doesn't think anything of trying to spoil me," Jasmine explained as she fiddled with the beginnings of a hangnail.

"You know the saying about looking a gift horse in the mouth; most women in your position wouldn't question it. Not that I blame you, as I know I'd be one to wonder myself. I'm glad to hear that what little I have to offer seemed to ease your mind."

"Yeah. Well, I should probably get back home; I got all these pretty fabrics calling my name and some projects I should get started on. Next time I come in here, it'll probably be for a few of those clasps you have in that basket in the corner." Jasmine turned and made her way to the exit, already distracting herself by going over her thread collection in her head to see which one would pair best with such nice textiles.

"... wait."

Jasmine was almost to the door when Mr. Brodeur called out to her suddenly. She lifted an eyebrow and turned back to look at him, and it seemed as though he was as surprised as she was that he did so. "What's up?"

"I have seen him before. Leon. But..."

She started to feel the beginnings of an odd twinge in the pit of her stomach at his hesitance. "But what?"

"It was in this shop, actually." He ran a hand through his mostly grey hair as he recounted. "He was with two others at the time. I assumed one of them to be Leon's father, taking a beautiful woman on a tour of all the fabrics we had to offer. They were all dressed quite formally. It was odd, but not so much as to make me dwell on it. Most of the people who patronize here tend to be fancy types, as you can imagine."

Jasmine nodded carefully, slowly coming back up to the counter. Her mind had already put together a scene of Leon's late father and who she assumed to be Selene, from what he let slip days before. "Did he speak to you at all?"

The shopkeeper shook his head. "No. Leon preferred to stay in a corner closest to the door while the couple remained entirely engrossed in their own world." His lips turned up in a faint smile. "If you could picture the embodiment of love between two individuals... something so tangible that you could feel like all you had to do was reach out and grasp it in your hands... that was what it was like, being in the same area as that couple. Of course, it was already palpable being in the presence of three immeasurably dazzling people. I felt as though the walls of this shop would burst from trying to contain it all."

Jasmine continued compiling images in her mind revolving around a group of people that would most likely serve to make her realize how unremarkable she is even after cleaning up, through their mere presence alone. Her first impression of Leon was enough to make her double-take. But then, hearing the owner wonderfully recant his visitors also made her remember what Leon divulged to her about his father meeting someone that changed him, and it was heartwarming. It also relaxed her to know that what Leon told her and what she was hearing from Mr. Brodeur matched up.

"It had been awhile, so I was shocked to see your companion come back into my shop."

"Oh, like a few years or something?"

Mr. Brodeur hesitated before replying. "I'd estimate forty, give or take. I was around ten years old when they visited this shop, then owned by my late father."

Jasmine just stared dumbly at him, understanding the words said but finding it difficult to parse what they meant. "*Forty* years ago? I mean..." her brain struggled to do the math. "Was Leon a baby?"

"The man you came in with was the same one I witnessed all those years ago. I'd say he hasn't aged a day, by my estimation."

What the fuck. This is NOT real life. She wished she had somewhere to sit. Her mind was spinning with the reveal, and it was making her surroundings sway with it. She wanted to believe that he was pulling her leg way too hard for whatever reason, but the more she stared with wide eyes at the older man, the more she was scared that he was as earnest as he appeared to be. "How...?"

"My father made sure to instill everything that he thought I would need to carry on the family legacy of providing the best fabrics and service to the city. I listened to him well in his final years, even as he rambled on about the existence of certain people that were more than what they seemed; tragically beautiful, timeless, and full of a grace that seemed to have ebbed from the shores of society long ago." Mr. Brodeur reached up and removed the glasses from his face, rubbing a knuckle underneath one eye. "I believed it was a fever dream, to be honest. I hadn't given much of a thought to his words until that day you walked in with him."

"You know what you're telling me is unreal, right?" Jasmine's voice sounded odd to her own ears.

"Oh, undoubtedly. If I were in your shoes, I would write all of this off as the inane prattling of an old man losing his mind. But, against my better judgment, perhaps I saw something in your curiosity that offered me my own selfish out to tell you things that I haven't even shared with my own wife." He gave a small laugh. "When you two left that day, he came back into the shop to arrange shipment of the materials you appeared interested in. Chancing being too familiar with him, I wished him happiness in his relationship with you. Would you like to know his response?"

Jasmine could only give him a half nod of assent.

"'She has yet to choose me. I can only hope that she would, but if not... then I can be comforted by the fact that I was allowed her presence for whatever borrowed time she gifts to me.'"

Jasmine just stood there, a blank look on her face as she went through a flurry of emotions on the inside. "That... can't be right. I'm-"

"Nobody?" The shopkeeper lifted an eyebrow. "Often-times, it's others that see the light in us that we're blind to. Leon comes from a family that obviously appreciates the exquisite. Why would you ever stop to believe that his interest in you would be an exception?"

Jasmine didn't have an answer to that. It was one level of disbelief that she had to suspend to consider that Leon was evidently some type of immortal or had invested in a fair amount of plastic surgery only the best Hollywood stars could dream of acquiring. The other incredible revelation was that he allegedly liked her for who she was, which wasn't something Jasmine could wrap her head around. She wasn't a model. Her hobbies were obscure and involved a lot of sitting around inside looking unkempt and stressing over the fit of a sleeve. She worked a stressful customer service job that paid both just enough and not enough, and her undergraduate degree had been no help in getting her anywhere. There was nothing about her that she could see that would be intriguing enough to catch Leon's eye.

"I guess I have a lot of things to consider, Mr. Brodeur," Jasmine murmured.

"You do. And please, call me Kevin. Formalities don't matter when you find you share a connection with a mysterious soul."

The bell dinged from the front of the store, and he straight-ened up as a few potential patrons wandered in. Jasmine let the noise and presence of other people snap her out of her daze. "Well, let me get out of your way. I'll uh... still be back for those clasps, though."

"I look forward to that. Take care, Jasmine."

The cold air on her cheeks was negligible as she made her way back down the sidewalk, her mind numb from everything she hadn't planned on hearing. After walking a block in a daze, she took out her phone to call an Uber to her location, but instead found herself calling Kim.

"Ayyyeee, girl, what it do?" Her friend's voice drawled in her ear. "I ain't had time to catch you at work with all this holiday rush shit popping off and all these damn customers."

"Yeah. My bad about all that. I..." Jasmine's hand shook as she held the device to her ear, but she told herself it was mostly from the cold. "Girl, I just... it's starting to really get to me that I barely know anything about Leon."

"Why?"

"Girl, this fool legit bought me tons of ridiculously expensive fabric from the most premiere shop in town and had it shipped to my place without me knowing. Who does that?"

"Someone who wants to fuck you, duh. If he's anything like Elliot, you in for a helluva time. In fact, he may be even more freak nasty. You know what they say about them quiet, proper types."

Jasmine let out a sigh, knowing that Kim wouldn't be as concerned as she was. "I'm glad you had fun with Elliot, though. He does seem very much like your type."

"Whew, you don't *even* know. I shol did thank Leon as I was leaving they crib the other day, even though I know he ain't expect to see me coming out the room in nothing but Elliot's t-shirt."

"Wait, you know where they live?" A risky idea was brewing in her mind. "Do you happen to have the address?"

"I mean, I do, but like... why not ask Leon?"

"You could say I want to surprise him."

Kim snorted. "Oh, aiight then. You trying to get it in, you don't need to tell me twice. I'm finna text it to you." There was a slight rustling during the gap in conversation, and Jasmine's phone buzzed with the incoming message. "You headed over there now?"

Jasmine slowed to a stop on the sidewalk, her heart pounding. A part of her wanted to just rip that band-aid off and go straight over, but her rational side was fighting against it. "... no. I'm... I should sleep on it, first. I'll let you know when I do, though. For safety's sake."

"That's fine, you know I got your back, girl. Both him and Elliot just seem like rich kids living off they daddy trust fund having a grand old time. I know you not used to it, but listen; just have fun. A fine ass man wants to be your sugar daddy for a lil bit? Go on head and let him. Have him blow ya back out. Get him to buy you a car, fuck it. This could be the come up you need, but you too busy fussing to take it."

Jasmine wished she could believe her. The mind-blowing conversation she had with Kevin not too long ago still had yet to settle completely in her mind, and she knew that Kim would call her crazy for even entertaining it. *Maybe I am nuts, and I should just let this go.*

She kept that in mind as she ended the call and finally made her way back to the safety of her apartment. She mulled it over as she looked once again at the pile of fabric she had to play with, taking the time to lay each piece out carefully to get any creases out. When Jasmine showered and climbed into bed later that evening, her head was filled with replaying Leon's unexplained swordsmanship, his formalized speech patterns, and the odd things that she did know from him directly.

After twisting and turning for most of the night and waking up not feeling any better about it, Jasmine decided that she couldn't ignore her gut anymore.

For better or for worse, she was going to find things out from the man himself.

CHAPTER EIGHT

J asmine shoved her hand in her coat pocket after depressing the doorbell button, nervous but trying not to show it. She was expecting to pull up to a place that housed something ridiculous like a marble fountain and a circular driveway, stunned when instead they pulled up to the secluded abode just on the outskirts of town. It was still way nicer than anything she had ever seen, the brick seating nicely into the foliage that almost made her feel as if she had stepped into another world.

Worst case is that I got played by a shop owner and Leon is going to feel bad enough about it to actually tell me what his life is really like. But as she studied the leaded glass in the windows to the trees that enveloped the property, her nervousness became apparent and she found herself thinking that she should go right back to the driver still politely waiting in the curved driveway and pretend she never came.

Just as she was taking a step back off of the porch, a shadow could be seen on the other side of the frosted glass in the heavy wooden door, and it opened to reveal a stunned Leon.

"... Jasmine?"

Immediately, she felt stupid for not even having the courtesy of telling him that she knew where he lived and that she was inviting herself over. "Sorry, I got your address from Kim. I... can I come in?"

"Yes, of course," Leon said quickly, stepping aside and holding the door open wider for her to slip in. Jasmine stepped past him into the foyer, glad for the warmth of the indoors and busied herself with taking off her shoes instead of looking at him. He was striking as always, and for some reason decided to look like a GQ model with a partly unbuttoned dark blue shirt and the sleeves rolled up on his forearms. *Did someone tell him that was my kink?*

"This is a surprise, but I can't say that it's an unpleasant one," Leon continued, and Jasmine felt his hands on her shoulders when she straightened up, barely suppressing a shiver as he removed her coat for her and hung it on one of the hooks right near where her shoes were. "What brings you here?"

Curiosity that I hope won't kill me. "Oh, you know... just returning the surprise of you making tons of expensive fabric appear at my doorstep unexpectedly."

Leon winced. "Ah."

"Oh? You thought I'd let you off the hook for that, didn't you?" She looked over at him with a smirk. "Listen, that was sweet... but don't do that again."

"But I thought it was the giving season, yes?"

"Already looking for loopholes, huh? The audacity. I think you bought enough to make up for ten future giving seasons."

"Aw, look at you two, already arguing like a married couple." Elliot appeared from around the corner, leaning casually against a doorway. "Good to see you again, Jasmine."

"Same. Thanks for entertaining my girl. She appreciated it."

"I've never left a woman disappointed," Elliot replied with a wink, then slipped into the kitchen that they finally approached. "She's a lot of fun. Gonna see if we can meet up again this week. Anyway, want something to drink? Leon made tea earlier... and if you put a splash of bourbon in it, then it's actually good."

"The tea without the alcohol is fine," Jasmine replied, laughing a little. Having regular conversation with the two of them helped ease her nerves, and she further distracted herself by looking around at the décor. It was someplace that reminded her of where she grew up, populated with French colonial houses that had plenty of character within narrow hallways and decorated moldings. She only paused to take the warm mug from Elliot and breathe in the earthy scent before taking a grateful sip, letting the warmth of the beverage settle into her bones.

"So, did you really just drop by to curse Leon out for spoiling you?" Elliot asked, bringing his own cup to his lips.

She stared into her drink for longer than she should have, realizing that she really didn't have a plan on how to tactfully broach the subject. "Umm... kinda? More like I had a question. But I don't want you to laugh at me if I ask it."

Leon gave her an encouraging smile. "No worries. Simply ask, and we'll do our best to answer."

Well... here goes, then. "Are you a vampire?"

The bit of silence that stretched between them just made Jasmine's face heat up in embarrassment. Then Elliot burst out into loud peals of laughter, and she whipped her head towards him indignantly. "Bruh, I *said* I didn't want to get laughed at!"

"Sorry! I just... whew," Elliot tried getting himself together, wiping a tear away. "I expected something serious."

"But I *am* serious!" Jasmine placed the mug down on the table in front of her and folded her arms indignantly across her chest. "I can't think of any other reason why someone deadass told me that they saw Leon forty fucking years ago looking the same as he does now!"

She felt the energy in the room change almost abruptly. Elliot's eyes widened, and Leon's expression became flat. The two men exchanged a long glance, and Jasmine switched her gaze back and forth between them, feeling more concerned by the moment.

"... okay listen, it's fine if it was a joke."

Leon and Elliot continued staring at each other, and Jasmine felt like they were having an entire silent conversation with just their eyes. It was almost as if she wasn't there at all, and definitely did not help to settle her nerves. *Is it too late to ask for that bourbon?*

Eventually, they broke their intense gaze, and turned their attention back to Jasmine. Leon still looked fairly sober, and while Elliot did give Jasmine a cheeky smile, she could tell that he was using it as a cover to hide whatever he was actually feeling. "I'm gonna leave you two to hash this out," the blond finally said, knocking back the rest of his spiked tea in one fell swoop. After placing the mug in the sink, he slipped out of the kitchen and had Jasmine sorely wishing that his lighthearted energy would stick around.

"Who told you this?" Leon asked in a voice too soft.

"It was Ke- ah, Mr. Brodeur. I went back to the shop and pressed him for any information about you, because I was tired of you dodging me." Jasmine fiddled with the hem of her sweater. "He said that I am the only person he's ever told, but I really don't understand how that could be possible."

Nodding slowly, Leon turned and left the kitchen, causing Jasmine to follow him to the living room. An inlaid fireplace crackled with life, sending warmth through the large room that was nicely decorated with ornate rugs and leather furniture.

She picked one end of the couch to perch upon while she stared at Leon, whose hands were in his pockets as he paused on his way to an armchair to stand in front of the mantle, the light from the fire sending shadows across his face.

"If I explained to you how it was possible, would you believe me?"

Jasmine regarded him silently for a few moments, her face neutral while she thought back to Kevin's words. ...*the existence of certain people that were more than what they seemed; tragically beautiful, timeless, and full of a grace that seemed to have ebbed from the shores of society long ago.* "I'm gonna be honest with you, chief; I don't know. I've had to suspend a fair amount of belief just to come here. I'm still not quite convinced that I'll not end up dead in a ditch somewhere for asking too many questions."

Leon did give a small snort at that, the faint hint of a smile upturning the edge of his mouth. "You are far too precious to be killed. In fact, I consider it my responsibility to ensure that no harm will come to you."

"Why is that?"

He reached inside of his pocket and unearthed a chain with a teardrop shaped jewel hanging from it. It was almost easy to miss with the flickering of the light from the fireplace, but Jasmine recognized it as the cell phone charm she saw on him days ago. The more her eyes focused on it, she noticed that it contained an inner glow set to a rhythm.

"This is the Spark. It is a fragment of a very special Flame that my people currently possess, and its purpose is to identify the one who will reignite it. That person is you."

She let out a nervous laugh. "Wait, what? Hold up. *Please* tell me that this is just all one big elaborate joke. If Kevin was in on it too, that's aiight. I'll take the L on everything and we can move past this."

The wood popped a few times in the fireplace, filling the awkward silence that settled between them. Jasmine's eyes drifted back towards the necklace he held, feeling slightly mesmerized by the pulsing of the light within the jewel.

"I'm sorry. I know it would be easier for you to believe that you were pranked. But," Leon gave her a wan smile. "It is not the case. You are the Prime, Jasmine; a human that is chosen to mediate a treaty between two ancient races that has been in motion for thousands of years. You are not the first and will not be the last to shoulder this fate."

A few more moments passed before Jasmine abruptly got to her feet and started walking towards the door. *Why didn't I just leave his weird ass alone from the start? He's hot, but he's obviously fucking crazy.*

"Jasmine, wait!"

She didn't respond, focusing instead on lacing her shoes up on her feet as fast as she could. She didn't know how long it would be until she could call a ride to pick her up, but she was fully prepared to do so while power walking away from the suburb she was in.

"Jasmine..."

She reached for her coat and was stopped by Leon's hand over hers. She was gearing up to be violent until he came around in front of her and actually got down on one knee, clasping her fingers in his.

"Please. I know this is surreal for you. I've admittedly practiced countless times on how to approach this, and it gives me no joy to admit that I didn't find the right words before the gods made moves for me. I have asked much patience of you, and still I ask for one more; give me the opportunity to prove that what I've told you is true."

Jasmine stared down at him, taking in his pleading expression and nothing but naked earnestness in his brown eyes. She could tell that his guard was completely dropped, which was strange to see after dealing with such a composed individual any other time. But she felt as though she were at a crossroads and couldn't figure out what the right decision was. Her mind was yelling at her to make an excuse, exit, and never speak to him again. But something kept her rooted to the spot, and it wasn't just his plea that made her hesitate.

Throwing caution to the wind, she heaved a heavy sigh. "You've got one shot, Leon. *One*. And I shouldn't even be giving you that."

Nodding, he got to his feet, and still didn't let go of her hand. "Thank you. I will make it count."

Leon led Jasmine deeper into the house and up a flight of stairs. Normally, she would have been more curious about the layout and how many rooms it actually held, but her mind was a bit preoccupied with other things. It wasn't long down the hallway before he opened a door, revealing a cozy study with many books that Jasmine was automatically curious about. A reading nook laid tucked into one side of the room, the ambient light from the window nicely illuminating an ornate full-length mirror not far from there. It was gilded and seemed out of place for what was essentially a small library, but she watched as Leon finally let go of her hand and stepped up to it, watching what he did next.

Lifting a hand, Leon took his pointer finger and began tracing faint etches that Jasmine just noticed blending into the frame. They glowed like bioluminescence as he continued doing so, following the arch just above his head and coming back down to the other side. The mirror looked no different when he was done, but Jasmine watched as he put his hand through the silvered surface as if it wasn't even there.

"Are you ready?"

Jasmine wanted to say no; it would have been nothing but

the truth. There was no way, shape or form that she was ready for anything that she unknowingly walked into. But as she gazed upon Leon's face that was trained upon hers, she knew that she wasn't turning back. When he extended his hand like he had done so many times before, Jasmine placed her own in it and took small comfort in the familiar warmth of his palm as she did so. She likely didn't have to, but she closed her eyes as they both stepped through the portal waiting until both of her feet were on the ground on the other side.

CHAPTER NINE

J asmine opened her eyelids slowly, first seeing Leon in front of her before she took in her surroundings. Like the house she just left, it was a study, but far more ornate and with books that piled to the high ceiling and as far as the walls could reach. Jasmine took in the Victorian feel of the decor, ranging from the sculpted molding lacquered in deep mahogany to the filigree that dotted the ends of the bookshelves inlaid to the wall. She looked down at her feet, which were standing on an immaculately polished stone floor. Turning, Jasmine glanced back at the mirror they stepped through and only saw her reflection. The runes that allowed them passage slowly died down to fade into the mantle.

Leon then motioned for her to follow him. Jasmine let him lead her to a heavily curtained section of the wall, where he reached for a braided cord. The drapery parted inch by inch to bring in the soft glow of moonlight until it encompassed a fair amount of the room. The window was wider than Jasmine expected, made of leaded glass that was immaculately clear and gave her the view she needed to look upon the city below.

Gothic spires jutted into a night sky that seemed just on the edge of twilight in a strange way, framing the moon that caressed the land with its silvered light. Columns intertwined with vines were flanked by ornate statues of figures she assumed to be angels reaching upwards, faces peering towards the heavens they couldn't reach. The cobblestoned streets were lined with lamps that put Jasmine in the mind of something she might have seen in a documentary from old France, but the incandescence they emitted didn't seem to be powered by gas at all. She stepped closer to the window without touching it, not wanting to mar the surface with her fingerprints even though she gaped at how vast and elaborately dark the lay of the land was.

At the very least, Jasmine knew one thing for certain; she was tragically underdressed, and her companion's unreasonably picky nature when it came to clothes made a whole lot of sense just by glancing down at the people walking idly down the road.

"Welcome to Hellenia."

Jasmine wasn't sure if she had passed out somewhere along the way and this was really just one big dream that her brain was concocting to answer all of the mysterious things. "I... I need to sit down."

"Certainly." Leon gently took her arm and led her over to a chair upholstered in black velvet, where she gratefully let her shaky legs rest.

"What... I don't even know where to start. I just..." Jasmine gestured vaguely to her surroundings. "Our meeting definitely wasn't a coincidence, I guess."

"No. I went looking for you specifically; the Spark I have in my possession assisted me." He paused. "I do apologize for my initial deception. I would have liked nothing more than to be immediately forthcoming with my intentions and your purpose, but I fear that would not have been taken well."

You got that right. I'm not even taking it very well right now. "Yeah. Saying that you really are a vampire would have just gotten you ghosted off jump."

Leon's brow furrowed. "But vampires don't exist. I am Hellenian."

Jasmine supposed that it was a mixture of the shock she was feeling and his matter-of-fact tone that set her off into manic giggles. *This man who legit had me walk through a mirror to another world just looked at me crazy for suggesting that vampires are a thing.* "Okay. Then what *are* you? Outside of not human."

"For simplicity's sake, I suppose you could label me as a demon."

Jasmine's eyes nearly popped out of her skull. "I, uh... would never have guessed that. Demons don't look as pretty as you are."

Leon let out a slight chuckle at that, looking strangely bashful at Jasmine's appraisal of his looks. "Thank you. There is much that must be explained, but I would rather show you than tell you. Are you alright to stand, or do you need more time?"

She nodded, slowly getting to her feet. The logical part of her was oddly calm, as if it were awaiting more information that it could assimilate into something understandable and normal. Her emotions, however, were the most wrecked part of her. It made sense that the only reason someone like Leon would have ever approached her was because of some higher purpose, but it also made her feel disappointed in a way that she didn't want to fully acknowledge. "I'm as good as I'm gonna be for this."

"I'm glad to hear it." He held up the Spark. "May I? This is yours, after all."

Jasmine shrugged then stood up, allowing Leon to approach her. She managed not to shiver as he stepped behind her and carefully laid the silvered chain along her collarbone to clasp behind her neck. It was nearly weightless, and she looked down at the jewel that pulsated like a living thing against the shirt she wore for only a moment before following Leon out of the study.

Walking down the ornate stairs of the mansion she was in was surreal. Everything that she saw of Hellenia from her spot in the study was intimidating yet extremely beautiful to witness in ways that she didn't have the words to describe. It was hard enough for her to keep her head from swiveling about, and she only paused when she recognized a familiar figure idly sitting in an armchair near the bottom of the steps.

"Elliot?"

The man in question looked up, giving her his trademark smile as he stood. "Hey there, welcome to the dark side!" He waggled his fingers in a cartoonish manner before stepping up to Jasmine as she reached the bottom and encasing her in a hug. "I was worried that you would have just punched Leon and walked out of our lives forever."

"... I mean, that was almost what happened," she murmured while staring at him. He was dressed in the same casual clothes from earlier, but that's where the similarities ended. With all of his hand flailing, she noticed that his fingernails were black and taloned as if he had just come back from an acrylic salon, although they looked much less polished and more organic than that. When she looked up to his face, curved horns that reminded her of a ram's were poking out from the shock of bleached hair on his head, curving elegantly back to end at a point just below his earlobe.

Elliot caught her gazing at him and winked one of his red

eyes at her. "Like what you see? It only gets better from here, baby."

Jasmine blinked a few times slowly. "Uh huh."

Leon's voice sounded from beside her. "Could you do me a favor and take Jasmine to *De Igne Altaris Gratiarum*? I'll follow shortly."

Elliot nodded. "Will do. Maybe if I'm lucky, Viviane will be there."

Jasmine raised an eyebrow at the tone in his voice, grasping onto anything else to focus on that wasn't the fantastical realm she stepped into. "Oh? Who's that?"

"She's only the most stacked, voluptuous, sexy-"

"-high priestess that would like nothing better than to see you hung," Leon finished, turning to go back up the stairs. Jasmine snorted at that, and Elliot pouted.

"I mean, she can definitely see me hung in another way. I've offered multiple times."

"Looks like you finally came across a woman who doesn't fall for your charm and good looks, huh?" Jasmine said in amusement. "Never would have thought."

"Oh, she wants me. How can anyone *not* want me? She just doesn't want to seem easy, so I get it." He ran a hand over his horned head. "Well, let's get going on our little mini-tour. It's actually just beyond the courtyards of the estate, here."

The heavy, ornate doors parted with ease as Elliot opened them, and they walked out into the night air along a cobbled walkway. It was warmer than the world she just left, and she was glad that she was distracted from bringing her heavier coat that was still hanging in the foyer of Leon's other abode. But despite the temperature change, it was still just on the side of chilly, with a touch of humidity in the air that rose goosebumps on her arms under her long-sleeved shirt as they walked. Feeling oddly exposed now that they weren't surrounded by walls, she stuck close to Elliot's side, looking around for anyone else while admiring the carefully trimmed bushes and flowers that lined the path.

"So... I knew Leon was bougie, but I didn't know it was like *that*."

"Yeah, of course it is. Nothing but the best for a royal, after all."

Jasmine stumbled mid-step. "Excuse me? He's *royalty??*"

"Oh... I guess he didn't get around to telling you all that yet, huh?" Elliot winced, then shrugged. "Well, just act surprised or something when he tells you. I don't really know what I'm supposed to be telling you or not."

This shit just got even more wild. "Sure." Jasmine looked up as she saw a couple of figures approaching. Their entire bodies were draped in diaphanous dark material, giving them the illusion that they were merely floating by. As they got closer, she could make out feminine figures beneath the fabric, and was surprised to note that they didn't seem to have anything on underneath the layers of gossamer. She tried not to stare, but her head swiveled with their passing even as they kept their heads down, and she felt Elliot doing the same.

"Damn. Not her. But always a good view," he glanced back over to Jasmine. "Those are the priestesses. They tend to altars, do holy ceremonies, and any kind of magic shit that we need. My favorite part is the fact that when they're in service, they wear as very little as possible."

Jasmine gave him an odd look. "Don't you consider it sacrilege to look upon holy women like a lecher?"

"No. Why? It's just appreciation. And even though I know you've probably got the idea that Hellenians are all sticks in the mud like Leon, we actually don't have the hang ups humans have regarding sexuality."

"I see." Jasmine looked up as they approached another

building. It almost reminded her of an old chapel, but there was no bell tower, instead sporting the ornate accents that mausoleums would have in grand cemeteries. The light from the moon shone on the combination of granite and marble, giving it an otherworldly glow along with the pair of lamps that stood on either side of it. "Um, random question, but does Kim know that you're a... uh..."

Elliot shook his head as they climbed the few steps to the door. "Nah. She never will, either. I may push a lot of rules, but even I know not to truly reveal what I am to a human. I should probably duck out of here for a bit and check on her, though. Did you know she makes a mean plate of hash browns?"

"Yeah, she does." Jasmine sighed, resigning herself to the fact that she had unknowingly introduced her friend to a demon. "Oh... shit. When you see her, can you tell her that I'm okay? Make up something, I don't know. I don't want her thinking that I actually did get kidnapped."

"Don't worry; as you've probably guessed, we're all well versed in coming up with excuses on the fly to cover our asses." He reached for the brass handle and turned it, pulling the door open and gesturing Jasmine to go in first. "After you."

When the door closed behind her, Jasmine automatically felt somewhat claustrophobic even though the building itself wasn't very small at all. But simply being in a passageway that was lined with actual torches was unnerving. She walked by the sconces, feeling the warmth of the crackling flames go by her cheeks as she went the only way available. Everything was very well kept, and she quickly put together that the priestesses that they passed likely had shifts to come in and tend to the area they were in. Eventually the hallway opened up into a large chamber, and the only thing that sat in the very center of it was a stone altar surrounded by intricately woven iron bars, keeping the fire within its perimeters safe from anyone who may accidentally get too close.

"Alright... so. That right there? That's the Flame. It's the bigger portion of what you have on right now." Elliot gestured to Jasmine's necklace, and she tore her eyes away from the Flame to the jewel laying on her chest. It seemed brighter now that it was in proximity of the blaze, but she also noticed that the Flame itself didn't seem to give off any actual heat.

"Believe it or not, it used to be a lot bigger. This whole room could be illuminated like daytime easily. But it's reaching the end of its lifespan right now, which is why Leon had to go out and find you."

Jasmine trained her brown eyes once again on the ethereal Flame in front of her. It was a brilliant shade of blue, dancing in air as if there was a constant breeze buffeting it, and needed no kindling to stay lit. "Why is it going out?"

"The last Prime passed. The Flame is connected to the Prime's life force, so once they're gone, the Flame chooses another host."

This is insane. "So. As this... new Prime, I have to get this thing lit for you again? How do I do that?"

"Uh, you go on a little pilgrimage up a mountain called Hyperion. There, you'll find the actual spirit of the Flame, commune with it, and then bring it back."

"How steep is this mountain? Do you know I live a very sedentary life and have gotten out of breath doing too many laps around the track at a gym? How the hell do y'all expect me to climb a *mountain*?" Jasmine shook her head, quickly becoming overwhelmed once more. "And you guys can't do it?"

"No. The place where the Flame resides on the mountain is sacred and only appears to the Prime looking for it. And I don't think you'll be needing hiking gear or anything. It's a special kind of mountain. Hard to explain, but you'll see what I mean when you get there."

Jasmine took a deep breath. "And if I refuse? Prefer to just go on back to my customer service job and small apartment and be oblivious to everything I didn't know I signed on for?"

Elliot crossed his arms and looked at her. "There hasn't been a Prime in history that's shirked their fate, and you definitely aren't the only human who has felt that they shouldn't have to do it. But no matter what, the Flame chooses who it does for a reason; it wouldn't bond with the heart of someone who had it in them to just walk away from this."

Jasmine opened her mouth for a rebuttal, but then realized that she didn't really have the words. She hated the idea that her life wasn't her own; she lived a low-key, mediocre existence, but it was one that she built herself. She wanted to be contrary for the sake of exercising her own personal autonomy. She was pushing back on everything that had been dumped on her in a futile effort to make her feet feel like she was on solid ground. But when Elliot told her that, Jasmine knew that she had made her choice the moment Leon revealed himself and she didn't leave. She could chalk it up to simply being in shock, but there was an odd pinprick of surety in where she was at that moment despite the whirlwind of thoughts and emotions that sat below the surface of her mind.

"Fair enough. I guess since I'm already here, I might as well learn why y'all have to go through all of this in the first place."

"There are two races of beings that once walked the Earth alongside humans; Hellenians and Draconians." Leon's voice echoed down to them, and Elliot turned to the source. "Earth and the humanity that dwells upon its surface are precious, coveted entities that naturally draw our respective kind to your soil. Simply put, both of our races could not abide peacefully upon the same Earth. Legends dictate that our battles nearly tore the world asunder. As such, the gods that were invested in keeping the world intact instated an accord that we've kept for millennia. The Prime decides which race mingles with their own for a time through the power of the Flame, as we've long lost the privilege of choosing that for ourselves."

Leon finally stepped fully into the chamber they occupied, and Jasmine was back to gaping unattractively at him. Gone was the man that sheepishly adored French fries, and in his place stood a rather imposing figure with wardrobe choices that blew anything that she had previously seen on him out of the water. Her eyes went to his head, looking at the horns that were narrower than Elliot's, and curved in a spiral fashion towards the back of his head. Then she took in the arabesque pattern that laid into the suit he now wore, subtle in its dark colors but serving as the perfect accent to the piece itself. The black button up shirt that laid under it seemed to shimmer slightly in the light cast from the Flame, but the coup de grace was definitely the color of his eyes. Jasmine was shocked enough to see Elliot with red eyes, but it was even more of a change to look upon Leon with gold irises that were reflective in their intensity.

"I see, but..." Jasmine turned back towards the Flame, gesturing lamely at it, herself, and then back at them. "I don't know what to think. I don't even know *how* to think right now. I should be asking more questions, because I got a lot of them. But for right now, I think I need to let what I've learned settle a bit more."

"Seems fair to me," Elliot said finally. "Unwinding will probably do you some good. Hey, you think Sustina would be able to help with that?"

Leon nodded in agreement. "She would. I should check to see if she's available for a summon." He turned to go back down the hallway that would take them outside once more, and Jasmine suddenly shrieked.

"What the *fuck*? You... you have..."

"Ah. Yes," Leon gave his wings a small flex from their tightly tucked position against his back, still careful not to extend them to their full span. "I do."

"... may I touch them?"

Leon nodded. "If you'd like."

Stepping forward, Jasmine got into his personal bubble and reached out and gently laid her fingers on the membrane of a wing in awe. They somewhat resembled bat wings, featherless yet covered in thin peach fuzz that was buttery to the touch and gave the wings a darkened appearance. She felt the skin beneath her touch quiver when she moved, and that fascinated her while encouraging her to lay her entire palm on the wing and skim it downwards in a gentle petting motion.

"Do a lot of Hellenians have wings?" She asked softly.

"Nope," Elliot chimed in, his eyes sparkling. "It's why he's royalty, and why everyone in Hellenia knows who he is."

For whatever reason, just the simple motion of touching something as spectacular as his wings was grounding. Up until that point, it felt as though Jasmine was in nothing but a dreamy daze, struggling to find her footing. Now she was able to tell herself that for better or for worse, this was real, and she had to do what she did best and make the most out of it.

"Oh, okay." Jasmine removed her hand and looked him up and down. "Everything suits you, honestly. And as weird as all of this is to me, it's nice to see you in your natural habitat."

Leon gave her the same dazzling smile that he was capable of in his human form, and she couldn't help but feel doubly struck by his beauty once again. "Thank you. I hope to make your introduction as smooth as I can manage... and I suppose that starts with introducing you to others who are less facetious than I." Leon extended his hand to her, and she reached to take it like she had done many times before when she thought he was nothing but an oddly behaved human.

"You two are so *cute*," Elliot tittered under his breath as he followed them out of the altar.

CHAPTER TEN

Jasmine sat in a chair that was just on the side of uncomfortable as she watched Leon light a candle with only his fingertips, pause for a few moments, and then extinguish it. "Is that y'all way of texting?"

Leon chuckled. "I suppose. For Hellenians, we do have the ability to psychically contact one another. It usually involves imbuing an object of importance with a link that can be activated with a small bit of magic, closing just as easily. It is a one-way communication sort of device." He gestured to the candle. "This is the key Sustina chooses to represent her."

"Do you and Elliot have something like that?"

"We used to. But we are so close that a physical object is no longer needed. I can always reach for a part of my consciousness like a string and strum it, expecting feedback."

Jasmine nodded. "Wow. So you both know what the other is thinking all the time, or something? Does that ever get awkward?"

He moved to a chair nearby Jasmine, carefully tucking his wings as he sat down. "There have been a few... unfortunate times I've regretted the timing of opening our link, but as a whole our connection does not grant each other full range of each other's thoughts." Leon lifted his hands, long elegant fingers tracing the shape of a circle. "There are many layers to a Hellenian's mind; you keep what you wish deep within you, away from others. On the surface, there can be a thin layer of immediate emotions, speculation, ideas. You may create as many levels as you desire, as many chambers for different aspects of yourself for you to feel comfortable. Hellenians are a naturally private people, and we follow a strict code to ensure that every one of us will not feel imposed upon... this includes respecting your private counsel as well."

"Good to know," Jasmine took a deep breath and tried to relax. "So, um... when were you gonna tell me that you were royalty?"

Leon gave her a sheepish smile. "Only when I absolutely had to, if I'm being honest. I didn't want you feeling intimidated by me."

Jasmine snorted. *Like everything else I've been exposed to thus far is any easier to swallow.* "I'm assuming you have no siblings?"

Leon crossed his legs and placed his hands on one knee. "Correct, in a sense. I am not my father's only child. However, I am the only one with wings. A High Lord requires a male heir with that trait to be named as a royal."

"So... how many kids did your daddy make before you came into the picture? Do y'all have family reunions or whatnot? Do you live in this big ass house by yourself? Do *you* have kids?" Jasmine paused in the rambling of questions that just fell from her lips. "Sorry. I know I said I needed time for things to settle, but there's *so* much I don't know. If I'm being too nosy, then just tell me to shut up."

"I wouldn't dare," Leon reassured swiftly. "I am happy to

answer any and all questions you have for me. It is already unfair that you must go through this as abruptly as it's turned out to be. Now, I suppose I should answer inquiries in the order of which they came? The number of children my father has created isn't..." he trailed off then, then directed his gaze towards the door. "You may enter."

"Oh no, go ahead. I'd definitely like to hear your take on Vretiel's various progeny. I want to see if the stories match up with my experience with a few of them."

Jasmine looked over to the voice at the door to the room they were currently in and witnessed the first female Hellenian she laid her eyes on. She swept into the room in a long, shimmering maroon dress that clung to every curve on her and moved as if it were an extension of her body. The curled horns on either side of her head were almost like buns, the small point protruding just next to her mahogany-colored eyes. Jasmine wished that she would just stop staring at every single Hellenian that came into her view, but she couldn't get over how ethereal all of them were. *She has wings, too?*

Standing from his chair, Leon extended both hands to meet Sustina's, whose palms were facing upwards. His long-nailed fingertips brushed her wrists gently as he leaned forward and touched his cheeks to hers in greeting. Jasmine was slightly enamored with what had to be a common gesture for them to make, since both of them moved with the type of grace that made it seem like they were dancing.

"Thank you for answering the summons on such a short notice." Leon turned to Jasmine then, gesturing with a flourish. "Sustina, may I introduce you to Jasmine, the latest Prime. I... might have overwhelmed her with the gravity of her task, and I believe she would do well with a bit of a pampered distraction."

Sustina looked over at Jasmine then, and the latter hastily

rose from her chair, uncertain of the proper way of greeting. She wrung her fingers nervously, grinning awkwardly as the woman walked towards her. Just as Jasmine was about to stick her hand out in a handshake, Sustina's arms enveloped her into a warm hug as if she were a dear friend rather than a confused human who stumbled into what appeared to be a gothic Narnia.

"It's a pleasure to meet you, dear," Sustina said affectionately, and Jasmine automatically felt the tension ease out of her shoulders. She had the urge to return the hug, but didn't know how to do so without bumping into her wings, so she just stood there with her arms at her sides while breathing in the cloying scent that Sustina brought with her. It had a floral hint and a sweetness that Jasmine couldn't place but didn't find to be off-putting like most perfumes were to her. When the hug broke, she looked up into Sustina's eyes and perplexed by the depth she found in them. Jasmine had definitely seen some pretty eyes before, but when she looked into a Hellenian's, their irises seemed to pop out at her in 3D.

"Ah, same," Jasmine said lamely, causing Sustina to chuckle.

"Please, don't worry about formalities." She brushed a few strands of her wavy hair behind one shoulder as she turned back towards Leon. "I'll be sure to return Jasmine to you adequately refreshed, safe and sound."

Leon nodded. "It is greatly appreciated. I should see what duties I've neglected in the meantime." He smiled at Jasmine. "You're in good hands."

It's not like I really have a choice in the matter. Waving at Leon, Jasmine turned and followed Sustina out of the room, back down the stairs to the main hall that led to the entrance of the chateau, and out of the door. Instead of walking the path that Elliot had used when taking her to the Flame, they followed another that led to a cobbled road where a sleek black stagecoach was parked. The inner rims of the slender wheels were coated with the same red that Sustina wore, gleaming in the moonlight that coated the street. A man stepped down from the front of it to open the door for them as they approached, stairs smoothly unfolding as he did so. Jasmine tried not to look too astonished, but there weren't any horses to pull the vehicle that she could see, and kept her mouth shut about it until they were seated in the plush seats of the caravan with the door shut securely behind them.

"Y'all don't do animal labor, huh?"

Sustina shook her head, causing her black-to-red tipped hair to sway. "Magic is employed for transport; it is much cleaner and preferred." She looked at Jasmine out of the corner of her eye. "Ask your questions; they'll only multiply the more you sit on them."

Jasmine knew that the point of even being with Sustina was to not think about the outlandish situation she had found herself in. Yet the presence of another woman who had almost a maternal feel despite her obvious allure was already de-clouding her mind. "Alright. Well, um... what do you do here in Hellenia?"

"I am a courtesan. I've made a name for myself in the years that I've been in service, and that has granted me a fair amount of prestige in the realm. I am able to pick and choose my patrons with scrutiny, devoting the majority of my time to training other courtesans, namely those sequestered specifically for royal use."

Elliot wasn't lying when he said that Hellenians didn't have human hang ups on sex work. "What do you mean, royal use? How many royal families are there?"

"Only one, by the name of Exousia. There are other

powerful families scattered throughout Hellenia, but only one High Lord." The coach moved along the road, getting away from Leon's abode. "But, considering that the royal line requires a male winged heir to continue, I'm sure you can understand the necessity for a catered line of what are essentially concubines."

Jasmine's eyes moved to the wings on Sustina's back. "Why can't women lead, again?"

"Because Hellenians are stubbornly tied to tradition even if it does not always serve us in the most efficient manner," Sustina laughed, her mirth musical as it reverberated off of the coach walls. "However, leading an entire realm is not a responsibility that I'd like thrust upon me simply due to the matter of my birth; I will never envy Leon his burden. Having wings elevates me to just the right amount of access here without being beholden to staunch customs."

Jasmine looked out of the window on her side of the coach, taking in the buildings and structures that they passed. The towering spires that poked the sky and the flying buttresses that connected them were marvelous, yet as she trained her eyes on street level, she noted that things seemed more ordinary than she thought. Cafes and markets could be seen, filled with Hellenians going about everyday activities just like any human would back home. "You and Leon are related, I guess?"

"Perhaps; my birth was a fluke, and my mother never disclosed who my father was. It is quite possible that I could have been a lovechild of a saucy Exousia heir. It doesn't matter in the end, however. I've built my life within the freedom of not being concerned with lineage." Sustina smiled at Jasmine. "Leon will be the third High Lord I've lived through, and the one I've felt the closest to."

Third? Do I even want to know how old she is? Jasmine

studied the woman next to her that looked no older than thirty-five at the most. "He's lucky to have you in his corner."

"Oh, don't I know it. I do not miss any opportunity to remind him of that, as well." The coach trailed off to a smooth stop. "Let's get you properly relaxed and back off to your highness before he starts to worry."

The building that they came to was less intimidating than Leon's mansion, but was still ornate with stained glass windows and a moderately sized courtyard filled with nicely shaped bushes interspersed with various statues. If Jasmine looked long enough, she realized that a few of them were mildly risqué, and she kept her eyes on the door in front of them and Sustina's figure as she climbed the few steps before pushing it open.

"Welcome to my pride and joy, Haven. Please be sure to leave your shoes at the door."

Jasmine bent down and peeled off her sneakers while gazing at her surroundings in an awe that hadn't abated since she stepped through that mirror. Ornate chandeliers hung down the hallway, giving the place a glow that was just bright enough to be enjoyable without being overwhelming. Peering into one of the curved alcoves, she saw a small gathering of women practicing their posture. Having the eye for fashion as she did, her eyes were immediately drawn to what they were wearing. The layered mesh tulle that encompassed the majority of the dress hung to the floor, hiding their feet while miraculously not appearing like a princess type of skirt. It was embroidered with interspersed gems that glittered like stars along the entire dress, providing nice accents to the fishnet bishop sleeves that belled elegantly around their arms. The empire waist of the ensemble gave way to a v-neckline that came back together to form a choker, and immediately Jasmine started wondering if there were patterns she could acquire for such a masterpiece.

"So, where can I get me an extra one of those? For science, of course."

"Hmm? The dress, or the woman within it?" Sustina lightly teased, laughing at Jasmine's flustered reaction. "The Quattuor style has been coined as the most preferred for courtesans, however I am proud to say that I've normalized this particular rendition for my adepts in particular. Dark grey is worn by those in training, while black for fully fledged courtesans. Dark purple is worn by those in teaching roles."

"I've never heard of that style, before." Jasmine's brain was on overdrive now, having considered the possibility of discovering a new realm of fashion she could delve into and modify for her own projects.

"It's named for the four snaps that hold the piece together. One on each wrist, and two along the spine." Sustina winked. "Once all four are undone, the entire dress falls off as if sheared from the one wearing it. Very useful in our line of work. That being said, I would be more than welcome to acquire one for you... but I would be mindful of wearing it in the presence of Hellenians. It speaks for itself."

They went through another doorway, and the steam hit Jasmine's face before her eyes told her where she was. Once she was able to focus, she stood on the tiled floor and looked all around at the various pools of water that were available to soak in, many of them ranging in color. Her feet moved past a purple-hued bath that smelled similar to lavender and a hint of something she couldn't place, and in the back of the room she could make out the figures of a few women talking amongst each other while lounging in the warm waters. Their conversation paused for a moment while they noticed additions to the mini bathhouse, but thankfully returned their attention to each other once more before Jasmine could feel even more self-conscious than she already was. *Everyone here is on a different level of gorgeous. I knew I was a potato, but now I can't even say I'm a good potato.*

"Here," Sustina instructed, pointing to a partitioned area off to the side of the main pools. "If you were worried about being on display, then you can release those worries here. I'll bring you a few towels. Soak yourself in the waters; it does wonders for weary minds and bodies alike."

Jasmine waited until she disappeared around the corner to start peeling off her clothes. Although she figured that there was nothing to be ashamed of, being naked in front of alluring strangers wasn't going to be something she got used to immediately. She stepped inside the blue-tinted water, the heat of it nearly uncomfortable but she forced herself to acclimate by sucking in her breath and dousing half of her body in all at once. Hissing a little, she took a little more time to sink herself into a seated position on the submerged ledge, bringing the water up to her collarbone.

She watched tendrils of steam rise from the bath idly, not noticing when Sustina returned until the woman pulled up a small stool and sat upon it near the edge of the pool, resting fluffy black towels on her knees. "How do you like it?"

"It's nice," Jasmine said honestly, sinking down a bit further so the water could wash over her shoulders. "I feel pampered, that's for sure."

"As you should." Sustina's eyes turned softer. "How are you doing, honestly? The burden of being the Flame's chosen surely weighs heavy."

Jasmine was silent as her brain compiled many different sentences, and then tossed almost all of them away the moment she came up with them. "I... don't know. Before now, the most complicated thing I encountered was ten consecutive item returns in a row. I get that this is something I have to do, whether I like it or not. But I don't understand why it had to be me."

Sustina watched the curling steam rising from the pool. "No one understands why we were chosen to live the lives we do. The most we can do is accept the things we cannot change, and mold what we can. I am sorry if that isn't very comforting... but at the very least, I will try to be a shoulder for you to lean on."

"You're very kind, Sustina. Thank you." Jasmine paused. "I don't mean this to be rude at all, but... why are you going out of your way for me?"

Sustina moved some of her long hair behind her shoulders, sighing thoughtfully. "This is a fragile time for you, Jasmine. You will need someone in your corner without a stake in this cold war that you did not create. I'm simply presumptuous enough to place myself in that position for you."

"Ah." Jasmine watched the faint ripples in the otherwise calm water spread from where she lifted her hand and scratched the side of her head. "Are you saying Leon isn't trustworthy?"

"No, far from it. I am fairly certain that he wants nothing but the best for you. But by the nature of his position, he has motive. Elliot is loyal to him, as he always has been, and will follow with those motives. Eventually, you will meet others with power that may be more or less transparent with their goals. You've stepped on a chess board knowing nothing of the rules; being a courtesan that has been in many circles and observed how individuals work things to their advantage gives me the knowledge to try and assist you."

Jasmine tried to keep herself calm, although she could not help the worry that rose from the pit of her stomach at Sustina's words. "What do you suggest?"

"Know your worth. Room for doubt leaves room for others

to repackage their expectations disguised as a gift only to see you ensnared by them. As you learn more about what it means to be the Prime, you'll have to wrestle with a new idea of who you are that may make this difficult." Sustina folded her arms on her lap. "Being a human amongst ancient races may be intimidating, but you were given a gift that neither a Draconian nor Hellenian could accept. Do not think that you are inferior... or that you owe any of us anything at all."

Easier said than done. "Alright. I'll work on that."

"Good." She rose then, taking the towels from her lap and placing them on the bench she just vacated. "I'll leave you be for now. Don't feel like you must rush; I will return once I've checked on a few of my charges." Sustina smiled once more, the ambient light from the bathhouse making her olive skin seem tinged with gold. Jasmine smiled back at her and watched her leave the room, and she remained with the calming waters and her dazed brain.

She's no Kim, but I think she's aiight. Eventually, Jasmine was able to let herself enjoy the situation she was in. Just the small hint of luxury, as well as a break away from the crunch of work, was something that she could appreciate despite the circumstances. *Well, if they need this Flame lit, all I have to do is climb this mountain, bring it back, and then continue minding my business. Right?* It all seemed deceptively simple. She knew there had to be more to it than that, but until she was told otherwise, she let the tension and inner turmoil float into the comforting, fragrant waters of the bath.

By the time Sustina had returned to escort her back to Leon's manor, she felt properly invigorated and better able to handle her new environment. Leon also seemed relieved to see them come back, and he greeted Sustina in the same fashion as before.

"As promised, I've returned her safe and sound," Sustina said. "She has an open invitation to visit again any time."

"It is greatly appreciated." Leon turned his gold gaze to Jasmine with an apologetic smile. "You may want to capitalize on that sooner than you think."

Jasmine's gaze narrowed a little. "What do you mean by that?"

Leon sighed wearily. "I fear I have yet another thing to ask of you on short notice."

CHAPTER ELEVEN

"A fucking *ball*, Leon?" Jasmine sighed in exasperation as she followed him down one of the many hallways of the manor. "I swear, you stay *trying* me..."

"It is not my intention, truly, although I do understand why you'd feel that way." He led her to another inset alcove with another mirror similar to the one used to come to Hellenia. "I've been adequately scolded by my tailor for being unavailable in the weeks leading up to this event, and I've yet to adequately prepare for my role in it as well. My lapse in judgment has not gone unpunished."

"But you knew this was gonna be a thing before now, right? How come I'm just now learning about it?"

Leon gave her a self-depreciating sigh. "I did not anticipate you being in Hellenia in time for the fete, yet your arrival was foreseen by the High Priestess. She took it upon herself to notify my tailor, which caused him to contact me quite vexed at this new predicament."

Jasmine watched his fingers gracefully trace the appropriate sigils, and the surface of the mirror rippled again with the effect once he was finished. This time, she was more prepared for the transfer, keeping her eyes open and not shivering as the slight wisp of crossing over dusted her skin. The abrupt change of scenery was somewhat disorienting, but Jasmine found herself quickly distracted by her surroundings to the point where she nearly forgot to step out of the way for Leon to enter.

"Wow..." she murmured. Brodeur's was a dream come true for her when she finally stepped foot in that parlor, but her reverence for fabrics and the things that could be fashioned from them only tripled when she got a good look at what lined the walls in this premiere atelier in Hellenia. Bolts of glistening fabric were precisely layered nearly to the ceiling, causing Jasmine to clamp down on her urge to scurry over and touch the ones within reach. There were more than a few worktables in view, covered in a variety of fabric and sketches alike as well as essential tools that Jasmine had back in her own apartment for her projects, although from what she could see, the ones in the shop were of far higher quality than what she used. Wandering in a daze over to one of the mannequins closest to her, she took in a nearly finished elaborate ballgown and examined the design made with the thousands of seed beads carefully laid into the fabric, giving it the initial appearance of oil slick.

"Nithael is the most revered tailor in Hellenia; his attention to detail is unmatched, and his wait list spans months in advance," Leon told Jasmine as he stepped beside her. "He's worked closely with my family across generations, and there are few others I would trust with my wardrobe."

"No wonder you have such bougie tastes. You got someone customizing all your clothes with this amount of skill. Incredible," Jasmine tore her eyes away from the masterpiece in front of her before she gave in to the urge to molest it, focusing on another mannequin with the beginnings of a double-breasted jacket. "I've noticed that you guys don't do pastels or anything, which is fine. That would go against your whole aesthetic here. But I've seen nobody outside of Elliot wear white even as an accent. Why?"

"White is reserved for funeral rites only; it is the most sacred color Hellenians have. Elliot... is a unique one in that he shirks a lot of tradition."

"Unique? That is a nice way of saying 'abhorrent'," a stern voice clipped into their conversation. Both Leon and Jasmine turned their heads to address the one who entered, a tall and slim Hellenian wearing a simple black suit with the jacket unbuttoned, revealing a silver chain that held an antique pair of embroidery scissors laying against his shirt. His black hair was slicked back for the most part, with a few stray wisps brushing his forehead as he strode into the room, dark violet eyes studying Jasmine with an intensity that she was sure she herself had whenever she was formulating a new project in her mind. "It's about time you brought her here."

Leon winced. "Yes, I apologize for tarrying. Jasmine, this is Nithael. He'll likely want to get your..." he trailed off as the man he was introducing reached out and grabbed Jasmine by the wrist, nearly dragging her to a nearby pedestal.

"Very nice to meet you, Jasmine," Nithael said briskly as he produced measuring tape out of his pocket. "Please excuse my forwardness, but I haven't much time to get you properly outfitted for the Solstice Ball. It is *tomorrow night*, after all, and *someone* has gotten far too used to my efficiency for my liking."

Jasmine glanced over at Leon, who was standing there taking all of the verbal barbs as gracefully as he could. For as annoyed as she had been with all of the surprises in such a short amount of time, she couldn't help but feel a bit bad for him. "I mean, it's not all his fault. I was working, and it can be hard to-"

The tailor cut her off with a wag of his finger. "I'll not have you sticking up for him. Raise your arm, please." He held one end of the measure to her shoulder and spread it down to hand. "He could have had you here sooner, and most definitely *should* have. *Now* I'll have to work thrice as hard to have a number ready for you that is befitting of the Prime. There are a few pieces I have here that I could alter to make this easier, but nothing truly compares to making something from scratch."

"I craft clothes in my spare time, but it's nothing like what you've done for... well, likely longer than me and my folks have been alive by far." Jasmine chuckled awkwardly as he flitted around her like a hummingbird, stopping to jot down each new measurement on a miniature notepad that hung from his other pocket, attached by a chain. "Your work is awe-inspiring."

"There is a reason why those from all over the realm want to commission me," Nithael said, his tone pragmatic. "Nothing but the best leaves my parlor."

"I can see that. I... well, maybe after the ball or something, would you mind if I just watched you work? I promise I won't touch anything, I just... I love fashion. It's probably not too apparent considering I'm wearing stuff like this," Jasmine gestured to her plain shirt and her jeans before her hand was snatched and made to stay lifted while he worked around her waist. "But if I had the time and the means, this is all I'd likely be doing with my life. I can't help but admire you based on what I've seen in here alone."

Nithael paused and straightened, staring at Jasmine with an unreadable look on his face before turning to Leon standing a bit away from them. "I don't allow anyone but apprentices in my parlor."

"I am aware. I also know that it has been quite some time since you've opened your salon to an apprentice."

"The older I get, the less patience I have for ineptitude and general lack of drive for something other than the quick fame they think they'll get for working with me."

"Jasmine doesn't have those expectations, Nithael. She is simply a curious human with an eye for detail that I am sure would impress even you."

Nithael huffed. "She is also the Prime, and I don't make it a habit to employ someone with such a divinely touched fate."

"I'm not looking for an apprenticeship... although honestly that would be amazing, but... I mean, if you're not comfortable, I totally respect that." Jasmine interjected, not wanting to be discussed as if she wasn't there at all. She figured that she was being way too forward, but she couldn't pass up an opportunity to at least ask. *I've clearly lost control of my life, anyway.*

"I don't think that it would be much at all to accommodate at least a fraction of your request, would it?" Leon folded his arms and looked in amusement at Nithael, who turned back to Jasmine and studied her with a sharp eye once more.

"What color would you like as an accent? The base color of your final piece will be black, of course, but a personal touch can make it truly yours."

Jasmine was quick to answer. "Purple. Dark purple."

Nodding, Nithael scribbled into his notepad. "Are you opposed to steel-boned corsets?"

"Nope. I was actually researching the best way to make one from scratch not too long ago. They're great for posture."

"They are indeed. Tricky to make well, if you are unused to the process."

Jasmine shrugged. "Not so much tricky as it is time consuming. The paneling is always the hardest part, especially with nice materials. You just don't have much room for error once you get started, so it's best to go slow, I've found."

"And what would you say is the best base for a sturdy corset?"

"It depends... but honestly, I've used two layers of fine fabrics, like coutil, between the fashion outer layer and the inner lining. Works better than just one heavy layer of fabric, and it feels better, too."

Nithael straightened and glanced over at Leon. "Very good. I'll make you a deal; light the Flame once more for Hellenia, and you may have full access to my wares and knowledge."

Jasmine's eyes widened excitedly while Leon raised an eyebrow at the tailor. "That may count as unfair coercion."

"Incentives are acceptable, are they not?" Nithael's violet eyes flashed mischievously as he grinned. "I want the Prime to have something to look forward to when she returns from her pilgrimage, and it's not like she'll have the time to immerse herself in her craft before then."

"Sounds great," Jasmine stepped off of the platform. "The way to my heart is always good food and better fashion."

She spent the rest of the time watching Leon get fussed over next, and that's when Jasmine realized that the reason Leon got custom garments wasn't just because he was royalty, but also due to his wings. There were things that she noted that she never would have thought about until she saw Nithael draping him with garments and making measured adjustments, such as the extra hidden snaps or buttons that closed a suit jacket seamlessly around the base of the joint that protruded from his back. It made Jasmine wonder if Leon had assistants to help him get into anything elaborate.

"Excellent. That should certainly do it." Nithael ran a hand through his dark hair, carefully passing by the horns that protruded from the top of his head. "I'll have your suit ready for you by the morning. But for you, Jasmine," he pointed his pencil at her. "It will be a bit of a crunch. I'll send for you as needed, and I'll have others here to help properly outfit you. So don't go far."

Not like I was planning on it with so much to explore right here. Jasmine was fairly excited after they left his parlor and was back at Leon's manor in an instant. She looked up at him with her eyes wide as they walked into the main corridor. "Was he legit in his offer? Like, all I have to do is light the Flame, and I get *his* knowledge at my fingertips?

Leon sighed. "His word is a promise; he does not bargain often. I have no doubt that should you accomplish that, he will make good on it."

"You don't seem happy about it, though."

"It isn't that I'm not happy for your opportunity, Jasmine; your passion for your craft is admirable, and I immediately thought of how well you two might get along once I witnessed it for myself. I just wish that your duty as the Prime wasn't wrapped up in a personal pursuit."

Jasmine stopped walking and folded her arms across her chest, feeling annoyed with him again. "And *I* wish my life wasn't hijacked by this duty, but I'm trying to make the best with what's been tossed in my lap. Can't you let a girl enjoy something before pulling the rug out from under her?"

Leon turned to face her then, his gold eyes heavy with concern as he placed his hands on her shoulders gently. "As much as I'd admittedly want nothing more than for you choose Hellenia as the temporary home of the Flame, I also know that the Draconians will have their own bargains up their sleeves for you... things out of my reach. It would be foolish to assume that an offer of apprenticeship would be enough to sway you after spending time with them."

"I guess that's fair," Jasmine relaxed into the warmth that Leon's palms brought to her shoulders. "But it's just so hard for me to think about, you know? I spent a lot of time with you, and I will be more familiar with Hellenia than I'll be with these Draconians."

"Remember how we met? I was nothing but a stranger whom you nearly tripped over yourself in an effort to escape. What is Hellenia, really, except a wondrous new place that may surely lose its glamour once your initial shock and excitement has dissipated?" Leon lifted a hand and gently brushed a finger against her cheek. "This dance we have with the Draconians is eons old, and their differences with Hellenians can and will be flaunted to their advantage with you. I don't like to think of it, but if at the end of your journey you decide that the Draconians are more suited to you, then there is nothing within me that could blame you."

Jasmine looked up at him, trying not to shiver with his soft touches to her face. He wasn't wrong, and she supposed that she was foolish in thinking that anything about her quest was easy. As silly as it was, having something like an apprenticeship with a talented designer was enough to both distract her and encourage her. While she was huffing up the incline of the mystical mountain of Hyperion, she knew that the allure of making clothes would get her through it better than anything else she had been told at the moment.

"What do you know about them? The Draconians? Like, what should I expect?"

Removing his hand from her face and placing it in her grasp once more, he started walking again as he spoke. "It is difficult to say, exactly. We don't seek out communications with them for obvious reasons. But, from what I know, they are lavish and prideful creatures. In many ways, they are the opposite of Hellenians. It is not to say that we are immune to our own quirks... however, considering their origin, it is not incorrect to assume their taste for riches."

Tilting her head to the side, she almost didn't want to ask her next question. "What's their origin?"

"They are dragons, able to take on a humanoid form."

Jasmine started feeling lightheaded. "Excuse me? I've got to meet *dragons*?"

Leon chuckled as they rounded a corner and started ascending the staircase. "I truly do feel apologetic for the situation that you've stumbled upon. If I may be perfectly honest, I've never particularly cared for the method of designating a Prime to meddle in our affairs. It would be different if the human chose to be involved."

"I don't think I would choose this. I'm a practical woman who likes to keep things simple. This is anything *but* simple."

He nodded in understanding. "Most would not choose this fate, I believe. But... I am glad that it chose you, if only for the selfish reason in that it allowed me to meet you."

Jasmine paused, pretending to be enamored with the moderately sized bedroom Leon had apparently designated for her. But his words made her feel fuzzy, and also conflicted with what she knew. She turned from the elaborate chest of drawers and a window seat that overlooked the gardens silvered with moonlight to gaze at him in the soft lighting.

"You sure have a way with words, you know that?"

"I'm simply being honest."

"Mmkay," she turned back to the bed, running her fingers across the embroidered, silky duvet and wondered if she had ever laid on anything as nice as what was presented to her now. "Well. I suppose I should get some sleep so I can wake up and get dragged out of it the first chance Nithael gets. I shouldn't be as excited for that as I am."

Leon chuckled lightly, nodding before turning towards the door. "It's not surprising that you would look forward to it; I think you two may be kindred spirits. Please rest well, Jasmine. And... thank you."

"For what?"

"For trusting me."

CHAPTER TWELVE

"Holy *shit*..." Jasmine winced and sucked in her breath instinctively at the tightening stays around her midsection. Nithael was proving himself quite deft at a lot of things; lacing up a corset was one of them.

"Just a bit more. Try to breathe as naturally as possible, even though I know that is a challenge at this point." She could nearly hear the self-satisfied smile that he wore on his face as he tightened another lace. "The last thing we want is for the Prime to pass out on her plate at the height of the dinner."

"Sure." Jasmine tried following his instructions, but it seemed as though each time he pulled the strings, it was to prove just how badly she was screwed to survive the evening. *My tits better look bomb as hell at the end of this, though.* Even with her inward griping, she was full of excitement over the fact that she would be wearing something that was fitting for Hellenia as well as made by someone as skilled as Nithael.

Sustina had arrived at the parlor earlier in order to do Jasmine's makeup, happily painting her face like a world-renowned artist with a blank canvas at her disposal. Before

Jasmine could see the final product, a couple of other women filtered in and started fussing with her hair, surprisingly getting it into shape without destroying her coiled strands. They left just in time for Nithael to fuss over accessories and to finally get her into the dress he miraculously put together on such short notice. Jasmine idly wondered if he slept at all through the night.

"I must say, even I impress myself from time to time," Nithael hummed, working his way down the spine of the corset. "So many things could have gone wrong. There was only so much of this material I had to work with, so if I had miscalculated your measurements at any point... ah, it's best not to think on it. It would have been a nightmare, to say the least."

Jasmine shifted a little, giving herself a few centimeters of breathing room. "I can only imagine. You've earned your accolades for sure."

He stretched after finally tying the ends of the ribbon into a perfectly shaped bow at the base of her spine, letting his eyes go over the lay of the dress and nodding briskly in approval. "Alright, now slip into the shoes there, and I'll put you in the final piece."

"And then I get to see how I look?"

"Of course. You'll be all put together, then. There's really no sense in peering upon an unfinished product. I don't know why so many insist on doing so."

"It's a comfort thing, I think." Jasmine wiggled her toes into the heeled shoes, looking down as Nithael busily closed the ankle clasps and arranged the few charms that dangled from it nicely. "Watching it all come together is just as satisfying as the finished product."

"Perhaps for *you* it would be. But for fussy upper-class Hellenians, it turns out to be a disaster. They decide they don't like the look of it before I've even finished adding all the accents. They think at the final stages, when everything is already done and ready to wear, that they can request something entirely different. I've stopped allowing my clients to look upon themselves mid-process for my own sanity." He slipped a long overcoat on her shoulders, coming to the front to snap the single button adorned with silver chains that rested just at her belly button. "Now, put these on. Carefully, so they don't tear..." Nithael handed her a pair of fingerless black lace gloves, which Jasmine gingerly slipped on over her palms and adjusted the seams to lay appropriately.

"How am I supposed to eat in these?"

"With the provided utensils," Nithael answered without preamble. He held her hand as she delicately stepped off of the fitting platform and led her to the large mirror flanked by lamps that was tucked away near the back of the parlor. "*Now* you can see your transformation."

Jasmine did well to not look too hard at herself until Nithael gave his permission, not willing to break the whole vibe he set. When he moved fully out of the way and allowed her to gaze upon the work that had been done on her person, her mouth went agape at the vision that greeted her. "Well... damn."

The dress that Nithael fashioned was made of black lace, the embroidered flowers and abstract leaves providing enough coverage despite the translucent netting that allowed her brown skin to show through in intervals. It was also likely the shortest dress Jasmine had ever worn, with the hem a full hand's length away from her knees and wonderfully scalloped as it laid across her thighs. As she moved, the light caught the hints of iridescent purple thread that accented the design, a subtle addition of color that showed the complexities of the pattern. The overcoat that he had given her was almost like a duster the way it left the front of the dress exposed yet created a train that was a perfect half inch off of the floor with the heels on, black with a slight satin finish that ballooned elegantly behind her. The end of her sleeves were highlighted with frilled purple lace that just peeked out over the back of her hand, and matched the pattern of the gloves.

Surprisingly, Jasmine only found herself admiring how well her bust looked all laced up and fitted into the outfit for a little while compared to the number that had been done on her hair and face. Sustina somehow made her look deliciously sultry, which was never a look that Jasmine ever would have thought she could attain. Smokey eyeshadow and a perfect layer of mascara made her brown eyes pop, combined with the hints of highlight and other techniques that Jasmine always deemed too much out of her league to attempt. Her full lips were carefully lined and filled with a black that faded into purple. Jasmine stopped herself from reaching up and touching her hair, which had been arranged artfully in flat curls all around her head, pinned precisely with jeweled accents that gave the appearance that her dark hair was the night sky sparkling with stars. Silver cuffs climbed the outer cartilage of her ear, and the only other jewelry she wore was the Spark that Leon put around her neck right before they left for Hellenia, the jewel pulsing lightly at the spot right between her collarbones.

"Acceptable?" Nithael chirped as he went about triple adjusting the lay of the garment on her shoulders and fluffing out the train to lay how he wanted.

"Ah, yes. More than yes. I've never looked this good in my life." Jasmine turned a bit to the side, admiring the lay of the outfit. The train on her jacket shifted flawlessly with her, and she started examining it in the mirror to see how Nithael might have cut the pattern in a way to make the upper half form fitting while the bottom flowed like water.

"That's what I like to hear. Now, I hate to rush you, but

we've already cut it extremely close." He led her by the arm gently yet firmly to the portal mirror that would take her back to Leon's house. "Try to remember to lift the hem of your overcoat when going up or down steps so as not to drag."

"Gotcha. Thank you again, Nithael. I'm looking forward to learning all of your wonderful craft tricks and tips when I get back with this Flame."

"Just wait until you see how finicky I can get with my apprentices," he made a shooing motion with his hands. "Off with you, now. Hurry."

Jasmine wasted no further time stepping through the mirror and appearing right back into the alcove in the manor, blinking a little at the change in lighting before moving out into the hallway and clacking her heels across the stone floor at a brisk pace. She had no idea when the event started, or what time it was currently; her phone was her watch and it had been out of service ever since she crossed over into Hellenia. She just knew that it was crunch time, and she worried about making Leon late. Her own mind spouted worries at her, which made her increase her pace a little bit more and she whipped around the corner planning to climb the steps to call for Leon... just for him to be descending the final few steps in a bit of a hurry to come and collect her himself.

"Oh! Shit, sorry," Jasmine backed up a few steps out of near collision zone. "I was just coming to... you look really nice."

What she said was a complete understatement, but the more she looked at him, the more she realized that her world could never fit him as well as Hellenia did. His carefully embroidered black suit jacket fit him perfectly, the shiny material of the pattern itself gleaming almost silver in the light that caught it. The midnight color of his vest and dress shirt had just enough variance in material for Jasmine to differentiate between the different pieces of the ensemble, accented by a tie that had thin red flower patterns on it. The swallowtail curve of the jacket hung to the back of his knees, with the inner lining the same shade of red as the accents on his tie. She looked back up to catch sight of the accessories hanging from his horns, which seemed to consist of a delicate silver chain with a charm or two dangling with his head movements. Realizing that she was rudely staring, Jasmine straightened up and cleared her throat before extending both of her hands to him, palms up.

"Sustina told me about greeting Hellenians formally. You're male, and also overall in an elevated status here. Palms upward is to show that deference. Right?"

"Correct," Leon said after a moment's pause, lifting his own hands and placing them gently in her own. His gold gaze laid upon Jasmine's form intently, causing her to shift a little in her shoes and feel self-conscious underneath his scrutiny.

"Do I look okay?"

"Yes. You look beautiful, Jasmine. My apologies... it seems as though you've not only swept me off of my feet, you've eradicated my manners in the process." Leon's lips spread into a smile as he kept a hold of one of her hands, leading her to the front entrance. "We'll be arriving by coach."

At least Jasmine was familiar with the method of transport after being picked up by Sustina the other day, but the elaborate coach that awaited them as they stepped outside was something different. It was larger than Sustina's, accented with silver and accompanied by engraved accents and a large crest that must have been Leon's family sigil on the side. The driver hurriedly let down the steps as Leon helped Jasmine inside first before following her and having the door shut behind them.

"Are you nervous?" Jasmine asked, looking at how deceptively calm his hands were clasped in his lap.

"A bit. I enjoy the season, but I abhor the obligations this nets me. I also worry about overwhelming you, although I suppose that is unavoidable." Leon looked over at her, his eyes uncertain. "It is my fault that you are not more prepared."

Jasmine shrugged. "There was never gonna be a good time to let me know that all of this is real. Just tell me what I need to do to not embarrass you at this event."

Leon chuckled. "Let me lead. I would like to say that everyone's eyes will only be on me, but they will be curious about you, as well. Everyone knows their part, but I want to tell you that you are under no obligation to be made uneasy by way of any Hellenian." His gaze turned serious as he reached out and grasped her hand, giving it a reassuring squeeze. "If at any point you feel that way, please seek me or Elliot out. I do not intend to be away from you during this event, but I also cannot guarantee that I won't have to satisfy my royal duty by being pulled by one attendee to the other."

"Gotcha. What's the itinerary?"

"The first part of the fete will be dinner. Once the food has been served and cleared, we celebrate until dawn."

Jasmine did a double take. "Until *dawn*? Do we have to stay that long? I can't hang that late; I'm pretty sure my eyes are going start drooping closed long before the sun even thinks to rise."

"No. I've only stayed until dawn a few times, when my father was still alive and I was much younger and enthralled by the idea of being allowed to attend such a gala. Now, it seems as though I've pinpointed the ideal time to leave without looking as though I am making a grand escape."

"You're definitely an introvert. I can relate," Jasmine nodded while becoming distracted by the view outside just as she had done the first trip she took across town. "I know how to greet people. I know I'm the Prime. I guess I'm as good as I'm gonna be for this."

The carriage fell in line behind a few others headed to the

same place, an extravagant edifice flanked with ornate angel statues and other intricate stonework in the foundation. Jasmine saw the sheer extravagance of the building before they even pulled up properly to it, and that was when the butterflies started stirring in her stomach. She had never been to any formal function before, unless she counted the fake ones that the local renaissance festival put on that required everyone to show up in garb. But this was quite obviously something that was out of her league only a few days ago, and now she was all dressed up and going in on the arm of someone that should also have been out of her league. *Life sure does come at you fast.* Feeling the coach slow to a complete stop made her jitters worse, and by the time Leon was helping her out of the vehicle and to the first set of steps that would lead them to the grand hall, Jasmine was praying that she wouldn't be onset by a bad case of gas thanks to her wild nerves.

"It'll be fine, Jasmine," Leon told her as they approached the doors. He waited until she had properly gathered her train in the hand that he wasn't holding. "Remember to breathe."

"You're the second person today to tell me that," she muttered as they reached the top of the steps, greeted by the pair of attendants standing on opposite sides of the doorframe, holding the large brass doors open for them. Just inside, there were a few people milling about chatting, formally dressed in their best and making Jasmine think that this was the demon equivalent of attending the Oscars. She tried not squeezing Leon's hand to death as they approached, going unnoticed for a little while before a couple of them clued into who just arrived, and filtered over to greet them.

From that point on, it was a whirlwind of action. Leon only let go of her hand to meet others, his proper mannerisms and speech perfectly fitting the situation. When he introduced her, she made sure to greet them well, which seemed to incite pleasant surprise on the face of many Hellenians that she was paraded in front of. Jasmine was grateful that the introductions tended to go fast where she was concerned, since the attendees mostly watched to see how she interacted with them rather than engaging in small talk. Being on display was something that she mentally prepared for, so her sticking close to Leon and inching along with him into the hall proper was fairly easy.

When they emerged into the main area, Jasmine looked around at everything with wide eyes. Elegant draping swooped along the walls and high ceiling, accented by chandeliers that she assumed had to be lit by the same magical source that kept the gas-styled streetlamps that dotted Hellenia forever lit. Teardrop shaped crystals dangled from them, fading from black to clear at the ends, giving the entire room the appearance that stars were sparkling in midair. A small entourage had set up on the stage, playing ambient music that drifted easily over the mingling crowds of sharply dressed Hellenians talking amongst each other. Jasmine tried not to stare at them too hard as well, but she couldn't help but feel like she had landed smack dab into a fashion show, and the crafter within her was screaming about all of the inspiration that literally surrounded her at that very moment. Black was obviously the preferred color amongst many of the occupants, but the jewel toned colors that were used as accents to various ensembles stood out that much more. She blinked when she felt Leon give her hand a gentle squeeze to get her attention, and she sheepishly looked over at him.

"Keep pace with me while we make it over to our desig-nated seats," he nodded in the general direction, causing Jasmine to notice a table decorated fancier than the rest. "We will be slightly accosted on the way there."

His estimations proved to be understated. Jasmine felt as if she were an animal in a zoo exhibit, and her cheeks were starting to hurt with how often she had to keep a smile plastered on her face for everyone. Within minutes, she started wondering how she was going to take hours of that kind of treatment without visibly cracking.

"Thank god, a chair," Jasmine whispered under her breath as they finally got to where they were headed, and barely waited until Leon had pulled the seat out before plopping gratefully down into it.

"Do your feet hurt?" Leon asked as he settled into his chair next to her.

"No, actually. These shoes fit better than anything I've paid big money for, and I'm not quite so sure how Nithael managed that. But what hurts is my face at trying to appear cheerful through my urge to just run and hide from all of this attention. I don't know how you do it."

Leon laughed a bit, the charms hanging from his horns shaking with the movement. "Many years of practice. If there is any silver lining, it is that I was raised knowing that this would be my future, and navigating it is like breathing for me."

Nodding in understanding, Jasmine looked up to see a figure parting the milling people and approaching their table. The sultry sway in her gait automatically had Jasmine recognize Sustina, and she looked excitedly at the woman as well as the beautiful gown she was wearing. The strapless dress fit her shapely figure perfectly, the bottom of it flaring out with sequined lace. A matching cape laid upon her shoulders, glittering in Sustina's choice colors of black and red. She smiled warmly as she stepped to the chair on the other side of Jasmine and took a seat, nodding respectfully to Leon as she did so.

"Well met, Jasmine. I've watched your entrance, and you've been doing swimmingly thus far."

"Maybe all the practice I had doing customer service to irritating patrons prepped me more than I thought. Everyone here is loads more polite, at the very least."

"That's because everyone's fake as hell," Elliot's voice filtered over to them as he was the next to approach. He took the chair on the other side of Leon, and Jasmine leaned forward to look him up and down pointedly.

"Well damn, you clean up nice."

"I know," Elliot replied confidently, making a show of adjusting his tie. It was the first time Jasmine had seen him wearing something formally Hellenian, and the black suit with royal blue embroidery changed her entire view of him. Although his hair was still bleached and uncommon amongst everyone there, he had taken the time to impeccably style it so that it laid in a neat swoop back from his face. One earring dangled from the ear that was facing her, and she noticed that it held a smaller version of the crest that had been on the side of the carriage they arrived in. In the diffused lighting of the hall, Elliot's side profile was enhanced and affirmed for Jasmine that he was a man that never had to worry about being unattractive. "I can say the same for you, baby," his flirtatious mannerisms took over as he gave her a wink. "I wouldn't mind being in between both of you ladies for a night."

Jasmine glanced at Leon and found him completely unfazed by his best friend's propositions, and Sustina's melodic laughter pealed like bells on the other side of her. "My asking price is steep."

"Wasn't too steep last time," Elliot replied easily, looking as if he were undressing Sustina with his eyes.

Sustina simply answered with a cultured laugh, gracefully taking the champagne flute that was offered to her from the waiter that was making the rounds.

"It's blue?" Jasmine said out loud, lifting her own glass a little to stare at the bubbly contents.

"Specially brewed from Evlet berries that can only be found during this season. Equal parts tart and sweet, it is enhanced by the fermenting process." Leon supplied. "Its arrival also is my cue to formally start this fete."

Jasmine watched as he smoothed imaginary wrinkles out of his suit before standing up, carefully handling his beverage as he made his way to the stage. The constant hum of chatter died off as he took his place, and she couldn't help but take a quick glance at just how full the room was. *Whew chile... I could not be doing this kind of shit all the time.* Sitting up a little straighter in her chair, she followed suit with the rest of the guests and let her attention settle on Leon who had taken his place in front of the band.

CHAPTER THIRTEEN

"Welcome, all. It is an honor to stand before you tonight at what is the grandest of celebrations for Hellenia," Leon began, his voice carrying clear through the hall without aid of a microphone. "It is also bittersweet, as I would admittedly like nothing more than my late father here in my place, giving an introductory speech worthy of the occasion. I am woefully ill-prepared to deliver the masterful spiel that you all must be expecting, so I beg your patience and forgiveness as I grow into the role placed upon me.

I carry within me the tenants and dedication to the people that Lord Vretiel instilled. As your High Lord, I will continue to hold the best interests of Hellenians as my own, setting forth to actualize them to the best of my ability. As I stand before you on this longest night, I declare my vows to you as well as encouraging you all to partake in this gala to your heart's content. Our lives are long, but we must not take them for granted. Everything we have is a gift, no matter how they come to us. Let tonight ring our appreciation for our existence and the days to come." He lifted his drink, and everyone seated did the same in response. *"Orandi gratia dei nobis in tenebris luceat."*

The crowd recited the phrase back at him, and Jasmine awkwardly made up for not knowing that cue by just making sure that she took her obligatory sip at the same time as everyone else. It was sweeter than she expected, almost like a fizzy Moscato, but as the last bit of the beverage filtered off of her tongue, she was left with a pleasant kick of tartness that stopped just short of making her want to pucker her cheeks in response. "Whew. That *is* good stuff."

"It is. Take care to pace yourself; the spirits here tend to run much stronger than what you are used to in the human realm, as they are made for our physiology," Sustina advised as she took another sip of hers.

Jasmine could already feel the first tendrils of a buzz encroaching on her mind, and she'd only taken the first third of the beverage. "I'll keep that in mind. What's next on the agenda?"

"The Blessing," Elliot chimed in, just as the band started up a rhythmic, deep drumming. Leon took his leave, and movement off to the other end of the hall caught her eye as another figure approached the stage, carrying a silver rod from which two ornate thuribles hung from each end respectively. Clouds of purple incense billowed from the censers, enveloping the path the person was taking and bringing forth a mysterious air. Jasmine recognized the sheer robes of a priestess, although the material was shimmery and had a few more embellishments than the ones on the others she briefly saw while she had been on her way to the Flame. Instead of a raised hood obscuring her face, she wore a mask, the filigree on the front giving the appearance that she was faceless. The headpiece that seemed attached to the mask itself was impressive, fanning up and out and dangling with countless ornaments that glimmered with every movement. By the time she had taken her place on the stage, it seemed as though everyone was as enraptured as Jasmine was.

The beat changed subtly, and with that, the priestess began to move. The dance she did emulated water with the flow she had with every step, the incense swirling around her with each turn. The scent of frankincense and myrrh filtered to Jasmine's nose and tickled the corners of her eyes, but she hardly dared to blink in fear that she would miss even a moment of what was going on in front of her. The dexterity the priestess was presenting was incredible; she twirled the laden stick as if it were a baton, keeping it perfectly level as she spun it and herself in a myriad of patterns. The slight haze the incense brought to the establishment felt almost sentient as it settled, muffling further the sounds of anything save for the drums fueling the rite.

Jasmine lost track of how long she was staring until the priestess was bowing to the crowd, and only then did she allow herself to blink her very dry eyes as she joined everyone else in applause. "That was amazing."

"That's because the woman herself is a goddess," Elliot said. He had switched to leaning forward with his elbow on the table, dreamily staring at her as she left the stage.

"Let me guess... that was Viviane?"

He nodded, and Leon shook his head at his best friend. "You pine after a woman who wants nothing to do with you."

"I'm not convinced she doesn't want me. Not yet. You know how persistent I am."

"That, I do." Leon agreed wearily, sitting up straighter in his chair as plates full of food were placed in front of them.

Jasmine got right to her dinner as soon as she deemed it appropriate to dig in. It was a feast, both as visually appealing as it was delicious when she placed it in her mouth. From the appetizers to the dessert, there was nothing that she found to disagree with her taste buds. It became a bit of a task to be mindful of her lace gloves as well as not scarfing down everything like she would normally do if she were in the privacy of her own apartment. Having a five-course meal padding her stomach, Jasmine felt better equipped to go back to her drink and simply appreciate the flavors that danced along her tongue.

She was mid-sip when her attention caught on the figure approaching their table. The mask was gone, but the rest of Viviane's ensemble remained, and Jasmine was once again shocked speechless at the beauty Hellenians seemed to effortlessly embody. Her skin tone was deeper than the glimmering inky gauze she wore, adding to the ethereal vibe she carried with her. Her braided hair was pulled back into a high ponytail, accentuating her cheekbones and the natural contour of her face. When she finally came to the edge of the table, she was close enough for Jasmine to notice that her eyes were a dusky plum color rather than the dark brown she was expecting. Her horns were as elegant as the person she seemed to be, curving around to the front of her forehead and giving the appearance that she was always wearing a circlet.

"Oh, I've waited for this moment," Elliot preened, and the look the priestess shot him could have melted steel.

"Delusional to assume that I've come here for you. I'm here to see the Prime," Viviane replied coolly, then bowed her head to Leon. "I hope I am not interrupting, High Lord."

"Not at all," Leon replied. "Jasmine, this is Viviane Lilanthea, High Priestess of the Cloister. Priestesses are the backbone of Hellenia; any magical advancements and supplements to our way of life can be attributed to them, as well as overseeing our marriages and other sacred rites."

Jasmine nodded and scooted out of her chair to meet her. She was intimidated by her presence in a way that she wasn't when she was meeting a lot of highbrow Hellenians, and she attributed that to the aura that emanated from Viviane. Jasmine had been around a lot of religious figures growing up, but none of them seemed to embody the quiet but strong power that seemed to lie just below the surface of her skin.

"Hi," Jasmine said lamely, and extended her palms out in greeting.

"Remove the gloves, please. I prefer skin to skin contact."

"So do I," Elliot piped in, and Jasmine heard Leon heave a weary sigh. Viviane, however, simply kept her calm gaze on Jasmine as she worked the delicate gloves off of her hands and placed them in Sustina's care. Fighting the urge to wipe her sweaty palms on her dress, she held her hands out to the priestess again, watching as she laid hers on top.

Viviane's gaze was still focused on Jasmine, but the priestess's eyes became distant. Jasmine felt strange, put on the spot and worried about how many eyes were on them while this was occurring, but couldn't pull away from the draw that she felt. *Is it the booze, or am I really feeling energy swirling around where our hands are touching?* It felt like forever, but eventually Viviane withdrew her hands and blinked, which gave Jasmine the cue to breathe unhindered for the first time since encountering her.

"Well met, Jasmine," Viviane said as her eyes drifted towards the glowing pendant that settled between her collarbone. "The Flame makes no mistakes in who it chooses to be its champion. I'm pleased to have had the opportunity to see you before your pilgrimage."

"Thank you. I just hope I won't disappoint."

"You won't," Viviane answered with such surety that it caused Jasmine to blink twice. A hint of a smile appeared on her full lips as she gave a slight bow to her, but it disappeared fast as she turned and saw Elliot standing expectantly behind her.

"In the spirit of the season, can't I get a little love?" He lifted a flirty eyebrow and held out his hands, which Viviane looked down her nose at for a moment before gingerly accepting the greeting.

"In the spirit of the season, I will hold my tongue on the lashings it could give you, as the Solstice is most sacred. May that be a suitable substitute for you."

Unfazed, Elliot pressed on as he enveloped her hands in his. "You don't have to hold your tongue. I always like to see what it can do."

The closed-lipped smile she gave was enough of a dangerous flag for Jasmine to pinpoint as Viviane stepped closer to Elliot. "I would rather hold yours... once it's been removed from your mouth." She slipped her hands from his and moved around him fluidly, her robes shifting with her steps that carried her back across the hall from whence she came.

"Damn," Jasmine plopped back down in her seat. "Check your edges Elliot, make sure she didn't scalp all of them."

"I'm so turned on right now, I wouldn't even care if I was bald. I know I'd still look good, anyway."

Shaking her head, Sustina bade Jasmine offer her hands to her so that she could help slip back on the lace gloves. "It is sadly comedic, their interactions. No one else would dare pursue the High Priestess in this manner."

"Did he do anything to her?"

"Besides being openly appreciative of her figure and unabashedly vocal about his intentions? No. However, you would be hard pressed to find any two people as opposite as they are. It would not surprise me if Viviane found Elliot's existence to be anathema to her own. She is a woman steeped in the very traditions that he bucks regularly." Sustina gave a final minute adjustment to the glove before pushing back her chair and standing. "Please excuse my departure; I've a prospect that I must pursue that will undoubtedly garner me much better results than what Elliot has gotten from Viviane."

Jasmine noticed that since the dinner portion had been wrapped up and the dishes discreetly cleared from the tables, that people were beginning to mill around once more. The band had picked back up the musical score it was playing before the formalities began, and she felt her shoulders relax a bit more now that she wasn't as much on display.

Unfortunately, her relief did not last long.

"My position as High Lord comes with many responsibilities, one of which was opening the fete. Another one is christening the first dance of the evening," Leon said calmly, and Jasmine nodded in understanding.

"Seems legit."

Leon gave her an amused glance before pushing back his chair and standing, offering his hand to her as he usually did. Jasmine stared blankly at it, then up to his face, out to the empty dance floor, and back to his hand.

"You must be out of your damn mind."

Elliot burst out into laughter even as Leon shook his head. "I am not, I assure you. You are my guest for the evening, and unfortunately, this places you as a willing accomplice in this endeavor. I will only bother you for this dance, if it makes any difference."

Jasmine took a deep breath, examined the half-finished flute of champagne in front of her before picking it up and knocking the rest of the contents down her throat in an effort to give her the liquid courage she needed to not erupt into full blown panic. "Alright, then. Lead the way."

CHAPTER FOURTEEN

Leon escorted her with ease from the table to the dance floor, and Jasmine did her best to not let her eyes wander to anyone who was looking at them. She shivered a bit as they took their position, with one hand lifted in his as he slipped his other hand to rest at her waist. Jasmine grinned nervously, looking up at him.

"Suddenly, that little dance lesson you put on in my living room makes a lot of sense. Were you prepping me for this?"

"Not consciously. But I am glad that we had practice." He pulled her a bit closer, smiling softly at her. "Remember, you have a commendable dance partner."

Jasmine kept herself from tripping over his feet and her own by putting herself as much as she could into the mindset of them practicing in her apartment. While they moved, Jasmine allowed her peripheral vision to pick up on other couples that had joined them, which brought her anxiety down a little bit now that she had a bit of cover.

"Random question; do you have bodyguards?"

Leon nodded as he gently maneuvered her into a turn. "Of course."

"I haven't seen them, though. I would have thought that you lived in that big ass house on your own."

"The royal guard is trained in subtlety. Neither I nor they are empowered by a physical show of might. They make their presence known only when needed." He smiled at her. "They keep an eye on both of us here in Hellenia."

"Oh," Jasmine marinated on that, and how odd it was compared to what she was used to in her world. "Have you ever needed to actually use them?"

The lilting sounds of the band swept over them as they moved. "Not particularly. They are most important in adolescence, when wings are just beginning to emerge. There have been stories of Hellenians mutilating a child's wings to disqualify them from being named an heir."

"What? That's horrible! Who would even do that?"

"Usually, it turns out to be at the behest of the mother of the child that is unwilling to relinquish their progeny to the crown. Without wings, the claim to the title is useless, and they know that." Leon's gaze turned slightly somber. "It is an act of desperation, as it's against a mother's instinct to have their child stripped from them."

From Jasmine's limited viewpoint, Hellenia seemed like a utopia compared to the world she was a part of. But hearing just a hint of what he alluded to reminded her that every place had its problems. She kept the rest of her swirling thoughts to herself as she and Leon kept up with the other dancers, the ebb and flow of the band keeping their feet ensconced in pattern.

By the time there was a break in the music that allowed a spattering of applause to the entourage that played it, Jasmine was feeling partly numb. She didn't know if it was because of the dancing, the fact that she was doing it all in heels, or perhaps turning that last drink into a shot was affecting her in one fell swoop. But she was very glad to be done with her small duty for the evening, allowing Leon to walk her back in the direction of their table that was now empty.

"Thank you," he said earnestly as he pulled out her chair for her to sit.

"It wasn't too bad, actually. Not that I want to do it again or anything."

Leon chuckled and opened his mouth to reply, before his golden gaze shifted to see another attendee that seemed to have been waiting for him to leave the dance floor for an opportunity to approach. "Ah. Unless you would like to accompany me for more polite greetings for people you don't know, I plan on saving you the trouble this time and drawing that attention on my own."

"Say less," Jasmine waved him off to do more meet and greets. "I'll just be chilling until you say it's time to go, people watching in the meantime."

Elliot had wandered off sometime during the dancing, so when Leon took his leave, Jasmine found herself alone for the first time for the entire day. While there was comfort in being escorted around, and benefits to being able to ask whatever questions she had about her surroundings and the people in it, she was tired. She craved the type of recharge that she would get if she was in her pajamas hunched over whatever craft project she decided to whip up in the comfort of her own apartment. But with a pilgrimage looming over her head, she wondered when she would next be able to indulge in something that she took for granted.

Man, how much time off will I need to do all this? Jasmine stopped with her fluted glass halfway to her lips. *Fuck, ain't I supposed to work tomorrow? How do I call in without cell service? Will Leon let me pop back in my apartment for a little bit to handle things?*

She immediately felt panicked for not considering this before, as enamored as she was with what was literally a magical world running parallel to her own. Regardless of a Flame and a pilgrimage, she had to make sure she still had a life to come back to when it was all said and done. Her mind was slightly sluggish from the buzz she had garnered from the drink, but it was trying its damnedest to calculate how many PTO hours she had and how much ass kissing she would have to do to her higher ups to get the time off in the middle of a holiday rush. *I've gotta find Leon.*

Jasmine left the relative safety of the reserved table to meld with the guests, her eyes darting about for Leon's familiar figure. She felt nervous the longer she went without placing him, but she tried not to let it show whenever she was predictably accosted by other guests to engage in brief chatter. She had no idea how she was even managing, but the familiar strain of her mouth muscles told her that she was smiling a lot more than she normally did. The alcohol contributed to her feigned cheerfulness, allowing her to finally get away from the thick of it. Jasmine skirted the outer reaches of the large ballroom in order to catch her breath.

Wait... I thought I heard Leon's voice.

She crept further towards the sound, feeling more nervous than she thought she would be. Eventually, she found herself at the edge of a secluded hallway, mostly darkened but still allowing enough light to see that her ears hadn't failed her. But the person Leon was with had her preferring to partially hide herself behind a pillar.

"It's rather rude to stop me from introducing myself to the Prime," a honeyed voice filtered to Jasmine's ears, and she peeked again at the slender figure wearing what was probably the most daring dress that she had seen on a guest yet. The long red gown with belled sleeves was combined with a large split up one side of the dress, showcasing the entirety of her leg and the matching heels she wore.

"I know that anything you have to say to her would be better left unsaid."

"You've never given weight to anything I think."

"That is false, Rina," Leon said, a hint of underlying ire apparent in his reply. "But perhaps I should not be surprised, considering everything you've ever told me was a lie."

Jasmine pulled herself back behind the corner of the wall with a wide-eyed look on her face, ears straining to catch more of the conversation.

"It's easier to boil it down to that, isn't it? I understand. I cannot say that it isn't well deserved." The sound of a glass being set on a hard surface echoed briefly. "But you know I would do whatever I could to save you from the fate your father suffered."

"You speak absurdities. You don't know her. Don't pretend that what happened with my father had anything to do with your motivations tonight."

Rina chuckled drily. "Surely you know that the changes your late father went through coincide with how enamored he was with the Prime. It is not so far off to believe that she poisoned him."

Jasmine's mind worked in overtime as she eavesdropped, barely daring to breathe.

Leon sighed in exasperation. "Ridiculous rumors whispered in ill-begotten places.

I will not carry on such an irrational train of thought with you."

"Then why are you entertaining me?"

As Rina's tone changed, Jasmine became antsy. The way

Leon didn't immediately rise to answer her added another layer of uneasiness.

"You miss *us*, don't you?" Rina's voice had dropped to a softer tone, one that Jasmine had to strain to hear.

"I do not."

"You still are a terrible liar, I see." Fabric rustled. "I'm sorry that I was ever the foolish person to have taken you for granted."

Jasmine should have listened to her instincts. If she did, then she would have saved herself the sight of seeing the two of them in lip lock when she took a chance glancing around the column, again. She could have spared herself the awful feeling of her stomach dropping out from under her. But it was all that she focused on as she quietly slipped away, back into the brighter and more crowded areas of the ball.

If anyone wanted to get her attention, she couldn't have known or cared. It wasn't until she felt someone grab her arm that she stopped moving, looking up blankly at the familiar figure that intercepted her fast movement across the hall.

CHAPTER FIFTEEN

Jasmine stared down at her lace covered hands while the carriage she and Elliot occupied rocked on the road that carried them away from the Solstice Ball and everything there, not really knowing what to say. Upon finding her dazed figure wandering around aimlessly on the floor, Elliot drilled her for answers and didn't like what he found.

"Listen... I don't know if it really matters to say it, but I really fucking hate that bitch," he finally said, breaking the heavy silence. "I always had a bad feeling about her, but Leon was happy. Wasn't until I caught her with her tongue down another man's throat that I went to him about it. He didn't even want to believe me... but I think he always suspected."

Jasmine nodded slowly, still feeling half numb to it all. "That's... wild. Who cheats on the High Lord?"

"Someone who thinks she's sly enough to do it and get away with it. She played his heart like a harp, and that burned him. They ended things forty years ago, and I think she regrets the poor press her name got over it rather than what she did to him." Elliot glanced over at her then. "Sorry that you had to see all that. But I know Leon well enough to know that he didn't want to be in that situation."

She made a non-committal noise and stared out of the carriage window. Her mind was full of too much, and with the ebb of her previous buzz quickly exiting her body, she thought about what Sustina said about Elliot being loyal to Leon above all else. She also thought about how the only reason she was there was because she was needed for some higher purpose. Jasmine took a deep breath and let it out slowly, not wanting to get into the fact that even though she was always a bit suspicious of Leon, she got attached to him despite everything.

When they arrived at the manor, Elliot thankfully didn't press her on anything else, leaving her to take much needed time by herself. She climbed the stairs to the second floor, intending to go to her room, but let her feet carry her right past that doorway and into the study with the mirrored portal. Standing in front of it, her eyes traced the inactive sigils before realizing that she had no idea what combination would get her home.

Gathering the overcoat and the train that went with it in her hands, Jasmine went over to the window seat overlooking part of Hellenia and sat down, kicking off her shoes and tucking her feet underneath her. *So, it's rumored that the last Prime killed Leon's dad, if what Rina said holds any weight at all. But that doesn't even make any sense.* Her brow furrowed as she tried putting puzzle pieces together.

The Prime brings this Flame to whichever race they want to have direct access to humanity. Was there a set up within Hellenia to paint the Prime in a bad light? The more she thought about it, the more she realized that whatever Elliot and Leon had told her wasn't enough information. It didn't make her feel any more prepared for embarking on such a journey, either. Jasmine juggled the same things around in her mind, hoping that they'd fall into place as she watched errant clouds go by in the moonlit sky from the window. She lost track of how much time she spent mulling over things, abruptly jolted out of her stupor by the sound of the study door opening.

"Leon..." she stared at his stiff form hovering in the doorway. There was so much that she wanted to ask him, but felt her chest tighten with the things she had admittedly tried to ignore in the midst of it. Standing up slowly, Jasmine walked over to him, then lost whatever train of thought she had when she saw his face up close.

"Shit, are you *bleeding*?" Jasmine peered at the cut on his lip. If Leon came home looking that disheveled, she could only imagine how involved their make out session got after Jasmine made her exit. Forgetting any sense of subtlety, her feelings still roiling from what she shouldn't have witnessed, she let her next words fly off of her tongue without thinking. "Did Rina do this to you?"

In only an instant she found herself pinned against the opposite wall. She knew she had been trying not to make eye contact with Leon, but she swore she didn't know the man could move that fast. The palms of her hands were pressed against the cool stone in an effort to center herself, even though she had all but stopped breathing as her eyes stretched wide in shock. He was too close to her; Jasmine swore that there were only a few inches between them at that point.

"Do not mention Rina," Leon growled, and Jasmine felt her body cool in anxiety. His golden eyes seemed to shine too bright, boring into her and making her feel caged. When she opened her mouth to meekly apologize, he evidently took that as a cue to kiss her before any other foolish things could spill from her lips.

Out of all of the times that Jasmine may have fantasized on what it would be like to kiss Leon, she did not think it would have been fierce and full of a hunger she could barely comprehend. Jasmine's toes curled at the intensity of it, moving her lips against his and tasting the coppery tinge of his blood on her tongue in the process. She wasn't given much time to process how she felt about it before Leon closed what little distance remained between them by fitting the entire length of his body against hers.

"O-oh," Jasmine gasped as soon as he had given her the opportunity to breathe. Her crush on the man burst out of the box inside her and rushed past her worries, giving her body an intoxicating buzz as she gave into it. Her breaths were coming out in labored pants, every new sensation throwing her brain for a loop. It wasn't too long before his knee snaked between her legs and pushed them apart, giving him room to slip a hand underneath the hem of her dress and feel along the thin material of her panties until he came across what he was searching for.

Jasmine felt as though she should have been embarrassed by how aroused she was. But with the way Leon's fevered gaze never left her, all she could do was tighten her grip on his shoulders with a moan. He quickly drove her to a powerful release, making her knees buckle in the aftermath. As Jasmine began to slide down the wall, Leon caught her by the arms and lifted her as if she weighed nothing at all.

They swept out of the study in the wake of Leon's urgency, quickly sequestering in his quarters.

Once they were in his room, Leon's sexual energy seemed to triple. His eyes never left Jasmine's form as he took off his clothes in a methodical manner. When it came time to remove her own, Leon examined the ties on her back that held the bodice together before he made good use of his long talons to slice through it like butter. Jasmine's eyebrows nearly disappeared into her hairline as her well-made dress fell off of her upper body like a petal, her hips the only thing stopping the whole garment from sliding to the floor. She admittedly looked down mostly to see if Leon had done what she feared and ruined the work of art, but at her slightest movement he entrenched his fingers into her hair and pulled her head back, knocking some of the jeweled hairpins loose in the process. He continued directing her until her back was flush to his chest and her head was resting on his shoulder. Jasmine would have found it a terribly uncomfortable position had he not kissed her hungrily, making the awkward craning of her neck negligible with every swipe of his tongue against her own. By the time he let go of her, she dizzily tilted forward and stumbled, only to be given a firm shove that ended up with her on her hands and knees on the mattress.

Jasmine never imagined that Leon had this side to him. All she knew before was his calm, somewhat pretentious demeanor, full of etiquette that kept their relationship tame. She was incredulous with the stamina of a man so transformed by lust that it had entirely torn his mask of decorum.

Jasmine considered herself blessed to see his facial expression as he came. The fluttering of his eyelashes, the way his head dipped, and the groan he emitted were definitely things that she was committing to memory. But just as she was starting to feel the first twinge of post-coital awkwardness, Leon moved his hips and brought to her attention that he was still quite erect and most definitely still inside her.

"What the fuck, how are you still hard??" Jasmine whined, her head lolling on the pillow. Leon gave a little chuckle at that, but it held a darker seductive energy than his usual show of amusement. Lifting his upper body off of her, he took the same talon that had ripped her dress and traced a feather light caress on her chest right beneath her collar bone before applying enough pressure to leave a shallow cut in his wake. She found herself shivering as his lips and tongue lapped up the blood that he drew from her, holding Jasmine's gaze the entire time.

Out of all the kinks that she could think of, a blood kink was not something that she would have ever thought would be palatable to her. But watching Leon indulge in erotic bloodletting was doing things to her she hadn't anticipated. Noticing her blood mingling with his on his lips was entrancing. And finally, when he kissed her again, she could taste the metallic hint of it all as he moved within her once more.

After her third orgasm, her consciousness waned. Jasmine remembered mumbling to Leon that she needed a nap right before drifting into a dreamless doze, waking up at some point later to find him gazing at her intently. She learned quickly not to make any sudden movements, as Leon was prone to growling in warning right before pouncing on her, keeping her right where he wanted her to be. Regardless, the sex was constant; he didn't say much outside of one or two words, the passion making his usually verbose tendencies nonexistent. But it didn't take verbal communication to infer what it was he was after, and through every position he took her in, Jasmine learned to anticipate as much as she could.

Eventually, Leon allowed her to rest in earnest when his superhuman endurance seemed to wane, and she fell into the deepest sleep she had in some time. It was with trepidation that she peeled her eyes open hours later, with faint traces of the twilight that served as daytime in Hellenia creeping in through the half-shrouded windows. But she didn't have to brace to be jumped immediately after regaining consciousness as she had trained herself to do through that carnal stint in the sheets.

The spot that Leon held next to her in bed was empty.

CHAPTER SIXTEEN

It would have been brushed off as a vivid fever dream, if the prominent stickiness between her legs didn't tell her otherwise.

Jasmine didn't want to see the kind of state she was in. She hadn't washed her makeup off, her body ached in places that she didn't even know could hurt, and her hair felt like it needed a literal pound of conditioner to save it. Her elbows popped as she used her arms to get herself upright, surveying the room in a daze. Leon's clothes had vanished, but she saw her dress laying over the back of one of the chairs.

The longer she sat in the bed that was much too large for her small frame, the lonelier she felt.

She could still smell the remnants of sex in the air, almost hear the memories of their combined moans echoing through the walls. As surprisingly pleasurable as the previous night had been, the morning brought her the misfortune of feeling like a discarded object. Jasmine didn't want to feel that way, but so many things happened to her in such a short amount of time that her vulnerability was causing her to spiral.

A knock resounded through the bedroom, causing Jasmine's heart to skip a beat. *Leon?* Her attention was drawn to the entrance she was carried through last night, but it was another door on the opposite side of the room that opened instead.

"Sustina?" Jasmine was simultaneously disappointed yet relieved to see the courtesan's face.

"Good morning," she tentatively replied as she stepped fully into the room, smiling with visible concern on her features. "Apologies for surprising you like this; the High Lord called upon me to assist you once you'd awakened. I've drawn a bath for you, hoping my timing wasn't too ill. I am glad that it wasn't." Sustina's eyes searched Jasmine's form, lingering for a moment on a visible bruise. "The waters are still hot. Would you like me to help you?"

"No, I'm good. I can get there." Jasmine discarded the blanket and slowly stood up, doing her best to ignore her last hope of seeing Leon leave her tired body. She was sure she would feel more embarrassed if it was anyone but Sustina, but the knowledge that the Hellenian ran a high-class escort service likely meant that she was no stranger to seeing bare bodies in post-coital disarray. The urgency to get to the promised hot bath water drove her to shuffle quickly to the bathroom, only sparing a moment to admire the grandiose bathtub before getting in. The scent of lavender hit her nose as she gratefully sank in the calming waters and sighed.

"I've ointment for your wounds; once the skin has been cleaned, I'll apply it liberally on the affected areas. For what it's worth, it is odorless. But it may sting quite a bit as it helps accelerate healing. Or at least, I hope." Sustina placed herself on a stool behind Jasmine, reaching forward and starting to coax the hairpins from her tangled strands. "I've only ever used this on Hellenians."

"Thank you," Jasmine said, letting herself enjoy being pampered for once. She didn't have the fight to refuse it. Her heart felt heavy, and she could only stare into the colored water as Sustina's motherly touch gently washed her body. She didn't know what to say.

"I'm sorry, Jasmine."

"For what?" Jasmine's voice was bitter, and she herself nearly flinched at the sound of it.

"For not having the foresight to prepare you for weathering a Rut. But now, the only recompense I can offer in the wake of it is merely to ensure that your physical wounds heal cleanly." The sound of a discarded hairpin tinkering to the floor echoed off of the tiles. "I know Leon wasn't expecting this to happen, either."

"I... don't really understand."

Sighing softly, Sustina finished getting all of the ornaments out of Jasmine's hair before adjusting her stool to be on the side of her rather than behind. "Every Hellenian male experiences a Rut once they come to sexual maturity. It is cyclical, and unique to each man in how it shapes them. If a male is unmarried or otherwise uncommitted, then he often chooses forced isolation in order to ride the worst of it out. There are other ways to mitigate the heightened emotions a rut evokes in men other than sex, but all are solely dependent on the male to have safeguards in place to make use of them."

"I see."

"Jasmine... I hesitate to speak on behalf of the High Lord, but if there is one thing that I do know, it is that he left you in my care today out of necessity. He's of the age where ruts are unpredictable, common to last days in a row." Sustina tucked her hair behind both ears before bending down and retrieving a small jar filled with viscous, light yellow ointment. "Most Hellenian men are unable to possess the sheer willpower it took for Leon to leave you in the midst of it. You are human; aggressively mating over the span of multiple days would run the risk of gravely injuring you."

Jasmine winced at the first application. It burned like peroxide on top of a papercut, but she gritted her teeth and held steady through it as much as she could. "So, why did it happen now?"

"Considering how well Leon keeps his own counsel, I can only assume that his Rut was prematurely triggered."

Jasmine paused as she mentally recounted last night's events. "I came back here from the ball before Leon did."

"Oh? Why is that?"

"Let's just say that he and Rina were a bit preoccupied with each other."

"Ah. They were an item for a long time, and his body is likely primed to recognize their bond even if their relationship is currently dissolved. It would not take much for her to instigate the conditions that would bring about his Rut. However, Leon choosing to step away from her would not undo that which was put into motion; it would have to be sated somehow."

Silence fell between them as Sustina made her way covering marred skin with the balm, her touch light as she did so. Jasmine sat in her feelings, still heavy with what happened and how it happened. Sustina's explanation didn't make her feel better at all. If anything, it further pushed her into believing that she had simply been in the right place at the wrong time for Leon. *If Kim even knew what went down, I think she'd throw hands on my behalf.* She missed the comfort of her boring life more than ever. As nice as Sustina was, Jasmine was feeling overwhelmed with having to deal with non-humans for the time being. She wanted nothing more than to go back and pretend that she never had that fateful meeting with Leon in the park at all. As the last of the scratches were properly pampered, Jasmine figured there was only one way to get out of her supposed fate.

"Who do I talk to in order to start my pilgrimage to Hyperion?"

Sustina's busy hands paused. "You wish to embark on that now?"

Shrugging, Jasmine looked to the wisps of steam rising from the water. "I don't see much sense in putting it off, really. Now is as good of a time as any. I'd rather get it over with."

The courtesan lapsed into thoughtful silence before she tentatively nodded. "I understand. I can send for Elliot to escort you to the portal." Her hands dropped to her lap then. "Always remember what I told you before. I hope it will serve you well in my absence."

Once she was finished with her bath, Jasmine made her way back to her borrowed room and pulled on the regular clothes she had with her from before. With all the makeup washed off, Jasmine felt more like herself than she had in the few days she had been in Hellenia. She took a moment to look at herself in the mirror, feeling a bit better for recognizing her normal self within it.

By the time Jasmine got down to the main floor, she saw Elliot waiting for her. He too decided to go back to what was comfortable for him, which evidently consisted of a Louis Vuitton hoodie and jeans.

"You ever get tired of being the odd one out here?" She asked nonchalantly, not wanting to have to go through another awkward exchange, especially when it had to do with Elliot's best friend.

"You mean, do I ever get tired of being the hottest man in

Hellenia? Never," he replied smoothly with a wink. "You ready for this?"

"As ready as I'm ever going to be for something I've never done."

"That's the spirit. That kind of attitude always means a good time," Elliot left the manor with her and down the walkway to a waiting carriage.

Unlike every other ride that she had taken in Hellenia, this one was quiet. Jasmine half expected Elliot to ask her about what happened last night, as she was sure that he knew with how close he and Leon were. But he surprised her by letting her keep her counsel, which she was grateful for. She peered out of her window thoughtfully, looking at how pleasant the scenery was in the muted daylight that covered the area. Eventually, the buildings and pedestrian lined streets gave way to trees and rolling hills. It was just as fascinating as being within the city proper, as Jasmine realized that her view of Hellenia was quite limited. They traveled for a bit longer before the carriage came to a stop, and Elliot stretched his arms above his head before opening the door.

"It's just a little bit of a walk from here, but the view is nice." He grabbed Jasmine's hand as she came down the steps. "Really peaceful."

"You ain't lied with that," Jasmine agreed, craning her neck all around to look at how the breeze rustled the leaves of the tall trees. She enjoyed seeing nature like this, even though back at home she rarely went outside if it wasn't for the sole purpose of getting from one place to the other. Yet, walking with Elliot to a small clearing in the forest made her feel like she truly was on a magical journey that had yet to fully start.

"Oh, I have been *blessed*," Elliot crooned as they approached an altar outfitted with a stone archway. Jasmine didn't even have to guess who it was as the priestess who was busily brushing some errant sticks and whatnot off of the platform straightened up and lowered her gauzy hood at their arrival.

"I knew you would arrive today," Viviane said, completely ignoring Elliot for the time being. She smiled, and Jasmine couldn't help but be dazzled in the wake of it. "My crystal readings told me as such."

"Ah," Jasmine replied awkwardly. "And here I thought that it was my own decision to decide to come."

"The universe is both blunt and subtle in the ways it steers us. Much of what we consider to be made of our own volition, is exactly how It was always intended."

"Can't wait for the Universe to intend for us to be in the same bed together," Elliot put in unabashedly.

Finally showing hints of irritation, Viviane turned and began lighting a series of candles on the altar in front of her. "One for the self. Another for Hellenia. And the final for Hyperion." The wax began pearling and dripping down the side into a well-placed bobeche as the priestess moved from there to the arch just beyond. She traced symbols that seemed far more complex than the ones that she was used to seeing Leon do for the portals set up in his own home, and they glimmered with green energy in the wake of the path her finger took along the surface of the stone. At first, Jasmine didn't see any difference, until a faint ripple in the space between the set columns caused her to take a step forward. Just the slight change in angle made a faint outline of what was beyond, and her heart started to beat a little faster in her chest.

"After you," Elliot gestured with a frivolous flourish of his hand, and Jasmine paused while glancing at Viviane.

"The door to your destiny has opened, Prime," Viviane said. "May your feet carry you to where you have always meant to be."

Jasmine didn't know how she felt about the implication that everything in her life was summed up to such an unbelievable circumstance, but she knew well enough to know that talking about an impending existential crisis with a priestess who likely saw the world through a mystical haze on the regular wasn't the way to go. Jasmine simply nodded to her before stepping across the threshold and into the land that housed the fabled Mount Hyperion.

There was snow at her feet, but the air itself wasn't chilly. The trees that dotted the scenery in front of her were likely the same as the ones that she just left, but they *felt* different somehow. Her eyes caught movement in one of the branches, and a small, furry animal with a russet hue peered curiously at her before disappearing into the leaves. Turning, Jasmine looked back at the gateway she came through, the foggy outline of the altar and lit candles still visible. But beyond that was an expanse of rolling hills with brilliant flowers, mesmerizing her eyes with the saturation of color that she wasn't used to seeing after being in Hellenia. Elliot came to stand next to her, hands in his pockets as he followed her gaze.

"I come here sometimes. When I just need to get away from everything. There's a peace Hyperion brings that can't be replicated anywhere else."

"Do other Hellenians come here, too?"

Elliot shook his head. "No. In fact, I'm not technically supposed to be here without real reason, as all of this is holy land in a way. But being best friends with the High Lord nets me a few privileges that I definitely capitalize on. Most of the priestesses know me and don't ask questions if I happen to show up."

Jasmine raised an eyebrow. "Oh, I'm sure you made yourself well acquainted with them."

"Not *all* of them. Give me some credit," Elliot laughed.

"But, yeah. This is Hyperion. This entire land here lays just outside of time, the only neutral ground that Hellenians and Draconians have between them. Legends say that when the gods put their foot down on our constant fighting, they carved this place out." Extending a hand to point behind Jasmine, he bade her to look at the top of the mountain that peaked through the trees and stood steadfast against the bluest sky she had ever seen. "The Flame is up there."

"Lovely," Jasmine muttered, realizing how long of a trek that would be, and uphill no less. "Glad I'm wearing sneakers for this. How long does it take to get there?"

"Not sure. I've heard it varies for each Prime, honestly. If anyone but you tried reaching it, they'd just end up right back where they started, eventually. This whole place is sentient in that way. It's apparently less about how far you have to go physically and more on how your spirit aligns with the destination."

"If this is the one area you and the Draconians can coexist, how come y'all haven't duked it out before?"

"Oh, don't worry; the gods worked that into their master plan." Elliot ran his hand through his hair. "No blood can be spilled here. If it is, then both races lose out on ever having the opportunity to visit the human realm for eternity. You can say that was definitely enough incentive to keep it cute."

Jasmine kept her eyes on the mountaintop. She wasn't religious or particularly spiritual in any way, but she felt an intangible pull the longer she gazed into the distance. Reaching into her shirt, she pulled out the Spark that hadn't left her neck since Leon fastened the chain, and watched it glow bright before dimming down again. It seemed as though it had turned into a beacon now that they were in the vicinity, and Jasmine swallowed tightly at the unknown task in front of her. "Well, then. I suppose... I should be off."

Elliot stepped forward and enveloped her into a large hug

that Jasmine tentatively returned. She felt odd about having close physical contact now, but she told herself that it wasn't his fault that she felt that way.

"Listen. I know this seems wild. And honestly, it is. But you'll do fine." He pulled back from her, hands on her shoulders as he smiled at her. "And if you do end up choosing the Draconians over us in the end, I'm not gonna blame you. Just make time to have tea and crumpets with me at the base of this mountain every now and then."

Jasmine laughed at the mental image of Elliot holding a delicate porcelain cup that was nearly too small for his hands, sipping its contents with a pinky up. "Alright, you got a deal." She gathered herself and stepped back, preparing to finally depart. Nodding to Elliot, she steeled herself for the next leg in her wild journey, fighting every urge in her to turn and look back.

CHAPTER SEVENTEEN

DRACONIA

Set in a beautiful natural basin, a crowd was gathering. Figures of varying features wearing colorful, elaborate garments of different cuts and styles filtered into the crescent moon shape of the coliseum, murmuring amongst themselves and choosing what they felt were the best seats for the very special performance they had come to witness. Jewels sparkled on fingers, oddly complimenting the beautifully colored sky above them as the stands filled, opening up to an expanse that lied past the finely pounded gravel directly in front of them and into a steep hill in the distance. A pole could be seen at the apex, shining faintly in the sunlight that washed over the land.

Once the stands were nearly full, a lone figure approached from the west, out of one of the many small enclaves the amphitheater afforded. Her robes were made of iridescent fabric, as if a large dragonfly itself shed its wings to lend her its beauty, although it did not discount the natural allure that the woman had all of her own. Her hair was bone straight, black, and fell down her back in silky strands, while straight cut bangs framed her petite face and complimented her countenance.

Upon her arrival, the chatter amongst the audience died down, even as her dark eyes trained themselves to the sky above them, as if searching the clouds for a sign. They drifted along the pastel heavens idly, casting faint shadows on the ground below as they passed. After a few moments, she blinked and tilted her head downwards to observe the audience, her expression impassive yet pure.

"Greetings." Her voice rang loud and true without help of an external amplifier. "The time has come. The sacred Flame that lies in the obscured heart of Hyperion has chosen its new host. As such, it is time for us to determine our own champion, the one that will bring the Flame's glory home to Draconians. Soon... we shall be free to wander the expanses of the human realm."

Applause sounded from the stands, which the woman allowed to naturally die off before speaking again. "The Trial begins today, with each of the four quarters of our realm represented by a member of the royal families."

She turned slightly to her right. "Nemeer Siar of Favonius, come forth."

From one of the alcoves, a large man stepped out. The material of his red tunic almost seemed too tight with the way his muscles bulged against it, yet he moved as if there was nothing hindering him at all. Carrying no weapon as he himself considered his body to be sufficient, Nemeer could easily lift and send even the strongest of beings flying with one well-timed throw.

He smiled widely, raising his arms triumphantly in response to the cheers that came from the stands at his announced presence.

Once the commotion died down a bit, the woman nodded once before pointing her attention in another direction. "Fouzia Boreas of Apartica, come forth."

Also wearing a training tunic, but with the color of the clearest ocean that was in stark contrast to Nemeer's bright crimson, a slender figure approached. Her long, wavy hair was pulled smartly into a ponytail that swung down her back, and also partly obscuring the opulent bow that was her weapon of choice. Draconians across all four corners of the land knew about her legendary archery skills that bordered on the territory of impossible, flung arrows cutting through the strongest of gales to still reach her target. She bowed her dark head in a demure manner to the jauntiness that greeted her from the crowd, even though the self-assured smirk that splayed on her lips belied the tenacious nature she encompassed.

The announcer gave Fouzia a head tilt of approval, then moved on. "Kai Witan of Apelion, come forth."

Kai took a moment to crack his neck before stepping out of his designated alcove, hearing the whistles and sounds of encouragement from his obvious supporters coming from the stands as well. The green silk of his tunic matched the sword he held in his right hand, polished yet worn with nicks that were well earned over the many years that it had been in his family. The hilt was fashioned with a mixture of gold and jade, tempered appropriately through a special sort of alchemy that his people were known for so that the decorative inlay would stay strong and unbreakable. He lifted his chin in acceptance of it all, while keeping his grip on his weapon and looking across towards Nemeer and Fouzia, his brown eyes shining in anticipation.

"Ciaran Anea of Notos, come forth."

When his name was called, the man jogged out, stopping in his designated place and giving a sweeping bow. Fouzia rolled her eyes at the display, but it was hard for her to hide her smile at the theatrics that she knew Ciaran could engage in. His part of the crowd really wasn't any better, whooping and generally being just as obnoxious as their leader. On one side of his hip, opposite a dangling length of fabric the same vibrant plum of his clothing, hung a narrow silver cylinder about a foot long that caught the sun's rays every so often and sent shards of light down the length of the arena. Straightening up from his bow, he gave a playful wink to the others before turning his attention towards the woman who was preparing to speak again.

"The rules will be repeated for clarity." Her dark eyes shifted from each of participants after holding their gaze for a few moments each. "You must keep your current form at all times. Weapons are allowed, bodily harm is to be expected, but intentional maiming is not advised." She lifted her hand and gestured to their waists, where different colored strips of fabric hung from their pants. "The Trial will have a winner when one participant gathers each of the opponents' banners and carries it successfully to the goal. The champion will earn the right - and the honor - to be heralded as the one who will formally court the Prime in our land."

Large scale clapping resounded through the arena, and at the announcer's cue, the four competitors walked forward to stand in a loose circle around her.

"Are you prepared?"

"You should be asking the others if they're prepared for *me*," Nemeer replied, puffing his chest out to the point where the already strained knot buttons on his shirt threatened to pop right off of his lumbering frame.

"You act as if you've never been taken down before," Kai said smoothly. "Don't let today be an embarrassment for you."

The large man simply let out a belly laugh, and the woman in the center took that as her cue to step out of the circle. Her flowy figure walked over to the sidelines, where a large brass gong sat. Closing her elegant fingers around the handle of the mallet that was placed on a small table next to it, she waited for all clamor to die down from competitors and the onlookers alike before raising it. It became almost eerily silent in that moment, with a breeze stirring the leaves on trees in the distance and rustling fabric on bodies.

"Begin."

At the rolling chime of the gong being struck, the fighters sprang into action. Kai and Nemeer immediately hopped backwards, out of possible range of any quick attacks. Ciaran popped his cylinder from his side, and with the flick of his fingers, it extended on both sides to become a sturdy staff. While he twirled it in one hand, Fouzia remained standing in almost the same position, hands at her sides in a deceptively casual stance as she raised a cool eyebrow at her compatriots as everyone sized each other up.

They stayed like that for a time, feeling the excitement build while not wanting to be the first one caught off guard. Fighting was in their blood, and the four of them knew each other's quirks like the back of their hands. Extremely close knit as each of the Draconian royal families tended to be, they trained together from the moment they each could hold a weapon. Bonded just as tightly as the generations of their individual families had before them, they served as a united front that bonded the myriad of Draconians in the land together.

Yet, their competitive nature would take hold during this time, causing them to temporarily be at odds for the grandest prize of all; the honor of courting the Prime.

Ciaran was the first to move, running at Kai and swinging out with his staff. Kai ducked underneath it, keeping his sword behind his back as he did so, and bringing it in front of him to block the next strike. The sound of metal clashing against itself resounded through the arena and caused a bit of a titter to kick up amongst the crowd as they watched. They seemed to move like coordinated dancers, telegraphing each other's moves nearly before they happened and dodging out of the way at the last minute. Ciaran was known for his agility, bounding around like a hyperactive monkey and letting his staff create blurs in the air as he pressed his opponent...

... just in time to get snatched out of midair by Nemeer, tossed as though he weighed nothing at all. He flew in Fouzia's direction, and she simply stepped to the side and watched his body tumble once before he used the momentum to turn it into a roll, landing in a crouch on his feet and looking terribly amused at how he had been caught off guard. Meanwhile, the much larger man turned his sights on Kai, lowering his center of gravity before thundering towards him and looking to do the same, but the man in green hopped backwards a few feet, holding his sword in front of him as a guard.

Flipping back into the fray, Ciaran poised himself to land a soaring kick to the back of Nemeer's leg to bring him down a few notches, just for the man to flex one of his large, tanned hands and exhibit his own agility that seemed unlikely for someone of his size to have and grab Ciaran's ankle before it connected. Kai switched gears, running back towards the two and using the opportunity to snatch the purple cloth attached to the upside-down man's side. As soon as his fingers curled around the fabric, there were cheers coming from his section in the stands, signifying him as the first to make headway in the competition.

Then there was a slight rush of air, enough for Kai to know that something had passed him, and then the scrap was gone. The tale-tell feathers that were attached to the end of Fouzia's arrows taunted him in the slight breeze, pinning the cloth to the ground several yards away, and he looked back at her with a raised eyebrow.

"Let's see how fast you can run," she said, reaching behind her for another arrow with a gleam in her eye.

Kai made a beeline for his prize, hoping to beat the woman and her deadly precise archery skills, but knowing that he was likely acting exactly the way she expected. Nemeer dropped Ciaran and chased after him, covering lots of ground with his long legs taking one step for Kai's two. Fouzia took aim, firing her shot first to Ciaran, pinning his sleeve to the ground with an arrow before quickly pulling out two more, breathing out slowly, and letting them fly. They both darted at the same pace, but at the last moment, seemed to catch the wind and veer in opposite directions; one grazed Nemeer's cheek, leaving a red line upon it and causing him to flinch, while the other singed across the top of Kai's sword-bearing hand and caused him to drop his weapon to the arena floor.

"Change of plans," the man in purple muttered before pulling himself up from the ground, hearing the tear of fabric as he got up from where the woman thought she had him pinned. She noticed his movement and nocked a few more arrows, firing them akin to a machine gun in his direction. Ciaran was prepared for them then, deflecting them all with well-timed spins of his staff before setting off towards her, figuring he would press her as soon as he was in range. In a way, he cursed their collective inability to take care of Fouzia before she surveyed the playing field like he *knew* she was going to do. If left to her own devices, she would certainly take advantage of her distance and make quick work of them.

Meanwhile, Nemeer and Kai had gotten to the fluttering amethyst cloth and reached for it at the same time. The back of Kai's hand stung from the arrow and he wanted to go back and retrieve his sword, but this prize was more important. They both grabbed opposite ends of the fabric and lifted it from the ground, leaving a hole in the middle of it where Fouzia's arrow had stapled it to the spot and took a moment to stare at each other in challenge. Ripping it in two wouldn't give them any sort of advantage.

"Drop it, or I *make* you drop it, Kai," Nemeer stated.

"Do it, then, if you can," the smaller man responded haughtily.

With a twist of his hand, Nemeer wrapped the cloth around his wrist and used it to pull Kai towards him in the same motion. Kai's feet dragged uselessly on the ground, kicking up errant dirt and pebbles as he tried to no avail at getting any leverage in the situation.

"Should've let go when I said." Muscles flexed below the red silk of his blouse, lifting Kai with little effort. In response, Kai simply doubled over into a roll in midair, hoping to use the momentum to get himself free and take the scrap with him. Unfortunately, it just got him into a better position for Nemeer to spin in a half circle and rocket the man to the other end of the arena, far out of reach of Ciaran's captured fabric. His brown eyes watched as Kai tumbled away, then hopped back a few steps to avoid another barrage of arrows.

Ciaran finally got near enough to Fouzia to slam the flat of his staff down on her head, and she blocked at the last minute with one of the curved limbs of her bow, fingers curled around the riser with a grip that wouldn't shake. A bit of sparks flew as their weapons connected, and she made a hissing noise of displeasure at anything striking her prized bow that hard. She pushed back against Ciaran's onslaught with a huff, and when he swung his staff at her again, she kicked out and rooted one end of it into the ground and quickly ran up the long weapon before he could get it unearthed and launched herself right off of his shoulders with a grunt. Using the momentum and height she gained, she twisted in midair and fired off another shot, this time cutting through the fabric at his leg.

"If you wanted to rip my clothes off, I could have given you the opportunity before now," Ciaran shouted, bending down to yank the arrow out of the earth. Fouzia responded by gracefully flipping her middle finger up at him while running at full tilt towards Nemeer and the flag he held, her brown skin ruddy with heat and exertion. She took a mental count of her stock of arrows, finding sixteen of them left and telling herself to be frugal.

Nemeer laughed a bit at how ferocious the small woman could be despite her size. Rushing someone like him head on never ended up well, even for those who were comparable to size and strength. Yet, she kept steady, nocking an arrow and taking aim at what looked to be the very center of his forehead. Letting it fly at only a few feet of distance, Nemeer's meaty hands grabbed it just before the point hit its target, and then realized too late that it was a distraction all along. Fouzia had gotten to her knees and slid on the gravel, shredding the knees to her pants as she snatched the fluttering red sash right off of his waist, rolled and got to her feet triumphantly.

More cheers sounded from the people of Apartica, prompting Ciaran and Kai to exchange a wary glance.

Fouzia had the advantage of having two sashes, now.

Kai casually walked back over to his discarded sword, picking it up and making a show of dusting the red braided tassel off in the process. "Nice. Enjoy this while you can."

Fouzia smirked while keeping her eyes on the field and those in it. "Oh, I will." She was relieved that she no longer had to make herself be in Nemeer's proximity, as he was by far her greatest threat. The other two were nimble and wily, but if they couldn't *catch* her, she could find a way to get their sashes and make a dash for the goal.

Ciaran leaned on his staff and assessed the situation with periwinkle eyes, his sandy hair drooping across his sweaty forehead. He could go toe to toe with Kai all day for his prize; they were the closest in battle technique and agility in that matter, but he would get tired out quickly keeping up with him. Close range with Nemeer was never advised, and he would ideally need help taking that giant down. Fouzia was formidable, but if he could wait out her stash of arrows, he could swoop in and clearly have the advantage.

Nemeer bent down and unearthed one of the firmly packed bricks that outlined the entirety of the arena, firing it like a cannonball at Fouzia. She dodged, and in the explosion of dust that it kicked up, she turned and hightailed it towards the goal. The others were quick to follow suit, and the roar of the crowd sounded behind them as they carried the competition out of the amphitheater and into the grassy hills beyond.

Fouzia huffed as the incline began, finding the softer grass and soil underneath a lot harder to keep her fast pace. She kept going, only stumbling once, and kept her eyes on the pole at the top. Meanwhile, Ciaran was gaining on her, far more accustomed to that type of exertion and managing to snake his staff out and trip her. She went down in a roll, kicking up blades of grass in her wake, and he ambled over to grab the colored fabric she had on her person.

The tip of Kai's sword brushed the top of his nose just as he was bending down, and Ciaran looked up at him. "Nice to have you in the same area," he muttered before grabbing a hold of both sashes Fouzia held with one hand, swinging the brunt of his staff with the other, using his body for an extra bit of power despite his lower ground. Kai dodged under it, stabbing his sword out to try and get the sashes that way, but Ciaran spun away before he could get them.

Unfortunately for the man in purple, he collided with Nemeer's broad chest, who grabbed the mass of fabric and yanked it right out of the man's hands. "Thank you, the delivery is appreciated." And he kicked Ciaran off to the side, his staff sliding in the grass in his wake.

Fouzia sat up then, seeing now who had the advantage and confirming that her sash and Nemeer's were liberated from her. She brought her bow back to the front of her, an arrow already set to fly. Yet, Nemeer dodged out of her range and past them, headed for the goal. Scrambling to her feet, she chased after him.

Kai pressed both of them, tossing his sword aside in favor of jumping and attaching himself to Nemeer's left arm and yanking down with all of his strength. It was enough to get the man to stagger, but then he pressed on. Ciaran reappeared and did the same with his other side, trying to slow the giant down.

"C'mon, damn you, *fall!*" Ciaran huffed. Nemeer's only response to that was to laugh heartily, grunting with the unintentional weight training he was getting while he slogged forward.

The sound of footsteps flattening the grass behind them was heard, and Fouzia relieved Kai of his green sash before literally leaping and climbing Nemeer's back as if she were scaling the icy, unforgiving cliffs of her homeland. Once she got to his shoulders, she tentatively straddled him from behind, wrapping Kai's fabric around his face and pulling backwards, causing his head to fall back and his footing to finally crumble. With a yell, the group of them collapsed to the ground, and immediately they scrambled for the advantage.

Kai reached for a blue sash, snatched it, only to get punched in the face by Fouzia and get it stolen from his fingers. Ciaran pried Nemeer's closed fist open to get at others, only to be nearly kicked by Kai. Nemeer rolled over, pinning both Fouzia and Ciaran underneath him, reaching his long limbs to gather the flags as he saw them. But his fingers grasped at nothing, and he blinked as he saw Kai with all four colors taking a running leap to the pole, latching onto it and shimmying his way to the top.

"Get. Off. Of. Me. You. Heavy. *Ass!*" Fouzia emphasized each of her words with a firm slap to Nemeer's side, her cobalt-colored eyes flaring with irritation and desperation. Ciaran had made multiple divots in the soil trying to get out from underneath the heavy man, but by the time the three of them had figured out which way was up, Kai had attached the fabric pieces to the top of the pole and let himself fall ungracefully back to the ground, the air getting knocked out of him on top of the adrenaline and exhaustion setting into his bones.

In the distance, back at the coliseum they left, the ringing of the ceremonial gong reached them.

Ciaran rolled over onto his back, splaying his body spread eagle as he looked at the sky. "That's that, then."

Fouzia sat back on her haunches and looked extremely put out, a pout clear on her full lips. "I cannot believe I lost because you fucking *sat* on me, Nemeer!"

"I didn't mean to fall on you, but you did that yourself," Nemeer replied. "Besides, it was a great workout. I should have you guys come to Favonius and help me train on the beach by hanging off of me like you did."

"Not everything is about you and building more muscle mass, you know," Ciaran said derisively. "We train enough on the regular."

The larger man shrugged good-naturedly. "Just a suggestion. Also, are you two seriously upset over this? This just means that Kai gets the responsibility of swaying the Prime. And if he fails, then it only looks bad on him."

"True enough," Kai finally said, rolling over and sitting up. Some of his black hair had gotten loose from the short ponytail it was gathered in, and he swiped the errant strands that were dusting his forehead and nose back from his face. "But at least we put on a good show."

The only woman in the group got to her feet and started scanning the grass, picking up her bow first and then looking for where her arrows had scattered to. "I guess you're right about that. I'm still gonna be pissed about that for awhile, though. I had you guys *beat*."

The group of them slowly got their sore bodies together enough to become fully upright again, foraging for their lost weapons. As Kai bent down and retrieved his sword, he caught a bit of his reflection in the surface of the metal, interspersed with the fine detail that ran down the center of the blade itself. He was half covered in dirt, cheeks flushed red, and sweat matting pieces of his hair to his temple.

Yet, he smiled. Kai had prepared his entire life for that moment; they all did, and they had done well. In the end, all Draconians won when the Prime chose to give the Flame over to them. He would just have the added honorary title of King when he succeeded, an honor that was only bestowed upon the one with the Prime at his side. Kai could almost taste it.

"Now that all of that is out of the way... I suppose we should prepare to show the Prime the glory of our lands." Kai looped one arm around Fouzia and Ciaran respectively. "But first, a bath."

CHAPTER EIGHTEEN

Jasmine reached out to touch the petals of a flower that looked like a hibiscus, boasting bright yellow edges that blended into a dazzling display of purple. She supposed with as little as she knew about botany, it could have been something that existed in some tropical place she could only dream of visiting. But considering the fact that it was sprouting gaily from a mound of snow, she didn't think that was the case. *Everything about this mountain is bizarre, but beautiful.*

There wasn't a way for her to accurately gauge how much time had passed on her journey; it didn't get dark. She also didn't feel hunger or exhaustion, and she knew it had been awhile since she had sleep or food. But whatever energy that held together that mythical place was affecting her, and she got up from her kneeling position next to the flower and kept heading up on the trail that seemed to materialize before her with each step she took.

Jasmine couldn't find the peak anymore, the forest density shrouding her view from much of what was ahead. She remembered Elliot's words; "*It's apparently less about how far you have to go physically and more on how your spirit aligns with the destination"*. She didn't know how to gauge her spirit compass so to speak, but she *did* know one thing; her mind was given all of the time in the world now to marinate on everything that happened in her life since Leon stepped into it. And unfortunately, the more she thought on it, the worse she felt.

The facts were plain to see; the only reason Leon approached her was because she was the Prime. He made an effort to infiltrate her life because Hellenians wanted to keep the Flame in their possession. *And the only reason he fucked you was because he was horny and you were available.* Jasmine bit her lip, hating how her heart sank into her stomach. She knew what Sustina had told her, and it wasn't like she thought the woman had lied to her... but there was so much Jasmine didn't realize about her role in all of this, that whatever the kind courtesan said held little weight in the face of everything else.

She couldn't shake the feeling that she was being used. She let her heart get attached to someone who wasn't even human, didn't have the decency to tell her the ins and outs of the whole Prime deal, and in the end left it up to his best friend to be the one to show her what little of the ropes he could. She might have gotten the best sex of her life, but just because he offered up his luxurious manor and plied her with pretty clothes didn't mean that he still didn't manage to "wham, bam, thank you ma'am" right after the Solstice Ball.

Jasmine kept her feet moving, but she found herself tripping over foliage every so often. It could have had something to do with the fact that her vision was blurry from the tears she was trying so damn *hard* not to shed. Eventually, she gave up, leaning against a tree trunk and taking a couple of deep breaths. Underneath all of the hurt, she felt extremely foolish. Foolish to think that someone that put-together, that handsome, and that important could ever truly care for her. If it had been anyone else, she knew that she would have shut them down. Jasmine prided herself on being self-sufficient and not overcome with desperation like many people in her age bracket that didn't think twice about loading up a dating app and trying their luck with cute strangers on the internet.

And now, there she was, literally in the middle of nowhere, having feelings she avoided for so long and being left knowing that it likely didn't mean a damn thing.

Jasmine slid down to sit on the ground, pulling her knees up to her chest and folding her arms over her legs. Despite the annoyances of everyday life, she sorely wished that she could just go back to her customer service job and talk to Kim about whatever she could think of on their shared breaks only to go home and draft up the next clothing project she wanted to do. She wanted her life to go back to normal, untouched by stupidly beautiful men and their gifts and persuasions. *I want to go back to not feeling so damned alone.*

Tears soaked her pants as her shoulders shook, but she remained as silent as the land around her in her leaked sorrow. It was strangely cathartic to let it out in that way, amongst nothing but the trees and the random animals that she spotted along the path.

Alright, that's enough. Pull yourself together, girl. The sooner you do this and get it over with, you can go home and let whoever the hell you give the Flame to run buck wild. She clung onto that grounding thought, redirecting her goal in mind to be back in her own realm, in her own apartment, being left alone once her usefulness to ancient races ran out. As she let that sink in, she felt the tension and hurt slowly ease out of her body, giving her the strength to get up and dust the snow off of her behind. Jasmine took a moment to wipe her face before getting back to the path, looking off into the trees randomly. If nothing else, she couldn't choose a better place to have a breakdown. The blue sky that peeked through the leaves was heavily saturated and serene, the ground was covered in a thin layer of snow that didn't seem to seep through to her bones, and the strange large fruit on one of the branches was also a nice touch.

... that was definitely not there before.

Jasmine walked slowly, peering out of the corner of her eye at it, trying to appear nonchalant. It wasn't like she had a sense that she was in danger, as she innately felt that nothing would ever come to harm her while she was on holy ground. But as she kept looking in that area, the more she was convinced that it wasn't normally a part of the whole Hyperion experience. Swallowing, she moved forward.

The "fruit" blinked.

Aw, hell naw. Jasmine didn't hesitate to break out into a full on run up the mountain after that. Her heart was racing in her chest, and she thought she heard branches cracking behind her. She didn't dare to look back, instead focusing on not tripping and falling while she rocketed up the path to put as much distance as she could between whatever that was and her person. Eventually, the foliage thinned out, and she was sprinting into a small clearing that brought the peak into view much closer than she was expecting.

And then she saw it, cutting through the clear blue sky with painted on clouds.

It appeared like the tail end of a kite, almost fluttering through the air but with an express purpose. As it traveled closer, details became more apparent... the largest of them all being the fact that it wasn't just some*thing*. Light from the sun glittered along the green scales of the serpentine dragon, showing off a shifting hue from viridian to gold as it flew, propelled wingless by a force that had to be innate to the being itself. Red spines lined in a perfectly arranged single-file row down its back, fluttering in the air as it briefly circled the tip of the mountain and perched there, staring directly at Jasmine.

She felt like she had to hold her breath despite her lungs protesting her compulsion to do so, considering she just ran however long she did. But she felt mesmerized by the sight of something that she had only previously seen drawn in heavily stylized art that populated campy antique stores. Red whiskers protruded from its face, accentuating the formidable visage that was both terrifying as it was enthralling. A large, five-clawed foot could be seen holding onto the rock face as the rest of its body curled elegantly around the bit of mountain it was resting upon, round eyes peering with far too much sentience at the woman who had stopped moving and was full on staring right back at it.

After a moment of a tense exchange of glances, the dragon lifted off once more swooping through the air before diving directly down, disappearing into the trees as if breaking water tension in a pool, the ripples fluttering the branches and causing quite a few birds to take flight in its wake. And then, after what seemed like an eternity, a figure stepped out from the forest from that direction, walking with a purpose.

His body held the sinewy strength of those who built and maintained a well-rounded physique. The base of the top was white, yet the closures, mandarin collar, and the large cuff of the sleeves held the same shimmering green and gold pattern as the scales of the creature that was just on the tip of the mountain earlier. He stopped just a few feet away from her then, brown eyes looking her up and down before folding at the waist in formal bow.

"The Prime, I assume," he said as he straightened.

"Yes?" Jasmine squeaked, suddenly feeling as though she lost control of her own vocal cords. Her gaze went to the long tail that protruded from his tailbone, swishing slightly from side to side before curling upwards and wrapping itself around the man's waist like a sentient belt, blending in and flattening before Jasmine's eyes to become a part of the garment itself. With a coordinated flick of both of his wrists, the belled sleeves circled his arms enough for him to gather the edges of them and place both hands behind his back in a casual manner.

"I'm glad you made it to Hyperion. We've been waiting for you." He smiled. His appearance may have been human, but he had an air about him that was nearly alien in nature, a far contrast to how comparatively easy Leon and Elliot could don a human disguise. High cheekbones filled out his slightly angular face, showcasing bright eyes within epicanthic folds that gave way to dark hair and slightly pointed ears. "My name is Kai." His head nodded to the trees just behind her. "And that is my friend Nemeer. Forgive him if he scared you; subtlety is not his forte."

On cue, a large crimson head peeked out from the treetops, looking over at them. Even though it was a humongous dragon, one could almost feel the embarrassment radiating off of him at having startled Jasmine earlier. "We've come to escort you to Draconia. We're allotted as much time as the Hellenians had of you, as per the ancient agreement." Kai's head tilted to the side. "But first... you have a name of your own. I'd like to know it."

For a moment, she was too busy trying to get her brain to restart that she didn't realize that she was fielded a question. Her wide eyes just kept staring at the red dragon and willing the rest of her brain to fully comprehend what she was looking at. It wasn't CGI projected into reality. It wasn't a hyper realistic animatronic structure in a theme park. It was an actual living, breathing *dragon* and she felt entirely too small in its presence. She forced her head to turn back towards Kai, and immediately trained her gaze downward, bowing awkwardly and wishing that she didn't look every bit of the hot mess that she did. "Jasmine," she relinquished finally.

She didn't look up until Kai closed the distance between them and lifted her chin with a finger to meet his gaze. Close up, his features were even more striking, a symmetry of beauty just on the side of inhuman radiance. He scanned her face, all the way down her chest, and to her feet. Once he met her eyes once more, it was evident that it wasn't a clinical and detached kind of examination that was occurring. He was taking stock of someone he had full intentions of claiming and already likely considered her his.

"No need for you to ever stray your gaze from me, Jasmine," Kai said, running his thumb lightly across her cheek before withdrawing his hand. "We are equals."

She fought back the urge to shiver at his touch. *You literally flew in and shapeshifted into a human wearing some sort of supernatural drip. I stumbled like a lost drunk into this area with my hair all knotted up, in dire need of tissue for my nose and lotion for my hands. We are not the same.* Before Jasmine could respond, Kai was moving away from her and gesturing her to follow him over to his very large companion.

"There is a shorter way to our land, but I thought it would be nice to have you experience the scenic route." His head turned upwards. "Nemeer."

At the mention of his name, the dragon lumbered forth out of the trees in earnest, showing off how ridiculously massive he was. He looked like the typical dragons depicted in fantasy novels, with large bat-like wings and shimmering scaled skin like an oversized, muscular lizard. The copper outline of his otherwise bright red scales showcased his own unique beauty, and even though he moved his wings only a little, the wind generated from that easily bent the tops of the trees as he approached. Moving his right claw, he exhibited an unlikely amount of care as he turned and opened it slightly, creating a gap within that would safely carry Jasmine without fear as he flew to their destination. Kai glanced back at her, giving another bow while extending his hand towards Nemeer. "Your chariot awaits."

Jasmine looked at where she was supposed to sit, then up at Nemeer, then over to Kai with a startled look of incredulousness. But instead of opening her mouth and saying something brash, she nodded as politely as she could and stepped up to the claw, noting that it had to be the size of a small car.

"Thank you, Nemeer. Hope I don't fall out or anything," she murmured as she reached up and patted his scales awkwardly, noticing how buttery smooth they were to the touch. Then she ducked her head inside the space allotted for her and sat down, getting as comfortable as she could.

As soon as Jasmine was settled, Nemeer sat back on his haunches before giving a few powerful flaps of his wings, and then he was soaring upwards, completely flattening the trees in the downdraft as he took to the skies. The winds grew slightly warmer the further they got away from the enchanted peak, and the clouds blended into a sky that changed subtly the longer they went. Jasmine squinted against the torrents of wind buffering her between the spaces left in his claw, trying to see clearer the change in the surroundings.

Eventually, Nemeer dipped gradually, bringing them directly into the middle of a large cumulous cloud, obscuring everything from view. But when they emerged on the other side, there was a whole new scenery that awaited them. Lush, green mountains created the perimeter of basin that was teeming with colors and life, vibrant flowers in random cliff places greeting them as they sailed by. Looking down, Jasmine could see the gleaming gold rooftops of structures, interspersed with walkways and roads that still appeared to be made for ants with how high up they were. But as the dragon kept a steady decline, it was easier to make out people going about their lives, with a few children glancing up at the massive figure sailing through the skies.

Finally, they came to a landing spot, and Nemeer had to truly make sure he landed softly without accidentally jarring the woman he held with him. Thankfully in contrast to how he blundered through the forest at Hyperion, he took most of the landing in his hind legs, creating a backdraft with his wings to slow his controlled fall as they finally touched land. His claw opened slowly, allowing Jasmine to step out in what seemed to be a wide, flat courtyard flanked by cherry blossoms and grass as sage as something seen in a travel destination magazine. Wisps of clouds passed by in the background, creating a picturesque vision of partially obscured mountains against the backdrop of a vibrant sky doused in pastel colors, with stars twinkling just beyond.

Jasmine was so used to darker and more subdued scenery from her time in Hellenia that the sheer vibrancy of her surroundings made her eyes sting, and she rubbed the back of her hand against her lids to clear them. *This shit don't even look real.*

Nemeer's head lifted towards what looked to be a side of a gilded palace, mostly obscured with more cherry blossom trees and other green foliage. But a figure stood casually by that wall, and just by the look of the clothes alone, she could tell it was Kai. Bowing his head once more he gave Jasmine a small little nudge with his snout in her back, urging her to walk over to him. Jasmine stumbled a bit, thinking that the dragon still didn't know his own strength, but turned back to him and waved at him sheepishly before making her way over to her host.

"It's beautiful here. Back home, I wouldn't see anything this nice for another handful of months with it being winter right now."

Kai smiled as he reached his hand out and hovered it at the small of her back, leading her inside the building. "Our realm has different regions, all leaning towards various climes that stay somewhat level within. Where you are now is Apelion, and what I believe to be the most temperate of the four corners. We receive just enough rain to keep the trees and blossoms blooming, but not as much as Nemeer's land of Favonius. It's ridiculously humid, there. However, for a taste of winter, I should have Fouzia take you to Apartica."

"...okay," Jasmine replied, too overwhelmed to fully parse his words. She could at least garner that the people she mentioned were important to him with the ease that their names fell from his lips, but she was starting to get a tad overwhelmed. Now that they were inside, they traveled through a brightly colored hallway, awash with heavily saturated pigments that were just as dazzling as the scenery outside. Partitions carried what seemed like a mixture between jade and stained glass, allowing natural light to shine through and send kaleidoscopic patterns on the richly carpeted floor. Perfectly spaced turquoise lanterns lined the ceiling, and if Jasmine listened closely, it was almost as if the tinkling of chimes sounded in the distance.

"I assume you've been well introduced to certain machinations beyond what you've experienced in your mundane human life, so I know you have questions." Kai turned a corner and came to a sliding door, opening it. "I'll be happy to answer them. But first, you must be properly dressed." He looked at her current clothes with a guarded expression, and Jasmine felt like it would be the perfect time for the ground to open up beneath her and just swallow her whole.

"Figured as much," she gave him a weary grin. An odd,

bittersweet twinge settled in her chest as she said it, remembering how much fun she had poking around Nithael's parlor and being promised an apprenticeship of a lifetime... if she gave the Flame to the Hellenians.

"You must present as your title allows." Kai gestured for her to step inside the room, where a team of perfectly coiffed handmaidens in matching flowy dresses waited patiently. When they saw Jasmine, they all gave a synchronized bow, stepping back to reveal a vanity, washing area, and what seemed to be an entire wall full of glittery gowns and the like. "I'll be waiting when you're finished." Kai bowed his head politely. "They'll know where to direct you."

For as much as she sorely needed a bath and a detangling brush for her hair, she was sure that she was never truly going to get used to being pampered in such a fashion. Turning to one of the women dutifully standing by, she asked a question. "Do I get to decide which one of these garments I get to wear?"

"Of course," a handmaiden replied politely. "Everything is at your disposal."

"Awesome." Jasmine took a seat on the stool in front of the vanity. If nothing else, she could always find a welcome distraction in pretty clothes. "Let's do this, then."

CHAPTER NINETEEN

B y the time Jasmine had left the quarters, she looked like a completely different person.

Her hair had been carefully combed out and done in hundreds of uniform plaits that framed her face, interwoven with strands of gold that tapered towards the ends and make it look like they were all dipped in the precious metal. The dress she had on, and the accompanying long jacket that she wore over it were made of gossamer, yet the many layers that made up the flowy garment concealed the most of her figure. Airy greens with a hint of gold composed the majority of the dress, and her jacket had a thick embroidered edge to it that sported vines and flowers in bloom. There was a light sash that defined her waist, and the rest was as free flowing as she assumed many Draconians preferred their clothes to be. Jasmine would always have an appreciation for the heavier Victorian-esque styles that Hellenia was known for, but she also liked not being weighed down for the time being.

She followed one of the handmaidens through the colorful halls, their footsteps muted by the plush carpet until they came to a set of screen doors. Once they were pushed apart, they were greeted by a large room meant for entertaining, with a large lacquered table and loads of seating scattered about. But Jasmine's attention settled on the occupants of the room, one of which she recognized as Kai, and the other being a burly man leaning against a wall facing him. At the sound of the doors opening, both of them turned their attention to the women in their midst, and the handmaiden bowed politely before stepping aside to give Jasmine the floor.

"This style suits you well," Kai smiled as he sat up from his casual position, then nodded to the other man with him. "Nemeer shows his regards."

Before Jasmine could respond, Nemeer crossed the room and enveloped her in a bear hug that lifted her at least a foot off of the ground. She squeaked in surprise, but he just seemed to glaze over it in his excitement. "I'm sorry if I scared you earlier... *really* feel bad about that," he sheepishly told her before letting her down. "I just wanted to see you for myself before you got here."

"It's all good," Jasmine replied, feeling her arms tingle from how tightly he had held her. *This man seriously does not know his own strength at all.* Yet, he had an earnest air about him that made it impossible to hold anything against him. Even for as big as Nemeer obviously was, she knew she had to get used to existing around beings that only wore a human skin and encompassed the spirit of the grand beasts they actually were. "Thanks for... well, giving me the first-class aerial view."

Nemeer grinned widely. "Of course! You're the guest of the hour, after all. When you get to visit Favonius, I'll show you the beaches we have and where I like to work out, and-"

"Don't overwhelm her," Kai chided gently. "As of right now, I believe the Prime and I have much to discuss."

Nemeer sagged his shoulders a bit in disappointment. "Jasmine, right? I'll see you soon enough; you'll meet the others too for dinner later." He rotated his arm, loosening up a stiff muscle and walked over to the door. "I hope you'll like us, really. We're a bit different, but it's not so bad." He gave another wave before disappearing into the hallway, leaving Jasmine and Kai alone. She looked after his lumbering figure in a bit of a daze, just now realizing that Nemeer wasn't wearing a shirt. But in his absence, she soon felt awkward once more, bowing her head as she fussed a bit with the long sleeves to get them to stop drooping over the tips of her fingers.

"Why don't you have a seat?" Kai gestured towards a nearby chair fashioned out of cherry wood and upholstered with silk. "And ask me anything you wish to know."

Jasmine made her way over to the offered chair and sat down, weary at the thought of having so many questions on her mind. She knew exactly what he wanted from her and why, and although she had come to her epiphany post-breakdown on Hyperion that she was only a tool to be used, it still left a bit of a sour taste in her mouth and made her not want to make the same mistake that she did with Leon in thinking that she would ever be anything more.

"I guess I should ask what's expected of me while I'm here," she started. "I know that I'm to bring the Flame to either you or the High Lord of Hellenia, but that's about it. I feel like I've been flying off the seat of my pants, and to have a bit of clarity in all of this would be appreciated."

Kai's brow furrowed. "I was under the assumption that you knew your purpose. Did the Hellenians not inform you?"

Jasmine couldn't stop the bitter chuckle that left her lips. "I don't think things went exactly as planned in that regard."

The Draconian nodded slowly, his face clouded in what was obviously something he didn't expect to hear before replying. "To put it simply, you are a conduit for an ancient power that allows us passage to your realm. Once you commune with the Flame itself at the peak of Hyperion, you make a decision to gift said passage to us, or the Hellenians." He uncrossed his long legs and stood up, pacing slightly.

"What you are doing here, and what you have done with the Hellenians, is deciding which race you deem fit for that prize. There are pros and cons to consider, of course... but in the end, it's your call." Kai studied her with an indecipherable expression. "I take this to also mean that you don't know what happens after."

Jasmine felt a knot start twisting in her gut. "Not really. I just know that both you and the Hellenians want to mingle with humans, but only one of you can at a time. I didn't know there was anything *after* I decided who gets that privilege." She took a moment to swallow. "What are you saying, exactly?"

"I'm saying that your choice doesn't just affect us, it affects *you*. For your time here, it is important that you get to know our society, what it's like... how to move and breathe like one of us. And if you bless us with the Flame, we take you the rest of the way."

She sat like a statue in the extravagant room, staring without blinking at Kai and clutching the sides of her garment into her fists. Jasmine rolled the words he said over and over in her mind, trying to find a loophole... *any* alternative, that would make that pill she was offered go down less harshly in her throat. "You're telling me that I can't go back home? That I'm stuck with you or the Hellenians?"

"You'll become a hybrid, for lack of a better term." Kai leaned against the lacquered table near her chair. "Your life-span will be extended to far longer than the average human's, as your communion with the Flame ties its longevity to your soul.

You will gain powers and abilities in line with the race you choose; for example, you will obtain a draconic form if you choose me." His lips turned up into a grin. "I am not sure of the particulars granted to a Hellenian hybrid, however. It was supposed to be explained to you already."

Jasmine just sat motionless with a blank look on her face, trying in vain to process the information given to her. The only thing that she had going for her was the hope that she would just be done with being tangled in a web she didn't choose as soon as she got the Flame. Now, Kai's words dashed that belief to the floor where it shattered into a million pieces. He looked at her dejected figure for a moment before heaving a consternated sigh.

"To be frank, this worries me. What have the Hellenians been doing to prepare you for this task? It's unheard of for a Prime to be released to Hyperion without knowing this."

Maybe the asshat was too busy making me think that he actually cared instead of just telling me just what the fuck was gonna happen to me. The weight in her stomach got heavier, and Jasmine couldn't stop the bitterness that she held when it came to Leon. She despised not being fully informed of something that clearly had such an impact on her life. "Sorry," Jasmine said, standing up. "Can we get some fresh air? I want to ask more questions, but I think I need to move."

Kai nodded, pushing away from where he leaned on the table and offering his hand to her. "There are gardens nearby. We can continue our conversation there."

Jasmine stared too long at his hand, remembering how Leon would insist on doing so everywhere they went. She didn't want to be rude, but she also didn't have it in her to accept such a simple gesture from a man who had his own motivations and stake in the Flame anymore. Pursing her lips together, she bowed her head again and then made a small motion with her arm for him to lead the way. For what it was worth, Kai didn't seem to take it as a slight, and simply led her out of the palace and back outdoors into the sunlight.

Being in open space and fresh air helped a little. Jasmine raised her face to the sky and took a deep breath, taking in the aroma of random flowers and the natural sweetness of the breeze that ruffled the beautiful clothes she wore. "What happens if the Prime chooses no one to take the Flame? Has that ever been a thing?" She could admit to herself that her curiosity on the subject was mostly motivated by pettiness. She still couldn't completely wrap her head around the fact that she was going to be physically altered in any way, and since she couldn't get out of being the Prime, she was looking for any alternatives to extricate herself while still technically fulfilling her duty.

"There has not been a Prime in history that denied both races access to your realm. And, if you knew how our influences directly impacted your world, I think you would hesitate on attempting to be the first to do so." Kai looked at her askance as they walked, his hands clasped behind his back.

"Why is that?"

They came to a circular fountain, the center of the white marbled structure fashioned like a seven-tiered pagoda, spilling crystal clear water out of each hole and splashing to the pool below. "The Hellenians have had control of the Flame for many years, hundreds of them, by your calendar. During this time, I can assume that you may have seen changes in your environment, likely for the worst. The earth is crying out for healing, yet... the changes seem irreversible."

Kai faced her completely then, the light from the sun shining on his hair. "This is something our influence can reverse. Dragons are native to the land. We were its rightful caretakers before our unfortunate war with the Hellenians that forced us to retreat. Those fallen angels may give humans the gift of accelerated spirituality, mysticism and the like... but what good is it if the land you live on dies while you pray to gods that have no interest in saving anything but your souls?"

Jasmine focused on the sprawling expanse of the gardens that were on the land, processing what she was just told. A part of her wanted to believe that he was lying, that he would say anything possible in order to convince her to relinquish the Flame to him. Yet, she couldn't deny that Kai had been anything but straightforward with her. She could appreciate it, despite the fact that the information that he gave to her made things more complicated. She had no idea that her realm was being passively affected by the ancient races' presence, but it all checked out; global warming was an issue, and it had been greatly accelerated even just within her lifetime.

But Jasmine wasn't so naive as to believe that he wasn't omitting anything that would make the Draconians look less favorable.

"You make a good point," Jasmine conceded. "But it seems like the one thing humans have that lies outside of either race's influence is that of technology. We've always been extremely adaptable no matter what trials come our way, even if we are the ones that make our own problems a lot of the time. So, I will definitely need more time to think about who I bless with the Flame."

Kai studied her for a bit, and then turned and continued walking down the path past the fountain, expecting her to follow. "The Prime knows when their heart knows, and not before. I didn't mean to imply that you would be able to make a decision upon simply stepping foot in our realm. But after some time becoming better acquainted with us... I'm sure it will become clearer."

Eventually, they came to an elaborate glass dome, filled with more trees and flowers. Everything was meticulously crafted out of leaded glass, reflecting the light at many angles and casting iridescent fractures on the outside grass. Kai opened the door and gestured for her to step over the threshold into the little haven it enclosed.

It was just only slightly more humid within the enclosure, but no less stunning. Many birds of different sizes and colors flew from branch to branch, unconcerned with visitors. Similar to the gardens they just left, it was full of greenery and interspersed with colorful flowers, many of which didn't have a human equivalent. Butterflies coasted through the air, flitting from bush to bush, only scattering when two individuals came walking slowly down the gravel lined path. The Draconian lifted a finger, and a red bird with long tail feathers dipped in purple swooped down from a branch to sit upon it.

"Despite me answering your questions to the best of my ability, this is not a substitute for your own instincts. I don't wish to tell you what to do." Kai turned to face her, outstretching his hand. The bird fluttered its wings and landed on Jasmine's shoulder, making a small trilling noise and getting itself comfortable. "The Flame chose you for a reason. If it were truly up to me or the Hellenians, we wouldn't have need for you as an intermediary in the first place."

Nodding stiffly in a way to not disturb her feathered companion, Jasmine thought about what else she could ask of Kai since he was being so forthcoming. *Let's play hardball and see how he bats.*

"Real talk; do you hate the Hellenians?"

Kai made a small noise at her question, training his eyes to the ceiling to gather his words. "Contrary to what they may believe, I don't hate them. Not many Draconians do anymore, I'd imagine. The battles between our ancestors are distant memories, and now we are little more than opposing teams for a prize."

Yeah. And I guess I'm the fucking prize. Jasmine let her eyes turn distant, even as the colorful bird happily hopped from one shoulder to the other, unperturbed by her dip in mood.

"Are you alright? This seems to be a bit much for you."

"You think?" Jasmine retorted before remembering who she was speaking to. "Sorry. It's a lot of information I have to make sense of. Thank you very much for your honest opinion. I might just be tired. I guess I did hike up a mountain before getting here."

"Your pilgrimage on Hyperion is a unique one. I knew that once you arrived here, you would be feeling the exhaustion catch up to you." Kai gestured for her to follow him back out into the garden. "Let me show you to where you'll be staying while you're here."

The bird reluctantly fluttered off of Jasmine as it noticed they were leaving, and she turned to wave at it before stepping back outside. The sun almost seemed too bright, and she attributed that to her fatigue. She wanted to keep talking as she had a bunch of questions still, but her brain had reached its limit. There was so much to consider, and she felt as if she was on a hamster wheel running to a finish she would never reach. "Thank you... sorry."

"No need to apologize," Kai reassured as they entered the palace once more and led her down a hallway before sliding open another door. The room on the other side of it was moderate in size in comparison to what Jasmine assumed the rest of the palace was like, complete with a four-poster bed and a rounded window that showed the beauty of the land and sky on the other side of it. A small table, nightstand, and a few chairs similar to the one she sat in earlier greeted her as well. She noticed that her previous clothes had been placed on one of them, and just seeing the mismatched familiarity of her own belongings grounded her a little.

"There will be dinner later, with the others. But please feel free to rest as long as you'd like. If you'd rather bow out for the night, then feel free as well. There's no pressure... as I assume you've got a lot to think upon."

You could say that. "It's fine. I think a few hours of shut eye would be great, and then I'll be back up to socializing. It's my first day here, after all; I can't waste the opportunity while I have it."

Kai gave a sound of assent, then turned to leave. "Then please, rest well. I'll send a handmaiden to you once dinner is ready, if you feel rested enough to join."

Jasmine nodded, watching him as he left and slid the lacquered wood and stained-glass door shut behind him. Then, and only then, did she feel her posture slump and some of the pressure leave her body. She was sure that Kai was being as gracious as he could, but it was still so odd. She didn't have time to process everything that happened to her in Hellenia before she decided to start her pilgrimage, and a part of her was regretting her haste in that manner. *Well, what were you gonna do there anyway? Wait for Leon to pull his head out of his ass and reject you to your face?*

She carefully peeled off some of the layers of her outfit, actually wanting to rest but not wanting to wrinkle the fabric. After she was left in just a plain silk shift, she flopped down onto the bed and curled up, listening to the birds outside and finding them drowned out nearly by her whirling thoughts. Eventually, the tears started falling; emotions flowing that she didn't allow herself to fully process even after her minor breakdown on Hyperion. As much as Jasmine hated crying, it was cathartic and helped her release some of the stress that had built up inside of her. Not knowing nearly enough about her situation and what she was supposed to do was wearing on her.

Eventually, she sobbed herself into a dreamless doze, face down into the pillow.

CHAPTER TWENTY

Jasmine was confused when she was stirred awake by a gentle hand on her shoulder, and she groggily pulled herself upright and looked around at her unfamiliar surroundings. She honestly thought that she would be waking up in her bedroom, patting around the covers for her cell phone to see what time it was and how much longer she would have before she had to get up. She stared blearily at the image of one of the handmaidens before her until the events from the world's longest day came flooding back into her memory, then noticed that the sun had set outside the window.

She wished that she could have real time to herself in order to not feel like she was performing in an unfamiliar place, but that wasn't in the cards. She smiled kindly to the woman who woke her for dinner, making sure that her face wasn't stained with either drool from her sleep or tears from her earlier breakdown. Then, she was smoothing out the wrinkles in her outfit which she got back into and was led down the hallway once more.

The dining area was brightly lit, with a circular table in the center and many chairs surrounding it. Only four of them were filled, and Jasmine recognized two of the people already. The others consisted of a man with sandy hair and a dark-skinned woman, and Jasmine bowed politely.

"Hi. I'm Jasmine. I met Nemeer already, but it's good to be able to be acquainted with the rest of Kai's companions that he speaks so highly about."

"Oh? He spoke well of *me*? Was he drunk?" The one with light-colored hair teased before leaning his head back and laughing. "Nice to meet you, Jasmine. My name is Ciaran, and I rule over the lands of Notos. Glad to see that Nemeer didn't crush you by accident."

Nemeer threw his hands up in exasperation, almost hitting one of the servers that was placing dishes on the table in front of them. "Listen, *obviously* she's okay! I don't know why you're being mean."

While Ciaran moved to clap the larger man on the shoulder to show him that he was just joking around, the woman turned her attention to Jasmine next. "I'm Fouzia of Apartica. If you can, please forgive the two loud idiots over here. Outside of me, Kai's the next best thing, so count your blessings that you ended up with him."

Jasmine nodded slowly, making her way over to the empty seat next to Kai and settling in. The smell of the food that was being brought out was delicious, and it seemed like her body was catching up to feeling hungry again after her journey. "Um, that makes it sound like we're a couple or something. I'm still learning a lot while I'm here, so is there something to what you just said, or am I looking too much into things?"

Fouzia lifted her eyebrows in shock, but before she could respond, Ciaran leaned forward in his seat to address Jasmine. "Kai didn't get around to telling you about how things work for the Prime, huh?"

Kai gave a tempered sigh through his nose, appearing carefully composed as he poured both himself and Jasmine a cup of tea. "There was a lot she didn't learn from the Hellenians. I don't seek to overwhelm her."

"Well, I'm rested now, so might as well let me have it," Jasmine said defensively. *Leon tiptoed around me about all of this. I'll be damned if I let any of these Draconians finesse me because of my ignorance.* She knew that for as hard as it was going to be settling with things, she couldn't avoid it. The best weapon she had at her disposal was knowledge.

Ciaran grinned at Jasmine, moving forward. "Well, as you can see, there's four rulers here in Draconia. It'd be rather messy for us to vie for your affections while you were here, so we have a tradition where we fight it out first. Kai won, so that's why you're staying with him in Apelion and not with any of us."

"I see," Jasmine lifted the tea to her lips. *An arranged marriage of convenience on top of revoking my humanity. This shit just keeps getting better and better.* She glanced over to her side and saw that Kai was studying her in concern, and she shoved all of her thoughts aside for the time being.

"Thank you for the information; I'll try to keep most of my questions at bay for right now. I don't want all this wonderful food to get cold," Jasmine said, looking down and reaching for the pair of chopsticks that was carefully laid out on the linen in front of her. "And, I'm starving. So please, don't wait on my behalf."

"A woman with an appetite. I like it!" Nemeer said cheerfully, starting to heap insane amounts of food on his plate already. Fouzia sighed and reached to do the same, shooting a look at him in the process.

"Leave some for everyone else, please. We know you could

put away this whole table by yourself if we let you, and I'm not trying to fight you over the last roll."

Jasmine naturally fell back in the midst of their regular banter, relaxing a bit as she observed. It was nice to see them all interact organically, and despite her situation, she found herself smiling at how pure their friendship was. Kai seemed to be the mildest of them all, but she remembered how easily he seemed to devour her with his eyes when they first met on Hyperion. *There's more to all of them than what I'm seeing, I know it.*

In the meantime, she let herself enjoy the different food that made its way on her plate thanks to Kai easily shuffling dishes through the rotation and placing portions for her on her gold-rimmed plate. She asked questions in intervals about flavors she didn't recognize, seeing a few things that reminded her of lotus root or glass noodles, but a lot of it was native to Draconia and had no human equivalent. Nonetheless, there wasn't anything that Jasmine found she particularly disliked, opting to finish what was set in front of her until she actually felt rather full. By the time she pushed her plate away and leaned back with a fresh cup of poured tea, she was happily satiated.

"Tell us about yourself, Jasmine," Ciaran poured himself some of the liquor that was also available as a beverage choice, but she had declined in favor of staying sober around strangers. "Obviously, we're not blessed to have a Prime in our midst except in a couple of hundred-year spurts, so don't be shy. We're on the edge of our seats, here."

Jasmine was comfortable being in the background as an observer, but once again she was reminded that the reason that they were all gathered there was because she was the guest of honor. Clearing her throat, she shrugged as nonchalantly as she could. "There isn't a whole lot to me. I work, pay off student loans, and sew some clothes in my limited spare time. Pretty sure this Flame chose the most unremarkable person, but it is what it is."

"Student loans..." Kai murmured. "Am I to assume that you mean prospective students are given money to *pay* for an education, and then are expected to pay it back?"

"That's how loans work, usually," Ciaran snarked after taking a sip from his cup. "But it seems silly to charge money to people who want to learn. Everyone should be allowed to learn whatever they wish with no barriers. It's how we function here."

Jasmine was going to say something about how admirable it is that Draconians seemed to have a better grasp on what it meant to care about society as a whole than humans did, when she was interrupted by an excited Nemeer.

"You sew? Clothes? You make your own? What do you think of the clothes you were given? Is it along the lines of the quality you make? What would you do different? What's your favorite color? Also-"

Fouzia laid her forehead down on the table in front of her. "Gods, here we go..."

Jasmine gave an amused snort. "While I'm really happy to answer any of your questions, I assume there will be time to discuss things about me, later. I actually want to learn more about you all. I know I'm in Draconia, but you rule over different areas of it, right? I want to see everything for myself." She paused to move her long sleeves back a little bit. "As the Prime, I have to know what I'm getting into. I don't know how much time I have with you all, but I want to make it count."

Kai looked at her for a moment before nodding in agreement. "That is a good idea. And it would be a great opportunity for us to show you the entirety of Draconia."

"I want to go first!" Nemeer's hand shot up, his brown eyes wide. "Is tomorrow too soon? Don't worry, I don't have to fly you there. We can just go normally through one of the passage-ways set up between regions. Unless... you wanted to fly again?"

Fouzia sighed heavily. "What, we don't want the Prime choose for herself? Is that how we're gonna do this?"

"Well, I mean... whatever's most convenient for you guys, I'll work with. I don't mean to be any trouble."

Ciaran grinned. "Oh, it's no trouble at all. You're the Prime, after all. We're *always* looking to entertain."

The rest of the dinner progressed easily, full of laughter and boisterous conversation. Jasmine didn't have much to add, but she did feel herself relax a little bit more into her environment. She couldn't help but compare it with Hellenia; for the exception of Elliot's easy exuberance, it seemed to be very rigid and formal. Now she was witness to four individuals acting no different than a tight-knit family despite their high positions in society.

It was nice. But it also made Jasmine miss the company she kept with Kim and how they would find ways to laugh together on break or over the phone.

"Would you like to turn in?" Kai's voice filtered into her thoughts, and Jasmine realized that she was zoning out into the recesses of her mind. "Once Ciaran starts drinking, we usually go long into the night. But I don't want you to think that you're obligated to do the same."

"Yeah. I should rest up for tomorrow, since I'm assuming that Nemeer will be here bright and early?"

Nemeer let out a belly laugh. "Not too early. I have to get my morning exercise in, first. But I'll be here before midday."

"Good enough for me."

CHAPTER TWENTY-ONE

L ifting her head to the sky, Jasmine breathed in the air tinged with salt and wondered how places like the one she was in now could exist, even outside of the human realm. She had seen loads of photoshopped travel pictures, with idyllic islands and water so blue that it made her feel like perhaps her eyes weren't sharp enough to pick up the depth present in it.

She didn't think that she'd ever have the chance to be transported to a place that made those magazine spreads seem obsolete. Apelion was wonderful in its own right, stunning her with cherry blossoms and curved rooftops that made her feel as if she were cosplaying on the set of a dramatic Chinese movie. But Favonius introduced her to the expanse of the ocean and a relaxed vibe that definitely matched the happy, carefree personality of the dragon who ruled it. Flowy clothing was still their bread and butter, but her arms and stomach were exposed in the red gauzy fabric that criss-crossed over her chest and ended in a beach dress that danced along her ankles in the breeze.

She looked over at Kai who was seated next to her on the balcony, the wind ruffling his short ponytail and tangling the loose strands that escaped in the air. He'd been nothing but polite, but the fact that he felt like he was entitled to her in some fashion was unnerving.

"You know, I figured Nemeer was all about fitness and everything, but I didn't think he was *this* dedicated," she said, gesturing to where he was on the beach in front of them. The Draconian in question was in the middle of another set of one-handed pushups... but this time, he had one of the local children sitting happily on his back while he did it.

"He is the most physically active of the four of us. The humidity combined with the soft sands of Favonius makes for good resistance training, something that I'm sure he thought would work to his advantage during the Trial. In fact, it nearly did; it still took all three of us to get him to slow down at the end there."

Jasmine blinked in astonishment, knowing that none of them were slouches even if Nemeer was a head or so taller than all of them. She looked back towards him then, finding that he had finished up that round of exercise and was brushing the sand off of him, while the child made his way back to them happily.

"Catch!"

Jasmine was not used to things being randomly tossed in her direction, and her first instinct was to dodge. But without making a fool of herself, she lifted her hand and caught the smooth object.

"What's this, Tahir?"

"Sea glass! Master Nemeer told me you might think that they're cool. We have a lot of it here in Favonius." Tahir put his hands proudly on his hips. "When it washes up on shore, they can be easy to find depending on the color, but it's better if you swim to find the best pieces."

"I see." Jasmine held the translucent stone up to the sun, taking note of how it sparkled through the light cerulean color. *Wow, with a few of these things, I could use them as accents on some of my projects... that I likely won't be getting back to any time soon.* "Thank you very much. It seems like Favonius has many natural treasures."

"We have quite a few artesian sea glass merchants who make just about anything out of these gems." Nemeer stooped to scoop up the child, placing him easily on his shoulders before he hopped over the barrier separating the beach from the balcony as if it was nothing. "But if there's treasures to be impressed by, I could show you stuff that's better."

Jasmine raised an eyebrow. "Really?" She wasn't the type to be overly impressed by material objects, but she would be lying to herself if she said that she wasn't intrigued at the fact that Draconians and the dragons she learned about in mythology shared their affinity for shiny things.

"Yeah. Let me take you to the vault. It's fine, right?" Nemeer looked over at Kai, who gave his friend a nod of assent before getting out of his seat. Jasmine fought hard to not be overly annoyed at the fact that Kai apparently had to be consulted before any actions were to be taken, but she knew it wasn't something that she was going to win at the moment. She simply stood with him, looking up at Tahir perched on Nemeer's shoulders to smile at him, instead.

With the white sandy beaches behind them, they made their way back to the large stone castle that Nemeer called his home. Attendants stopped and bowed their heads to them as they passed before carrying on with whatever duties they were attending to. The lush courtyard in the center of the square shaped palace sported many flowers, different plants, and featured a large apple tree whose branches reached just above the rooftop surrounding it, reaching for the sky. As they walked past it, Tahir reached out and grabbed hold of one of the branches, pulling himself off of Nemeer's shoulders and making his way further into the leaves. The prince caught Jasmine's concerned gaze and smiled.

"Don't worry too much about him; he's not allowed in the royal vault, and he really likes occupying himself with the tree. I think he's the most popular kid in his area because all his friends know that he brings back the sweetest apples Favonius has to offer."

Eventually, they came out on the other side, and another stone lined walkway led them to something that reminded Jasmine of a casita. She stood next to Kai and watched as Nemeer pushed open the heavy wooden doors, then beckoned them to come inside. It looked to be completely dark after being outside in the bright sun just moments ago, but when the doors swung shut behind them, flames that lined the walls came to life automatically, showing the grandiose interior. Jasmine stopped in her tracks and simply stared at everything with her mouth slightly agape.

There was gold... lots of it. Jewels sparkled on silk pillows, and marbled statues poised gracefully as they walked by. It seemed as though they had walked into a warehouse of fine arts and expensive things that came from many different areas of Jasmine's realm, all on display.

"Every Draconian family, royal or common, has a vault. The treasures within vary, but they all hold considerable importance." Kai looked over his shoulder at her, gesturing to one of the marbled busts to the side. "The Veiled Virgin, crafted by the artist Giovanni Strazza."

Jasmine blinked at him. "Excuse me, what?"

Nemeer laughed heartily at her shock. "My family spirited

all of this away long before I was born. It's a generational thing. We have a habit of hoarding, for lack of a better word. Draconians use special magic to whisk away things that hold great value, using alchemy to create a nearly identical replacement. You guys really would be none the wiser."

"I would garner a guess and say that the vast majority of monuments, art pieces, jewels, and other similar things are mere copies in your realm," Kai added, turning his head to look at the rest of Nemeer's family stash. "Save for any modern works that we haven't the chance to investigate for ourselves yet."

"Wow." She turned her attention back to the statue, taking in the exquisite detail that she had only ever seen in pictures online. She had a bit of trouble processing the fact that the Draconians had been spiriting away historical works just to keep in their coffers, but she knew that she wouldn't get anywhere dissenting. So instead, she let the two of them lead her deeper into the antechamber, where the light became somewhat dimmer. There was a smaller room set apart from the rest of the spoils, enshrouded in wisps of incense that seemed to muffle their steps as they entered. There were large, faceted jewels ranging from the size of serving platters to plates, propped up on individual stands atop a sprawling altar.

"These are the most precious of any treasures a Draconian could have. The jewels here are our ancestors, evidence of our family line through each generation." Kai gestured towards them, and Jasmine observed that they seemed to have a faint glow within, not unlike the Spark that still hung around her neck. "It is true that we live extremely long lives... but they tend to be lonely ones."

"What do you mean?"

"Ah, well... Draconians only have one mate for life, and get one child out of it," Nemeer explained, running a hand through his curly dark hair. "Normally, it's not really that big of a deal, as all generations live under one roof, and we are dedicated to our community as a whole. But for people who have royal blood like me, once that child becomes of proper age to rule, the parents voluntarily move on and become hardened dragon scales."

Jasmine studied the unique gems in front of her. "I can't even imagine. I mean, it explains why you guys and your assistants are the only ones I see around the palace and everything, but just leaving you guys to your own devices? It seems... cruel."

"Our lifespans much longer than a human's. It takes quite a bit of time before we reach maturity, and within that time, we are taught everything that we need to know to rule. It's less of an abandonment than it is simple tradition," Kai explained. "At any rate, it makes our connections with our neighbors and friends all the more important to us. I don't know what I'd do without my comrades; we've been together nearly since birth. Though our personalities may differ and we've certainly had our disagreements, I wouldn't change a thing."

"Same," Nemeer walked over and clapped a large hand on Kai's shoulder. "But I won't lie; I've always been jealous of humans and how they can just have multiple children. I know if I *could* change anything, it would be that."

"How many kids would you wanna have, then?" Jasmine asked.

"Me? Oh. Well... I'm thinking at least six. That's a good even number."

"... six. Whew," Jasmine laughed a little. "Well... maybe if in the event I *do* choose to bless the Flame to you guys, you'll be able to go to the human realm and find yourself a surrogate."

Kai shook his head. "Unfortunately, we cannot reproduce with anyone but a Draconian. While we are able to take a humanoid form, our physiology on a molecular level isn't compatible with humans."

"Ah," Jasmine murmured as they turned and made their way out of the vault. She wondered if it was the same with Hellenians, but that made her think about that fateful night with Leon, so she cut off that train of thought almost as quickly as it left the mental station. "So, what would happen in the event that a Prime becomes a Draconian? Does that change things?"

Nemeer turned around to close the doors to the edifice. "The Flame's power can only go so far from what I understand. It changes you just enough for certain traits to come through, like having a dragon form and a longer lifespan. But it doesn't do much in terms of reproduction." He pouted. "It's really a shame, though. Imagine if that *was* possible! Winning the hand of the Prime in the Trial would mean even more!"

Jasmine slid her gaze to Kai, her face unreadable. She didn't have anything against Nemeer and his almost childlike excitement when it came to the things he was explaining. In fact, she appreciated having the mind to ask these questions, and having both of them simply answer truthfully. But hearing that she was thought of as won from a competition she never consented to still bothered her. It was brought up so casually, and it was expected that she just... put up with it. *Maybe other Primes were down with this in the past, but I am not the one or the two.*

"I'm glad to hear that you've made a family for yourself in your friends," she said evenly, pushing her discomfort out of her face as much as possible. "You all seem pretty tight as a group."

"We are," Kai agreed, his face brightening. "Royalty has its lineage, but our companionship is what's strongest among us. Nonetheless, I'm happy that you're being given the opportunity to see each of our unique wonders in and of itself."

"Can't wait to see more." Jasmine looked at the bit of sea

glass that she still held. It was easier than meeting Kai's gaze, as the light hit his eyes just right to show the depths of mahogany within them. Despite all of her reservations when it came to him and her place, if she wasn't careful, she would catch herself staring at him. *You'd think after all of my time with the Hellenians, that I'd be used to being around such fine ass people.* It may have been born out of avoidance of going back to Apelion and twiddling her thumbs until the next day came, but she looked up at Nemeer's hulking figure and showed him the stone.

"So, you mentioned merchants do stuff with these things? Mind taking some time out to show a girl what that's all about?"

Nemeer's grin was contagious, and Jasmine found his large arm circling her shoulders as he steered them towards town. "Oh, I think you'll love it. I'll introduce you to Senria, who is the best sea glass crafter in Favonius. The stuff she makes with a few of these things... you wouldn't believe it. Then, I can also show you some of our signature foods, which are a combination of things from the sea and local fruits. If it sounds weird, it isn't. Okay, *some* of them may be, but they taste good, honest!"

Kai simply followed along, and the rest of the day went by easily. Jasmine put her worries to the side, allowing herself to be distracted by the boisterous market along with Nemeer's accommodating personality. She didn't speak much to Kai, not sure of how best to get over her slight awkwardness when it came to him.

When the following day arrived, bringing both of them to Ciaran's land of Notos, she found she couldn't avoid talking with him any longer.

CHAPTER TWENTY-TWO

"May I ask you something?"

Jasmine looked up from her hands that were folded into her lap to Kai, who was sitting across from her appearing more graceful than what she herself could manage in the lavish, yet cramped litter. *Must come with the territory of being royalty.* "Sure. Might take my mind off of how freaking *hot* it is here."

"What is your attachment to remaining human?"

It was asked with the innocence of a being that had no concept of humanity, and while that was better than being confronted in a derisive manner, Jasmine still had to fight to not automatically be defensive in the face of it. "It's who I am, and quite frankly, I never wanted to be anything else. Maybe some humans have fantasies about being gifted beings with special powers or what have you, but that's never been me. The most I've ever wanted was a solid month's worth of vacation time, no guilt trips from my superiors for taking it, and enough money to live a comfortable life sewing outfits to wear for particularly niche events. And considering how the human world works, that's already asking for a lot."

The litter jostled a bit, reminding Jasmine of the fact that they were seriously on their way up a mountain range carried on the shoulders of Draconian attendants. She had wanted to outright refuse, considering how extra it was and the fact that she had climbed a mountain by herself prior to arriving to Draconia in the first place. But not only had Ciaran waved off her concerns, she was secretly relieved that she wasn't allowed to let her modest sensibilities get in the way of reality. The desert landscape of Notos would have probably had her passed out not even a third of the way up, drenched in her own sweat.

"I see," Kai mused. "Nothing about being chosen by the Flame entices you?"

"Not really. It's kind of been a monkey wrench in my life, to tell the truth. Things like being 'the chosen one' only sound good in a movie or something where you don't have to see the inconveniences that come with it."

"But these so-called inconveniences are blessings."

"Are they?" Jasmine settled her braids behind her ears to keep them from swaying. "Let me put it to you this way; if someone arrived at your door tomorrow and said that you were chosen to leave your entire life behind and become something else, how would you react to that? Would you think it a blessing?"

Kai opened his mouth to reply, and then stopped. Jasmine could almost hear the gears turning in his head at what was a simple question, starting a chain reaction of responses that he had to weed through before simply offering one to her. She figured he was smart enough not to say anything to her face that would insinuate that humans were in a place that was below Draconians, even though she knew that was the general unsaid consensus amongst them. She could also tell that Kai was unused to not centering his beliefs in conversation, which was a little bit funny when it came to him actually taking his words into account.

"I guess I wouldn't," he said finally, his expression still thoughtful.

"Don't get me wrong; y'all are alright from what I've seen thus far. I like getting the tour of your lands and learning more about you while I consider the task that's ahead of me. Since I know that either Draconia or Hellenia will be my new place of residence, I like to be informed." She straightened her shoulders. "But I'm not the type to be swayed by fancy things alone."

Kai blinked at her, and then gave a chuckle. "If there's one thing I've noticed, you're swayed by exceptional clothing. With that, I'm sure I can get farther than you anticipated."

Jasmine felt her cheeks get hot at the unexpected read, forgetting how transparent she was when it came to exquisite designs. Each day she spent in Apelion she was given her choice of the nicest outfits that came in no less than three flowy layers, and when she visited Nemeer's realm, she had been presented with clothes that represented his lands. Today was no exception, draped in the sandy hues that most of the people of Notos sported, save for a few brightly colored accessories. It was something that got Jasmine excited to visit despite her initial wariness, and she thought she was doing a better job of hiding it.

Thankfully, she didn't have to reply to Kai's smug observation, as the litter slowed to a stop and she could feel it being lowered to the ground. Kai disembarked first, pulling back the heavy curtain that blocked out the worst of the sun's rays and allowing Jasmine an unobstructed exit.

The view that greeted her was breathtaking, much like everything she had seen in the lands thus far. At first, she thought Notos to be rather barren after the rich colors of

Apelion and Favonius, the tan hues that made up most of the landscape save for the oasis the brunt of the population and the palace itself resided in were lackluster under the harsh sun. But in the higher elevation of where they were in the mountains, she was greeted by desert flora that wasn't present in the city proper. The indigo bushes and ocotillo flowers reminded her of the beading that she wore on her wrists and along the waistline of her clothes, and as she walked forward close to the edge of the cliff, she observed a magnificent landscape of craggy mountains carving the valleys below against a bright sky.

"Wow..." Jasmine took in a deep breath, letting the cool breeze flow across her face. "This is amazing. Oh, wasn't Ciaran going to meet us here? Did we seriously beat him to the top going a snail's pace in that caravan?"

"Knowing him, he likely wants to make a grand appearance. We shouldn't have to-"

Seemingly from out of nowhere, a grand creature came galloping towards them, its long body reflecting the sun shining down on the area in royal purple shimmers. Its build was very similar to a Komodo dragon with the way it lumbered along with clear musculature on display. Yet, there was a lissome grace to its motions that was somewhat surprising to Jasmine. Its long tail tapered off into bushy fur, similar to the mane that circled its neck that appeared white but shone almost fiery gold in the light. Broad bronze bangles sectioned parts of its tail along with around the wrists of its claws, and it skid to a stop before them, kicking up rocks in its wake. The gigantic horn that sat right in the middle of its forehead curved up and back like a crescent moon, and it bowed its head to blink at Jasmine with generous eyes that confirmed to her who he was.

She didn't know how she wasn't startled into tumbling right off of the edge of the mountain after all of that, but she chalked it up to absolute shock freezing her into place.

"Let me tell you about the Run," Kai said casually, drawing Jasmine's attention back to him. He held in his hands an elaborate but sturdy saddle, given to him by the attendants that carried them to the meeting spot. "As you can see, this area in Draconia is rife with mountain ranges, some of which are volcanic. A tradition that those of Notos embark upon involves flying through the tight caverns and across the peaks as fast as possible."

Kai walked over to his friend to secure one side of the saddle on his back, then walked around in front of Ciaran's transformed face to get to the other. "Those who are young, or who have never done it before ride along in human form on the back of a seasoned participant to get to know the route. Races are held with prizes offered to those who win or beat established records. Ciaran currently holds the fastest time, closely followed by me."

Jasmine could see where this was going, and her heart started hammering hard in her chest as she watched Kai finish the preparations before walking back over to her.

"He should know better than to be too wild with you." Kai gave her a lopsided smile. "However, I still do recommend you hold on during the duration of the ride."

Jasmine lifted both of her hands and looked down at the ground for a bit, giving an incredulous snort. "Hold up. You seriously want me to get on the back of this dragon?"

Ciaran flicked his tail, and Kai nodded. "Yes. Don't worry, you won't fall off. There are straps to keep you situated on the saddle, and the seat itself is secure on his back."

She looked at the long, scaly body, then up at the saddle before looking back at Kai. There was a fair amount of trepidation when it came to going through what he described, but she also couldn't help but be a bit excited for it once the initial shock died down. A thrilling ride through mountains on the back of a dragon seemed like something straight out of a fantasy movie. *Well. YOLO.*

Her garments offered her the movement needed to climb atop Ciaran's back, and once she was settled, she realized it was sort of like being on a horse for the first time. She felt the straps tighten around her legs as Kai adjusted them.

"Please don't be too ambitious with the Prime."

Ciaran snorted, tossing his head a little. Jasmine reached forward and grabbed the horn of the saddle in surprise of just how much that movement rocked her.

"I mean it. This isn't an exercise in making her more terrified than she already is."

Ciaran snorted again. Kai rolled his eyes and turned his attention back to Jasmine. "I do hope that at least you have some stomach for excitement." He backed up a few yards, giving them a wide berth, and placed his hands behind his back. "I'll see you soon."

Jasmine nodded tentatively at him before facing forward, her nerves rattled as if she were getting behind the wheel for the first time.

Ciaran carefully ambled a few steps back, rocking her a little in the seat that she looked comically small upon, before rushing forward at a full sprint towards the edge of the cliff.

"HOLY SHIT!!" Jasmine shrieked, hunkering down as much as she could with all of the jostling before she felt him allow his body to free fall into a swan dive, speeding past the rockface at an alarming speed. The feeling of her stomach dropping out from under her was intense, and tears blurred her vision at the wind that ruffled his mane and blew past her face. Then, at the last moment, he soared upwards, flying through the air and aiming for the natural passageways between the mountains.

The journey was like a high-powered roller coaster mixed

with the excitement of being on the back of a powerful animal steering the entire ride. Even though Jasmine was sure that her screeches could be heard echoing all through the canyons, eventually her screams of fear turned into squeals of delight mixed with loud, joyous laughter. There were times where Ciaran dove down, low enough to a shallow stream where she could lean over and skim the surface of the water with her fingertips. Then he would switch it up and go above the clouds, cutting through the wisps with his body and letting the dispersed plumes brush their faces.

The scenery flying by her was exhilarating. The wind whipped her braids around with every sharp turn they took, and Jasmine learned to anticipate when they were coming and lean with the curves as best as she could. Eventually, he slowed his speed and gently coasted by sand dunes and other wildlife, making his way back to the spot where they embarked.

Kai's figure could be seen sitting cross legged on a nearby rock, with closed eyes and his face turned to the sky in a calm sort of meditation. Ciaran landed surprisingly soft back on the cliff, only jostling Jasmine for a little bit until he came to a stop.

"Doesn't look like you passed out during all of that, so I can only assume Ciaran did as I suggested," Kai said lightly, coming over to unstrap her from the saddle. "How did you like it?"

"That was... the most lit thing I have ever done in my whole life," she replied breathlessly, still processing the rush that came with the whole experience. "So... is it okay to go again? Or is it just one ride per Prime per day?"

"It is usually one ride per person. A young Draconian is expected to memorize the pathways, and then show proficiency in navigating it themselves." His hands were deft, undoing the snaps and carefully helping Jasmine off of the saddle and then removing it. Ciaran turned, brushing his large face against Jasmine's side like a cat giving affection before scampering off.

"Aw," Jasmine couldn't keep the disappointment out of her voice at the news.

Kai gave her a sidelong glance. "If you happened to give us the Flame, you could be flying through these passages yourself. Perhaps in the future..." Kai trailed off, giving her a sidelong glance with a knowing smile. It made Jasmine laugh heartily for the first time since arriving, and it felt as though a bit of the strange wall that was between them came down.

"Okay, maybe y'all have *two* things that will hook me into this Draconian life." She followed him to the litter to be carried back down the mountain. "So, what's next on the agenda? I don't think anything can top what I just experienced, though."

Kai pulled back the drape to the entrance. "Don't tell Ciaran that. I'm sure he'll find a way to rise to the occasion."

CHAPTER TWENTY-THREE

Jasmine adjusted the sleeves of her light duster, looking out to the city beyond where she stood in the front of the palace. She had actually fallen asleep on the way back down the mountain, letting the rocking motion of the litter lull her into a comfortable doze. She felt refreshed and eager to see what else was in store... and if she was being honest, she looked forward to spending more time with Kai.

It helped seeing how he interacted with his royal companions. If they couldn't do much at first but exchange stilted facts and misunderstand each other, then she observed how he patiently indulged Nemeer's excitement for both food and fitness alike or shooting Ciaran as much snark as the Notos prince could dish out himself. Kai was rounding out in her eyes, and it made her lower her guard a little.

"I'm not sure if it's considered rude, and if so, please forgive me. But I was wondering why I don't actually see you guys like... transform?"

Kai came to stand next to her, peering at the pleasant hues of reds and orange in the setting sun on the horizon. "It's uncouth to switch in front of guests. It also might be a bit jarring on your senses to see us change from what you see now in front of you to the large beasts we become. Switching between forms takes a lot of control to do smoothly, and often is draining on us. Consistently maintaining our dragon form is not something we are able to do without intense training, and we are arguably at our most vulnerable in the moments following a switch."

"Makes sense." Jasmine was going to ask something else, but she was caught off guard by Ciaran coming around the corner and whisking her off her feet in a hug, spinning her around once.

"You wanted to go again! I *knew* you had the spirit of a dragon in you!"

"Hey, I dunno about all that," Jasmine sputtered, but she couldn't help but smile at his enthusiasm. "But I didn't die, so the adrenaline rush was totally worth it."

Ciaran's lavender eyes twinkled as he moved to stand between her and Kai, looping his arms through their respective arms before moving forward and down the steps that would lead them past the courtyards and into the city. "I've always wanted someone new to fly with me on the Run. Nemeer has done it a couple of times, but he doesn't like it because the tight turns don't suit his large frame. Fouzia would probably give both Kai and I a run for our money if she actually tried, but she prefers her blisteringly cold mountains instead. If you would join me as a fellow dragon, it would be an honor."

"We'll see. Anyway, you said something about these night markets?"

"They're the lifeblood of Notos. As you can tell, the afternoon sun is too hot for much activity, so we claim the night as ours. Plenty of beaded jewelry I think you'd like, fruits you can only find here in this region... oh, and of course, the wine. Lots of wine. You'll have to try all of them."

Kai chuckled, shaking his head at Ciaran's unwavering enthusiasm. "It doesn't get terribly rowdy until the wee hours of the morning, and I assume you'll be safely back in Apelion by then. At any rate, you'll sleep as soundly as possible tonight."

I have no doubt about that at all. This has been more action than my sedentary ass has seen in years. Jasmine was whisked into the whirlwind of Ciaran's chaotic aura and found herself shuffling to keep up with his pace all the while trying to absorb everything around her. The lights of the street market started to come alive, the sounds surrounded the three of them as Draconians were setting up their stalls. As soon as she saw accessories and clothing, she was instantly flitting from one place to another, looking at their wares and asking about the craftsmanship that went into everything, avoiding Kai's smirk as he watched her.

"Oh! Let's stop here."

Ciaran gestured to a draped tent, with flowing sashes moving in the breeze. When they were parted to give way to the entrance, the inside seemed much larger than it appeared from the outside. The cushions that littered the ground surrounding quaint low tables greeted them, and a few other people were in their own groups, laughing around what looked to be the Draconian equivalent of hookah. While Kai took Jasmine to a spot off into the corner to get settled, Ciaran went to the front and chatted gaily with the person who seemed to be in charge, only to return with a large faceted bottle, enough matching cups for each of them, and a deck of cards.

"... oh no," Kai said wearily as the items clunked noisily on the table in front of them.

"Oh, *yes*," Ciaran continued unabashed, organizing the

deck of cards. "It's only fair we end this magnificent evening with a game of Khartopai. Let me explain to our guest of honor here." Skilled fingers spread the cards on the table in a neat fan, picking out four cards to show Jasmine.

"The rules are quite simple. These four are the royals, represented by each of the corners of Draconia. If you look closely, you'll even see that they are fashioned into our likenesses. I happen to think I'm *much* more handsome than this." He held up the stylized card, his signature color of purple prevalent amongst all else. "But whatever. Each of us will get our own pile, evenly distributed. You'll leave them face down, and only turn up one card at a time to a center pile. Once one of the royals appears, you must be the first to slap your hand down on it... but there is an exception."

Jasmine understood the game as a different form of slapjack until she was told there was a catch. "Oh, boy."

Kai reached over and neatly showed her each of the cards. "If you are the first, you must also make sure you shift that card in the direction the royal designates." He tapped the face of them in order. "Apelion goes to the East. Favonius goes to the West. Notos goes to the South, and Aparctia goes to the North. If you fail, then the center pile is shuffled out amongst us all to try again. If you succeed, you take the pile to yourself. If you are the one with all of the cards at the end, then you are the winner."

"Don't forget the rest."

Kai sighed, gesturing towards the bottle on the table. "This is a game that all Draconians know, but Ciaran has his own way of playing. Each time you aren't first to tap a royal, you take a drink. Each time you are the first, but move the card in the wrong direction, you take a drink." He gave Jasmine an apologetic smile. "We're all drunk by the end of this. It's a terrible addition, truly."

Ciaran folded his arms. "I could have added some of the other flairs, like making us all switch spots with each turn. I figured this was a lot easier and less competitive. At least this way, the Prime also gets to have some of our best wine while we do this." He started pouring into the cups and passing them to each of his companions.

Jasmine looked down into her cup warily, remembering her experience with otherworldly alcohol. "Is it a good time to tell y'all that I'm kind of a lightweight? Will you go easy on me?"

Ciaran's "no" was countered with Kai's "yes", and both of them stared at each other.

"She's the Prime."

"All the more reason to drink up, right?"

"Have some decorum; she's been through valleys at high speeds and dragged through this market at your behest. Can't you allow her some liberties?"

"...this isn't even the strongest wine we have!"

Kai closed his eyes for a brief moment before continuing. "I'll drink whatever she can't. Is that an acceptable compromise?"

Ciaran tilted his head to the side, eyes trained to the ceiling of the tent, before nodding. "That's fine. Not like I haven't carried you back to the palace before."

Jasmine couldn't help but be *very* amused at the back and forth between them. It also reminded her of the dynamic between Leon and Elliot, even though Kai wasn't nearly as uptight as the High Lord always managed to be. *Ugh, you were doing so good not thinking about him until now.* She pulled herself back into the present just long enough to nod in agreement.

"Aiight, then. Let's do this."

Ciaran scooted up closer to the table, taking the cards and shuffling them. Then he got to work sorting it into three face-down piles, sliding one card at a time to each of them in a clockwise fashion until they were all distributed. "One more time for the Prime; these are the directions." He pointed them out carefully, making sure she knew where she was sitting in relation to them. "And now the fun truly begins."

Being a bit challenged in general when it came to directions, Jasmine knew that going to be her Achilles Heel. She watched the cards come flying into the middle of the table, keeping track of them and eventually got into a groove of how the game was played. It was fast-paced play, requiring her to stay in the moment and move as soon as she saw an opportunity. It didn't stop her from having to drink often as the two royals who had quite a bit more experience in the game than she did, however. She had taken quite a few sips of the wine before finally being the first to slap a card on the top of the pile and shifting it correctly.

"BOOM!" Jasmine shouted triumphantly, raking the pile into her hands. "Drink, bitches!"

Thankfully, neither Kai nor Ciaran blinked an eye at her brash outburst, picking up their cups and drinking with grins on their faces. She was already feeling the effects of the wine, and it became harder to keep up with the few times she was able to collect more cards. Jasmine didn't know when Kai had done his due diligence and began picking up her cup to take sips on her behalf, but when she looked over, she noticed his cheeks were getting rosy and his eyes had taken on a sleepy quality that she found rather endearing.

Jasmine found herself more distracted than she'd like to be whenever their gazes met as the game went on. *Maybe the wine was a mistake.*

"I feel like I have to keep telling you how much you enjoying the Run earlier meant to me," Ciaran spoke, speech only slightly slurred as he gathered all the cards after their game had ended and shuffled them again. "I don't have that many who can keep up."

"You're rather unpredictable," Kai said diplomatically, his fingers going for Jasmine's cup out of habit at that point.

Ciaran waved his hand carelessly. "You've said so before, but I don't believe it. I feel like what's happened is that many of us have lost the true spirit of a dragon. We take our lineage for granted. We aren't challenged, and don't challenge ourselves. It's irritating. Do you think our ancestors were *predictable*? Do you think this is all we're meant to be?"

Jasmine looked over at Kai, who took a moment before replying. "There is still the future. Who knows what changes will come."

"Who knows, indeed." Ciaran turned his bright gaze onto Jasmine. "Perhaps we'll be surprised this time around."

Normally, Jasmine would have had the wherewithal to just be quiet and let the moment pass. But the wine she consumed didn't do much for her filter, so she let her words fly without thinking too much about them. "I can't speak for your ancestors of course, but I think as long as you guys do whatever makes you happy, you can't go wrong in the end."

"Whatever makes me happy, huh..." Ciaran swallowed the rest of the wine in his cup before setting it down, gazing at her thoughtfully with a hint of something unreadable in his eyes. But before Jasmine could look too much into it, he was back to smiling brightly. "Well, hearing the slur in your words doesn't make me believe them any less, but it *does* let me know that we should probably be getting you back to Apelion. Kai, could you get her some water?"

Kai nodded and stood, and for the most part, was able to walk in a straight line to the bar. Coming back with the water in question, he poured a new glass for Jasmine and slid it to her before pouring himself and Ciaran some. "It has nectar from a flower native to the region added to it, to keep the fluid in your body longer. The people of Notos spend enough time consuming it and find that they can go a lot longer without needing water on average. The added nutrients should help you sober faster."

"Oh, it's like Gatorade!" Jasmine said, taking a long swig. There was a tangy flavor beneath the surface of the beverage, but other than that, it was the smoothest and most satisfying drink of water she'd ever had. "Damn. Y'all sell this around here? Am I allowed to take some home to my apartment? I'd have to ration it, but this *slaps*."

Ciaran burst out into peals of laughter, and Kai stood up, wobbling only once before helping Jasmine to her feet next. Automatically, she put most of her weight on him, wrapping her arm around his waist for further support as her eyelids fluttered at the end of a large yawn. A small part of her was panicking at being so familiar with him, but it wasn't like she had much of a choice considering the amount of alcohol she consumed for the night.

"You can lean on me and Ciaran as we make our way back to the portal. We're well versed in helping each other in these very circumstances."

Jasmine barely remembered the way back to the palace. The only thing she registered was the temperature change that signified their passage from Notos back to Apelion, and it made her shiver in the lighter clothing that she wore.

She clung embarrassingly to Kai the entire way back to her room, letting him get herself situated in her bed before making sure the drapes were covering the windows in her chamber. Jasmine wasn't aware of how long he lingered before leaving, as she was out almost as soon as her head hit the pillow.

Her dreams were wild, blurs of her flying without assistance through the caverns in Notos, over the blue oceans of

Favonius, only to land in the cherry blossom spotted lands of Apelion. She truly felt as if the world was her oyster, unfettered by the worries she once had as a stressed human trying to make ends meet in a lackluster job. The alcohol she had imbibed allowed her to be lucid through all of this, letting her choose to remain in the blissful unconscious fantasy that she was unsure she'd ever let herself pursue when she woke.

Dreams were safe. No responsibilities, no consequences.

Unlike the kind she suffered when she woke up the next morning with a headache and a handmaiden at the door, arms full of clothing that she had to change into as soon as possible.

She'd forgotten all about her scheduled plan for today.

CHAPTER TWENTY-FOUR

"Wow, you look exhausted. What the hell did you guys get up to yesterday? Or do I even want to know?"

Kai actually had the shame to look a little embarrassed, even though Jasmine was absolutely sure that he handled any lingering hangover much more gracefully than she was. The outfit she was given was the heaviest she had worn since arriving in Draconia, and it already gave her an idea of what to expect. Although, she figured the beads of sweat appearing on her forehead had less to do with how warm she was in those layers and more to do with how her body was rebelling against actually having to function.

"Ciaran roped us into a game of Khartopai. I'm sure you can understand the consequences of that."

Fouzia snickered. "Playing with him means there are no winners at the end. He involves alcohol because he knows he sucks otherwise, and if everyone's drunk then no one can call him out on his lack of skill. It's something I've always suspected."

Kai gave a noncommittal shrug, and then started making his

way to the portal in his courtyard. "Well, I suppose we should be off."

"What do you mean, 'we'? Let this be a girls' day off, please. Go lay down and drink that bitter tea you like so much and let me handle the Prime."

Jasmine watched in dazed amusement at the staring contest between the two of them. She couldn't get enough of the dynamic between Kai and everyone else, and the one between him and Fouzia at the moment was definitely one of a sister telling her brother confidently what she was going to do whether he approved of it or not.

"Fouzia... I've escorted Jasmine through each quadrant by now."

"And?"

"I should continue to do so."

She raised an eyebrow. "Why? There's no rules to this; we're doing this because the Prime suggested it. It should be her that has a say in whether or not she is going to be escorted like a child. What do you say?"

Jasmine blinked slowly, trying to avoid looking directly into the sun that was too bright for her throbbing head. "Um... sure. I mean, I think I can handle it on my own this time."

"Then it's settled!" Fouzia grinned triumphantly, making her way to the portal. "I'll have her back in one piece, and a lot less groggy."

As Jasmine went to follow the princess, she turned and looked back at Kai. Perhaps it was simply because she hadn't fully come to her senses yet, but she felt a pang of longing creeping up on her and didn't know if it was picked up from seeing Kai standing there seeing them off. *I can't have gotten attached to him that fast, come on.* But she couldn't deny that it was odd not having him by her side like he had been since she arrived.

"Watch your step; there's ice all over the place, and it wouldn't do me any good to have to haul you back over to Apelion if you slip and hurt yourself within five minutes of arriving."

Jasmine wasn't a stranger to snow or cold, considering where she lived and how often she had spent standing at bus stops in the middle of winter while bitter winds made her cheeks go numb. But after getting used to nicer weather all around, it was a shock to step over the threshold and immediately feel her muscles tense from the chilly, sudden drop in temperature. The boots she was given kept her footing in the few inches of snow that blanketed the area, and she saw her breath leave her lips in cloudy puffs that slowly dissipated amongst the lightly falling precipitation.

"It's beautiful here," Jasmine said honestly, scanning the mountains that made up most of the area. "But I'm glad I didn't wait until I got here to change, because I would have frozen my ass off."

"Oh, I figured. That's why I had them delivered beforehand." Fouzia winked at her. "The castle is this way, just over the bridge."

Jasmine made sure to place her steps surely as she was lead over an ice draped bridge, marvelous to gaze on but had her nervous to walk upon. She tried not to glance over, but she couldn't help it. The drop was so steep that she couldn't see the bottom, and it made her wonder how high up they even were.

The castle itself seemed like an extension of the cliff face, with spires reaching almost as high as the peaks of the mountain itself. Servants opened the thick doors as they approached, and Jasmine could feel her muscles start to untense from the cold just from the hint of warmth that radiated from inside.

"First things first, let's get you some of Apartica's special tea. I hope you have a sweet tooth, since we happen to be pretty heavy handed when it comes to that." Her cloak was off of her shoulders, revealing a long-sleeved blue top with fur along the dipped neckline. The ends of it nearly reached the floor if it weren't for Fouzia's heeled boots, but the splits up the sides revealed close-fitting pants underneath that allowed for freedom of movement. Jasmine immediately wanted a pattern for everything she saw, not noticing that Fouzia had turned around with a saucy look in her eyes.

"Are you checking out my ass already?"

Jasmine coughed, redirecting her gaze. "No, I was just-"

"Don't worry about it, I'm teasing you. I do a lot of that, and you won't get special treatment just because you're the Prime." Fouzia led them into a large seating area, complete with a grand fireplace that crackled comfortingly against the wall. Most of the room was otherwise taken up by large windows, showcasing the winter wonderland that made up the land of Apartica.

"That's okay. It's refreshing, actually. I never wanted to be placed on a pedestal, but it doesn't stop literally everyone I've met thus far from putting me there. Maybe it'd be different if I earned it, I don't know." Jasmine took a seat on one of the plush seats across from Fouzia, liking how it seemed to meld to her frame as she sank into it.

"I get it. Well, as much as I can. As you can see, some of us are raised with this kind of life. But I learned early on how to sneak off without prying eyes to do things that probably wouldn't have been looked upon too kindly as a member of Draconian royalty. Sometimes, you just need a breather from it all. I'm glad I could pry you away from Kai for a little bit."

Jasmine smiled, realizing that the brisk walk from the portal to the castle did wonders in clearing up her muddled brain. An attendant came by with a silver tray balanced with a teapot, snacks and other containers to place on the coffee table between them.

"Don't eat the treats by themselves; they're salty to offset the sweetness of the tea." Fouzia instructed as she poured a steaming cup to slide over to Jasmine. "And as you relax, you can also tell me how you've enjoyed Draconia thus far."

"I like it here. I mean, it's been a tad overwhelming, but I think I've been pleasantly distracted from everything that's on my plate just learning about how you guys live. You all are free with your information and I'm grateful for that alone."

Fouzia hummed thoughtfully, lifting her cup to her lips. "Kai did make mention that the Hellenians didn't prepare you as they should. Maybe you don't want to tell me because I'm Draconian, but I can't lie and say I'm not curious as to what happened there."

Jasmine paused to take her first sip of tea, letting the hot liquid warm her from the inside out and appreciating how rich and sweet it was. Perhaps it was because Fouzia was a woman, or it had more to do with the fact that she already felt significantly more relaxed around her alone rather than next to Kai, but she didn't mind being a little honest with her predicament. "Ah... well, they weren't that clear on anything. When I met the Hellenian High Lord, he came to me in my realm and sort of integrated himself in my life. I had different expectations of what was going to happen even after being told I was the Prime."

"Oh, so he made you fall in love with him, is what you're saying?"

Jasmine nearly choked on her beverage, feeling hot in the face at how easily Fouzia cut to the heart of the matter. "I..."

"Listen, I don't blame you, but I also won't lie to you. That's a common tactic used to get a Prime to come around. Things like decency, overarching effects, and even the prettiness of our respective lands don't matter as much to humans as attraction." Fouzia tucked a bit of her wavy hair behind one pointed ear.

"After all, that's what got the last Prime in Hellenia's corner. I wouldn't be surprised if his son went the same way with you."

"I suppose." Jasmine started thinking about the rumors involving the previous Prime again, then was startled out of her thoughts when Fouzia sat her cup down on the table.

"You want to know how you guard yourself from that? Fuck a lot of people, and nobody will be able to use desire as a weapon against you. It works for me."

Jasmine slowly lifted a biscuit to her lips to wipe her palette clean before she continued drinking her tea. Fouzia was terribly frank in a way that reminded her of Kim, and a pang of nostalgia came over her. "Umm... yeah, I don't get out much."

"You're out now. So why not take advantage of that and cut loose a little?"

What is she saying? "You want me to just... go and find folks to bang, or whatever?" Jasmine's cheeks started tingling.

"Yes. Don't worry, I'll help you out." Fouzia sat back in her chair with her tea. "I was thinking about taking you to a pleasure house in town. Everywhere in Draconia has a few of them, if you know where to look... but I happen to think ours is the best."

Jasmine gave up all pretense of finishing her beverage and instead tried to process the apparent opportunity that was casually laid in front of her. After spending time with Sustina and learning how things went with courtesans, she could say that she did mental work to undo some of her learned biases after being in a place where sex was properly integrated into society as normal and not taboo. But she couldn't help but feel like she was back in her freshman year of college being tempted by upper classmen to go to an off-campus party.

"Will Kai be mad if I do this?"

"He may have won the Trial, but he doesn't yet own you. So why do you care?"

Fair point. Jasmine wanted to call herself crazy for even considering it. She wasn't sure if she could even do what Fouzia was suggesting and detach herself from Leon just through casual relations with others. *It would be nice, though.*

She stared into the depths of her half-finished cup of tea, seeing her dim reflection in its shallow depths. She had been on an incredible journey thus far, and even survived a ride on the back of a dragon. All that she experienced was so far out of her usual scope, and she had taken it in stride.

Jasmine looked up to meet Fouzia's gaze.

"You'll be there too, right?"

The smile Fouzia gave her unexpectedly made her feel a little hot beneath the collar. "Oh, I wouldn't miss this for the world."

CHAPTER TWENTY-FIVE

Jasmine couldn't take her eyes off of the buildings that laid on either side of the half-frozen stream, illuminated by lamp posts that gave off a warm glow against the snowy backdrop. She never truly learned to appreciate snow, considering how she was long past the times where school days made it relevant. But walking beside Fouzia along a path that seemed magical just in its natural state was just as surreal as the gold rooftops in Apelion or the crystal blue waters of Favonius.

It was *almost* enough to get her to forget what they had come into town to do.

"Hey so, question. I know y'all can only have one mate for life. If that's the case, how do these uh... brothels work?"

"Draconians can only truly mate in dragon form. There's this whole ritual surrounding it; it takes weeks of prep, days of initiation, and is sacred in and of itself. Sex is something entirely different. Physical, not spiritual." Fouzia glanced over to her as they moved to make room for a few passing people on the walkway. "Never had to explain this to someone before, but then again, not like I get the opportunity to spend time with a non-Draconian."

While Jasmine added another entry to the index of facts that she had collected over her time in their realm, Fouzia slowed down and walked up to building that looked no different than the others in the area. There was a discreet placard hanging over the doorway, but all it held was a symbol that wasn't in any language that Jasmine knew. Either or, she was rather surprised that a pleasure house was just right along the main pathway along with all of the other shops, and not down some shady alley. *I guess I still have a bit more of my internal prejudices to work out.*

When Fouzia opened the door and led her inside, that was when Jasmine blinked at how much the outside décor did not match what she walked into. There was a faint smoky haze in the air, but not enough to make her eyes sting. The lighting was muted, and the entire place was outfitted in deep purple and maroon drapes that created a cozy, sensual atmosphere. A man stood as the host in the foyer, recognizing Fouzia and bowing deeply in acknowledgement.

"Lady Fouzia, your presence is always a welcome sight. I see you've graced us with new company, as well."

Jasmine didn't know what to think about what she was getting into, but she did know one thing; that man's voice was sinful to listen to. It rolled like silk off of his tongue and made Jasmine feel like she was being caressed, which was something she never experienced before. Not only that, but the flowy pants hung so low on his waist that just a tug would probably get her seeing more than she bargained for.

"She's a very special guest. I thought it would be nice to show the Prime a bit of our fun side."

His eyes shifted to Jasmine, drinking up her figure slowly.

Even in all the layers she was in, she felt naked in just that casual perusal. "Understood. Should I have your room prepared as usual, or should I make adjustments?"

"No, keep everything the same. We'll be in shortly."

Fouzia pulled back a shimmering partition to reveal a general area with compartments for belongings, and she got started unclasping her cloak. Jasmine followed suit, undoing her boots and placing them out of the way, and hanging her overcoat in a space next to Fouzia's.

She started getting nervous when she saw the princess undoing her shirt, next.

"Um..."

Fouzia raised an eyebrow. "You didn't think you'd be going in the main area *clothed*, did you?"

Jasmine's heart rate started picking up again. "Well... I didn't think it was going to be a thing to just walk in naked! I thought there was gonna be a lead up, or something!"

Fouzia tittered at her distress, then cocked a finger to draw Jasmine's attention to another set of drapes. Without another word, she opened it a few inches for Jasmine to peek at what was on the other side.

Jesus Christ. It was one thing knowing vaguely what she was getting into. It was another to see it in front of her. There were a few people idling around, going from one partition to the other, and they were all as bare as the day they were born. It didn't help that she also got a glimpse of what was going on in one of those side rooms when someone stepped out, and it was enough to make her jump back from the opening with her eyes wide as saucers.

That time, Fouzia gave a full laugh at her expense. "Oh, you'll be fine. I just wanted to show you that it would be odd if you went in with clothes on." She went back to undressing after dropping that bomb, and Jasmine had no choice but to mechanically follow suit while her mind spun.

In what seemed like both an eternity and a blink of an eye, Jasmine stood in the middle of the room completely naked and attempting to trick herself into thinking that she was in a fancy bath house so she didn't launch herself into cardiac arrest. She avoided the gaze of the attendant from earlier, who let them into the main hall. Fouzia boldly took the lead, her long dark hair brushing against her bare back as both of them drifted down the plush carpeted path to get to her private room.

Jasmine did not know for the life of her how she could be so casual with all of the pornographic sounds that drifted out of the areas on either side of them as they walked.

"I get that you're nervous. You probably want to turn around and run right out from this place... well, after you get your clothes back on, of course." Fouzia said, pulling back a curtain at the end of the hall. The rugs were plentiful, and draped fabric culminating to a single chandelier on the ceiling closed in the area further. The smoky scent from earlier was a bit stronger, and Jasmine wondered if there was incense.

In fact, she was looking for something other than the five gorgeous people lounging around in the room on the myriad cushions to focus on, lest she feel more out of her league than she already felt she was. Jasmine felt Fouzia gently take her by the arm and lead her to a low table off to the side of the room, and she forcibly tore her eyes away from the curious ones that didn't stray from her.

"If it makes you feel any better, almost no one is automatically comfortable in these environments the first time. Even the most promiscuous Draconians get a bit of a shell shock when they realize that the things that they dreamt about in their fantasies can be offered right here." Fouzia lowered herself on a cushion, pulling an elaborate hookah over to her and taking a puff. Jasmine watched the faint purple smoke plume out of her nostrils, wondering if it was the lighting or if Fouzia was just as sensual as some of the people who worked there.

Jasmine's eyes wandered before she could stop herself, and she saw a man and woman making out not too far from where they were seated. She became entranced by their lips moving slowly against each other, and she became keenly aware of how long it had been since she had kissed someone like that. As if on cue, the man slid his gaze over to meet Jasmine's without breaking stride, winking at her.

"Hey," Fouzia's voice came into focus, and Jasmine felt fingers on her chin turning her head away from the scene. "Take a little hit of this. It'll help you relax."

Her fingers shook slightly as she took the offered pipe and breathed in the heady smoke. It was surprisingly cool going down her throat, which made her not think about how big of a pull she was taking until Fouzia pulled the end of it from her lips. Jasmine held it in her lungs as long as she could before exhaling at the end of a few coughs, her entire face feeling like it was on fire.

"What... is this?"

"Dragonroot. The berries are best for desserts, and the leaves are good for things like this." Fouzia explained, taking another hit herself. "Alcohol is forbidden in pleasure houses, because it dulls the senses and you need to be fully aware of what's going on around you." Her lips turned up into a grin. "But *this* is a gem."

Jasmine waited to feel any kind of effects of what she just inhaled, wondering if it was something that only worked on Draconians. She did note that she felt less tense than she was when she first entered, which was a good thing. She was just about to chance looking around the room again when Fouzia asked her a question.

"What's your limit, by the way? What's not allowed?"

"What? Like, as in... kinks?"

Fouzia licked her lips, and Jasmine became extremely focused on that simple action.

"Let me be clearer. Where *don't* you want a dick to be?"

"My ass," Jasmine replied, then blinked at how easily that rolled off of her tongue. But then, she became distracted by her own mind constructing a vivid scenario involving the man that winked at her, and his member slowly inserting itself in the place she explicitly had just told Fouzia she did not want it. She sucked in a sharp breath, feeling her nipples harden at the imagery alone.

"Got it. Best to get that out of the way before the dragon-root takes full effect. Otherwise, you'll end up doing just about anything." Fouzia moved from the cushion across from her to settle next to Jasmine, her blue eyes shining in the low light. Jasmine always thought that Fouzia was beautiful from the first time she saw her, but now it seemed like her dark skin held a glow to it, and her eyes went right to her breasts that moved as the Draconian princess leaned in close.

"I've got a little confession, Jasmine. I've wanted to know how those pretty lips of yours fit against mine. Glad to know that I'm getting my chance."

Jasmine didn't even have time to give the full body shiver Fouzia's words sent through her before she was being kissed, and she was lost in how quickly she melted right into it. Her hands came up and laced themselves in Fouzia's dark hair, deepening the lip lock and moaning a bit as their tongues danced together. She had never kissed another woman like this in her life, but now that she had, it was all that she wanted to do.

She very quickly understood the effects of the dragonroot in that moment.

Fouzia broke the kiss, letting out a contented sigh before looking around at the rest of the room's occupants. "Our special guest tonight is the Prime. Her name is Jasmine, and you can only touch her ass, not stick anything in it. I'm going to be extremely disappointed if all of you aren't moaning or screaming her name by the end of tonight, okay?"

"Are you including yourself in that?" Jasmine asked before she could stop herself.

The Draconian princess tilted her head back and laughed before pulling Jasmine down to lay on top of her on the cushions. "Kiss me like you just did a few more times, and I'll see what I can do."

Jasmine lost track of how many times she kissed Fouzia, but she remembered how the Draconian's breast felt in her hand as she took a chance and kneaded it lightly. She was abuzz with arousal, something that didn't abate even after someone made her orgasm twice over just with their tongue alone. There wasn't a moment that went by that she wasn't being touched by someone, or multiple someones, letting the sounds of pleasure mingle with everyone else's without abandon. Jasmine discovered first hand that the man who winked at her in the beginning wasn't just skilled at giving exceptional kisses. She also realized that she liked feeling a woman's soft hair as they moved together, chasing a mutual release. She didn't have the experience of being in that type of situation before, but it didn't stop her from moving fluidly with everyone there. Jasmine traded partners as she pleased, even watched Fouzia handle three individuals at once like it was her calling while her fingers found their way between her legs at the scene.

Not once did she think about Leon. Not once did she feel ashamed of her actions.

A part of Jasmine wanted to blame the Dragonroot for that,

but as its effects started to wane in the brisk winter air on their way back to the castle, she realized it wouldn't be entirely true.

"Before I let you go back to Kai looking fucked out of your mind, I want to show you one more thing," Fouzia said, pulling the brunt of her long hair out from under her cloak and letting it fall around her shoulders. "It'll be worth it."

CHAPTER TWENTY-SIX

"I bet you could hit a target blind."

"Sometimes, yes. It's not preferred, though." Fouzia let another arrow fly, and it scattered the snow that was falling a little heavier since they arrived back at the castle. The target that was hanging out in the middle of the canyon, swaying with the wind, was only just visible if Jasmine squinted. But even then, she could tell that the arrow hit it even from that great distance. For someone who was quite ignorant on archery as it was, what she was watching Fouzia do might as well have been magic.

"How long have you been practicing?"

Fouzia fired off another arrow. "Since I was old enough to hold a bow. Royals often have to choose one weapon to master in their lifetime, and I knew this one was for me. I learned how to anticipate the change in winds before taking a shot. I'd come up here all the time with my parents, letting them set targets as far as out as they could manage to see if I could find a way to hit them. By the time I was able to hit the center of the smallest target we had at the longest distance across this gorge, they knew I was ready to take over the estate as my own."

"Amazing," Jasmine breathed. They fell into a comfortable silence as Fouzia emptied her quiver, then moved to crank a lever that reeled in the target that had been set out in the distance. As it came closer, Jasmine confirmed that the princess had indeed hit the center of the mark, some arrows sitting precariously on top of others.

"It's how I meditate. Being up here alone, with the snow muffling every sound, staying until my fingers get numb from holding the string... it's like nothing else. But I don't mind you sitting here with me while I do this." She gave Jasmine a small pout. "It's really unfair how Kai won the Trial. I could have had so much *fun* with you."

"Sorry. If I do end up choosing y'all, then maybe Kai will let me sneak away for a visit or two."

Fouzia finished carefully plucking the arrows out of the target's surface to place back in her quiver. "Getting my hopes up, are you? You're sweet, but cruel." She folded her arms and pursed her lips, even though her eyes were playful. "Maybe I can show you what you'd be getting into if you became Draconian. Having a dragon form is pretty neat, after all."

Jasmine blinked in surprise since for the second time that day, Fouzia was casually disrobing in front of her. "Girl, what are you doing? Are you trying to get frostbite on your coot?"

"It's fine, I won't be bare for long." Fouzia gave Jasmine a flirty glance. "And maybe I just want an excuse to show you my ass again, I don't know."

After the day they had, Jasmine couldn't even find it within her to blush at a comment like that. "I'll be the last to complain, boo. Show me what you're workin' with."

The princess blew Jasmine a kiss before taking a running start and jumping fearlessly right off of the edge of the cliff.

Jasmine couldn't stand up fast enough. Logically, she knew that Fouzia knew what she was doing. But on the other, there was a visceral reaction to seeing someone toss themselves into an abyss with no abandon. She crept up to the edge, careful to keep her footing and ignoring the vertigo she experienced as she craned her neck to see if she could find her figure.

"Oh, shit!" She scrambled backwards, falling on her behind as a large gust of air funneled upwards from the gorge, closely followed by the twining body of a dragon. Jasmine gaped in the presence of it, watching its snake-like body spin and disperse the falling snow in hypnotizing patterns as it rose. She noticed that Fouzia had a feathered stripe directly down the center of her body, the plumes glittering iridescent lavender blue against her silver scales. Slender horns mirrored the long whiskers that trailed along on either side of a vulpine face that opened to let out a haunting call that echoed through the mountains before flying off.

After seeing everyone's dragon forms, Jasmine knew what to expect. But that moment was the first time that Jasmine felt like she wanted to be a part of it. She watched Fouzia dip and spin, preening like a show horse and truly wondered how it felt to inhabit a body that was much bigger than her own.

It occupied most of her thoughts even after she had been safely deposited back in Apelion as promised, all the way through dinner, and had Jasmine staring restlessly at the ceiling of her borrowed room as moonlight filtered through the window next to her head.

Giving up on sleep for the time being, she got up and slipped out to the gardens, finding a gilded bench and sitting down. She noticed after her first night spent that the sky reminded her of high-res pictures that people in her realm took in where there was no light pollution and the hues of the milky way could be seen. Jasmine didn't know much about planets and constellations outside of the basics, but she wondered if anything that she was seeing now would match up to what was in the night sky back home.

"You've been in a daze since returning from Apartica. I assume that's a good thing?"

Jasmine glanced at Kai as he sat down next to her. "Yeah. We had a great time."

"I'm happy to hear it." Kai looked to the sky himself, leaving a moment of comfortable silence before he spoke again. "What humans need telescopes to see, Draconians don't. While stargazing may not be in your subset of interests, I'm sure you can imagine the boon it would be when it comes to fashioning clothes down to the minute details."

Jasmine laughed a little. "You're a great salesperson, you know that? Going right for my throat on everything."

"If nothing else, I'm persistent." Kai let his smile fade into something more contemplative. "I've done some thinking on what you told me the other day. I don't know much about what it means to be human, but I suppose I don't need to understand the particulars of that to respect your attachment to it. I feel slightly foolish for not considering it from your point of view before."

"Thank you for considering it. I'm... getting used to the idea of giving it up the more time goes by, mostly because I know at the end, I don't have a choice. But it helps to know that you don't look at my humanity as something to throw away."

"Not anymore. I'll admit to my previous ignorance. Now, I wonder if it would help you to think of it as an expansion."

Jasmine tilted her head in confusion. "What do you mean?"

Kai lifted his hand, pointing to the dusting of bright celestial bodies over their heads. "Dragons aren't like Hellenians, who are made in an image similar to your own. We come from the stars; true celestial beings that expand endlessly like the universe itself." He met her gaze again. "You won't be fully divested from your humanity. But if you truly want to test the limits of what you can reach, there is only one choice for you."

Jasmine contemplated his words, long after he had left her to her own devices to retire. When she first arrived in Draconia, she was presented with the knowledge that each race subtly influenced her realm just by virtue of existing within it, and that was her focus on deciding who to give the Flame to.

Now, after becoming more familiar with dragons than she felt she was with Hellenians, it made her go back to thinking in more of a selfish scope, much like how she initially thought that Nithael's parlor was enough to have her running back to Leon with the Flame in record time.

Jasmine realized she had grown a lot, without having the time to sit and process the changes she made and what it meant to her moving forward. Unconsciously, she reached up and fingered the Spark that hung around her neck. Resolving to spend her last day in Apelion focusing on herself in that manner, Jasmine stood up from the bench to make her way back to the palace for a good night's sleep.

She was almost to the entrance when she noticed something glimmering out of the corner of her eye. *Is that the portal? Why is it open so late at night?* Jasmine furrowed her brow, changing course to go over to it and inspect it up close. She didn't notice how ethereal it looked without the sun drowning out its luminance, and she reached out to brush her fingers against the misty surface as she tried to make out what was on the other side.

Jasmine barely had time to register quick movement shifting behind her before a sharp pain took over her senses, and she crumpled to the ground.

CHAPTER TWENTY-SEVEN

J asmine opened her eyes slowly, a dull throb pulsing at the back of her head that made her wince in the effort of pulling herself to a sitting position. *Did I drink a lot, or something? Why can't I remember what happened?* Sifting through her confusion, she let her eyes adjust to the dim lighting that surrounded her, and also made sense of why she was sitting on something lumpy and hard.

She could tell that she was in a family vault by the obscene amount of riches that were piled up on all sides, including the gold coins she was perched upon. It didn't look like the inside of Nemeer's however, as she didn't see the Veiled Virgin bust that had caught her attention. Just as she was going to stand up, she heard footsteps approaching from the right, and squinted in that direction with her heart in her throat until the chamber brightened a bit more.

"You slept through the whole night. It made me think that I did lasting damage on accident. *That* would have been awkward," Ciaran's jovial voice filtered to her ears before his body came into view. Jasmine blinked dumbly up at him as he pulled over a gilded footrest and sat upon it, his arms on his knees.

A few more moments passed before Jasmine decided to respond. "So... you gonna tell me why you kidnapped me, or nah?" She kept her voice even despite her rising concern and trepidation, casting an unreadable gaze upon the Draconian prince while he acted as though nothing was amiss at all.

"Just doing whatever makes me happy, as you suggested." He gestured around the room. "From a young age, all Draconians play a little game where we borrow riches from each other. You could say it's practice for when we have access to your realm again and can peruse what goodies you wonderful humans concocted in our absence. Only, we don't announce what we took, or even that we've done the taking; you have to realize it for yourself, then sneakily recover what was stolen. Usually, it can be pretty difficult to tell what was taken the more populated your vault is. I'm sure there are treasures I have yet to retrieve from my peers that I don't know are gone. But since this is *you*... well. I don't think it'll take Kai very long at all."

Jasmine continued studying him with a shuttered look. "I didn't think I was on the same level as inanimate objects, but go off, I guess."

Ciaran laughed. "Believe me, you are far above a jewel in any vault in the whole of Draconia. I knew you were likely to leave soon, and I couldn't miss the opportunity. I'm not quite so sure why you're offended at your value. For a Draconian to treasure you in this manner is the highest compliment, Jasmine. If it helps..." He reached out and brushed a few of her braids away from the side of her face in a caring manner that had Jasmine too shocked to flinch away. "I could show you in ways that better translate that appreciation."

Thanks to everything she experienced in Apartica, Jasmine

wasn't so easily rattled by sensuality anymore. She wanted to slap him for violating her human rights that he didn't seem to grasp. But she also was very much aware of the power difference at play. "It's fine, I'll just take your word for it."

"Somehow, I'm not surprised that you'd say that." Ciaran withdrew his hand, but not his gaze. The more he looked upon Jasmine, the more she could see something that belied a sharp edge. "Since you'll be here for a little bit, I was wondering if you would like to hear my theory about the Flame you'll be communing with soon."

Jasmine bluffed as best as she could by giving him a nonchalant shrug, keeping her guard high. "Sure, go for it."

"I've spent a fair amount of time reading lore surrounding that little anomaly. It's a hobby the others never shared my enthusiasm for." He combed his sandy hair away from his face. "It's rumored that the gods who created our little arrangement decided to borrow power to keep the pact intact, rather than maintain what they wrought on us themselves. Deities often have better things to do than babysit beings they consider to be below them, after all."

She blinked at the undercurrent of bitterness in Ciaran's tone, but stayed silent as he continued.

"There is no bit of ancient magic recorded that could emulate what is assumed to be an eternal flame. Each time it's given to one of our races, it runs through its cycle just to die and be reborn through another host. I'm sure there is still some legitimate study of mythology in the human realm; what fits that description?"

Jasmine paused, not because she didn't know the answer, but because she was somehow afraid to give voice to it. "A... phoenix?"

Ciaran grinned widely. "Precisely. I believe they created

such an elaborate, beautiful prison in the form of Hyperion for this creature."

"I don't see how that would matter, even if it is true."

"Do better, Jasmine; humans pride themselves on thinking outside of the box, correct?" He finally dropped his jaunty facade and fixed her with an unnerving stare that made her shiver. "You have more options than what you were told – what we were *all* told. Imagine if you could negotiate with the phoenix to grant both Hellenians and Draconians freedom. Imagine if you could go back to your home as yourself. Isn't that something worth trying for?"

Jasmine felt as though she was a small child being scolded by her mother for not catching onto her homework fast enough. She wasn't sure if she fully bought Ciaran's theory, but she was too off-kilter to even come up with a rebuttal at the same time.

"And what if you're wrong?"

The prince shrugged, a reaction far too laid back for the heaviness of the subject. "Then I suppose the cycle continues as the gods planned."

Jasmine let her eyes drift from Ciaran as she digested what she'd been told. Even with all the time she had spent wracking her brain for ways to escape her fate, there was also a strange comfort in knowing that the path before her was set. Yet, Jasmine didn't like the idea of some other poor human being manipulated between two ancient races after she had passed, either. Now she had to recalibrate her expectations once again, without fully being settled.

She was so incredibly tired of having the rug pulled out from under her at every turn.

"I..." Jasmine began, but she never got to finish her thought as the door to the vault opened, bringing light and a fair amount of desert heat flowing into the room. She squinted at the figure illuminated in the doorway, and sensed Ciaran get up from his seat across from her.

"Oh, you *really* didn't waste time. I think you set a record, actually."

As her eyes adjusted, she could better see Kai's figure making his way towards them with purpose in his pace. Once he got a few feet from them, he stopped, and looked down at Jasmine first with a hint of relief in his eyes before fixing a glare upon Ciaran.

"The Prime is off limits."

"Is she? I was under the impression that it was only the family ancestors in the innermost chamber that was forbidden." Ciaran grinned and put a hand on his hip. "Besides, I'm most proud of this heist."

Kai reached down and grasped Jasmine's hand, helping her to her feet. "She's not a treasure to be pilfered, Ciaran."

"I beg to differ."

"You've never begged before, but it would be curious to see." Kai's voice had been measured before, but now came tinged with steel. "Jasmine is under my care, first and foremost."

Ciaran tilted his head slightly. "As is everything else in your possession, Kai. Why is the Prime different?"

"Because she is *human*. With all of the time she has spent with each of us here in Draconia, you would think this is the most important lesson we could learn from her presence. How else are we to know how to respect the realm in which we wish to integrate?"

Jasmine glanced over at Ciaran, who was still looking upon his long-time friend with a bit of humor. "We are born knowing how to rule the realm that our ancestors once held. Don't tell me that the Prime has you thinking otherwise?"

Jasmine pursed her lips together into a thin line. She never liked being talked about as if she weren't right there in the room, but it was salt in the wound to also hear Ciaran assume so much. *Between this and the fucking abduction, he ain't earning no brownie points with me.* But before she could finally open her mouth in rebuttal, Kai calmly started leading her out of the vault.

"We'll discuss this later." Kai pushed open the door.

Jasmine glanced back as they were leaving, and Ciaran waved as if nothing that had transpired was out of the ordinary at all.

The two of them remained silent as they made their way to the portal, their respective discontent palpable on their faces. It wasn't until Kai was spinning the corresponding armillary spheres that Jasmine realized that he never let go of her hand. *This is the first time I've even let him take it the entire time I've been here.* She looked down, blinking at his palm laid over her own and actually liking the feel of his fingers curling to land on the back of her hand.

I haven't let anyone hold my hand like this since Leon.

Crossing over into Apelion was like finally breathing free of both the oppressive heat and the entire jarring situation she had found herself in. They walked a few paces across the courtyard before Kai slowed to a stop and turned to face her, his brown eyes full of apologies.

"I'm truly sorry that you had to experience that. When none of the handmaidens found you anywhere on the grounds..." he shook his head, letting that drop.

"Do you think that he would have harmed me at all?" Jasmine was hesitant to ask, but she had to know.

"Gods, no. Ciaran is a jokester, but we still have our honor." Kai sighed, and he let his hand slip from hers. "It doesn't mean that he didn't cross a line, however. I'll have that uncomfortable conversation soon enough."

"I'll hope for the best for y'all, for what it's worth."

Kai gave a snort, the corners of his eyes crinkling with a small smile. "You would? Even after that scare? You're more selfless than I imagined."

Jasmine shrugged. "My beef with him can be addressed at another time... I guess, depending on who I give the Flame to." Her mind drifted back to the weird conversation that she and Ciaran had in the vault, and she mulled over it a bit more before shoving it to the side. "So just make sure y'all are good for me, okay?"

After a moment of just gazing at her, Kai reached out to take her hand again and gently lifted her fingertips to his lips in a brief kiss that sent a series of tingles coursing through her body to end at her feet. "Thank you, Jasmine." His smile widened before his expression melted into seriousness. "Having said all of that... I think it's time to relinquish you back to Hyperion. I don't mean to end your experience here in Draconia on an awkward note, but I do know that your duty to us here is over. Keeping you for longer in the wake of it seems wrong, somehow."

She didn't know how she felt about going to Hyperion now. It was true that it was something that she couldn't avoid, but she never got to have the time to come to terms with her life and the direction that it was fated to go. "I understand. Thank you, though... for the tour. You provided me with invaluable information that's shed some light on my purpose, as well as welcomed me into the fold as much as possible. I'll truly miss it, here."

"Well, depending on your choice, you won't have to miss it for long." Kai said playfully, starting to walk back towards the palace. "My wishes aside, it's enough that you do what you feel needs to be done, no matter the result. We will carry on, regardless."

When Kai said that, Jasmine honestly felt that he meant it. It may have been difficult in the beginning, when both of them were guarded for different reasons and with different motives, but she truly felt that she finally came to an understanding with the Draconian Prince. And with the way that her body had started responding to his touches, for a moment she could actually see herself growing into a relationship befitting the arrangement that would await her should she give the Flame to him.

It was strange getting back into her regular clothes after spending so much time in different elaborate outfits. Yet, it grounded her once again to herself, which is something that she needed after being bombarded with the weight of her destiny. Looking back once at the room within Kai's palace that had been her temporary home, she bowed politely to the handmaidens as she left the abode and made her way back to the portal.

"Oh, no first-class flight back to the peak?"

Kai laughed as he spun the appropriate armillary spheres that corresponded with Hyperion. "If that's what you wanted, then I could have arranged that. But I figured that less theatrics would be better this time around. You've suffered our Draconian lavishness enough."

Once the pathway was opened, they stepped through, and once again Jasmine's sneakered feet were upon the lightly snow dusted ground of the mountain. She could most definitely tell the difference of energy between where she was now and where they left, and she breathed in the clear air before turning to face Kai.

"I guess you'll know when I've made a decision, right?"

He nodded. "Both races will know when you've communed with the Flame, and there will be an area on Hyperion in which we will all gather to watch the rest of the ceremony." Kai folded his hands behind his back. "The rest is up to you."

Jasmine didn't move to continue her journey. Kai just stood there, a serenely regal figure amongst the forested backdrop, and she took a moment to appreciate it. She remembered all too well the intimidated mess she was when she was first encountered by him, and now they stood apart from each other on what felt like more of an equal standing. After a moment of mulling it over, she squared her shoulders and cleared the distance between them to lay a chaste kiss on his lips before she could psyche herself out of it. Kai jerked slightly in surprise, but didn't pull away, letting their lips pillow together softly before she finally withdrew.

"I can't say that I was expecting that. But I would be lying if I said I didn't appreciate it," Kai replied softly, his brown eyes warm.

"If it helps, I did that on a whim because I wanted to." Jasmine backed away from him, her cheeks warm but feeling proud of herself for taking control of things, rather than waiting for everything else in life to do it for her. "Take care, Kai."

She watched as Kai gave a final bow of his head, and then turned to disappear back into the portal. In the quiet that remained, Jasmine turned and faced the summit that was well within her reach.

It won't take me long now before I'm doing what I came here to do. But... She turned her head up to the sky, looking at the clouds idly drifting by. Jasmine had gone most of her time in Draconia pushing her unease about Leon to the back of her mind. Knowing that she would have to face him again when the time came to relinquish the Flame didn't set well with her. In any other circumstance, Jasmine wouldn't bother investing in any sort of closure. But she could tell that it wasn't serving her to carry that burden with her into a sacred space that would be deciding the fate of the races as well as her own realm.

With one last glance at the peak, she turned her back to it and let her feet carry her downhill, back along the path towards the passage to Hellenia.

CHAPTER TWENTY-EIGHT

It did not seem to take her long at all to reach her destination. Jasmine knew that Hyperion wasn't a normal mountain, but she couldn't help but feel odd that time and space seemed to have shifted around her to allow her to arrive at the stone archway that had been her first introduction to the sacred place in a fraction of the time that it had taken her to get to the summit. Her eyes drifted to the wildflower fields just beyond, seeming to disappear into rolling hills of infinity laced with colors. She didn't know what she was waiting for, or even that she was waiting at all, until the portal shimmered to life before her.

I guess I was expected. Taking a deep breath, Jasmine crossed over the threshold and stood once again on the altar in the dreary forest in Hellenia, blinking at how muted everything seemed after the highly saturated colors of Draconia.

"You've returned."

Jasmine looked to her right, taking in the forever ethereal stature of the high priestess Viviane. She was less intimidated than before, but it still awed her to be in her presence. "I have. You probably saw me coming though, right?"

Viviane moved to extinguish the ceremonial candles on the pedestal with an elaborate bronze snuffer. "I see many things in my visions. Not all of them come to pass. However, some become deeply etched into the stitches of time, which allows me to prepare for when those visions become reality."

"I see. Well, I..." Jasmine paused, not truly knowing what to do. Her instinct was to go to Leon's manor, but just the thought of facing Leon again put a heavy feeling in the pit of her stomach. She knew that it was what she told herself she was there to do, but all of the awkwardness she escaped before came back to haunt her.

"Perhaps you should see the courtesan. She has been a boon to you." Viviane lightly touched the back of Jasmine's arm, a surprising show of relative care from the normally aloof priestess. "You may ride with me back into town."

Jasmine nodded silently, waiting until Viviane had tidied the space before following her along the worn path back to the road beyond. Despite everything, Jasmine was rather relieved at the prospect of seeing Sustina again, knowing how easy her energy was and the advice she gave her the first day she arrived. *Maybe I can soak in one of those fancy tubs and contemplate life before figuring out my next step.*

Settling into the seats, both of them traveled in silence back to civilization. Just like before, Jasmine's eyes stayed glued to the window, taking in the change in scenery and watching buildings with tall spires slowly drift back into view.

She couldn't not find Hellenia to be macabrely beautiful. A part of her missed the brightness of Draconia, but she couldn't even begin to pit one realm against the other; they were too different and striking in unique ways. With her mind drifting back to her upcoming choice, it was becoming obvious that it would be much harder than she thought in choosing one of them to be the victor.

If what Ciaran said holds any weight, there's a loophole I can take advantage of. She shook her head slightly, wiping that hope from her mind. Ciaran was a known trickster and she had nothing to go by but his word alone, which didn't seem smart. Jasmine glanced briefly across at Viviane, whose eyes were closed in what appeared to be a meditative state, unperturbed by her company and the rocking of the carriage. *I wish I felt comfortable asking Viviane what she knew about the Flame, but even if she knew, I'm not sure if she'd tell me straight one way or the other.*

Eventually, the carriage slowed down in front of the steps of Haven, and Jasmine glanced once more at the priestess who didn't make a move to acknowledge anything at all. Shrugging to herself, she opened the door and stepped out, looking around at her surroundings that were both familiar and foreign to her now before slowly making her way to the front door.

Her hand was poised to grasp the weathered bronze handle when it swung open, causing her to gasp and take a couple of steps back without thankfully taking an embarrassing tumble. A familiar figure stepped out, flushed and slightly disheveled while winking at whomever it was on the other side.

"A pleasure as always, Chellane. Give my regards to the lady of the house, will you?" He seemed to realize that he wasn't the only person on the stoop then, staring blankly before his eyebrows shot up to his bleached hairline.

"Jasmine? It's been a... wow, I *love* the hair. Gold is sexy on you."

She blinked before remembering that she still sported the elaborate braided style that Kai's handmaidens bestowed upon her when she arrived in Draconia. "Ah. Thanks." Jasmine shifted from one foot to the other awkwardly. Running into

Elliot unexpectedly was better than his best friend, but everything seemed to just remind her how much of a mess she left Hellenia in that had yet to be resolved.

"So... made your decision? Come to let us down gently before the big day?"

Jasmine shook her head. "No. I... I don't really know what I'm gonna do, tell you the truth. I feel stupid as hell standing here."

Elliot nodded, his flirty countenance fading to the rarely glimpsed side of him that was more serious than he seemed. "For what it's worth, *I'm* happy to see you. I wish I had answers for you, but the most I can offer is a drink. Wanna come?"

Jasmine's shoulders relaxed once she assessed that Elliot wasn't going to start drilling her on anything she wasn't ready to confront. "Y'all got any more of that blue fizzy stuff from the ball left over?"

He laughed, reaching out and draping his arm around her shoulders as they descended the steps of Haven. "Sadly, no. But I can take you someplace that can make equally tasty things."

Instead of his carriage awaiting them, Elliot preferred to walk on foot, which was a nice change. Jasmine didn't have to worry about fancy shoes or a petticoat this time, and it was easier for her to weather walking on the cobblestoned streets. She slipped her arm through his, surprised that they didn't seem to be getting as many overt stares as she expected. *We both aren't dressed properly for this realm, but maybe they're used to him just being this way.*

"Let me tell you... *Vinea et Malum* has the best food Hellenia has to offer. It's always busy, bougie enough to only take reservations, and the head chef is hot as hell. And then this little bakery here only does walkups. See the line? But it's worth every moment you wait for one of those morsels."

Jasmine let Elliot play an excited tour guide, pointing out different places and adding on commentary on how much he did (or did not) like it. For as much as Jasmine had observed from her carriage rides, nothing compared to being sure footed on the ground amongst the people to get a feel for an area. She realized that she considered herself more familiar with Draconia now because of all of the interaction she had with everything there, and it would do well for her to at least try and get the same sort of feeling with Hellenia. She responded lightly to his introductions, letting her eyes drift over the styles of clothing passerby wore in between it all. It was then that Jasmine was reminded of her agreement with Nithael, and she barely stifled a sigh to herself when she realized how naïve she had been.

Eventually, the alleyways became narrower, and the people sparser. Jasmine looked around at how dim things had become, looking up at Elliot with unspoken questions swirling in her gaze.

"Don't worry, you're safe," Elliot told her easily. "I like to stick to pockets of places that cater to people like me who don't need all of the fancy bells and whistles."

"You mean, like slumming it?"

"It's... well, not quite. Poorness by human standards is an affliction on the ruling class, and it is not something anyone of the Exousia line would ever tolerate in all of Hellenia. So, there isn't any real 'slum' here." He gestured to the closely packed buildings, humble in comparison to the main stretch of Hellenia that Jasmine was more accustomed to seeing. "For many, this is simply enough. It's not a reflection of someone's character."

Jasmine was quite shocked to hear his explanation. It was embarrassing for her to admit to herself that she could barely wrap her mind around a society that didn't have poor people. In hindsight, she didn't remember seeing any of that either in Draconia, but abundance was simply normal life for them. It was a bit different to learn that for Hellenians, a good standard of living was something that they actively sought to maintain for all under the Exousia rule.

She pulled herself out of her thoughts long enough to notice that they were standing in front of a weathered door, which Elliot confidently pushed open. The warmth from the inside immediately suffused her bones, and it became obvious that she was in a cozy bar. Rounded tables made shiny by the multitude of hands that likely laid upon its surface greeted her, illuminated by lanterns on the walls in set places to give the entire area a warm glow. It wasn't busy, but there were enough Hellenians dispersed throughout the bar that made Jasmine think of restaurants back home just before happy hour hit. Some of the patrons glanced curiously in their direction, but most went back to their business after nodding their heads in acknowledgement to Elliot.

"I take it this is one of your regular spots?" Jasmine asked as she settled onto one of the cushioned barstools.

"Oh, yeah. If I'm not fooling around in your realm, napping at the base of Hyperion or trying to get in Viviane's pants, I'm usually here." Elliot waved at the bartender, who automatically started mixing together a drink. "So, do you like fruity, sweet things? More bitter?"

"Eh, surprise me. As long as it doesn't taste like motor oil or anything really rough, I'm game." Mulling over all that he said, she propped her elbow up on the bar top. "I'm not drunk enough to ask about Leon right now, but have you talked to Kim? I have no idea how much time has passed. Pretty sure I don't have a job anymore, either."

After taking his glass with a smile and taking a moment to instruct the bartender to make another drink for his companion,

Elliot turned his head back to Jasmine. "Well, you haven't lost as many days as you think you have; once you disappear into Hyperion, time functions way different. You could spend months running around that mountain and find that only a few days have gone by." He paused to take a sip of the amber liquid in his glass, wincing a little at the sting. "But I have been in contact with Kim. She's worried because your phone is out of service, and I had to pull a lot of tricks out of my sleeve to keep her properly distracted."

"Oh? What did you tell her?"

"Tell her what? We just had a lot of sex, really. Always works."

Jasmine closed her eyes and shook her head, but she couldn't help but laugh. "Well, okay then, I'll take it. I'll need to make an appearance back home soon, though. I'm sure she'll be chewing my ear off no matter how good of a pipe you're laying down. And... I know I left a few loose ends I should clean up before..." she trailed off, thinking about all of the things she learned about her destiny and what awaited her.

"I get you. Here, try this and see what you think." Elliot slid a glass in front of her, filled with a purple liquid. "I know it looks like cough syrup, but I promise you that it's a lot better than that."

Jasmine curled her fingers around the glass and lifted it to her lips, taking a tentative sip of what he had ordered for her. She couldn't quite place what the flavor was, but it wasn't unpleasant; there was tartness that reminded her of pomegranate combined with something else just on the edge of bitter, relaxing her tense muscles all the same. "Not bad."

They sat in comfortable silence, listening to the idle chatter of those at tables behind them and drifting into their own thoughts. Jasmine had so much she wanted to ask, and she knew that this was as good of a time as any to put those questions forth. But she found herself wary of even broaching the subject.

Thankfully, Elliot did it for her.

"Leon's been kinda... not himself since you left. For one, he goes to the human realm of his own accord, now. I'd have to force him to go with me in any other case." Elliot kept his drink a few inches from his mouth, staring thoughtfully ahead at the back wall lined with different bottles of libations. "But all he does is gorge himself on French fries. Isn't that insane? He even went to a McDonalds. Wish I was there to see the look on the employees' faces when his cultured ass walked through the door."

Jasmine couldn't hold back a giggle despite her tumultuous feelings regarding the Hellenian lord. Just the thought of him showing up dressed to the nines in a low-class fast food chain restaurant was enough to send her. "That's pretty amazing."

"Yeah. And sometimes, I know he tries to avoid me, even though he can't because I know him too well. But he doesn't really like what I have to say these days."

"Mmm." Jasmine took another sip of her drink. "Like what?"

Elliot's red gaze moved to her face. "Like about how he majorly fucked up with you. He's always been an idiot when it comes to interpersonal relations that aren't scripted and steeped in ceremony. But I was still hoping he would've done better."

Jasmine shrugged despite her roiling emotions that were stirred up now that they were on that topic. "He only fucked up in not letting me know that he was only in it for the Flame. Now that that's clear, I can move forward."

She ignored Elliot's stare that seemed to see right through her bluff, drinking more and liking the hazy feeling she was getting from the alcohol. She remembered how booze was stronger for Hellenians, and idly thought about slowing down because of it. Yet, she also needed something to get her through hashing out a complicated subject.

"Listen," Elliot started, and then seemed to rethink it. "We both failed you, honestly. I left a lot up to him to explain, and he didn't. I could give excuses for it, but it won't change a damn thing. I just wish more than ever that we were human; that would cut out a lot of the bullshit that makes this complicated. I mean, Leon would *probably* still be a bit of an idiot, but I'd have a little more hope, then."

"Isn't the goal to get me to become a Hellenian, though?"

"Formally, yes. But if you ask me, I wouldn't wish that on anyone." Elliot finished his drink in one smooth gulp. "It's probably different from your point of view, though."

Jasmine frowned a little. "Y'all seem to have a few things right that humans don't, and also have a banging sense of fashion. Sure, there's some drawbacks, but overall, it's difficult for me to understand what's so bad about it."

Elliot smiled in response, but it didn't reach his eyes. "Did you want another drink?"

She nodded, finishing what was left in her glass so that Elliot could put in for a refill. Once the bartender expertly crafted the next round and slid them over, the blond sighed heavily and seemed like he was mentally preparing himself.

"Christianity's pretty popular in your realm. Do you have an understanding of Genesis? You know, 'God created the heavens and the earth in seven days and then fucked off', or something?"

Jasmine snorted. "Yeah, that about sums it up. Wish I'd have had you as my Sunday school teacher."

"I'd be terrible at it. God didn't just cast out Adam and Eve; He actually had an entire meltdown and tossed out every one of His angels as well. He decided to leave all of creation like a deadbeat father that went to the corner store for smokes and just never came back."

Jasmine's eyes widened in shock, and she took another sip of her drink. "Oh. Well, damn."

Elliot nodded with a sardonic look on his face. "Damn is right. As you can probably imagine, the angels didn't know what to do after being severed from their creator. They had no purpose, anymore. Grew out of the wings that they once used to soar amongst the heavens. Learned some stuff from humans but could never really integrate. Oh, of course, got into beef with the dragons along the way trying to find their place somehow. So, that's how Hellenians came to be. We don't move like free beings, because we're still chained to the past in a lot of ways. Humans have a lot of problems, but... believe me when I say that you guys have a brighter future than we do."

Jasmine sat in a bit of silence, processing this origin story and finally understanding some of the things Kai had mentioned offhand when explaining things about the two races. "That's... wild. Is that why you need a High Lord that has wings? Because it's a throwback to your origin?"

"Yep. It's also why a lot of older Hellenians have angelic names. Leon lucked out though; his father didn't put *that* curse on him, at least." Elliot chuckled and drank some more. "But yeah... I say all that just to let you know that I completely understand if you end up giving the Flame to the Draconians, instead. I joke a lot, but you have to make this choice for yourself."

"Not exactly. I've since learned that each race has its own boons that gift humans just by virtue of whoever holds the Flame that I have to consider. So, it's not really about me; I'm just a cog in the wheel." Jasmine explained this easily, but still felt odd about resigning herself to such a fate. "My role is making sure that humans stay having the best path to that brighter future."

When she looked over at Elliot again, she was struck by the residual sadness in his red eyes. It wasn't quite pity, but she could tell that he wished he could save her from it all. Jasmine prepared to ask him why he personally felt so indebted to her humanity when she saw his gaze flicker from her face to a place behind her.

Jasmine also noticed how quiet the bar had become.

She feared turning around, even though her gut has already told her who was there.

"Jasmine."

CHAPTER TWENTY-NINE

Seeing Leon again felt as if someone had poured cold water over her entire body. She just stared at him as if they were frozen in time, taking in his familiar posture and impeccable clothing. Everyone else in the establishment also found it very interesting that the High Lord himself decided to grace the local bar, directing attention towards him as well.

However, it was obvious that Leon only had eyes for Jasmine.

"Really?" Elliot asked wearily. "Here?"

"You aren't inconspicuous, and you know as well as I how fast rumors travel here. And... I could sense her the moment she stepped foot in Hellenia."

Jasmine didn't know why his remark set her off so badly. Perhaps it was just the natural breaking point that she had been hedging upon since she woke up alone in Leon's bed in what felt like eons ago. With the combination of the alcohol coursing through her system, she narrowed her eyes in a glare and let the words fly out of her mouth without care.

"That's cute."

Leon started getting that kicked puppy look that Jasmine used to find so adorable, but now only served to incense her more. "I needed to see you."

She snorted, placing her glass down a little bit too loudly and folding her arms across her chest. "Oh? Cause I thought a man that hit it and quit it said something."

"I left you in Sustina's care, knowing that she would tend to you in my absence."

"Just say you used me for a better shot at the Flame and go."

"Hey, um..." Elliot hissed from behind her. "Maybe not the best place to disc-"

Leon closed his eyes for a moment, swallowed, and then continued despite his best friend's caution. "That wasn't the case, Jasmine. I understand how it might have appeared to you, but I apologize for how careless I allowed the situation to--"

Jasmine scoffed. "Apologize to Rina; I'm sure she'll care about all those pretty words you like weaving more than me."

Even through the haze of inebriation, she could tell she crossed a line even though she was too stubborn to walk it back. Leon's eyes narrowed.

"You know nothing about Rina to even have the grounds to speak about her."

"I just think it's funny how you got all the smoke about her, but none of that energy when it comes to letting me know where I stood with you, my duty as the Prime, or anything that actually mattered."

Leon assessed her coolly. "You seem to have done well committing to your own foolish notions without my 'pretty little words'."

Jasmine smiled too sweetly in response. "Well, a girl's gotta commit to *something* when a man proves he ain't worth the effort, right? Might fuck around and give the Flame to the Draconians after all, because at least *they* respected me enough to let me know what was up."

"You two are fucking *children*, I swear," Elliot grumbled, right after finishing his drink and the rest of Jasmine's during the entire debacle. "Read a damn room! Is this really the stage you want to set??"

Jasmine blinked at him before looking around the bar, really noticing how much attention they were getting. Upon feeling the first hints of true embarrassment start to leak through, she hopped off of the barstool with a mumbled 'sorry' in Elliot's direction and weaved around Leon to get to the door and step out into the fresh air.

Her emotions were raw, and she had started to shake from the adrenaline after the argument. The way her surroundings shifted in her vision told her that she should have stopped after the first drink, but she couldn't undo that any more than she could undo the spectacle she caused. Just briefly thinking of Kim and how effortless her friend could handle causing an entire public scene made Jasmine long more than ever to just be back in that small break room at work with nothing but employee gossip to share with her best friend.

I want to go home.

She pushed away the impending tears borne both of longing and frustration, picking a direction to start walking. However, she got intercepted by a firm grip on her arm, which made her automatically swing with her other on whomever dared to put hands on her.

"Stop it," Leon's stern voice cut through the alley as he held both of her hands flush to her sides. "You're drunk, and we both should vacate. You aren't getting anywhere good on your own."

Jasmine wanted to keep fighting. She wanted to unload all of the unresolved hurt she still held within her over how they ended up. But being that close to Leon once more was more cloying than the alcohol she consumed. The tension seeped out of her bones and made her shoulders sag in defeat, and Leon moved to support the brunt of her weight against him as they walked to the main street where his carriage awaited.

She barely remembered the ride back to the manor. Everything within her seemed worn out from dealing with such heavy emotions, and she didn't speak to Leon at all. Silently, she just allowed him to navigate her from the carriage to the mansion, then up the stairs she didn't plan on seeing again until they came to the room she first stayed in. Jasmine barely got her shoes off before she climbed into the plush bed, flopping unceremoniously onto the pillow.

She forgot that Leon was still around until he was gently coaxing her to sit up to drink some cool water.

Just having him be kind to her after everything was worse. It would have been better had he treated her with the iciness she knew she deserved after her outburst in the bar. After half the glass was cleared, Jasmine's vision started blurring with tears she did not want to shed.

"I'm sorry. I'm an emotional bitch, right now. You didn't--"

"Shhh," Leon brushed a few of her braids behind her ear. "Yes, I did deserve it. Your anger is understandable, and I should have conducted myself better on all counts."

Jasmine tried to stop from crying, but her cheeks became wet anyway. "Elliot probably wants to beat both our asses right now, huh?"

Leon gave her a hint of a smile. "Most likely. We've tarnished his reputation at one of his frequent establishments. This isn't counting the public scandal I'll have to address in the wake of it."

She started laughing through her tears, getting out a couple of chuckles before laying back down. "I'll help if I can. It's the least I can do after going off like that."

"Don't worry about that. Rest, Jasmine. There will be time for all of that later."

For all of her earlier posturing about not caring for his words, she believed him, then.

CHAPTER THIRTY

J asmine opened her eyes with only a minor headache, looking to the window that shone gentle light through the gap in the heavy curtains. She didn't rest deep enough to not remember everything that happened, but she was still within sleep's lingering embrace to not panic about it.

But what she saw when she turned to her left shocked her. Leon was sitting upright with his closed wings against the backboard, hands clasped over his outstretched, crossed legs as if he were waiting for something. Yet, his head was slightly canted to the side and his eyes were closed.

Did he stay here all night? Jasmine carefully sat up, not wanting to disturb the vision in front of her just yet. Since hearing Elliot's explanation of Hellenian's origins, she could only see how angelic Leon looked as he dozed, his black hair laying across his cheek with his chest slowly rising and falling. She didn't know how many minutes she let pass with just her staring at him, nearly committing the vision to memory before reluctantly reaching out and nudging his shoulder.

"Hey... you can go back to your room to get better rest. I'm pretty okay, now."

Leon's gold eyes fluttered open, and he turned his head to look at her. Jasmine realized that it was the second time they shared a bed, only this time, he was still around in the morning.

"It's fine. I..." he trailed off. "I feel whatever rest I've gotten next to you makes up for the nights I haven't."

Jasmine stared longer at him before shaking her head. "You still know the right words to say, don't you?"

"Obviously not. If I did, then you wouldn't feel the way you do now. My words always seem to come too late."

She couldn't argue with him, there. She was conflicted enough as it was, feeling oddly comforted by his presence while still feeling a bit wary of his intentions. Turning her head, she stared back at the window. "Is it possible for me to go back home for a bit?"

Leon nodded, swinging his long legs off the side of the bed to stand. "Of course. I can connect you to the portal in my house, which is the closest to your apartment. We can depart as soon as you're ready."

Jasmine didn't need to be told twice. Pushing the remnants of her headache aside, she got her shoes on in record time and waited for Leon to do the same. He led her to his study, which invoked odd feelings all on its own considering what happened the last time she was within it. But she ignored it as best as possible as she watched Leon retrace the runes that he undoubtedly practiced many times before, opening the pathway.

"Ah. I nearly forgot..." Leon murmured, and then fiddled at the brooch that was pinned to his lapel. Then before Jasmine's eyes, she saw the glamour he always wore in the human realm take shape, melting away his horns and wings, negating his talons, and transitioning his irises to a warm brown. It was shocking to watch it happen, and she felt that he looked odd as a human now.

When he offered his hand to her, Jasmine could tell that he was acting on impulse, and the look of hesitation clear on his face confirmed it for her. She looked down at it for a bit before tentatively placing her hand in his, and feeling his fingers encase it. Together, they stepped over the threshold and was greeted with the familiar sight of her own world. The sun shone brightly through the window, showing off that the first snowfall had occurred since she had been gone, leaving the bare tree branches glistening with ice.

The relief Jasmine felt was palpable.

"Let us go downstairs. I should be able to summon an Uber for you from my phone. I expect that your device hasn't been charged in some time."

She nodded and followed him out of the room, eventually ending up in the living room where the warmth of the fire met her cheeks and crackled peacefully. Jasmine sat stiffly on the couch, somewhat in a daze and feeling like she just lived the longest dream she'd ever had. But Leon's presence alone was a reminder that things were not over despite her overwhelming urge to just bury herself in her covers and not come out for a long time.

Looking up wearily as Leon returned from the kitchen with a hot cup of tea, Jasmine grasped the ceramic and looked down into the brown liquid thoughtfully. "Have you ever wanted to be human?"

There was a long pause before he responded. "I am quite settled into who I am and what I know, and there are many aspects of humanity that don't fit quite well with me." Leon settled into an armchair across from her. "It is true that I went into this only with my original purpose in mind; to find the Prime and get them to light the Flame once more for my people, regardless of my own personal reticence at the thought of temporary integration."

"But?"

"But... it has been an unexpected boon for me. I've begun to understand Elliot's proclivity towards humans, the yearning to shuck off the weight of expectations that only exist for Hellenians." He gave her a self-depreciating wince. "But overall, it is your presence in my life that drove me to delve into selfishness that unfortunately made your transition rocky and incomplete. I cannot begin to make up for that."

For what it was worth, Jasmine didn't rush to reassure him. The brunt of her anger at him had faded with her outburst and consequent hangover, and she was back in her own realm with clarity she never would have gotten otherwise. Taking another sip of her tea, she looked at him contemplatively.

"Wanna play hooky?"

Leon blinked. "Pardon?"

"You got a whole lot of shit to deal with the moment you go back to Hellenia. So do I, for different reasons. I'm not trying to handle all of that right now. I want to pretend for a moment that the person I am, the life I have here, is all that I gotta worry about. Even if it's only for a day, I'm reclaiming my time while I can." Jasmine paused, taking a deep breath. "If you want to escape with me for a little while, that's fine."

For a moment, he looked like he wanted to refute everything that she said. But eventually, his shoulders relaxed and he let out a soft smile. "I'd be honored, Jasmine."

Once the car arrived, both of them left Leon's temporary home to travel back into the city proper. Much like she did when she was in Hellenia, Jasmine stayed glued to the windows as the city she adopted for herself in her adult years passed by, glancing at the regular people wearing clothes that were normal going to establishments she recognized. She never thought she would appreciate so much about things that were a part of her everyday life... until they suddenly weren't, anymore.

Stepping into her apartment was another layer of comfort that almost brought her to tears. She looked around all of the knickknacks that she had collected, the stack of fabrics she had just started getting through, smiling gratefully to herself.

"Home sweet home." Jasmine looked over her shoulder at Leon. "Do you want pizza? Well, wait... have you *had* pizza before?"

"It's been quite some time. The last one I had was in Italy."

"Oh, Mr. Fancy Pants, I don't have anything like that for you. But I can get you some trash from a local place I like." Jasmine reached for her phone, then sighed when she remembered it was dead. "And I'll use your phone to do it, if you don't mind."

While her cell charged and the food was ordered, she got to work digging out the rest of the bottle of wine she saved and dumped the remainder of it into two coffee mugs, bringing it over to the couch where Leon had taken a seat.

"One of the scariest things about doing what I have to do is knowing that I can't come back to this life. It's isolating to think about." Jasmine took a healthy sip of her wine, happy to not have to worry about being plastered after one cup of it. "It really makes me want to chuck away this whole Prime business."

"If there was a way, I would help you find it."

She raised an eyebrow. "Really? Even though your people would likely call for your head over it?"

"My people whispered ill things about my father when he fell in love with Selene and refused to hide it. Then, once he passed, they did the same in blaming her for his death. I love and have a duty to Hellenia and those within it, that will never change. But if it were something so precious as to your autonomy and happiness, I would bear their criticism for the rest of my days."

"Okay but, you *do* know that no Flame means no way for you to get McDonald's french fries, right?"

Leon started laughing. "Somehow, I knew Elliot would make mention of that to you. And the thought of that certainly is sobering. But..." He paused, his eyes lowering slightly, and Jasmine waited for him to finish his thought. Unfortunately, before he did, the buzzer to the front door of the complex rang, signifying that their pizza had arrived.

What followed afterwards was a relaxing day filled with introducing Leon to other things about modern human life that he was only vaguely familiar with, starting with the meal itself. It apparently was a big jump for him to accept that fries were to be eaten by hand only, so the look of panic on his face when Jasmine unabashedly lifted a greasy, cheesy slice to her lips was hilarious to her. Once he got over that, she introduced him to the wonders of reality fashion TV shows, and she definitely admitted to herself it was only to watch him nearly throw something at the screen at some of the "aberrations" he was forced to see lauded as high fashion.

Everything made Jasmine feel like she used to back when Leon was just a handsome stranger that landed in her lap by some odd twist of fate. She only took a break from basking in the security that brought by picking up her partly charged cell phone and giving Kim a call, just to give her friend the opportunity she needed to chew her out for being AWOL and following it up with an outpouring of work gossip that had Jasmine feel like she had a connection to normalcy. Apparently, she *had* missed a bit of work, but it had been covered up by Kim making an impassioned plea to management on her friend's behalf while using Elliot as a "distant family member" of

Jasmine's to confirm that there was an emergency to get her qualified for FMLA.

"I guess I can thank my near perfect attendance for the past few years and a friend that looks out for me no matter what to save my ass in the most unlikely of circumstances," Jasmine said when she wrapped up her phone call and settled back on the couch next to Leon. "Kim and Elliot pulled the largest strings to cover me with my job."

"Oh? I hope he didn't--"

"No, Kim doesn't know anything particularly incriminating. She's actually assumed that you whisked me away to some private island and chained me to your bed these past few days. Her words, not mine."

Leon blushed almost immediately, looking down at his hands. "To be honest, that might have been your fate if I hadn't the fortitude to leave you the night of the ball. I know it caused extreme distress and misunderstandings, yet... I don't trust myself when I'm in that state. I would rather you think I used you than come out of a Rut and find you harmed by my own hand."

Jasmine felt her body tingle, being brought back to such a pivotal moment in whatever their relationship happened to be. "I understand. In hindsight, I didn't make it easier on myself when I just decided to leave right after. Sustina explained what went down, but I wasn't really ready to settle with it then."

"Jasmine..."

"Hmm?"

Leon's hand was over hers now, and she glanced down at it before looking up at him. Immediately, she wished that she had continued to look anywhere else, because the way he was looking at her made her feel uncomfortably warm.

"The Rut was ill timed, unfortunately brought on by the

hasty actions of my ex. She felt that engaging the primal part of me would net her what she once lost. I'm sure she's still shocked that it did not." He gave a small chuckle. "But... I wanted you long before I walked into the study that evening. I simply wished that my first time with you was more controlled."

Jasmine swore that there was a slow ringing in her ears. "First time?"

"Yes." His eyelids dropped slightly, which directly affected her increased heart rate. "I did not intend on you being in my bed only once."

She was out of wine, but that was probably a good thing. Her mouth was dry as she stared dumbly at him and absorbed everything that he was saying. "I see."

"I am adept at asking things of you that I likely have no right to. But I can't help but want the chance to redo things with you, if you'll have me."

Jasmine laughed nervously. "Which part did you want to redo?"

As if he was waiting for that question that had an obvious answer, Leon's hands left Jasmine's to reach up and cup her face between them, gently tilting her chin at the right angle to comfortably meet his lips with hers. Unlike the first time, they parted tenderly against her own as he deepened it only just past the point of chaste, giving her tingles that arose from the tips of her toes all the way to her fingertips. Jasmine's hands became braced on his chest, feeling the smooth material of his shirt and brushing up against the brooch that was pinned there. They remained in that lip-locked dance for a moment longer before Leon finally disengaged.

"Does that make it clear?"

"Oh... yeah. Yep. Really clear." Jasmine cleared her throat, and then took a moment to make up her mind. She unraveled her legs out from under her on the couch to get up, tugging on Leon's arm for him to follow her.

"You're on my turf for now, Leon. And I hope you don't mind if we do things my way."

Jasmine felt a strange combination of nervousness and confidence when she got Leon into her humble bedroom. But the anxiety faded away bit by bit as she unbuttoned the luxurious shirt he wore, once again exposing the chest that had her heart palpitating the first time she mended a button for him in her apartment. She let herself explore the planes of his chest with her fingertips, eventually coming to the dips of his Apollo's belt when it came to remove his pants.

She had time to fully appreciate and shiver in anticipation when Leon moved to take off her own shirt in return, giggling a little as he tossed it carelessly to a corner.

She did miss his remarkable Hellenian features that once seemed so alien to her senses. She wanted to have the freedom to touch his velvety wings, or marvel at his horns when he dipped his head to kiss along her neck. However, Jasmine did enjoy being able to properly straddle him as he laid flat on the sheets, gazing up at her as she moved with his mouth slightly agape and eyes full of adoration.

Jasmine remembered still her entire romp in the pleasure house with Fouzia, and how good it felt to be desired simply for desire's sake. But she never had someone who looked at her the way Leon did.

She stayed awake for as long as she dared, curled up in the crook of his arm as they laid together in her bed, with the moonlight filtering in the windows and seeming brighter from the snow that coated the world outside. With his hair strewn across her pillows, Jasmine thought about what it would be like if they were just two normal humans hooking up.

It'd be nice. But... not in the cards, I guess.

By the time the morning rays filtered into the room, rousing them out of sleep, Jasmine felt like she had a proper heading on her path, for once.

"Rise and shine, sleepyhead. I don't have French fries for you... but, I think I could make something that you may like for breakfast."

Leon must have slept deeper than he did since last time, as the sight of him with mussed hair and barely open eyelids nearly sleepwalking into the kitchen after her was something completely adorable. Jasmine started by fixing him a strong cup of tea, placing it in front of him as she got to work taking out a frozen bag of tater tots to spread over a cookie sheet.

"I should be treating you to breakfast, not letting you scurry around a kitchen to--"

"Shhhh, don't start with that," Jasmine cut him off gently, adjusting the temperature of the oven. "My turf, remember? I'm doing this because I want to, and you're gonna have to just deal with it."

His shoulders sagged in defeat, even though his languid smile told her that he didn't mind relinquishing that. "Understood."

If Leon wanted to justify how he felt, he seemed to have learned better and let it be. This made Jasmine happy, because for once, it meant that Leon had to put down all of that rigid, Hellenian culture he had been steeped in and just learn how to exist. She may have really pushed it when the tater tots were done and insisted on feeding him the first few morsels, but she chalked it up to the power of crispy potatoes winning him over in the end.

Everything about their casual morning was nice. Jasmine didn't want it to end, even though she knew it had to; there were things that neither of them could avoid for much longer than they already had. Leon seemed to notice where her mind had wandered, sliding a comforting hand over hers after she had cleaned up the dishes.

"Thank you. For everything." He said as he met her eyes. "In such a short time, I feel like I've learned so much... grown more than I have in the past few decades of my existence. It's incredible if I think on it."

"I feel you. I'm just a regular girl, Leon. Never in my whole life would I ever have thought that something like this would happen to me."

Leon laughed, rubbing his thumb over her knuckles before withdrawing. "Ah... even now, you don't believe that you're anything but 'regular'. Astonishing."

After a few quick texts to Kim to let her know that she would be out of contact again for a few days, she took one last look over her apartment before following Leon back out into the winter air to head back to his house on the other side of town. She felt nervous with anticipation of finally fully climbing Hyperion and communing with the Flame to complete her duty. Yet, Jasmine knew once it had been done, somehow... she could move on.

Those were the thoughts that occupied her mind as she followed Leon back through the portal to Hellenia, crashing right into his back when he stopped suddenly only a couple of steps over the threshold.

"Shit, I'm sorr- ... Leon?"

Looking up at his face, even in the ambient light of the grand study, Jasmine could tell that he had gone completely pale. His eyes were wide, darting back and forth wildly, and she kept trying to follow where his gaze was going and not seeing anything other than the rows of books lining the walls. Tentatively, she reached out and took hold of his arm, giving him a gentle tug.

"Leon? What happened? Talk to me."

Finally, he moved his head to look down at her; it was a jerky motion, almost as if he were forcing himself to turn away from whatever it was that was occupying him. The panic in his eyes was palpable, and Jasmine's heart seized at whatever it was that made him feel that way.

"I can't feel Elliot. He's gone."

CHAPTER THIRTY-ONE

Jasmine didn't think she fully understood what Leon meant, but it didn't help the feeling of trepidation that formed in her belly as she followed his figure out of the study and down the hall, quickening her pace to try and catch up with him.

"What do you mean?"

Leon descended the steps at a pace so fast that she was afraid he'd trip. "Our connection. That tether, I can't strum. I don't know why." He stopped in front of the table that also held Sustina's key, as if he were contemplating if there was some physical object he could use to try and fix it all. "This has never happened before."

Jasmine let out a breath, trying to rationalize something that wasn't a worst-case scenario. "Maybe he closed it? For privacy?"

"This isn't a shuttered connection, it is a *missing* connection. The difference is clear. I don't know how to simplify it further than that."

She couldn't help but feel a bit peeved at how short Leon

was being with her. *Did he forget that I don't know how all of this shit works, or...?* She frowned, but she tempered herself when she saw him nervously comb his hand through his hair multiple times and pace from one end of the foyer to the other.

"Do you think Viviane could help? She's a Priestess, and she's... well, she's always connected to all sorts of stuff, right? Is it alright to ask her to do a little bit of missing person work?"

Leon stopped his pacing and looked up at her, blinking once. "Perhaps. I usually would not call on the High Priestess for such trivial matters, but..."

"Nothing trivial about how tight you are over this. You're the High Lord, I'm sure she'll understand."

The ride to Viviane was tense, and Jasmine didn't know where she stood with Leon. At her suggestion, he simply set forth into action, and she had to scurry along to keep up with him as he blew out of the manor. He sat rigid in the seat, staring straight ahead at nothing at all, his breathing deceptively controlled. After a bit of time with nothing but the sound of wheels moving on the cobbled streets to occupy them, Jasmine chanced reaching over and touching Leon's hand.

She didn't realize that she was holding her breath until he finally grasped hold of it, almost tight enough to hurt. His fingers were clammy, and Jasmine tried returning the grip as much as she could to convey that she was there with him. But in stark comparison to how they were that morning and even the previous night before, she felt like there was a wall erected between them.

Eventually, they pulled up in front of the priestess alcove, and Leon wasted no time exiting the carriage and letting his long legs carry him straight up to the door, knocking heavily. The woman that answered looked at Leon strangely, and Jasmine realized that with everything going on, he hadn't even remembered to remove the human glamor from earlier.

"Is Lady Viviane available?"

"A-ah, yes, High Lord," the priestess pulled herself together and bowed quickly, opening the door further to let them in. They were led through sconced halls until coming to a larger chamber, where the priestess in question was seated in front of a table strewn with various ceremonial objects.

She turned to look up at them as if she had known they were coming. "High Lord. How may I be of service?"

"I need you to locate Elliot for me. I cannot contact him through our link."

Viviane's dark eyes shifted to meet Jasmine's for a moment before settling back on Leon. "Do you believe something has happened to him?"

Leon's lips parted hesitantly as if he were embarrassed, but then quickly stated his case. "I'm not sure. But my spirit is worried. If it is nothing, I wholly apologize for the intrusion, and will seek to reimburse you for the trouble. I know the work you do for the coven and all of Hellenia far outweighs my selfish requests."

Holding his gaze for a moment longer, Viviane then simply turned to her workstation and unearthed a dowsing crystal. Taking the long chain that held it in one hand, she moved over to what looked like a complicated chart laid flat on the table and let the crystal hang, closing her eyes. Jasmine watched as the pendulum swung idly, not really knowing much about the art but hoping that whatever she was doing would procure results.

Minutes passed. The crystal swung, passing over and over the symbols and lines, never stopping. Eventually, Viviane opened her eyes and palmed it, turning to a set of cards next.

Jasmine wasn't sure if Leon noticed it at all, but she swore she saw the high priestess's brow furrow in concern as she worked.

Once Viviane had settled on another method of divination that seemed to involve an intricate web set within a wooden base, Jasmine was fully worried. She hadn't done anything but smoothly consult one thing after another, but she felt like if there was an answer, then it would have been found by now. Just a glance over at Leon gave her a view of his stony, shuttered expression as his eyes never left Viviane's work.

Until at last, the High Priestess broke her silence.

"Elliot is not in any realm I can reach."

Jasmine blinked. "What does that mean? I'm sorry for my ignorance on everything, and I know it's likely not my place. But I don't understand what's happening here."

Viviane's gaze settled on her. "I cannot place his spirit in Hellenia, nor the human realm. The space between where Hyperion rests holds no echo I could hear. I hesitated on consulting the afterlife, but I wanted to confirm there as well." She looked at Leon. "If it is any comfort, there were no traces of his soul's passage."

Hearing that did seem to take some of the tension out of Leon's shoulders. "It is. But it still does not explain why he's apparently ceased to exist. Surely there must be *something*."

Jasmine didn't know what to say; she felt like a spectator in the middle of an act that had spiraled off script, leaving her standing on the set with nothing to do. She wanted to ease Leon's desperation somehow, but everything was out of her hands. Her eyes shifted back to the High Priestess, and she noticed that her expression was pensive, looking slightly askance back at the web she had last consulted.

"I said that he is not in any realm I can reach. There is only one I cannot."

It took her longer than she would like to admit to piece together the reluctant words that Viviane spoke. *No.* Jasmine looked in alarm at Leon, who met her gaze with pursed lips and something she didn't want to see come to fruition right behind his hardened gaze.

"Okay, uh... listen. Let me... let me talk to them."

"You would be the only one able to, as it stands," Leon said coolly. "Although, it would not spare them the consequences of such a grave overstep."

Jasmine could only shrug helplessly at that. "The least I can do is try to confirm for myself if anything happened. Then we can only move forward from here, right?"

Viviane folded her hands in her lap. "Jasmine... this alone is grounds for war. In many ways, it would be better if he simply did disappear with no explanation."

For once, Jasmine could tell that she said that without any of the usual ire that came with referring to Elliot. And that just served to scare her even more. *A fucking war? Like the kind that caused Hyperion to even be a thing in the first place?* She shoved that out of her mind as much as she could, preferring not to think on it.

"Alright. Get me to the portal, please. I'll do what I can."

CHAPTER THIRTY-TWO

Jasmine worked her way up the path that she was becoming quite familiar with for as many times as she traversed it. A part of her noticed that a few things with the scenery were different than when she first was there. She couldn't remember if she passed the spot where she had her previous breakdown. The flowers she had stopped to sniff were on the other side of the path than what she remembered. But that strangeness faded away as she continued on her way, remembering that the entire mountain was likely sentient in a strange sense.

She definitely reached the summit much quicker than before. It was almost as if the land shifted to suit her urgency, and she was stepping out into the clearing where she first encountered the Draconians. Making her way over to the portal, Jasmine paused when she realized that she had no way of activating it. Her heartbeat quickened in her chest as she stared at the series of carefully crafted armillary spheres set in the arch, wondering what all the markings meant.

"Jesus, this is dumb," Jasmine cursed, reaching her hand up

and touching the Spark that laid against her chest. She closed her eyes, hoping against hope that she would get some sort of magical insight to allow her access to Draconia. A slight breeze blew calmly by, but nothing else greeted her.

She felt ridiculous. Huffing an exasperated breath, she dropped her hands from the necklace and squinted up at the archway again. *Wait... the last person to use it would have been Kai, right? So these would be set to the last location, technically.* It was a bit of a long shot, but it wasn't like Jasmine was getting any other ideas standing there waiting for divine intervention that wasn't coming. Tentatively, she reached out and moved one of the spheres to a new position before moving it back to how she found it.

When the center of the portal rippled to life, she almost jumped out of her skin. Staring at it for a moment longer, she tiptoed over the threshold and found herself on the other side, standing in the familiar courtyard in Apelion. Happy that she didn't end up somewhere terribly uncharted, she set off towards the gardens, looking for Kai. Jasmine wasn't sure where she'd find him, and thankfully bumped into one of his handmaidens and asked to be escorted to where he was. As she moved through the colorful halls of the palace, her nerves got even more of a hold on her, realizing that she didn't know how to phrase what was likely going to come across as fantastical.

Eventually, the handmaiden pushed open a set of ornate wooden doors, and the circular room that greeted her stopped her in her tracks for a moment. The smell of fragrant dried leaves hit her nose, and all along the walls was the largest collection of teapots that she had ever seen.

Arranged from size to material of construction, the shelves neatly faded into carefully rationed and labeled drawers, full of the tea that was wafting to her nose. The whole room was illuminated through the skylight above, settling on the pearl-inlaid lacquered table that held a fresh pot of tea for the individuals sitting within. Both of them turned once they heard the door open, staring in shock at Jasmine as the handmaiden bowed politely and then scurried off, leaving her to her own devices.

Jasmine glanced at Ciaran for a moment, then cleared her throat. "Uh... hi, again. Sorry to barge in."

"It's fine. I'd ask how you managed to decode the passage here, but that obviously isn't the most important thing to note." Kai set his teacup down, arranging his robes to stand. "Is everything alright?"

Nope. Not at all. Jasmine fiddled with her cuticles nervously before shrugging. "Ah, y'all wouldn't happen to have seen a Hellenian walking around here or anything, right?"

Ciaran squinted, and Kai blinked before replying incredulously. "A Hellenian? Are you kidding?"

"I wish I was, actually. But one of them has gone missing, and he just happens to be the current High Lord's best friend. Can't find him anywhere, and now they're... uh... assuming that... he's... here." Everything sounded ridiculous the more Jasmine forced out the words. *I will never be cut out to be a diplomat, that much is for sure.* "I'm sure you can see why that would be bad, for them to get that idea. So, I convinced them to just chill out for a bit while I see for myself. Because honestly, I don't even see how a thing like this could happen."

Ciaran exchanged a concerned glance with Kai. "This accusation is pretty baseless."

"But no less serious." Kai walked over to Jasmine and placed a comforting hand on her shoulder. "There has never been a Hellenian on Draconian soil in the history of its conception. We may not have the overall tension our quarrelling ancestors shared, but we aren't allies, either. I'm sure there wouldn't be the need for a Flame and a chosen Prime if things were otherwise." He paused, sighing through his nose. "Should I meet with the High Lord to attempt to clear the air?"

Ciaran crossed his arms, leaning back in his seat with a frown on his face. "It could be a set up."

Kai's brow furrowed. "How so? Believe me, I don't look forward to this, knowing what they assume. But on Hyperion, there can be no foul play lest we both lose what is most precious to us."

The other Draconian let out an amused snort, shaking his head and standing up to walk over to them. "I worry about how trusting you are sometimes, Kai. Talk with him then, as you insist. I'll gather the other two and meet you there in a bit." Ciaran's eyes drifted over to Jasmine then, and she couldn't help but tense a little. She was glad to see that the two of them had their talk and were okay, but she still didn't know how to process their last interaction. As if noticing her discomfort, he gave her an easy smile and a wink.

"With the Prime as your good luck charm, you probably won't be in danger at all."

Jasmine watched him exit, then placed her attention back on Kai. "I'm sorry this is happening; I can't believe it myself."

"It isn't what I expected to encounter in the least. I wasn't planning on actually seeing the High Lord himself until the Transfer of Passage ceremony, and while that isn't without its minor tension, I would do that five times over than this confrontation." Kai sighed, then gestured to Jasmine. "Well. Shall we go?"

She had a heavy feeling in her stomach as they crossed back over to Hyperion. All she could think about was how shuttered Leon had become. She distracted herself briefly by making Kai stop and teach her how to work the spheres properly to open the access point to Apelion, not wanting to chance lacking any more knowledge than she already did. But once that was over with, it was only their footsteps crunching through the light dusting of snow that coated the path in intervals that occupied their thoughts as they descended.

For whatever reason, Jasmine felt that the environment was too quiet now. Perhaps she had been distracted by her solitude and overly invested in the ambiance of Hyperion, but it seemed as though the mountain itself was holding its breath. She glanced over at Kai as she could, sometimes wanting to hold his hand, but always defaulting on letting him keep to himself. She didn't envy his position; even with her testimony and the other Draconians speaking truth, Jasmine couldn't figure out what the next course of action was if in the event Elliot had actually disappeared without a trace. A part of her was still hoping that there was a misfire in the psychic waves that would resolve itself, and Elliot would be just fine.

Kai didn't offer any conversation, simply walking beside her with his face unreadable. By the time the ground beneath them evened out, and she could see the first hints of lush flowers that signified the field beyond, his expression had smoothed into the mask she saw when they first met.

It was easy to spot Leon's silhouette amongst the bright flowers contrasting against his darkly clothed form. His long hair stirred around his shoulders, buffeting the top of his wings as he stood there, seeming to watch the clouds go by. Jasmine's heart quickened, and she realized that didn't know where to place herself during this conversation. She was on Leon's side as much as she could be, but she also truly felt that Kai and the other Draconians were innocent in any wrongdoing.

As comfort, she reached up and rubbed her thumb and forefinger along the smoothness of the Spark, feeling its warmth.

Jasmine made herself stop at a distance that was between the two, trying not to fidget while both men acknowledged each other with a cool formality that was heavily tinged in mutual apprehension. She noticed that both Leon and Kai were similar in how they held themselves, projecting an air of mysterious regality that made her feel more out of their league than she had ever been before.

"I am Leon Exousia, current High Lord of Hellenia. I assume Jasmine has apprised you of the situation at hand?"

"She has, and I came as soon as I heard. Kai Witan, Prince of Apelion, the eastern quadrant of Draconia." He bowed his head, but his eyes never left Leon's person as he did so. "I understand your friend has vanished?"

Leon took a moment to adjust a cufflink. "He has, unexpectedly. I've known this person for much of my life. No matter where he roams, we both know that there will be no time that we are not in contact with each other." His gold eyes cut over to Kai, then. "In consulting many methods of divination that are used to tie the Hellenian people together for many generations, it is thought that he is where we cannot reach... which is within your jurisdiction."

"There are problems with that assumption, Lord Exousia. No Hellenian can even find the passage to Draconia unless escorted by a Draconian themselves. And even if there were any of my companions with the inclination to extend an uncanny welcome to your friend, where would we meet him to instigate this?"

"Elliot often comes to Hyperion for quiet introspection, which is a space both of our races can freely occupy. It is not as presumptuous as you say to come to this conclusion."

Kai furrowed his brow and placed his hands behind his back. "Strange that someone who isn't the Prime was allowed special privileges to dally on sacred ground before the Transfer of Passage occurred."

Leon's eyes flashed in warning. "Are you implying a lapse of judgment on my decision to afford him passage?"

"No more than you are implying foul play on me and my people."

Jasmine tried curbing her nervous ticks, but it was impossible when the tension could be cut with a sharp knife. She had never seen Leon so frazzled before. Even though everything was said with precise diction, a straight back, and poise that didn't waver, she knew him well enough to know that he was on edge. Kai was handling it well, but she could also tell that his charity was wearing thin. She supposed that with the amount of pride Draconians had for their sense of honor, it was hard for him to hear this from Leon.

"Well, then... this would be a good time to clear the air, right?"

CHAPTER THIRTY-THREE

All three of them turned around, and Jasmine tried to make sense of what she was seeing. Ciaran had joined them, but he wasn't with Nemeer or Fouzia.

"I hope I'm not late." The Draconian sauntered up to them, colored petals drifting in the air along with his footsteps. Once he got within a safe distance of them, he stopped, and let the person he was escorting fall to his knees. Jasmine was already making her way over when she was stopped by the tip of what looked to be a spearhead pointed directly at her face.

"Don't worry, he's fine. Just a little groggy." Ciaran glanced down at Elliot, who was slowly blinking as if he couldn't quite pull himself out of a deep sleep. "I hope you understand why I had to subdue him."

Both Leon and Kai were frozen, staring in different levels of shock at the newcomer and the scene before them. Leon's eyes were locked onto Elliot in a mixture of horror and relief, while Kai's put-together mask fell completely apart as he looked with his mouth agape at Ciaran.

"... what... what have you done? Why have-"

Ciaran waved his hand in the air casually, as if he wasn't currently destroying his longtime friend's whole perception of him with every second that passed. "Kai, really. I *told* you that your naiveté was a concern. But, thanks to the Prime showing up, I really didn't know how valuable of a contingency I had." He grinned widely at Jasmine, nodding.

"Release him now, and I'll do you the honor of sparing you any suffering when I kill you." Leon said in a voice that seemed much too calm for the situation at hand, edged with intent that made Jasmine shiver in the aftermath. Ciaran's reaction was to laugh heartily, unphased.

"Oh, I'm sure... if I didn't know that you wouldn't dare throw away the right to the Flame just to get your hands on me. So why don't you spare me the dramatics while I let you know what you want to hear from me, yes? We don't have much time, anyway; Fouzia and Nemeer should be arriving soon, and this will *really* become more of a party than I want it to be."

Jasmine just looked down at Elliot in concern, and when he met her eyes, she gave him a small smile. She was glad to see him physically unharmed, but his sluggishness was a great concern. *What the hell happened to you?*

"I often come to Hyperion myself, you know. It's just *fascinating* that this is one of the only things the gods left us. Draconia is beautiful, and I have no doubt Hellenia is as well. But they're gilded prisons, with this mountain as the lock with the key hidden within it. And I yearn for freedom." Ciaran casually flipped and caught the spearhead he carried in his palm. "*True* freedom, not the bits that are meted out to us every few hundred years. Wouldn't you agree?"

He was met with silence from everyone, and he took that as a license to continue. "The Prime is the closest thing we have to breaking these silly chains that dare to hold us. Unfortunately, the last Prime failed to do so, like all others before her. She was a beautiful thing, however. What was her name? Selene?" Ciaran's purple eyes slid to Leon. "I think I remember my father saying as such. He really thought that he had her... until it was *your* father that ended up with her heart in the end."

Jasmine felt as though she could see Leon become more tense by the moment, and her own sense of foreboding weight didn't ease the more Ciaran blithely continued his monologue.

"She liked to come to Hyperion as well. I suppose it's a place of comfort for any Prime who traveled its unique trails to the summit. I never interacted with her on my visits. I just paid attention to the particular shrub she often picked leaves from before returning to Hellenia. I knew enough to figure out that she was using it for tea that can't be found anywhere else. Oh! Kai, I should have thought to bring some to you as well; you would have appreciated having something so rare added to your marvelous collection, right?"

Kai blinked, looking like it was hard to remember how to speak. "Tea, Ciaran? This is what you see fit to tell me on the heels of instigating such a betrayal?"

"You like tea the most out of the four of us. Why *wouldn't* I let you know? Now, where was I," he tapped the spearhead thoughtfully on his lips for a moment. "I decided to try a little alchemy with a theory of mine; it involved adding a near undetectable compound to the bush itself that included residue from this spear here.... which, if you don't know, is the famed Spear of Longinus. Serendipitous to find this in my family's vault, actually. Given a Hellenian's origin, I assumed that those of angelic blood wouldn't react kindly to ingesting something that defaced the Son of God."

Jasmine finally found the courage to speak. "You killed Leon's father."

Ciaran looked blankly at her for a moment. "Did I? Oh... well, if so, then that's an unfortunate side effect. Selene was my only target, seeing as though she chose to become Hellenian. I just needed a new roll of the dice, a chance to convince a new Prime to go the extra mile for me." He smiled at her, and Jasmine swallowed tightly. "So, I guess my question for you Jasmine... is whether or not you'll make all my hard work worth it. Will you choose between these two?" He gestured towards Kai and Leon. "Or forge your own path to free us all?"

Suddenly, the strange conversation that took place between them following her abrupt kidnapping was brought into focus. Ciaran truly did spend time researching obscure lore and obsessing over what lies in the heart of Hyperion, and it led them to this moment. Jasmine didn't like being put on the spot for something that held more in the balance than what she initially bargained for, and she didn't want to go along with anything Ciaran had concocted.

Nothing's fucking easy. I don't know why I tried tricking myself into thinking it would be.

A large shadow was cast quickly over them all, and they looked up to see a pair of dragons circling above, gradually lowering altitude in preparation to land. Jasmine recognized both of them to be Fouzia and Nemeer, and a bit of hope came to life within her.

"Listen, I still think you're crazy for risking all of this, but..." she looked down at Elliot again, and shoved her frustration with Ciaran aside. "If it means you let him go back home, I'm willing to do whatever I can to break this cycle."

Jasmine looked back at Kai and Leon, seeing both of their unreadable gazes on her. She didn't know if they considered her complicit or an unfortunate chess piece just by trying to negotiate with him, but it seemed to her that everything rested on her shoulders.

"For what it's worth, I do have faith in you, Jasmine." Ciaran said softly, his gaze losing a bit of the manic sheen it had during his entire tirade. "I could feel from the moment we met that you would be different."

Jasmine nodded, feeling uncomfortable for being the focus of what had to be Draconian obsession. She knew that he could only see her as a shiny object to complete his impracticable goals. Kai at least took small steps to consider her as an individual and not just a prize, which made her appreciate him in the end.

"However..."

She furrowed her brow in apprehension to his yet unspoken caveat.

"Draconians don't rely on faith alone."

Before she could find any sort of motor function in her own limbs, Ciaran reached down, grabbed Elliot by his hair, and slit his throat.

CHAPTER THIRTY-FOUR

Things seemed to shift in slow motion for Jasmine in the moments that followed.

The scream that she couldn't emote outside of her head rang loudly in her mind, staring in horror at the blood that coated the leaves and petals of the flowers that surrounded Elliot's limp body.

There was the sound of another weight hitting the ground just behind her, and when she was able to tear her eyes away from the scene in front of her, she saw that Leon had fallen to his knees as if he were shot.

Kai was shouting, but she couldn't understand what it was that he was saying. It was if her mind had trouble grasping onto the words that left his lips, but the anger and pain was easy to intuit.

Nemeer and Fouzia had rushed in finally, having shed their dragon forms only to gaze upon the aftermath with mixed looks of shock and horror on their faces. While the larger man approached Kai and placed a hand on his shoulder in an attempt to ground him, Fouzia wasted no time marching up to

Ciaran in fury just to lay a wicked right hook to his cheek that sent him falling to the ground.

"What have you fucking *done*, you..." she stopped mid-rant, glaring down at him with her piercing blue eyes that seemed to be overwhelmed by too much emotion. "I can't believe you. I just... *can't* believe you."

Jasmine caught movement out of the corner of her eye, seeing that Leon had started to stir. He chose to crawl, making his way through the flowers until he got to Elliot's fallen body, where he folded himself upon his knees and cradled his friend's upper body in his lap. She was still frozen in place, the deceptively calm breeze brushing along her skin as her chest ached every moment she looked upon the horrific scene. A part of her still couldn't comprehend what happened; it wasn't like she was accustomed to seeing people get killed in front of her. But as she looked down at Leon curling his upper body protectively over Elliot, long hair shielding his face from everyone else as he grieved, the weight of finality was settling over her quickly.

Ciaran was picking himself up off of the ground now, rubbing the side of his face. "You're lethal at more than just the bow, I see."

Fouzia was pulling back to unleash another hit, only to have her fist engulfed by Nemeer's much larger palm. With him being uncharacteristically somber, she huffed and didn't try again, allowing Nemeer to walk past her and place Ciaran's hands behind his back to put in what looked to be an elaborate set of cuffs. For what it was worth, the prince didn't even try to resist, and Jasmine figured that it had something to do with the fact that his larger companion would have put a stop to that faster than anything Fouzia could have done in her fury.

Eventually, Leon began to stand. He took Elliot's body up with him, cradling him in his arms as his wings flexed once, buffeting the air with a pop before settling. When he turned to face them, Jasmine took one step back. His face was impassive despite the redness in his eyes, and the evidence of freshly shed tears shone on his cheeks. But he was more shuttered and intimidating than he'd ever been, switching his hard, golden gaze to each of the Draconians.

"You have three days to prepare for war."

Jasmine blinked, and then turned her head to look at Kai. He met her gaze with his own, his face pale and highly transparent to the trepidation that he was feeling in the wake of Leon's announcement.

She was struck with the urge to console him, somehow. But she was frustrated at her utter uselessness in the wake of everything that happened. Jasmine didn't even know where she stood between them, or what she should do.

Leon turned away from them then, making his way back to the portal to Hellenia without another word. Jasmine looked after him dumbly, her feet feeling like they were encased in concrete shoes and unable to move. Movement to her right signified Nemeer walking past her with Ciaran in his grip, maneuvering him to stand next to Kai and now Fouzia who had relocated herself next to him.

With a final glance to her, Kai fished what looked to be a jade pendant on a red string from his pocket and rubbed his thumb in a pattern along its surface. Within the space of a blink, the four of them had vanished.

Logically, Jasmine knew it was due to the very imminent emergency that had settled upon them that they all made an abrupt exit. But combined with the shock of everything and her sense of helplessness, it felt like she was abandoned.

Making her feet unroot themselves from the ground, she was able to move to catch the portal back to Hellenia before it closed, not knowing where else to go.

CHAPTER THIRTY-FIVE

"I'm sorry, Jasmine."

She wanted to shrug but couldn't quite get the gumption up to do so. It was taking everything within Jasmine not to simply slip the few inches it would take to immerse her head into the steamy waters of the lavender-scented pool she was in and not come back up. It had only been a day and a half since Leon had declared war on the Draconians, and all of Hellenia was in an uproar in preparation for it. It made Jasmine alternate between panic and states of disassociation, the latter of which was settled upon her now as her body buoyed listlessly in the hot water that surrounded her. Sustina was gracious as ever, offering her shelter at Haven and making sure that she had everything that she needed without question, as well as offering her a shoulder to cry on when everything continually hit Jasmine like a truck.

Despite everything Sustina offered, Jasmine would much rather have been curled up on Kim's worn couch with a glass of cheap wine and finally watching one of those movies that she tried so hard to get her to watch what seemed like ages ago.

God, what if I had taken her up on her offer that day, instead of going to the library? Would I even have run into Leon? Could I have somehow avoided all of this even happening? Jasmine tried stopping her downward spiral, but it was near impossible to do so when the cold, lifeless Spark laid on her chest as a reminder that there was more to the untenable situation than before.

She couldn't go back home.

As Elliot had mentioned before when she first stepped foot on the holy mountain, the right to the Flame would become forfeit to both races should any blood be spilled on the land. Jasmine didn't make the connection that it also meant that passage from Hellenia to her realm would be shuttered as a consequence. When Leon informed her of that, she felt like she couldn't breathe. And unfortunately, she knew that the High Lord was in no position to comfort her in the wake of his best friend's murder and an upcoming battle. Not knowing where else to go, she found herself at Haven's doorstep, where Sustina took one look at her and ushered her in its halls without question.

"I just... feel so fucking *helpless*," Jasmine said. "I never asked to be the Prime. But I tried like hell to get things handled despite it, because I didn't have a choice. And now I'm an ex-Prime, which means nothing except 'useless' in an official sounding way. I watched Elliot *die* in front of me and didn't do shit but stare. I keep thinking about my family and friends who will think I've been abducted. There's gonna be more people getting hurt, more people dying. What am I supposed to do with that?"

Sustina simply sat there with her hands folded in her lap, a calming presence despite the look of concern on her delicate features. "I am not sure if there is anything you're 'supposed' to do with that. It is simply how the cards have fallen, I'm afraid.

But, despite how dire things seem, I hesitate to agree with the assessment that you are worthless."

"Well, it's hard not to think of it that way. My only purpose for being here is gone now."

"Was it your *only* purpose? You were someone before you were the Prime, Jasmine. That hasn't been stripped from you. And while you may be isolated from your world, you aren't isolated from those of us here that care for you."

Jasmine bitterly couldn't stop herself from thinking about how much of a fool she was that she was isolated from those of her own kind because of her entanglement with Leon. "You sure about that?"

"I am. And if I only have to speak for myself, then I will. But..." Sustina sighed. "I feel I must beg your patience with the High Lord. He is too clouded with rage and grief to show you for himself."

Jasmine sat on her words, turning away from Sustina and letting the warm water filter through her fingers as she moved to glide through the scented pool thoughtfully. She understood, as much as she could, the pain Leon was going through. But it also hurt that Leon didn't seem to allow her past the emotional wall he erected to have her help him. "How much patience do I have to give this guy, though?"

"Have you tried conversing with him since returning from Hyperion?"

"He's, uh... not the most approachable person right now." Jasmine felt embarrassed to admit that she wasn't doing the best job at making herself feel better with her own avoidance. "But I guess I should."

Sustina looked on in pity. "It may help you both. Leon has a habit of falling in on himself at the slightest hint of disruption. The only one who was successful at pulling him out of it was Elliot. But it doesn't mean that I think you shouldn't try. I've told you before, when you were in this very spot, that you should know your worth. It is more imperative than ever that you take that to heart."

Jasmine shook her head, remaining silent. She remembered those words, but her journey had been full of so many twists and turns that it was hard for her to put it into practice. *How the hell can I be confident in my worth when everyone around me keeps telling me what it is?*

"Well. I suppose I should stop wallowing and get to it, then. It's not like I have the time to avoid it any more than I already have." She made her way to the edge of the pool and pulled herself out of it, taking the towel Sustina had ready for her. "Thank you. You've had to deal with my grumpiness this whole time, and you handled it with grace just like with everything you do. If I don't seem grateful, I'm really sorry. It's just been... a lot."

"There's no need for apologies." Sustina smiled kindly, grasping Jasmine's hands in a comforting manner. "I said I was here to be in your corner, and I meant it. That hasn't changed simply because your title has."

Jasmine kept those words and the warmth they brought close to her chest as she got dropped off back at the manor that looked more imposing now. Taking a deep breath, she made her way up the walkway and pushed open the heavy door, looking around the foyer.

At the ball, Leon made mention to the fact that he did have bodyguards, but they always remained unseen unless needed. Now, it seemed as though they had dropped their proverbial invisibility cloaks and made their presence known. Tall, imposing Hellenians dressed in all black save for a hint of red on their person were stationed conspicuously throughout the manor, and it made Jasmine extremely nervous. She couldn't help but feel acutely aware of the fact that she likely wasn't worthy to be there anymore, even though none of them lifted a finger to stop her.

But as she progressed through the manor to find the man she was looking for, Jasmine considered that it felt worse that she could move through them as if she didn't exist at all.

Eventually, she reached the room she was looking for, and pushed open the door with a hand that shook slightly. It was a different study than the one she was familiar with, a grand desk the focal point of the room with a large window facing the courtyard right behind it. Leon sat at the desk there, his eyes going over documents and murmuring to a man on his left that looked more decorated than the men she had seen before. On the right was Viviane, standing with her hands clasped in front of her and watching the two men interact thoughtfully, until she noticed Jasmine had arrived. Leon was next, looking up and blinking at her.

Jasmine hated that she held her breath and wholly expected to be dismissed.

"Maltrien, Viviane; please give us a few moments, if you will."

Both of them bowed their heads politely, making to leave. Jasmine stepped out of the way so they could exit through the door, and she caught Viviane's gaze for a moment before she left.

Perhaps Jasmine was looking too much into a moment that lasted only a second or two, but she felt as if the high priestess was trying to convey something to her.

"Jasmine?"

Pulled out of her thoughts by Leon's voice, she turned her attention back to him as he stepped out from behind the desk to approach her. At the last moment, Jasmine opened her arms to be engulfed by a hug that she melted into, even though the wall of desperation and pain was still palpable in every touch.

"I'm sorry I didn't go with you to Elliot's memorial. It... I..." Jasmine tripped over her words. She couldn't bear Leon thinking that she wasn't able to support him, or that she wasn't bothered by Elliot's death. But she also couldn't tell him that a lot of her decision was wrapped up in her own insecurities about intruding on something sacred to Hellenians when she didn't have the label of Prime anymore to justify it.

"It's fine." Leon touched the side of her cheek softly. "Elliot's father was in attendance of course, and I fear he might have misdirected ire at you had you attended. His opinion of humans after his son started emulating them leaves much to be desired. Things are fraught enough as they stand."

Jasmine nodded, pulling back a bit to look up at him. "I wish there was a way to fix this."

Leon studied her for a moment, and gently withdrew. He walked over to the picture window and stared out to the garden beyond, his figure striking against the light that entered. "Do you say that on my behalf, or the Draconians?"

Jasmine bit her lower lip, feeling like she already messed up before she even started. "Why can't it be both?"

Silence stretched between them, and so did the gulf that Jasmine had been feeling ever since Elliot had gone missing. She felt desperate to bridge the gap, but she couldn't seem to find anything to grab hold of to do so.

"Because unfortunately, Jasmine, my heart is not as large as yours. I've suffered great losses in my life to date; Rina was foreshadowing, although she remains physically present to remind me over and over again of that loss. My father followed, and shortly after, so did Selene."

Leon's fingers traced the paneled glass in front of him, his talons clinking slightly upon the surface. "The one who was there to pull me out of each shard of despair was Elliot. He was my constant in a world that continued to shift out of control."

Jasmine watched him tap the glass thoughtfully with a finger before letting his hand fall to his side. She wanted to say the right words, but she had none.

"This war is for Hellenia's honor. There would be no way for me to keep the people's faith in my position as its leader if I opted to negotiate with the Draconians in the wake of such a violation. I would expect the same had the shoe been on the other foot. This is how it is, and it is a burden to all who are in power to accept it."

Leon turned back to face her then, and his gold eyes were hard, laced with determination steeped in the anguish he had been feeling for many years.

"But to ensure that anything remotely precious is ripped from their fingers, to take perverse pleasure in knowing their last smiles were squandered to the depths of the earth they can no longer claim, to raze the skies with their blood that will fall like rain... *that*, will be for me alone."

It scared her to see him like this. She knew that Leon was more than just the overly polite, fashionably picky person he mostly presented himself to be, but ever since experiencing a hint of his darker side thanks to the Rut combined with the unfortunate aftermath of Elliot's death, Jasmine was feeling overwhelmed.

Leon seemed to pick up what was in her expression, and he closed his eyes and let a close-lipped, doleful smile splay on his lips. Seeing it made tears spring to Jasmine's eyes, which he moved from his place at the window to come over to her and carefully wipe them off of her cheeks. For what it was worth, she managed not to flinch at his touch, but she felt like the damage had already been done.

She couldn't reach him. No matter how much she cared for him, it wasn't enough.

"You've shed too many tears on my behalf, Jasmine. Let these be the last."

And then he was moving around her, exiting and leaving her standing in the middle of the room feeling more alone than she did before.

CHAPTER THIRTY-SIX

Jasmine didn't know how long she stood in the middle of the study, breathing deeply and trying to get herself under some semblance of control. The beautiful, twilight-like light streaming in from the window cast a soft glow through the room, and her eyes focused on the errant dust particles she could see floating within it. Just having something mundane to distract herself with like that finally made the tears stop flowing and her heart stop feeling like it was going to break in two.

She had just started feeling semi-normal when there was a knock on the door behind her, and shortly after, a regrettably familiar figure stepped through.

"Ah... I expected to find Leon here."

"Just missed him," Jasmine said shortly, turning her face away from the woman and taking a few more steps to put some distance between them, swiping at her face to make sure all evidence of tears was gone. *I can't have her of all people seeing me like this.*

"I see." Rina's voice was measured and reserved, but still held that sugary quality that Jasmine remembered hearing that night at the ball. "Forgive any perceived rudeness in my question, but why are you here?"

Jasmine let a thousand responses to that fly through her mind, almost all of them being highly inappropriate, before settling down. "I don't know, really. Why are *you* here?"

"My uncle happens to lead the Hellenian military, and I last heard that he was to meet with the High Lord. This room is where battle negotiations are handled."

"Ah, cool. Well, I'm assuming that they'll be back eventually. Maybe they broke for lunch or something." Jasmine turned around, facing Rina. Bitterly, she noted that she and Leon must have made the most handsome couple. "I'm gonna head out now, so... you be easy."

She was just to the door before Rina spoke again.

"You should be grateful that you are no longer the Prime. Feeling this disappointment now has saved you an incredibly long lifetime of being in a ceremonial relationship with someone who will always hold you at arm's reach."

Jasmine kept her gaze on the door in front of her, noting the intricate patterns in the bronze door handle. "I guess you'd know something about that, huh?"

"I would. If you had been around to see Leon's father, you would fully understand why Leon is the way he is despite his best efforts to present otherwise." There was movement as Rina casually walked across the room. "Lord Vretiel was an intimidating man. He was a strong and silent type, could cut one down with a glance alone, and held true to his values and his people at all costs. Even after becoming soft due to Selene's influence, it is how the brunt of Hellenians choose to revere him."

Jasmine reluctantly turned to look at Rina, finding the woman had taken a seat on the edge of the desk.

"Leon remains oblivious to how easily he can seduce someone. Unfortunately, with that lack of awareness comes lack of emotional care. I thought I could change that in him... much like how Selene seemed to change that in his father." Rina placed her delicate hands in her lap. "I was wrong."

"Why are you telling me this? It's not like Leon and I are a thing, anyway."

"Because I've seen the way you look at him. I see the frustration in your eyes, even now as you try to conceal it. You may not have the best view of me, and I wouldn't blame you. I abhor the woman I was when I was with him." Rina sighed and looked off to the side. "I did foolish things to get a rise out of him, thinking that if I couldn't have what I truly wanted from him, then I would settle for making him as desperate for me as I was for him. It was... destructive, in the end."

Silence stretched between them before Rina looked back at Jasmine.

"If you are here to save him, I am here to tell you to protect your energy. Take this circumstance as a boon; you have no further obligation to Leon and neither does he to you. Trouble yourself no longer."

Jasmine thought of the last words Leon spoke to her, and how they matched with what Rina was telling her now. Her heart felt squeezed too tight, and she nodded stiffly before finally leaving the room. She was on autopilot, moving through the quiet corridors of the manor before stepping back out of the front door, making her way down the steps and to the road without much of a care of where she was going.

"Jasmine."

She blinked, turning her head to the left, and saw Viviane standing nearby, nearly blended in with the foliage and the shadow that was cast over the yard. She only managed to raise an eyebrow in confusion before the high priestess walked past her, motioning to be followed.

"Your time here has ended. I must return you to Hyperion."

"What?" Jasmine said incredulously, moving to catch up with her anyway. Viviane's long legs glided effortlessly to her personal carriage, opening the door and looking pointedly back at her to enter.

"The path narrows. I must do my part to place you upon it before it vanishes. Come."

Knowing well enough not to question the vague musings of a priestess, Jasmine kept her mouth shut and simply entered the carriage. The two of them made their way out of the city proper again, with Jasmine feeling a bone-weary ache in how she still managed to be yanked around by powers she couldn't see. She kept her thoughts close to her chest as they arrived back to the forest that held the portal, allowing Viviane to go through the motions lighting the candles and tracing the runes.

"Pay attention to the patterns. This will be the last you see of me for some time."

Jasmine made herself focus enough to commit the runes to memory, watching them glow as Viviane activated them. "Why?"

The priestess didn't speak until the portal was opened, and the shimmery image of Hyperion came into view.

"I am forbidden to speak on any of my visions, lest they not come to pass. I am, at my core, a watcher of powers far greater than I. While consulting the universe for Elliot, it gave me myriad premonitions, a legion of outcomes. The only thing central to all of them was you."

Jasmine's hands turned clammy. "I'm not even the Prime anymore."

Viviane gave her a wan smile in return. "It seems as though the gods do not care."

Not having anything to say to that, Jasmine simply followed through to the other side staring at the snow-covered ground that inexplicably gave way to colorful flowers and bountiful trees that hardly ceased. She looked back just in time to see the portal close behind her, then down at the defunct Spark that she still wore around her neck for whatever reason. Then she proceeded to scream in frustration at the top of her lungs, kicking rocks, stomping around, and overall letting out every single bit of absolute dissatisfaction she held at the way her life was being yanked around.

"What the *fuck do you want me to do??*" Jasmine yelled to the trees. "This shit is *not* my problem!"

The mountain itself only answered in a sigh that came in the form of an unseasonably warm breeze that didn't match the light dusting of snow at her feet.

Resisting the urge to pull her hair out, Jasmine made her way back up the mountain, angry with no outlet except to feel the burn in her legs from the workout she was subjecting them to. She kept going, pushing through foliage, taking turns she didn't have to do before, and followed her weary heart just to end up at the clearing she knew all too well. Somewhere beyond it, upwards to the peak with wisps of clouds obscuring it, was where she thought she would go in order to commune with the Flame.

Would it even accept me now, as the pact has been broken?

Sucking her teeth in exasperation, she turned away and instead fiddled with the armillary spheres on the portal nearby. Perhaps it was out of spite that she did so, or maybe it was where the universe wanted her to be all along. Regardless, Jasmine stepped through to Kai's courtyard in Apelion, breathing in the scent of cherry blossoms and fresh air.

She couldn't reach Leon, that was certain. But perhaps she could help another.

CHAPTER THIRTY-SEVEN

When Jasmine came across Kai, he was looking just as bad as she felt. He was sitting listlessly in the aviary, birds chirping gaily in juxtaposition to the absolute look of despondence on his features. He didn't even move to acknowledge her at first when she sat next to him, opting to stare at the same spot on the ground for a long time.

"None of this is what I wanted."

"You could say that again. It's a bit of a clusterfuck."

Kai snorted in agreement, straightening his posture a little and placing his hands on the bench on either side of him. "It should embarrass me to have you see me like this, a shell of my usual self."

Jasmine raised an eyebrow. "You still concerned about appearances when y'all are at the brink of a whole war?"

"Force of habit." He looked askance at Jasmine. "It distracts me from what Ciaran has done."

Jasmine winced at the flashback of seeing Elliot's throat cut open in front of her as easily as one may rip open an envelope. "Unforgivable."

Kai got up from his seat and took a few steps, clasping his hands behind him. "Ciaran is currently being held in a single cell at the place where our quadrants meet, awaiting trial. But the outcome of said trial will be the same; he will be executed directly following the eradication of his ancestral line. His vault will be redistributed amongst his former constituents, and a new leader of Notos will be installed."

Jasmine stared in horror at Kai's figure, shocked by the weight of that decision. "Are you serious?"

"Draconians are raised with the knowledge that we are not individuals; we are representations of all those who came before us, and we uphold that honor through our actions and how we live. Ciaran spat on that the moment he did what he did. He knows what awaits."

"And... what about you? How do you feel about it?"

A few birds flit from branch to branch, darting through the space between them completely unbothered by the somber mood. "I feel like I'm losing a brother." Kai's fingers tightened into fists at the small of his back. "He was always the most radical of us four, but never did I imagine he was capable of something so extreme. We grew up together, trained together, laughed and cried together... to watch all of that burn to ashes..."

Deciding to take a page out of Sustina's book, Jasmine sighed. "Are you able to see him? Like... yeah, I know he's a traitor or whatever, but if you get some closure, then maybe it would be easier."

"Or it would simply drive home the fact that a person dear to me will leave my life and the history of Draconia as soon as the war is over. Nemeer and Fouzia are doing better than I in distancing themselves, although I know the pain strikes them just as hard." He tilted his head up to the sky filtered through the clear panes of the aviary. "I wish I was stronger."

Standing up from her spot on the bench, she walked over to Kai and put her hand on his shoulder. "Strength looks different for different people. If what you want is to see him, then don't talk yourself out of it just because your friends have, or you think you gotta put on a brave face. Save all of that energy for the battle that's coming and get all this messy shit out now."

Kai turned to face her, and she was caught off guard from all of the emotion that was evident in his face. He might not have been human, but Jasmine could clearly read and understand everything that was presented in his eyes in that moment.

"Would you accompany me?"

Before, just the thought of encountering Ciaran again would make her uneasy. But now, she felt driven by the need to help Kai carry his burden. "Of course. Are we flying there?"

"You seem rather attached to flight. Did we create a monster, Jasmine?" Kai joked despite the heavy atmosphere, causing Jasmine to grin and shrug.

"Just asking. It's not every day you get to fly with a dragon, you know." She stepped up next to him, following him out of the aviary. "We can save it for another time." *As long as you don't get yourself killed in this war, that is.*

The portal Kai opened dumped them right on the outskirts of an intimidating fortress. Much like Fouzia's homeland of Apartica, it was built inside the cliff of the mountain itself, a barren, tan colored edifice that was much smaller in appearance than the energy it presented. Cool winds buffeted their figures as they walked along a winding path, leading them to an inlaid passageway that shielded them from the sun and other elements alike. The echo of their footsteps was eerie to Jasmine's ears, but she held tight to Kai's hand as they moved through the dimly lit building. Eventually, they came to a cell that was lit through a square-cut skylight open to the elements, with bars etched through with symbols and designs that

Jasmine supposed kept a Draconian in place. Ciaran lounged on the single cot within, looking much like he was sitting in his own living room and not awaiting his future execution.

"I didn't expect anyone to visit me. Warms my heart, really." Ciaran sat up and faced the door, his lavender eyes scanning Kai before flitting over to Jasmine. "Two of my favorite people, no less."

Jasmine frowned at Ciaran's convivial attitude that he fielded like a well-oiled suit of armor even now. "You're mighty happy about being in your position, I see."

"How is it different than the one I was born into? Yes, smaller, perhaps. Quite lacking on the scenery. And I *do* miss being able to choose my own food. But overall, I've always been imprisoned."

Kai's jaw flexed, but he didn't say anything. He just stared at his friend, eyes frank with all of the things he couldn't vocalize. Ciaran stood up then and walked over to the bars, raising his hand as if to lean against them. When it came within an inch of the enclosure, sparks flew and popped against his fingertips, causing him to flinch and drop his hand to lay at his side.

"Kai, it hurts me to see you like this. But I know in the end, I made the right decision."

Kai shook his head. "You've forfeited everything. Your kingdom, the Flame, us... I know you think this was worth it, but it wasn't."

"It was."

"It was *not*."

"It WAS!" Ciaran raised his voice so that it echoed off of the stone walls. "Open your eyes! I've lost nothing but fancy illusions. I seek to strip the walls that hold us."

"That was what earning the Flame would have gotten us!"

Ciaran scoffed, turning his head away from them and looking up to the sky. "Who, or what, decides that *dragons* must earn the right to be free? We've been culled by the gods thanks to the mistakes of our ancestors, and it is due time we railed against it all. The Hellenians may feel differently, considering they were born supplicants. But *us*? Who deserve all that the heavens and earth have to offer?" He sighed. "If my life is to be sacrificed so that we can do better than this ridiculous cycle, then it will be the greatest thing I'll have ever done."

Kai clinched his hands into fists at his side, averting his gaze momentarily. "Why did I come here?"

"Why did you?"

Both men stared at each other then, on opposite sides in more ways than one, but Jasmine could see that there was genuine care in Ciaran's gaze despite the mania that could glaze it when he spoke on such things. Eventually, Kai took a deep breath, straightening his shoulders.

"Because I love you, Ciaran. Losing you is like losing a limb. This freedom you speak of... it doesn't matter if all of us aren't there to fly through it together. *Nothing* matters if we're not all together." His voice cracked a little, and Jasmine bit her lower lip when she heard it slip.

"Kai, I..." Ciaran paused, then shook his head. "More things matter than just us. I know, strange coming from a Draconian. But if there was ever a time to be less self-centered, to expand our horizons, it is now." He slid his gaze over to Jasmine. "I trust in the Prime."

Please don't. I'm not even the fucking Prime anymore thanks to the horseshit you pulled. She kept her thoughts to herself, watching as Kai gave another wistful glance to his longtime friend before turning to leave.

"No trust in the rest of us? We have a war to clean up, thanks to you."

Ciaran tilted his head back and laughed. "I don't need trust to know that it won't be *our* blood running in rivulets down Hyperion's pristine hills."

Leaving the prison and coming back to Apelion was a somber experience, yet it was strangely void of the dread that permeated their initial departure. Jasmine could tell that a part of Kai was at peace having seen Ciaran, but he obviously was not happy with the outcome. She couldn't blame him; it was horrifying as an outsider to understand what was to become of Ciaran. Knowing how solitary the royals were in general and the way they all grew up together as a way to alleviate that underlying loneliness made it something unfathomable. She already refused to think too much about how she was cut off from her loved ones in her own realm.

"I'm not gonna ask you if you're alright. But I *will* ask if you want my company."

Kai looked over at her, his brown eyes grateful behind the internal conflict he was wading through. "I'm not in a place to refuse it. Thank you."

She followed him through his colorful palace to his quarters, a sprawling room with lacquered furniture, and a circular bed scattered with pillows. Jasmine moved to sit herself in a chair nearby while Kai instructed one of his handmaidens to bring him some tea, watching as he sat down himself. "So, umm..."

"Yes?"

"Do you curl up in your dragon form on that bed every night? Is that why it's round?" She was finding it hard to stop her lips from twitching in laughter as she fielded her inquiry.

Kai looked over in confusion to the mattress in question. "I wouldn't even fit in this room if I tried it. But I also didn't realize until you said something that I still manage to curl up as if I were." His eyebrow raised at her barely contained giggles, cracking a smile himself. "Your laughter is healing."

"One thing my mom told me is that it's better to laugh than to cry, if at all possible. Things are messed up all around... in more ways than one," Jasmine sighed. "But it's alright to have a bit of levity to make it not seem so crushing."

Kai nodded in agreement, and a couple of handmaidens returned with the tea he requested. He poured two cups, handing Jasmine the delicate, nearly transparent demitasse steaming with liquid.

"What are you going to do?"

Jasmine stared into her tea before lifting it to her lips and taking a sip of the rich, earthy flavor. She didn't immediately reply, honestly thinking about it in length. She couldn't go back home, where she truly wanted to be. The truth of that stung in ways she couldn't let herself dwell upon, and admittedly, she was using the mess between the Hellenians and Draconians as a way to distract herself from that. Leon was unreachable, his mind only on revenge that Jasmine couldn't blame him for feeling despite her not knowing how to handle such intensity. And now, she sat beside Kai with his conundrum that she didn't initiate and couldn't fix, feeling powerless in the face of a war.

"Might feel cute and climb the rest of Hyperion tomorrow trying to find this Flame anyway, I dunno."

Kai blinked. "It's closed off to us, now. There is no reason for you to continue that pilgrimage."

"It's closed off to y'all. Nobody said anything about me. Since I don't relish having a front row seat to this war, I might as well occupy my time doing what I originally was summoned here to do." She took another sip. "Maybe Ciaran is onto something."

"If he is, then what do you hope to accomplish?"

Jasmine shrugged. "Not sure. I'll figure it out when I get there."

Kai studied her thoughtfully. "Jasmine..."

"Nope. Whatever it is, save it. Respectfully." She put her teacup down and got up, beginning to pace the room. "I literally have nothing to lose. If I go, and there's nothing there, then at least I'll know for myself. That's worth something. If there *is* something there that's sentient, then I might just cuss it out for putting me in this situation without my consent. Either way, I'm not sitting around and doing nothing. I plan to do shit on my own terms for once."

Kai finished his tea and stood, walking over to her. Jasmine couldn't help but brace herself for some sort of admonishment or advice she didn't ask for, considering what she had been subjected to the last few days. But instead, he placed his hands on her shoulders and gave her a reassuring smile.

"I was going to offer you the palace to rest before embarking on your journey. I don't intend on stopping you. I was simply curious as to your reasoning."

"... oh."

"You seem surprised."

Jasmine felt her cheeks get hot. "Well... yeah. Kinda got used to people putting in their two cents when it comes to me."

"As a Draconian who spent my entire life serving a purpose and has now seen you released from your own, I wouldn't dare to do anything but give you what you need to see it through." Kai let his hands drop from her arms. "And if you don't have need, then that's fine as well."

She stared at him in disbelief before barking out a little laugh. "Incredible."

"What is?"

Jasmine leaned forward and kissed him. This time, she lingered at the end of her impulse, and Kai moved his lips against hers in kind, turning his head slightly to the side to better accommodate her approach. "You telling me what I needed to hear, is all."

He made a sound of assent. "I'm glad. For the kiss and what you said." Kai's eyes searched along the features of her face. "This is the second time I've been caught off guard by your advances."

"But this time, you kissed me back."

"I did."

They stood there in the center of the room in pregnant silence, just before opening their mouths at the same time and interrupting each other. This caused Jasmine to start laughing again.

"Okay, listen. One of us has to be the smooth one here. I think it should be the dragon with literal hundreds of years of experience under his belt."

Kai chuckled, moving to rest his hands on her hips. "Jasmine, if there is anything about Draconians you should understand, is that we don't have to be smooth when we are given everything that we could ever want, and simply take what's left."

Jasmine bravely wrapped her arms around his neck. "Then what's stopping you from taking me?"

"Your humanity," he said without missing a beat. "You aren't a thing to be claimed. I understand that better, now."

"It's different when I'm actually *asking* you to take me, though." She giggled. "I *like* you, Kai. You're hot as fuck, too. And while I wasn't ever going to give myself to you just because you assumed that I was yours, I think we're both in need of a good distraction."

Kai trailed a finger along her jawline thoughtfully. "Yet another offer I am not in any place to refuse."

CHAPTER THIRTY-EIGHT

It was still dark when Jasmine opened her eyes, her body lying languidly on the plush bed next to Kai. The sex had been incredible, and she wasn't surprised. For as much as Kai had said that there was no need for smoothness, he didn't waste any time performing the most exquisite bout of cunnigulus before their bodies joined together, and it made Jasmine dizzy just thinking back on it. *I think I've gotten laid more times in the past few weeks than I have in the last couple of years of my life.*

She also liked the simplicity of it all. She knew they were on the same page, and it was a relief.

What she did *not* like, however, was the fact that Kai was evidently a blanket hoarder. Somehow, he had wrapped himself in it and curled up around a pillow, sleeping peacefully with his back towards her. Jasmine frowned, but she couldn't be annoyed at him for long. *It's really cute how he does actually curl up like a lizard.* She looked at him for a little bit longer before shuffling to the edge of the bed and standing up, gathering her clothes silently.

Sunrise would bring the start of the war. She figured she didn't want to be around for that part.

She was straightening her shirt when Kai rolled over to look at her, his eyes bright in the moonlight filtering in through the nearby window. "Already?"

"Yeah. Unless you wanted to go another round."

Kai chuckled, sitting up and combing the hair that had fallen loose from his ponytail back from his face. "You've already tempted me enough with this, Jasmine. It's fairly bittersweet to know that this is something I could have had all to myself, if things had progressed as it should have."

"You're confident that I would have chosen you in the end?"

"Yes."

"Bold. But I'll let it slide."

Kai shrugged easily, and Jasmine had to snort at that. *He may have progressed a lot, but I guess a Draconian will always be Draconian.* "Want to walk me back to the portal?"

"Of course."

The stroll across the grounds under the silvered moonlight was fairly romantic despite the circumstances. Jasmine's eyes looked up to the beautiful night sky, feeling lost in its depths as she had done many times before. Her fingers were intertwined with Kai's, and she could almost pretend that this was nothing out of the ordinary.

"Don't die, okay?"

"I won't." Kai said simply, kissing her hand before letting it go to adjust the spheres on the portal to point back to Hyperion. In just a few moments, the archway shimmered to life, and the hazy image of the mountain's summit could be seen on the other side. Both of them looked at it in silence, knowing that their paths would split as soon as Jasmine stepped over the threshold.

"I'll also do my best to make sure the Hellenian lord doesn't meet his end in this war."

Jasmine froze, Leon's words to her filtering back into her mind in frightening clarity. "You know he's not gonna be as gracious in return, right?"

"I'm aware. He is operating off of vengeance married with grief, not glory." Kai slid his knowing gaze to her eyes. "But I know that you'd rather see him alive at the end of this. Consider it my gift to you for the grace you've given me."

She pursed her lips together and swallowed, having nothing to say to that. Kai smirked, reaching out to touch her cheek.

"Love from exceptional humans like you moves mountains. Perhaps it will move this ancient one yet." He stepped back, folding his hands behind him. "Good luck, Jasmine."

It was hard for her to turn away from him and cross over. It was even harder for her not to instinctively look back at him before crossing the summit and scouring the area until she found a faint pathway leading up, where the trees became scarce and rocks were abundant along the cliffs.

It was embarrassing to still be attached to Leon despite all of the convoluted things that had happened between them since she first came to Hellenia. And yet, the growing fondness she had for Kai wasn't impeded by that fact at all. Her entire upbringing, up to and including her previous responsibility as the designated Prime, told her that her heart would know who to choose.

Jasmine was quickly coming to the realization that perhaps some of the things she was raised on were lies. She wondered if it was something about Hyperion that made her contemplate these things, or if it was just the solitude and physical exertion she put out while climbing the heights required to get to her destination that caused her to do some soul searching. Either way, it was nothing but her thoughts and determination to reach a foregone goal as company, moving on through wisps of clouds that brushed the mountain's face.

Time never mattered on Hyperion, but it didn't even cross Jasmine's mind at all until she paused to gasp for air at the jagged entrance to a cave right in front of her. Her thighs burned, she was sure she was developing a blister somewhere on the sole of her left foot, and she could have sat right down on the hard ground and considered it a welcome reprieve.

But even though the cool, lifeless glass that once held the sacred Spark brushed against her chest as a reminder of what had already been lost, Jasmine felt drawn inside to see what awaited her. She kept moving, the light disappearing behind her as she reached her hand out to feel along the jagged edges of the rock face, slowing her pace so she didn't trip over anything in the darkness.

There was a moment where she thought there was nothing there. The entrance was but a pinprick of light behind her, offering no solace to what might await her within. But eventually, the wall she was leaning against fell away, and no matter how far she reached to find it, her fingers no longer brushed it.

Shit, I hope this isn't an edge I'm going to walk off to my death. Jasmine shuffled forward, listening for any evidence of a drop by following the scattering of pebbles in her wake.

Before she could go much further, the cave came alive. Swirls of bright blue flew by her face and surged along the perimeter, giving her an idea of just how large the chamber was. Jasmine's eyes couldn't keep up with the multitude of them, leaving trailing marks in their wake as they raced towards the center of the room. The ball they made grew, spinning together tightly until it exploded outward. The shape of wings unfurled on either side, the color of the flames that made them fading to orange before settling to white.

Jasmine's eyes started watering, and she sought to avert her gaze to something less imposing and terribly bright.

You have come.

She blinked, feeling unnerved by the fact that the disembodied voice wasn't just heard by her ears, but also seemed to emanate from inside her head. Jasmine would think that she was making it up of her own volition, but her inner voice didn't sound like that. "I... have."

The pact has been severed. I am barred by the gods from offering my power as passage.

"I know. But this is for me."

Why?

"To see for myself what the Flame actually is, and to ask why it pulled me from my life to be thrown in the center of this."

Pawn in the gods' games. I am no different.

"You're a phoenix."

What I am matters not. Still, a pawn.

Jasmine wanted to knock the entire hypothetical chess board over. "You're telling me that you can do nothing to get all of us free?"

Not as I am.

Her heart sank a few inches into her stomach, even though she knew that would be the answer. She closed her eyes for a moment, turning away from the mythical beast. "I see."

You can move freely between the realms.

"My mobility hasn't done anything for anyone, least of all myself."

I can give you the power to accomplish your goals if I am freed.

Jasmine felt a bead of sweat roll down the side of her face as her mind raced. She wasn't stupid; she knew there was a catch. There were so many things she wanted, and while she embarked stubbornly on this final journey just to see what was on the other side, she didn't expect to be granted this sort of audience. She wanted to go back home, to her shitty job and her best friend and the hobbies that made Kim call her a hermit. She wanted her realm to not be overly affected by the absence of the two races that were careening towards a war, knowing what they each represented. She wanted Leon's warmth. She wanted Kai's happiness.

She wanted it all. And she felt with the amount of shit she had gone through that she deserved a fair shot at attaining it.

"How do I free you?"

There was a breath of silence before it responded. *With you, born anew.*

Jasmine's heart was hammering hard against her chest. "I don't understand."

You do.

Everything came at a price, it seemed, and what the phoenix was offering did not come from a place of benevolence. It had its own wants, forged into permanence for however long it had been kept in captivity, and saw Jasmine as a tool to get them accomplished. Sustina's words from so long ago filtered back to her mind, about how she stepped onto a chess board while being unaware of the game being played. It was obvious now that nobody was aware save for Ciaran's highly educated guesses.

"Why me?"

Nothing to lose. Much to gain.

"My humanity is not 'nothing'."

It is a necessary exchange for what you seek. Your heart knows. Do you accept, Prime?

Jasmine looked down to the empty jewel on her chest. She thought the absence of light from within meant that she no longer had the favor she once did. She didn't consider until that moment that it wasn't something she was given, but something innate that she was.

Tears sprang to her eyes, and she blinked them away fast before squaring her shoulders and facing the entity in front of her.

"I accept."

Wind in the cave picked up at an alarming rate, and Jasmine covered her face to protect it from the debris that was kicking up in the wake of it. As if she were standing right in the middle of a tornado, the sound became deafening, and her footing was lost somewhere along the way.

She heard something shatter, and darkness settled into her vision before silence reigned.

CHAPTER THIRTY-NINE

Jasmine dreamed that she was floating alone through the depths of the universe, past planets and stars that had come and gone, awareness widened farther than she could have ever imagined. Her mind felt uncomfortably full, still pressing outwards, struggling against the bounds of what she knew to be true. Information she didn't understand came and went, and she tried moving her hand to grasp at a meteor moving by.

She did not have hands.

Instead of panicking, she felt at an odd sort of peace. The vast expanse that surrounded her was infinite, but she was, too. She could not be lonely, as she was everywhere, and everything was in her. The only one of her kind, a spontaneous gesture of life, imitating the expansion and entropy of existence.

Slowly, the planets around her became eclipsed. No matter which way Jasmine looked, she couldn't see what shadowed them. The stars winked out one by one, and confusion set in. Eventually, all went dark, and Jasmine felt her body sinking, wrapped up in a cool cocoon of nothingness.

She shivered. *It's so cold, here.*

When she opened her eyes, she didn't immediately recognize where she was. Her body felt damp, and she sat up slowly to raindrops falling on her cheeks. Jasmine felt extremely disoriented, like she just woke up from one of those naps that took her entire afternoon away from her and she didn't know what day it was. She stayed seated on the hard ground, looking around at the thick blanket of trees that rustled with the precipitation that weighted its branches.

Hold up... am I in Hellenia?

Jasmine's knees cracked as she got to her feet, her body stiff from being out in the elements for so long. She recognized the altar she was on, spinning briefly in a circle checking everything out before dazedly walking down the stone steps and to the path that would lead her to the street beyond.

Did I dream all that shit up, or something? Jasmine didn't think she did even if part of her hoped that it was fake. At least then she could hope that the mess that transpired days ago was nothing but a figment of her stressed out, overactive imagination. But it didn't explain how she apparently took a nap in the middle of a forest right in front of the portal to Hyperion. She bit her lip, reaching the end of the pathway and seeing the sky open up before her, the rain falling harder without any resistance.

She didn't even have a ride into town, and she knew that while it was technically walkable, it wasn't something that she wanted to do for hours in that dreary weather.

Fly.

Jasmine yelped and jumped backwards a few steps. "What the fu--"

I do not know this realm. I could only deposit us this far. Fly to where you seek.

She tried not to shake. Fragments of her memories came filtering back to her, but they hurt to make sense of. "How?"

Think of where you want to be in this realm. Then there you will be.

Jasmine took a deep breath through her nose and closed her eyes, fixing her mind's eye to a familiar location. She brought it into focus, filling in the expansive courtyard, the pillars that spanned the front near the door that opened into a grand foyer...

She became dizzy. Her body felt like it was swaying, buoyed on waves that eventually made her feel weightless in its grip. But she held on tight to her vision, grasping hold of it like a linchpin through it all.

Until her feet were steady on solid ground, and she opened her eyes to the familiar sight of the Exousia manor.

"... whoa." Jasmine gave her shoulders a bit of a shake before putting her hand on the bronze handle and pushing it inwards, walking inside.

It didn't take her long to realize that the place was vacant. Not like it was ever the bustling hub of activity before from what she could remember, but Jasmine couldn't sense anyone in the house, the grounds, the building that once held the Flame...

Jasmine blinked. *Am I actually picking up on all of this, or...?*

Your awareness is growing. Mine is shrinking. We are changing.

"Okay..." She shook her head a little and started making her way up the steps, operating on nothing but auto pilot.

Her steps slowed to a stop before she got to the first landing. *Fucking shit, there's a whole war going on right now. I should make sure that he's actually going to come back after this, no matter what Kai told me.* Jasmine clamored back down to the main floor, wondering what she could do. She wasn't a fighter, and even if she was, there was no way that she could take up a sword against the Draconians. But she wasn't keen on sitting around like a helpless babe for news, either. She made a huge sacrifice to get where she was now, and while she still majorly felt like herself, sharing a body with a mythical creature was an odd thing for her to get used to.

Hey, you'll let me know before I fail at trying something crazy, correct?

There was a span of a few breaths before the other voice within her responded, sounding much weaker than before. *Feel; do not ask.*

"Awesome." Jasmine put that tidbit off to the side where she could dissect it, later. She paced from one end of the foyer to the other, her footsteps echoing off of the walls as she considered the situation at hand. Supposedly, she now had the power to accomplish all of her goals. It was just that the being within her wasn't going to do much to tell her how to do it. Her eyes drifted to the table with various trinkets upon it, remembering that Leon said they were used for communication between select individuals. Walking over, she picked up the candle that was linked to Sustina.

Lighting this thing should be easy, all things considered. She pinched her fingers over the wick as she remembered Leon doing, and willed it to light. *Sustina?*

The wick exploded in a high flame, causing her to jerk back in shock and nearly drop it. She fumbled the candle clumsily, the fire licking at her digits and causing her to panic, the wax dripping over her hand and causing a sticky mess. Jasmine was actually in the middle of blowing on it when she realized that she didn't feel burned at all. *What the fuck am I doing?* She calmed her heart rate down low enough to concentrate again on the candle, willing the flame she lit to go out.

Placing the sad, slumped candle littered with marks from her hard grip back upon the table was enough to make Jasmine start to giggle uncontrollably. *This is a fucking fantastic start. I'm losing my mind.* She meandered over to a chair and sat down, picking the remnants of wax from her skin and watching the flakes of it fall to the polished floor and wondered what she should do if her attempt at communication didn't work. Jasmine figured that showing up as she was in front of a bunch of Hellenian escorts would cause more of a stir than she bargained for, but she didn't know what else to do.

Just as she was beginning to get antsy, she felt a tickle of something at the edge of her consciousness. Focusing on it drove her eyes instinctively to what was outside the manor, and she could feel a distinct presence approaching. She remained staring even though she couldn't see through the stone walls themselves, clutching the armrests of the chair she was in until the door to the manor swung open and Sustina's concerned face peeked through.

"Thank god you're here."

"Jasmine?" Sustina frowned, stepping fully into the foyer. "I thought that was your voice, but I didn't think..." Her voice trailed off as she approached, and Jasmine felt a feather-light ripple wash over her. She realized it was the Hellenian gently probing the very surface of her consciousness.

"Yeah, it's me. I can explain, but I also need your help with something."

The courtesan stared at Jasmine as if she couldn't understand what was in front of her. Jasmine saw her eyes drift to the necklace on her chest. Instinctively, she reached up to grab hold of it like she had done many times before, and nearly cut herself on the jagged remains of the jewel that once held the Spark.

Both women regarded each other silently, a hint of mutual wariness between them as they each tried gauging how the other would respond. Eventually, Sustina nodded, dropping her initial guard enough to let Jasmine relax.

"I will do my best."

CHAPTER FORTY

When the carriage arrived at their destination, Jasmine stepped out before it fully stopped moving, taking in her surroundings. Sustina followed shortly after, coming up to stand next to her with her eyes set to the distance.

"Hellenians are not laid to rest within the earth. It is our belief that we can only reach Heaven once again in death, so our bodies are raised." Sustina gestured to the myriad forms of pedestals, ranging from quaint to elaborate monoliths that spread out before them. "For a set mourning period, magic preserves the bodies before eroding naturally, allowing birds and other wildlife to feast on the carrion."

Jasmine nodded, her eyes tracing the floral arrangements and vines that accented the raised coffins. Like much of Hellenia itself, the macabre was made hauntingly beautiful. "Let's go, then."

They walked through the inverted graveyard, the scent of night-blooming flowers tickling their noses. Jasmine knew that they weren't alone; she could sense other Hellenians spread out, paying respects to the memories of their loved ones. Even in her changed state, Jasmine felt like the ground she was walking on was too sacred for her feet, and she was glad that Sustina was with her the whole way.

Eventually, they came to a stop in front of a pyramid, silvered steps with white flowers placed on either side of the incline. Sustina pointed to the top, and Jasmine's eyes drifted to land on a placard that was fixed on a post next to her.

Arma in caelis: Luciel Irin

"Luciel?"

Sustina nodded. "His father likely insisted on keeping his birth name for memorial. I do not believe he ever got his preferred name formally legitimized." She clasped her hands in front of her. "I do not know how to properly process your change, Jasmine. I also do not have the scope of what you intend to do to even find it possible. But, in honor of our friendship, I have said that I would be there for you if you were in need. I'm happy to be able to provide in what little ways I can."

Jasmine reached out to hug her, still finding comfort in the courtesan's embrace. "Thank you, Sustina. And if it makes you feel any better, I don't know what I'm doing, either."

With that, she started her climb, concentrating on a few steps in front of her at a time. Jasmine estimated that it was about three stories tall, nothing compared to the miles she probably trekked on Hyperion, but without the magical buoyancy granted by that sacred land it was easy to feel like it was longer than what it was.

When she crested the top, her pace slowed, and her eyes started watering at the sight in front of her. It was a beautiful setting: the glass coffin laying open and flanked by a pair of lanterns glowing with calming blue light. Elliot was laying peacefully within, dressed from head to toe in white that was carefully inlaid with silver embroidery that Jasmine could recognize instantly as Nithael's work. The silk ascot covered the gash she knew was there from Ciaran's spear, and she fingered the brooch with the Exousia family crest that held it in place.

"I'm so sorry I couldn't do anything to save you then, Elliot. But I hope I'm able to make it up to you now."

Closing her eyes, she laid her palm on top of his cold hands and breathed deeply. She focused her energies, reaching for the spark of power within her core that would allow her to do the impossible. The woozy feeling washed over her again, and she felt oddly detached from herself as another world opened up in her mind's eye. Streams of light hung like canopy tethers, drifting down from the sky to touch upon the many bodies that laid in the graveyard. Some were brighter than others, and some were so faint that they seemed to evaporate into granules to spread on wind. Jasmine was distracted by the vision for a moment, before refocusing to see the line that connected to Elliot.

It was more solid than the others, testifying to how recent it was since he passed. Jasmine reached out and wrapped her fingers around his individual thread, tugging experimentally. C'mon. She kept pulling, each attempt more stubborn than the last. Finally, she concentrated a pathway of flames licking upwards, rooting her non-corporal grip on the tether and pulled as if she were hauling the biggest pallet of goods across her store's floor.

A large ball of light erupted from the heavens, traveling down the energy rope at a startling speed towards Elliot's body. Jasmine was barely able to let go in time, falling backwards on her rear as her physical eyes shot open.

She waited the span of a few ragged breaths before slowly climbing to her feet, wondering once again if she just hallucinated the brunt of everything she was trying to do. She felt shaky, like she just expended a significant amount of energy.

It wasn't until she saw Elliot slowly sit up as if waking from a deep sleep that she let the weight of what she actually did wash over her, and she put her hands over her mouth as she started to cry.

"Jasmine?" He looked confused, staring around at everything before gazing down at himself. His hand touched his neck, and a moment passed where it seemed like he was processing reality. "... *shit.*"

"Shit is right," she agreed, wiping her face with the back of her hand. "I didn't even know if I could help, or if it was too late. But I had to try."

Elliot climbed out of the coffin, flower petals falling from his clothes as he brushed himself off and then looked at his hands like he was seeing them for the first time. Then, he was using those hands to pull Jasmine to him, kissing her deeply enough to be shocked clear out of the emotional landslide she was spiraling in.

"What the hell?" Jasmine sputtered as soon as she was allowed up for air.

"Did you expect anything else from a man who just got brought back from the afterlife?" He gave her his familiar grin. "It's *me* we're talking about."

Jasmine felt her cheeks heat up, and she cleared her throat. "I guess so. Um... well. I'm happy to see you, too."

Elliot winked, and then let his expression fade into one of concern. "Where's Leon?"

"... yeah. About that," she turned and started heading down the stairs. "We should bounce."

"What happened? Did he do something stupid? *Please* tell me he didn't do something stupid."

"I plan to intercept the worst of it, if I can. But I need you with me to do it, because if anyone has a chance of pulling his head out of his ass, it's you."

Seeing Sustina's look of absolute shock when both she and Elliot came rushing down the pyramid made Jasmine feel oddly proud of herself. She was still learning the ins and outs of her newfound capabilities, but knowing that she was one step closer to fixing things gave her the strength to push forward.

"You know, white *really* looks good on me," Elliot said once they were seated in Sustina's carriage. "It sucks that I had to literally die for me to get a fit like this."

"You are behaving quite casually for the miracle that has occurred," Sustina carefully stated.

"It's how I roll. Also, I have a feeling that I don't have time right now to process what happened." He looked at Jasmine. "Your aura is *crazy*. You don't look any different, but you feel..."

"It shocked me as well. But it seems as though she made a pact with the Flame. A different one from that of the other Primes before her."

Jasmine scratched her head. "Yeah. I'm still figuring it out myself, honestly. I'm going with my gut and hoping things pan out. I don't have a clear instruction manual for this. Thanks for giving me the benefit of the doubt, though. I know shit's wild."

Sustina reached over and patted Jasmine's hand. "With a war on our hands, I suppose this could be the dawning of an era filled with unimaginable things."

"Wait, a *war*?" Elliot looked horrified. "What the fuck?"

"Well, looks like we're here!" Jasmine said suddenly, gazing out of the window and seeing the forest come into view. With the way she left the carriage behind, one could say that she was literally running away from trying to explain exactly how bad the situation was. "Sustina... thank you for everything. I think I can take it from here."

"*Orandi gratia dei nobis in tenebris luceat*, Jasmine. I'm lucky to be alive to have met you."

Jasmine felt as though she were nearly dragging Elliot

down the pathway in her haste to get them to the portal. She took the altar steps two at a time, dropping his arm in favor of lighting the candles necessary before tracing the runes to grant them passage.

"Did my girl teach you how to do this?"

"Sure did. I have a feeling she saw all of this play out already in one of those crystal balls of hers, too." She finished her handiwork, seeing the portal ripple to life. "You ready for a grand entrance?"

Elliot shrugged nonchalantly, but the crinkles at the corners of his red eyes told a different story. "Baby, I don't know any other type of entrance to make. Let's do this."

CHAPTER FORTY-ONE

HYPERION

For as much as Hellenians were a cushy race, settled into ballrooms and banquet halls with frilled attire that blended the best of the past with touches of the present, they still had the blood of battle angels in their veins. And as Leon moved through the cluster of bodies around him, throwing himself headfirst into each opponent that dared to challenge him, the smile that spread upon his face was virulent.

The Draconians likely did not prepare for what the Hellenians brought to the battle. It began with lots of posturing, being surrounded by dragons looking as imposing as possible combined with flanks of soldiers in neatly color-coded armor that he figured represented each ruler's contribution.

But it was the legion in black that waited until the first descent of the dragons to activate a spell formulated by the high priestess herself to render their monstrous transformations useless. And as confused Draconians fell from the sky, that was when Leon drew his sword and had his people attack.

He made sure he held the far-reaching gaze of the Draconian royals as he commanded it.

Having an outlet to unleash the years of repressed emotions was what he needed, even though it was not ideal. Leon would have rather been listening to Elliot ramble on about the last human woman he was obsessed with than watching his sword strike home, sending a torrent of Draconian blood spurting in the air before he spun to another target. He would rather his father still be alive, living out the rest of his years with his love.

He would have rather had Jasmine by his side, listening to her laughter and enjoying simple things. Leon had considered her to be a fresh start, a blessing that arrived at the right time. Yet, he shouldn't have gotten attached so quickly. He didn't know how to tell her that the exchange of blood with a Hellenian was a bond linking them for better or for worse. She was a part of him, even as he did his best to push her away in hopes that any sort of distance between them would save her from meeting the same fate as anyone precious to him did.

But the look she had in her eyes cut him deep. And rather than fix it, he simply internalized that pain, transmuted it into every step that led him to the battlefield and married it with the pre-existing malaise that made his heart hard and his strikes sharp.

Leon's blade swung in an arc, severing the tendons in a Draconian's arm.

Yet, he knew he had been foolish in too many ways.

Something tickled the corner of his consciousness, and he turned and lifted his hand in time to catch an arrow that had been fired in his direction. Leon stared at the blue feathers at the end of the projectile for a moment before using magic to incinerate it to dust. His eyes scanned the conglomerate of battling bodies, looking for the one who dared aim for him.

"Keep your eyes here, High Lord."

Leon regarded Kai's sudden appearance, straightening his posture to address him. "Where is the one you call Ciaran?"

"Not present. You'll have to deal with me occupying your time in his stead."

Leon's eyes narrowed slightly before getting into a proper stance, his blade moving to cover his center. "You'd be first in line to shed your blood on his behalf?"

The tassel on the end of Kai's sword flicked through the air as he twirled the weapon. "Always. But let's first see if you can do that."

It didn't matter to Leon. He truly meant to work his way through each and every Draconian that breathed. If Kai wanted to volunteer to be the next, then so be it.

Their weapons clashed over and over, and Leon had the passing thought that if things had been different, Kai would likely be someone he respected despite their differences. He could tell the Draconian lived off of the traded blows, and Leon felt pushed to his limits keeping up with the deceptively flashy strikes that he intercepted. Yet despite how eagerly Kai jumped into the duel, Leon had the rising suspicion that he was simply being toyed with.

Formulating a quick burst of magical energy, he fired it in Kai's direction, and saw the prince twist in midair to avoid it. He then took the opportunity to slice a gash along his opponent's side during the evade, and Kai quickly tumbled to the ground and away, springing to his feet but unable to hide the blood seeping into his clothes as a consequence.

"You certainly are more nimble than I expected. Most find it hard to keep up with me."

"Your attempt at avoiding death for as long as possible is admirable. You should have been resolute in your attacks."

Kai barked out a short laugh, lowering his center of gravity. "It's more fun this way."

Leon blocked the next flurry of attacks, feeling the muscles in his wrist tense and release with each jarring collision. Then he suddenly dropped his guard, gauging how Kai would react, and found that the Draconian didn't take a clear shot at what would be a maiming hit.

"You dishonor your people by underestimating me."

"Oh, believe me; I don't underestimate my opponents." Kai kept his gaze on Leon. "I just have a favor I'm inclined to keep."

Leon answered by firing another blast of energy at Kai, noting how the blood loss was finally starting to slow him down. "Ridiculous. You'll die by my sword, and I will keep going until the rest of your kin take their last breaths."

Kai straightened himself. "I still have fight in me left. Come."

Leon launched himself towards him, narrowing his focus to a pinpoint to put his all into defeating Kai. He didn't know why he was acting so foolishly. In fact, it irritated Leon to find him so lackadaisical. *Does this war mean nothing to him?* He pressed his attack, interchanging between magic bursts and precision strikes. He watched Kai falter in intervals, handicapped by not only the magic veil that draped the area but also the sustained injury on his side, and prepared to end it all by cutting his neck and leaving him to die as a message to the others.

What is that? Leon paused mid-strike, shifting his gaze to something above them. It looked like a shooting star, growing in size as it descended to the battlefield.

It was only within the span of a few moments that it would make impact, and it seemed to be aimed directly at where the two of them were standing.

Both of them dodged away from each other at the last minute, shielding their eyes from the blinding light that appeared in front of them, swirling with licks of flame that dissipated into the air like drifting leaves. The brilliance was slowly fading, but there were spots in his eyes as he strained to refocus on what was there.

"Wow, I'm gone for like, two minutes and you start a whole war. I knew I couldn't leave you alone, but this is a bit much."

Leon stopped breathing for a moment, wondering what kind of spell was being placed on him to make him hallucinate something so cruel. Yet, he watched the familiar figure step out of the dome of light that materialized in front of him. He thought it was God himself who was presenting one of the dearest people in his life back to reality.

"Elliot?"

"Yeah?" He reached out and touched Leon's arm. "It's me. I had a little help though."

Leon looked past Elliot's shoulder and saw the being that seemed to be the source of all of the light that materialized. She smiled back at him, dazzling in her awareness and causing his vision to blur with the tears that finally threatened to fall down his cheeks. Elliot pulled him into a tight hug then, and even though he was sure his soiled hands would leave marks all over his white suit, Leon couldn't help but return the embrace with vigor.

"Okay, I'll admit it; I *am* actually touched that you would go this far for me. But I think it's time you pulled back a little." Elliot's grip got tighter. "Don't go down this road, Leon. Please."

As Leon felt the bonds that had been wrapped tight around his heart loosen little by little, he watched Jasmine move past them to kneel beside Kai and place her hand on his wounded side. More light emitted from her touch, and when she withdrew, all that was left of evidence was the tattered bloodstained cloth that laid around his newly healed skin.

"I see you've swayed the spirit of the mountain after all," Kai murmured, slowly getting to his feet.

"Something like that." Jasmine moved her gaze to everything around them. It was then that Leon realized that the fighting had stopped, with the eyes of soldiers transfixed by what was in their midst. When he looked at her, he saw the same human who he met before she embarked on her journey properly as the Prime. But her aura was something spectacular, burning with something bigger than the small frame she carried.

And it only burned brighter the more her eyes settled on each fallen body.

She raised her arms to the sides of her, and the flames began accumulating once more, enveloping her body until Leon had to look away. Even from behind his closed lids, the warmth was encompassing, and the darkness was illuminated to where all he could sense was muted orange.

Rebirth.

CHAPTER FORTY-TWO

J asmine stood in front of the rocky cave where she came across the phoenix, the winds from Hyperion stirring her hair around her face as she gazed. Every day that passed since merging with the mythical beast, she felt like she was living in a fever dream of sorts. Her dreams were complicated visions that felt familiar yet alien, and right beneath her skin was the thrum of power she wasn't yet accustomed to having. She didn't know how much more she would be changing, and at that point, only time would tell.

Was it worth it? She turned around then, looking at the individuals who had accompanied her to a place that they previously had never been allowed to reach.

Yeah. I think I'm good.

"Interesting chain of events, I'd say," Ciaran said, examining the cave with his amaranthine eyes. "I hope you're making the right decision."

"Slightly better than having you killed."

"Is it?" He met her gaze then, and for the first time since his betrayal, Jasmine felt like she could look at him without flinching. She saw within his swirling depths the pride of a Draconian, the lingering lust that he had for the precious and unattainable, and the quiet resignation to his fate brought on by his own actions. She could tell that he didn't regret anything, even now. In chains he might have been, but his stature of a royal dragon didn't waver despite it all.

Jasmine found she had to respect it.

"It's funny."

"What is?"

"I fought so hard to free us of a prison, just to be shuffled into another." Ciaran smiled wistfully. "I remember the day I told you that I hoped you'd soar through the Run with me. I meant it, even though it can't come to pass now. In my absence, I hope that you can use the wings you found on your own to fly through it in my memory."

Jasmine didn't know how to respond to that, outside of giving her own wan smile in return. She wished that it didn't have to be so bittersweet. In some aspect, her powers may allow her to do the impossible, but the consequences of his actions weren't within her realm of correction.

She turned then and nodded at the other Draconian royals in attendance, and they stepped forward to escort Ciaran within the depths of the cavern. Jasmine walked back to stand next to Viviane, with both Elliot and Leon standing a bit off to the side as observers. After some time had passed, the other three emerged, and once they were clear of the entrance, she reached her hand over to grasp that of the High Priestess as was planned.

"I will be the conduit to direct the ritual. Remain steady, Jasmine."

Jasmine nodded and reached deep within herself, a

smoother process than it was for her before, pulling up tendrils of power to feed to Viviane as she used her skills to weave a web driven by incantations over the cave itself. Fog began to settle in, and a heaviness blanketed everyone's shoulders as the magic seeped into the peak itself. During this, Fouzia started handing Nemeer glimmering medallions forged from Draconian alchemy, in which he used his height and power to embed each one into the rock face itself, from the top to the bottom. They glowed as they were set, merging with the spell being cast, and forming an invisible barrier that would be impenetrable by anyone who did not know the steps to reverse.

Once it was done, they all stood and observed their handiwork. Fouzia was the first to turn away, walking back over and bowing to Jasmine and Viviane.

"I know this eats him up to be trapped for eternity in that place. Death was the release he was banking on at the end of this." She reached up and wiped at an errant tear quickly, folding her arms and looking away slightly. "Can't blame you for coming up with it, though. It's appropriate."

"I just refuse to see any more people dying in front of me; that shit's traumatizing. And while I know it is in Draconian tradition to pass that kind of judgment, I'm glad that you guys heard me out on an alternative." Jasmine looked over at Kai, whose face was slightly withdrawn and contemplative. "You guys don't have to suffer that if I can help it."

Nemeer walked over next. "It's appreciated. I know we can't really visit him or anything, but... there's a kind of comfort knowing that he's here. Maybe it's selfish, I don't know. But I can handle this." He nodded at Leon. "Thank you for being gracious enough to lend Hellenia's aid."

"It is the least I could do, in the wake of it all. It will be the start in better relations overall between our races." His gold eyes trained themselves to the sky. "There is much work that must be done to undo countless years of being adversaries in a sense."

Jasmine nodded. "Where I'm from, we call it 'undoing generational curses'. As long as y'all decide that this is where the buck stops, then the future already is brighter. The lessons of the past will hit different from here on out, and that's important."

"Well... you've officially helped us clean up our mess," Elliot said, tilting his head to the side. "Passage between all realms is open thanks to you. You could go back home... although, honestly, if you do that, *don't* go back to your job. It sounded horrible."

"If I even *have* one at this point. There's only so long FMLA lasts before they start trying to check in on a bitch, you know?" Jasmine laughed lightly, then sighed. "I mean, I probably will. At least for awhile. I'm not quite so sure about the side effects of being a phoenix, yet. But I do know for as long as I can, I want to be in contact with my friends and family."

"Please do. It's all too often that we take them for granted." Kai smiled, even though his eyes were a bit sad in the wake of Ciaran's imprisonment. "The rest of us can visit."

She hugged him tightly, knowing that it would take time before things settled for him and the others. "You sure can. And with both you and the Hellenians able to play nice for the first time in forever, I'd like to see how this affects my realm in real time."

Leon clasped his hands in front of him. "My hasty actions did not help facilitate unity, even though you mitigated much of the damage with your abilities."

"Whatever I can help with, just let me know, okay?"

Nemeer raised an eyebrow. "Really? You can't give yourself

a little break? We'll be fine without you cleaning up our messes for a little while."

Jasmine opened her mouth to protest, only to be cut off by Fouzia. "Shut that pretty little mouth of yours. I know we've monopolized too much of your time and energy, already. Go chill out."

Even Viviane had a faint smile on her face as she turned to walk over to where her liege was standing. "You've been released from the strings of the Gods, Jasmine. I'd use that boon wisely."

She didn't even bother asking Leon for help, as the look in his eyes told her that he wasn't going to differ from the overall consensus. So instead, she threw her hands up in exasperation. "Look at y'all. Fresh off a war and already got unity in bullying me to sit my ass down, somewhere. I should be mad about it."

"Speaking of mad, maybe you should, uh... check up on Kim?" Elliot winced. "I was just a fucktoy, but you're like a sister to her. She'll want to know you're alive, even if she might make you wish you were dead for a little bit for disappearing without a trace."

"Oh, god," Jasmine actually wished she could throw herself into mending the relationship between the two ancient races, as that seemed better than putting herself at Kim's mercy. "Y'all *sure* you don't have anything for me to do?"

Her reply came in the form of everyone else turning around and making their way down the mountain.

These hoes ain't loyal. She sighed, looking back once more at the now sealed cave that changed her life forever. After a moment's pause, she reached up behind her neck and unclasped the chain that held the remnants of the Spark she carried with her every step of her journey to its end.

Jasmine walked up to the cave and hung it on one of the jagged rocks there, watching the sun catch the broken edges.

Taking a deep breath, she lifted her head, letting the warmth from the light steady her before focusing the flames that manifested around her body like a cocoon. After a few seconds, she launched herself into the sky, letting her soul direct her to where she wanted to be.

ACKNOWLEDGMENTS

First & foremost, I must thank my good friend Jenni. Without you, this novel would never have existed. I know you didn't expect your random throwaway comment on a viral tweet to turn into this... and to be fair, neither did I! Between that and offering yourself up to be an idea springboard in order to bring my characters to life, it's easy for me to say that you deserve the world.

It's my belief that every writer needs a hype man, and I'm lucky enough to have two particularly special ones who ate up both iterations of my manuscript with vigor while encouraging me to not doubt myself. Souha and Sarah, trust me when I say that you both are invaluable to me as lifelong friends. May I always support your dreams as hard as you've stood by mine.

To my wonderful husband, Justin, who is supportive of me and remains fully invested in my success, no matter the ups and downs. When I was let go from my full-time job and decided to throw my entire being into this work, you never dissuaded me from chasing my dreams. I love you to the moon and back.

G-fuu, my best friend of too many years for me to even quantify right now... I love you. Your steadfast support and level-headed nature are unrivaled in my life, and I wouldn't know what to do without it. To say the absolute least, I'm entirely blessed by the impact you've had on me.

To my Daddy, who told me "As long as I am on this Earth, I will do my best to support you." No matter how old I get, or when the time comes when you are no longer here with me, I will always be your Baby. When I say I have the best father I could have ever asked for, I absolutely mean it.

Shea, you took the time out of your busy schedule to read through the first iteration of my manuscript and had the patience to coach me through proper novel structure and enlighten me on how to navigate the publishing world. With your gentle critique, I was able to rewrite the core of my vision and make it into something I am proud to present to the public today.

To Lisa Kastner of RIZE and my wonderful editor Rebecca, thank you so much for taking a chance on me and making my lifelong dream come true. I cried in disbelief when you accepted my manuscript, because no matter how much I may be in love with my own work, it hits different when people who have the power to help get it in front of readers believe in it as much as you do. It was an incredibly validating experience, one that I will be holding close to me for the rest of my life.

Finally, to my mom. This book is the result of you making me use a collegiate dictionary in elementary school to do my English homework, taking me to the library every day, and supporting my obsession with handwriting hundreds of pages of whatever wild stories I could come up with. May the ancestors help carry my love and gratitude to your vibrant soul.

AUTHOR'S BIO

S.A. Gladden was born and raised in Detroit, Michigan, with an insatiable hunger for stories that can capture the soul. To create is to live, and she seeks to embody that through penning stories that mesh fantastical worlds with the diverse representation she and others like her crave to see. When she's not planning her next big novel, you can find her working hard with her friends & colleagues on Candle Glow Studios to port her visions into video games.

RIZE publishes great stories and great writing across genres written by People of Color and other underrepresented groups. Our team consists of:

Lisa Diane Kastner, Founder and Executive Editor
Mona Bethke, Acquisitions Editor
Rebecca Dimyan, Editor
Abigail Efird, Editor
Laura Huie, Editor
Cody Sisco, Editor
Chih Wang, Editor
Pulp Art Studios, Cover Design
Standout Books, Interior Design
Polgarus Studios, Interior Design

Learn more about us and our stories at www.runningwildpress.com/rize

Loved this story and want more? Follow us at www.runningwildpress.com/rize, www.facebook.com/rize, on Twitter @rizerwp and Instagram @rizepress